THE
VERGE
PRACTICE

Also by Barry Maitland

The Marx Sisters
The Malcontenta
The Chalon Heads
Silvermeadow
Babel

THE VERGE PRACTICE

A Kathy and Brock Mystery

BARRY MAITLAND

Arcade Publishing • New York

To the long-suffering spouse of the architect

FIRST U.S. EDITION 2004

First published in Australia in 2003 by Allen & Unwin

Library of Congress Cataloging-in-Publication Data

Maitland, Barry.
  The Verge practice : a Kathy and Brock mystery / by Barry Maitland. —1st U.S. ed.
    p. cm.
  ISBN 1-55970-713-5
  1. Brock, David (Fictitious character)—Fiction. 2. Kolla, Kathy
(Fictitious character)—Fiction. 3. Police—England—London—Fiction.
4. London (England)—Fiction. 5. Missing persons—Fiction.
6. Policewomen—Fiction. 7. Architects—Fiction. I. Title.

  PR9619.3.M2635V47 2003
  823'.914—dc22   2003020371

Published in the United States by Arcade Publishing, Inc., New York
Distributed by Time Warner Book Group

Visit our Web site at www.arcadepub.com

10 9 8 7 6 5 4 3 2 1

EB

PRINTED IN THE UNITED STATES OF AMERICA

Make no little plans
Daniel Burnham, 1846–1912

1

The Zhejiang delegation stood huddled at the foot of the great sheet of glass that hung between two brick warehouses, twisting out before hitting the ground to form a shimmering canopy supported on a spider's web of thin stainless-steel rods.

Sandy Clarke, senior partner of the Verge Practice, hurried through the glass doors to welcome them, the firm's information manager, Jennifer Mathieson, at his side. Stiff little bows, handshakes and business cards were exchanged, and the party moved from the chill May morning into the warm interior. Once past the low ceiling of the reception area, they paused for a moment to admire the sweep of the atrium that soared up above them, surrounded by floors of open-plan drawing offices, and to take in the view of the river through the glass wall on the far side.

'Rondon Bridge.' Cheong Hung, leader of the delegation, beamed knowingly at the structure to their left.

'Tower Bridge, Mr Cheong,' Clarke corrected politely, and drew his guest further to the right to point out the pinnacles of the Tower of London just visible beyond the bridge. He then turned to indicate the tiers of levels rising above them, all brightly lit and humming with activity, although it was only eight o'clock on a Monday morning. 'Would you care to inspect our facilities?'

Cheong's English wasn't that good, and he looked inquiringly at a woman at his elbow, who began to whisper a translation into his ear.

'Ah.' Cheong checked his watch and shook his head. He spoke to the woman, who then turned to Clarke. 'Mr Cheong regrets we are short of time. We are familiar with your facilities from your brochures. They are most impressive. Please to continue to the presentation of your proposals.'

'Of course.' Clarke was aware the party had three other presentations to attend that day before catching their flight back to the People's Republic, and that time was tight, but he knew that Jennifer was anxious to delay things until Charles could be traced. He led the way through a gallery in which models and photographs of some of their more spectacular recent projects were displayed: office towers, a football stadium, a dinosaur museum. Jennifer Mathieson described them briefly as they passed, but the visitors seemed more interested in her red hair and long legs. They came to a milky glass wall that parted with a mechanical sigh in front of them, and entered the auditorium that had been prepared for the formal presentation. While the Chinese accepted coffees and took them to their seats, Jennifer whispered urgently in his ear, 'Where the hell is he, Sandy?'

'He must still be upstairs in the flat,' Clarke said calmly. 'I saw a light on when I arrived this morning. I asked Elaine to call him.'

'I spoke to her. She says no one's answering the phone. There's no sign of Miki either.'

Clarke could understand her consternation. This wasn't at all like Charles. Normally he'd have been down in the office hours before, thrashing out the final details of the presentation with the media unit.

'Maybe he's in the shower or on his mobile. He's probably still jet-lagged from the States. Why don't you go up there, Jennifer? Take the key and winkle him out. I'll get things started.'

He fixed a confident smile on his face as Jennifer made for the door.

The audience was waiting. Clarke walked to the front of the room and introduced the other senior staff of the Verge Practice who were present.

'And Mr Verge?' Cheong asked haltingly. 'Will he join us?'

'Naturally, Mr Verge intended to join us. He has been totally involved in the proposals you are about to see. Unfortunately, he seems to have picked up a virus on a recent trip to California, and he has been unwell. He will join us if he possibly can.'

This was translated, producing an exchange of stony looks among the Chinese.

Cheong murmured a few words to the interpreter, who said, 'Mr Cheong is most disappointed. He very much wished to meet Charles Verge in person.'

'And Charles is very anxious to meet him. However, since time is short, I suggest that we start the presentation.' Sandy Clarke beamed another reassuring smile and nodded at the technician. Thank God for digital media, he thought; at least I shan't have to speak for the next fifteen minutes. Charles wouldn't have done it this way, of course. He would have worked the audience first, set the scene, hinted at the vision, created a receptive atmosphere. They had formed an effective partnership so often in the past, Charles's dynamism and his own poise, but today he was on his own.

Clarke moved to a seat against the wall and the room slowly filled with the sound of traditional Chinese music; the screen flicked alive to a scene of white clouds and the title, in both Chinese and English characters, came into focus: *The New City of Wuxang*. The titles faded and the clouds parted to reveal a patchwork of green fields, a rural landscape in Zhejiang province. Below could be seen a small village, rice paddies, a lake, a wood — and suddenly something else: an interchange, a row of towers, and then a huge city, digitally realised, stretching away in magnificent order towards the horizon, its buildings and highways glittering purposefully in the sunlight.

It was a lie to say that Charles had been totally involved in the development of this proposal. The truth was that he had shown little interest in it, though it was far and away the biggest thing they'd ever been called upon to design. The statistics were staggering, the quantities of concrete and steel and dollars, numbers with long strings of zeros. Yet Charles had remained remote from it all, attending design sessions reluctantly, offering advice only when pressed and then in a tone almost of amusement, as if the whole thing were absurd. And perhaps it was. As he watched the camera dive down to fly along one of the main boulevards leading to the centre of the metropolis, Sandy felt a dispiriting sense of failure, suspecting that though they had designed a vast and efficient beehive, they had utterly failed to grasp the possibilities of a city for two million human souls. And this feeling was immediately followed by a flash of anger. If only Charles had contributed a little more, set the team ablaze as only he could, things might have been different.

Fourteen minutes later there was still no sign of Verge, and Clarke was breathing deeply, maintaining his control. He saw Jennifer Mathieson's red hair at the glass door of the theatre. She was behind the audience, whose faces were fixed on the screen, and Clarke half rose from his seat, trying to make out what she was doing. She seemed to be signalling to him, waving her hand, but he made no move to go to her. Then something behind her must have distracted her; she half turned and the lights outside caught her face. Clarke was startled by its appearance. It was so white, eyes unnaturally wide, lips drawn back from her teeth, as if she'd had some terrible shock.

But the film was suddenly over, the room lights coming on to the sound of polite clapping from the guests, and Clarke rose to his feet. He invited questions, and it was clear that the party had prepared a list. One by one their questions were laboriously translated and then answered by either Clarke himself or one of the specialist team members. Traffic projections, construction methods, environmental concerns, pedestrian networks, densities, surface water management, each topic was worked over. Finally Mr Cheong spoke what sounded like a rehearsed line.

'I assume your fee proposal is negotiable.' Then he paused and said something in Mandarin to the interpreter, who translated: 'But Mr Cheong prefers to discuss this in person with Mr Verge, when he is available.'

Clarke felt humiliated, but gave no sign. He apologised again for his partner's absence, and the delegation began to shuffle their papers into their briefcases. The mood was not buoyant.

After he had seen them off, he hurried back to the reception area. 'Where's Jennifer?'

'She went back upstairs to Mr Verge's apartment, Mr Clarke. She wants you to meet her there urgently, and asked would you go alone.' The receptionist was watching to see how he would react to this odd message, and he forced himself to speak calmly.

'Very well.'

Clarke maintained his composure until the lift doors slid shut behind him, then he took a deep breath and wiped the sweat from

4

his brow with his handkerchief, aware that his hand was shaking. He vividly recalled the look of panic on Jennifer Mathieson's face, and wondered whom she'd spoken to and if she'd summoned help.

The doors opened and she was there, waiting for him outside the door to Charles's apartment.

'Sandy, thank God. I wasn't sure what to do. I thought I should wait here ... to make sure ...'

He went over and laid a reassuring hand on her arm. 'It's all right, Jennifer. What's up?'

'You'd better ... better look for yourself.' She could hardly get the key to turn in the lock, her hand was trembling so much. Then they were inside, and Clarke thought how deathly silent the place seemed. There was a strong smell of stale whisky, and he noticed a half-finished tumbler of amber liquid on a coffee table next to a copy of the Italian design magazine *Casabella*. A pair of women's shoes lay abandoned on the rug below.

'In the bedroom,' Jennifer whispered, as if the slightest sound might bring the ceiling down.

The bedroom was entirely white — white walls and ceiling, white carpet and blinds, white bed linen and furniture — and this made the glossy blackness of Miki Norinaga's hair and pubic triangle even more startling than it might otherwise have been.

She looked very young, Sandy thought, lying there naked in the centre of the double bed, the white quilt tangled round her knees. Her face was tilted up, eyes open, Japanese lids drawn back in that characteristic look of inquiry she had, as if doubting if the older men around her understood what she was saying. It was a look that her husband Charles had once adored, but which Sandy Clarke had found rather irritating. The symmetry of her slender figure was spoiled by the steel hilt embedded in her left side, immediately below her small breast. In death, her colouring had changed to a waxy yellow.

'What is that?' Jennifer Mathieson pointed an unsteady finger, her voice a mixture of panic and outrage.

'It looks like the handle of one of those rather beautiful carving knives that Miki and Charles brought back from Tokyo on their last visit.' Now that he had seen it, he felt very calm. 'Have you spoken to anyone yet, Jennifer?'

5

'No, I … I thought I should wait until the visitors had gone. She *is* dead, isn't she?'

'Oh yes. No sign of Charles?'

'No. God, this is so awful …' She looked as if she might pass out.

Sandy Clarke put an arm around her shoulders and led her out of the room. 'Look, this is what I want you to do. Take the lift down to the street and wait by the private apartment entrance for the police to arrive. I'll phone them now. Will you be all right? You'll feel much better for a breath of fresh air.'

After he'd seen her into the lift and made the call, he returned to the bedroom and stood for a long while, just staring at Miki. He had a disturbing sense that, dead as she surely was, she was still capable of explaining what had happened, that when the police arrived they would find the truth right there in her face. His eyes slid away from her, across the bedside cabinet to the chair, to the phone and flat-screen TV. He hardly saw these things, yet something must have registered, for his attention returned to the white cube of the cabinet beside the bed and focused on a pair of glasses. Neither Miki nor Charles wore glasses. The round lenses and fine dark frames looked familiar. He took a step closer, feeling heat rising up through his body to his face. He found he could hardly breathe. They were his own reading glasses, the spare pair he kept in his office. He couldn't remember bringing them up here. At his back he heard the hum of the lift, and he reached forward, snatched up the glasses and slipped them into his jacket pocket. Now his eyes began to dart wildly around the room. What else, dear God, what else? He heard the lift's motor stop. As he turned to leave he noticed a glint of silver beneath the pillow by Miki's head. He peered closer, panic rising in his chest. It looked like … it was … his silver pen, the one he'd mislaid. He heard the murmur of voices and leaned over, gripped the end of the pen between thumb and forefinger, and tugged it out from under the pillow.

'Mr Clarke?' A man's voice in the living room. He straightened, ramming the pen into his pocket, and turned to face them.

2

Brock marched quickly along Queen Anne's Gate, head thrust forward, a preoccupied frown on his face, and crossed onto Broadway.
The September morning was sunny and warm, but he hardly
noticed it. His current investigations were bogged down, there was a
problem with his budget, and the summons to headquarters had
been disturbingly vague. The bland office block was only a couple of
hundred yards away from the converted terrace annexe in which his
team was based, but in his mind the distance was much greater. He
reached the entrance to New Scotland Yard and unconsciously
straightened his shoulders as he presented his identification, signed
the book, accepted a pass and took a lift to the sixth floor.

Commander Sharpe was standing at the window of his office
when Brock was shown in. As the figure turned from contemplating
the panorama of the city northward across St James Park, Brock
was once again struck by the way his boss seemed to fulfil the
promise of his name. The same height as Brock, six foot two, he was
much leaner in build and thinner of feature, and in appearance, dress
and manner he was, decidedly, *sharp*. This impression was reinforced
by his excellent memory, by the intensity of his gaze and his precise
form of speech. The effect on Brock was to make him feel vaguely
crumpled. He tried to remember when he'd last had his hair
cropped and beard trimmed.

'Morning, Brock. I see our friends are patching their roof again.'
Sharpe gestured towards the window, and Brock looked out to see
which particular friends he might be referring to. Close by there

was the Art Deco headquarters of the London Underground, beyond it the Wellington Barracks, and in the distance the rooftops of Buckingham Palace.

'Home Office,' Sharpe said, referring to the building to the right of the barracks. Further to the right again, Brock could make out the chimneys and rear windows of his own outpost, and was uncomfortably aware that, with a powerful telescope, Sharpe would probably be able to read the correspondence on his desk. 'That's the reason I wanted to see you.'

The Home Office roof? Brock wondered, but said nothing.

'Coffee?' Sharpe went over to a cabinet and poured boiling water into two individual coffee plungers. He carried them to the circular table on a tray with cups, sugar and cream.

'I find this is the best way to get a decent coffee in this place. How's the knee?'

'Much better,' Brock replied, automatically rubbing the joint as he took the offered chair.

'Physio?'

'Yes. That seemed to sort it out.' It was over six months since he'd been attacked by a mob of skinheads in the East End, but the leg still ached at night.

'The commendation was well deserved, Brock, well deserved.'

'Thank you, sir. It was much appreciated. And by DI Gurney.'

'Bren Gurney, yes. And your DS, Kathy Kolla, she also performed extremely well, didn't she? In difficult circumstances.'

Brock shifted uneasily in his seat. Sharpe's memory for names was well known, but still, it sounded as if his boss had been checking up on his team.

'Couple of important things I need to discuss with you, Brock. You're familiar with the Verge inquiry, I take it?'

Of course he was — the whole country had been following it avidly since May, when the body of Miki Norinaga had been found in her bed, naked and stabbed through the heart. Her husband, prominent architect Charles Verge, had not been seen since, and the international hunt for the missing man had become a national obsession. The press carried regular reports of sightings from around the world, but none had yet resulted in an arrest.

'It's one of those cases that just won't go away.' Sharpe stirred his coffee vigorously. 'Tabloids love it. Today he's seen in Sydney, last week in Santiago. He's Ronnie Biggs, Lord Lucan and the Scarlet Pimpernel all rolled into one. And he's not just any architect. High profile, international reputation, knighthood pending — the very epitome of Cool Britannia.' Sharpe snorted and sipped at his coffee.

'It's all very embarrassing,' he continued. 'He had some extremely important clients. Significant buildings for the German and Saudi governments, for instance, neither of which are pleased to find that their glossy new landmarks are the work of a murderer. And our friends in the Home Office are particularly cheesed off. Their new Verge masterpiece is nearing completion, a Category A prison as luck would have it — Marchdale, out in the fens. The Prince was going to do the opening, but that's in doubt now, and the Home Secretary has been taking a lot of stick in the House. You can imagine what the press'll make of the unveiling.

'What particularly galls our friends isn't just that their golden boy is a killer, but that the world believes he's got away with it. If they can't hush the whole thing up, which they can't, then they want some kind of resolution — either his arrest and incarceration in one of their grubbier institutions, or, better still, proof of his innocence.'

'Is that possible?'

'Hardly, but you can't blame them for hoping. The point is that after four months we haven't been able to deliver on either option, which is a major embarrassment for the Met. So ...' Sharpe deliberately placed his cup in its saucer and sat back, fixing Brock with one of his scalpel stares, '... it's been decided that we need a fresh approach. A new team.'

A move of desperation, Brock thought, not liking the sound of this one bit. 'Superintendent Chivers has been leading the inquiry, hasn't he?'

'Dick Chivers, yes. The proposal is that he now hands the reins over to you.'

'I see.' Hell, Brock thought ... a trail gone cold, all avenues exhausted, the press watching every move, bosses demanding miracles.

'You sound less than thrilled.'

'Chivers is a thorough detective. I doubt he'll have overlooked much.'

'There's no suggestion that he has. In fact, I'm certain that he's conducted himself impeccably. But without result. What the inquiry needs now is a fresh mind to rejuvenate it, and you have a reputation for coming out of left field and getting results. It's not a criticism of Chivers, but it is an expression of confidence in you, Brock.'

Or of panic, Brock thought, but saw that he would have to make the best of it. He tried to look pleased. 'Thank you, sir. When exactly is the prison due to be opened?'

'Three weeks. The Palace will make a final decision on their involvement one week beforehand.'

Brock began to frame an objection, but Sharpe went on. 'Form your own team. Take any of Chivers' people you want. He's waiting to brief you now. Room 413, two floors down. All right? Now, the second matter ...' He sprang to his feet, reached for a glossy document lying on his desk and slapped it onto the table in front of Brock.

'You're familiar with this, of course.'

Protect and Respect: Everybody Benefits. Diversity Strategy of the Metropolitan Police. Brock recognised the cover. Everybody in the Met had received one and there had been extensive reports in *The Job*, but he hadn't got around to reading it. There had been a series of briefing sessions for line managers, but he'd always been busy elsewhere.

'What do you think?'

'Well ...' Brock said cautiously. 'A positive move, post-Macpherson ...'

'Yes, yes. But more than that. In the Deputy Commissioner's words, this is a *core business imperative.*'

Sharpe paused to let that sink in, then tapped the document with his fingertips and went on severely, 'It's that important, Brock, and we all have to embrace it.'

Brock was wondering now whether this was some kind of reprimand. Had his absence from the briefings been noted, or had he inadvertently committed some error somewhere along the line? Had he been reported for political incorrectness?

'The Diversity Strategy includes a six-point action plan, as you know. Six strategic areas, right?'

For an awful moment Brock thought he was going to be tested, but Sharpe lifted his left hand, fingers outstretched, and ticked the points off with his right index finger, one by one, for emphasis. '*Leadership, crime, processes, workforce, training* and *communications*. And to help stimulate debate and develop policy in each of these strategic areas, six Strategy Working Parties are being established. One which will be particularly close to your heart, Brock, will be the Crime Strategy Working Party.'

He opened the booklet and read, '"Resolving problems, investigating and preventing crime through a more inclusive approach ..." Now, Human Resources have been charged with bringing forward names, and from our point of view, you will agree, it is crucial that the voice of experienced, serving detectives is heard on these committees. Especially the Crime Strategy Working Party.'

While Sharpe returned to his desk for another document, a sheaf of A4 pages clipped together, Brock thought, oh no, I'm not going to waste my time on some bloody committee.

'The name of one of your team has come up, Brock, and I wondered what you thought. DS Kolla.'

Brock hadn't expected this, and Sharpe saw his surprise. 'No?'

'I thought you'd be looking for someone older, sir.'

'She's got quite a few years under her belt now, and we're after new blood. Over the next ten years the Met is going to have to recruit two-thirds of its staff over again, and people at her level are going to be crucial to that process. Besides, she's got an excellent record at the coalface, both in crime detection and in interacting with ethnic communities. There are a couple of recent letters of appreciation here from community leaders; one from a Mr Sanjeev Manzoor of the Pakistani community in Stepney, and another from Mr Qasim Ali of the Shiite community.'

Brock was familiar with the letters. Sanjeev Manzoor had deemed it politic to be nice to Kathy, hoping to avoid prosecution for making false statements to a magistrate, and Qasim Ali probably fancied her. 'Yes, I got copies of the letters. They were well deserved. And she's a woman, of course.'

Sharpe smiled briefly. 'That too. And with an ethnic partner, I understand.'

'How did Human Resources get hold of that?'

'We've run a bit of a check on her, and it all sounds good. So what do you think? You don't look certain.'

'No, no, I think she would do very well. She's intelligent and articulate. I'm just being selfish. I don't want to lose her, especially if we're taking on the Verge case.'

'Oh, it would only be a part-time commitment, and you wouldn't be losing her forever — at least, not unless she performs brilliantly, in which case it could well open up a whole new career path for her. But you would hardly deny her that now, would you?'

'Of course not.'

'Good, well I'll speak to her. Keep it to yourself until then, will you?'

'Bugger,' Brock muttered under his breath after he had closed the door behind him, and strode off down the anonymous corridor towards the lift.

Dick 'Cheery' Chivers was seated in the middle of the small conference room on the fourth floor, staring dolefully at a pile of unopened files on the table in front of him. He looked up as Brock came in and rose unsmiling to his feet. He was a veteran cop of the same generation as Brock, and had a morose look at the best of times. Clearly this wasn't one of those. 'Brock,' he acknowledged grudgingly, and took the offered hand.

'Sharpe's just told me,' Brock said. 'I'm sorry, Dick.'

'He dropped it on me at nine this morning. No warning. Out of the flaming blue.'

'He made a point of saying that it was no reflection on the way you've been running the case.'

'Bollocks. Course it is. Got to be.'

'If it's any consolation, I like it as little as you.'

'Yeah, well, it puts you in the firing line, doesn't it?' Chivers said. The thought seemed to cheer him up a little. 'I sent back to my office for these to help you get started.' He placed his large fist on top of the files as if reluctant to give them up. 'I've put a lot of hours into this case over the past four months, Brock. We all have. We've covered every angle. It's bloody ridiculous changing jockeys at this stage in the race. Sheer bloody foolishness. And bloody insulting to me.' His face was becoming darker as his anger found voice.

'What reason did he give you?' Brock asked gently.

'He needs fresh blood!'

'That's what he said when he told me he was taking one of my best young detectives from me to put her on a committee. He must have blood on the brain.'

'Bloody vampire,' Chivers growled, but the anger had faded as quickly as it had bloomed. 'I told him, with a case like this, you've got to have patience. If you haven't caught the runner within the first week then you have to be prepared to wait until he becomes careless or homesick or unlucky, and gives himself away.'

'So you have no doubt that Verge was the killer?'

'None at all. We considered all the alternatives — business partner, commercial rivals, a possible lover — but there were no other plausible suspects.'

'And you think he's still alive?'

'We've no evidence that he is, but I'd say it's ninety per cent certain. He was last seen on the morning of Saturday the twelfth of May, when he returned from a business trip to the States. His wife's body wasn't found until the Monday morning, between forty and sixty hours after the time of death, according to the pathologist, so he had the whole weekend to get clear. Later on that Monday his car was found beside a beach on the south coast, his clothes neatly folded inside, along with a handkerchief stained with his wife's blood, and a piece of paper bearing the single word "SORRY" in block capitals. There's been no trace of a body, and the whole business with the car looked dodgy.'

'Like the Stonehouse case.' Brock recalled another famous disappearance case, when a British cabinet minister had staged his own apparent death while holidaying in Florida, leaving a pile of clothes on a beach.

'Exactly. You'd have thought he'd have been a bit more original, wouldn't you? A bit more creative? I've gone over the case with Brian Ridley, who picked Stonehouse up in Melbourne, and there are definite parallels.'

'And with Lord Lucan.'

'The murdered nanny, yes. Though of course he's never been traced.'

'So you think Verge is hiding out somewhere overseas?'

'South America is my bet.' Chivers relaxed his protective grip on the files and sat back with a grim smile.

'How come?'

'He's a fluent Spanish speaker, and he could probably pass himself off as a native. He was actually born Carlos Vergés in Barcelona to a Spanish father and English mother, and spent a part of his childhood over there. Then his father died and his mother brought him back to England and Anglicised the name. He's still got family there, cousins and the like, and my bet is that he went there first and they helped him move on. We had one possible sighting in Barcelona a few days after he disappeared, and we've been working closely with the Barcelona police. I've been over there a couple of times, and though we couldn't shake anything out of the family, I'm pretty certain that's where he went. He had to have had help.'

'I suppose so.'

'Must have. This murder couldn't have been premeditated. I mean, this wasn't some loser doing a bunk. This bloke was at the peak of his success, a worldwide reputation, featured on TV and in weekend colour supplements, an ego as big as his bank account. Killing her must have been a moment of blind fury, and it finished him as surely as it did her. From that moment the good life was over. We've been monitoring every bank account and possible source of funds, and there's been no contact. Apart from what he had in his pockets, he must be relying on friends for everything. And that must be a pretty shattering thing for someone in his position, yeah? It's going to get to him, especially in about six weeks' time.'

'What happens then?'

'He has one daughter, dotes on her. She's pregnant and he knew it. Baby's due towards the end of October. That's what I told Sharpe. I'm betting she'll have heard from him between then and Christmas, and that'll give us the chance we need. But that's not soon enough, apparently. Politics. Too many red faces. So, good luck, old son. You're going to need it.' A sudden thought struck him. 'I don't suppose we could bring the birth forward, eh? Have the baby induced?' He seemed to consider this seriously for a moment.

'I think that may be beyond our powers, Dick.'

Cheery Chivers shrugged gloomily and pushed the pile of files across to Brock, and they set about making arrangements for the handover. They continued over a lunchtime sandwich and coffee, then Brock had himself a haircut and beard trim on the way back to his own office. There he worked through the afternoon, sleeves rolled up, reorganising case loads, reassigning tasks within his squad. It was a Friday, and they had agreed that Chivers would give a full briefing to a joint meeting of both their teams on the following Monday morning. That would give Brock the weekend to go through the files himself and try to form some initial ideas of where they might go from here, and also to make up his mind which of Chivers' people he would need to poach. By six he was finished with the rescheduling, all except the irritating blank against the name Kolla. He was staring at this when there was a knock, and she put her head around his door.

'Have you got a moment, Brock?'

'The very person,' he said. Getting to his feet, he stretched stiffly and waved her in.

She was crisply turned out in a black suit he couldn't recall seeing before, and the effect with a white shirt and her short, straight blonde hair was very smart, he thought approvingly. Sharpe would have been impressed, certainly a good deal more so than with himself in his perennial crumpled charcoal job. 'How did it go?'

'You knew? About the committee?'

'Sharpe spoke to me this morning.'

'What do you think I should do?'

'Didn't you decide on the spot?'

'I asked him to give me the weekend to think about it.'

In the reflected glow of the pool of light shining from the lamp over the desk he noticed a small, unfamiliar scar on the side of the bridge of her nose. Had she acquired this on one of the cases they'd worked on together? Why had he never noticed it before? She was gazing at him steadily, waiting for his answer. He looked away and thought, this is how we end up lying to our friends, wanting to do the right thing by them.

'Of course you should do it. It's an honour to be picked, and it's a great opportunity. If nothing else, it'll look good on your CV.'

'But I hate committees. I never know what to say. I hate listening to people who love the sound of their own voices.'

'You just do what we do on the job — you sit quiet and listen and observe, and when the moment comes you put the boot in.'

She smiled, but still watched him carefully. 'So you recommended me?'

'He asked my opinion and I told him you'd be excellent.'

'And you want me to take it?'

'No, I'd rather have you here to be honest, but that's not the point. Look …' he added brusquely, '… you make up your own mind, but if you ask me I say you'd be mad to turn it down.'

'Okay, thanks. I suppose I'll do it.' Her eyes passed over the papers on the desk, the job schedules and files. 'Has something come up?' She read the label on the top file. 'Charles Verge?' Her eyes widened. 'They're not giving us the Verge case?'

'They are. We'll be having a briefing on Monday.'

'But that's fantastic!'

Her enthusiasm was immediate and completely untainted by Brock's misgivings. He envied her optimism and wondered if he'd been infected by Chivers' gloom.

'No, it's not. It's an act of desperation. Chivers' people have been flogging it for four months and they've got nowhere.'

'Yes, but we're better …' She grinned suddenly and said, 'It's an honour to be picked, and it's a great opportunity.'

Brock acknowledged his own rather awkward words with a reluctant smile. Kathy's attention had turned to the job matrix lying beside the files, and she frowned at the blank beside her own name. 'I'll be on the Verge team, won't I?'

'What did Sharpe have to say about time commitments?'

'He said it would be a fractional commitment, about fifty per cent. I just have to give the committee priority if there's a clash with other duties. Oh, come on, Brock! You have to let me on.'

He pondered a moment, then said, 'Okay,' and took up his pencil, writing '0.5' in the blank space.

She smiled her thanks, then checked her watch. 'I have to run.'

'A date?'

'I'm meeting someone. Leon.'

'Ah yes. Would you describe yourselves as partners these days, Kathy?'

She gave him an odd look. 'I might. Yes, something like that.'

'Have fun.' He turned back to his papers.

When she had gone he repeated softly, 'Something like that …' What did that mean, exactly? Something unresolved? He shook his head and hoped that Leon Desai knew what he was playing at.

On the way home through South London he stopped at a supermarket and stocked up for the weekend with some pre-cooked lasagne, a pork pie, salad, eggs, bread, coffee and a couple of bottles of Chilean red. That evening he began with the crime scene file, and eventually fell asleep in his armchair over a copy of the pathology reports.

By the following evening he felt he had a reasonable overview of the case. Although he had been given only a small part of the huge volume of material that had been generated, it was enough to confirm his earlier expectation that Chivers' team had done a very thorough job. Once he had become convinced that Verge had indeed bolted, Chivers had set about constructing a huge spider's web of trip-wires that spanned the globe. Phones were tapped, mail intercepted, bank accounts monitored, passenger lists scanned, in the hope that one day, somewhere, a contact would register. Given the celebrity of the runaway and the crime, foreign police forces had been glad to assist, and liaison officers in over thirty countries had been identified, in addition to normal Interpol links. Particular effort had gone into working with the police in Spain and in a number of Latin American countries.

Brock couldn't fault the investigation, assuming the initial assumptions were correct, and there seemed nothing to suggest other-wise. The only thing that niggled was a certain vagueness about the forensic evidence, an absence of information, which Brock found unusual. The handle of the murder weapon had revealed no finger-prints or DNA traces of the assailant; the victim's body showed no signs of injury apart from the fatal wound; the bedding on which she lay had been recently changed, and offered no forensic data; and neither did a single driving glove, found on the floor of Verge's car. It was almost as if the murder setting had been sterilised, wiped of drama and significance.

He sighed, poured himself a glass of wine and opened the file containing a summary of each of the 1863 reported sightings of Verge from around the world which had been officially logged up to and including the previous Sunday, quite apart from the thousands more that had been recorded on the various Verge web-sites that had sprung up. He was interrupted by the phone ringing at his elbow.

'I thought we were going to meet this weekend.'

Brock recognised Suzanne's voice, sounding slightly peeved.

'Yes, I'm sorry. I was about to phone. Something came up yesterday, and now I'm up to my ears in files. I don't think I'm going to make it.'

'Oh dear. A new case?' Her voice softened, prepared to be mollified.

'An old one, but they've decided it needs a fresh look, and they've dumped it on me.'

'It must be important. It's not the Verge case, is it?'

Brock was astonished. 'Well … yes, it is actually.'

'Oh David, that's fantastic! And you're in charge of it now?'

'Well, yes …'

'Just wait till I tell the kids. They'll be thrilled. Stewart thinks he got away in a submarine, and Miranda's sure she's seen him in our shop. Of course, they both think you should have been on it from the start.' Then a thought struck her. 'But you don't mean to say you've been down here without telling us?'

'No … Why?'

'Well, to see the place where he disappeared. Bexhill. The kids are sure he would have come through Battle on his way down to the coast.'

Brock hadn't really registered the fact that Verge's jumping point had been quite close to where Suzanne lived with her two grand-children. 'No, I hadn't got that far yet.'

'Well obviously you must. We've been down there to look for clues. We can show you exactly where the car was found. Stewart found an ice-cream wrapper that he thought should have been dusted for prints, but our local nick weren't much interested. No doubt he'll give it to you. And we worked out how Verge could have got to the Channel ports from there, that is if he wasn't picked up by a passing submarine.'

'You seem to know a lot about this.'

She laughed. 'Of course we do! David, this is the biggest thing since Princess Di. The beautiful couple, the crime of passion, the dis-appearance. We follow every move. Stewart's got a map of the world on his bedroom wall with pins stuck in for each sighting reported in the papers.'

More than I've got, Brock thought.

'Anyway, you'll have to come down. Why not make it tomorrow? The forecast is fine. We can have a picnic on the very spot.'

Brock looked around at the papers piled around his feet and said, 'You know, I think that's an excellent idea. I'll be there by noon, and you can give me a briefing.'

And so the following day Brock found himself sitting on a tartan travelling rug laid out on the patch of beach just below where Charles Verge's car had been abandoned, holding a chicken drumstick in one hand and in the other the bulging scrapbook which Stewart and Miranda had compiled of the crime. He found their information a good deal more readable than the police files, especially concerning the principal characters. There was an amazing number of cuttings from magazines and newspapers, many recent, but some dating back years, scavenged by the children from junk shops and doctors' surgeries. Verge appeared most often, a short, stocky figure with a Napoleonic gleam in his dark eyes, a good tan, close-trimmed black hair and rather large nose, at the controls of his own helicopter about to fly his plans of the German Ministry to Berlin, or with a beaming Home Secretary examining the model of the new Home Office prison, or helping his wife out of their silver Ferrari. The accompanying articles made much use of phrases like *cutting edge* and *precocious talent*, and described him variously as domineering, passionate and obsessive.

'He's dishy, isn't he?' Suzanne said, offering him a glass of wine.

'Looks a bit full of himself to me,' Brock grunted, and read the headline of an article obviously written before the lethal termination of his marriage, *My wife is my greatest critic: Charles Verge reveals all*. Brock took a sip of the wine and gazed out to sea. It was placid, empty, a light breeze ruffling the low swell. Gulls wheeled overhead. There was something voyeuristic, ghoulish even, about sitting on that spot, poring over these pictures of the missing man.

'You're quite convinced he didn't really drown?' he asked the boy.

'Oh yes. Look …' Stewart flicked through the pages to an article cut from a local paper, featuring interviews with local fishermen and sailors discussing currents and tides, all agreeing that the body would have been washed ashore further along the south coast within forty-eight hours of a drowning.

What most disconcerted Brock was that the kids had never once mentioned to him their fascination with the case, or asked him for inside information.

'I had no idea you were doing all this,' he said.

The lad hung his head guiltily. 'We wanted to ask you about it, but we thought you'd be cross, because it wasn't your case.'

'I see. Well, I think you've done a very professional job. In fact, I'd like to borrow this for a while, to show some people at Scotland Yard. Would you mind?'

Stewart's face lit up. He gave a whoop and ran to tell his sister who was tracking a small crab along the water's edge.

There were pictures of the victim, too. Verge's wife was a Japanese architect, Miki Norinaga, who had come to work for him five years earlier, a couple of years after his divorce from his first wife. The articles made much of her looks (*svelte, waif-like* and *willowy*) and the fact that she was only thirty, twenty-two years his junior. She gazed unsmiling from the pictures, dressed invariably in black, looking very self-possessed.

'After you've caught him, the trial will be such an anti-climax,' Suzanne said. 'I mean, there's not a lot he can say, is there?'

Brock smiled at her confidence. 'I suppose not.' He recalled the photographs of the bedroom scene.

'They don't like her very much, the press ...' Suzanne pointed to a picture of Miki on her husband's arm. 'They always show her looking sulky and imply that she was a gold-digging bitch. Look ... *A family friend is reported as describing the dead woman as manipulative and possessive. "Charles adored her, and she had him wrapped round her little finger."* But it wouldn't necessarily have been easy for her, being married to someone like that, do you think?'

They packed up their picnic things and made their way back to the road, where Stewart pointed out where Verge's Land Rover had been parked, and the spot nearby where he had found the ice-cream wrapper, which he had preserved in a plastic 'evidence bag'. He handed this solemnly to Brock, whose phone rang as he accepted it. The voice was that of an elderly woman, speaking too loudly into the receiver.

'Hello? Who is that?' she demanded.

'Who are you after?' Brock parried.

'I want Detective Chief Inspector Brock.'

'That's me.'

'My name is Madelaine Verge. I am the mother of Charles Verge. I am told that you have been given charge of the investigation into the murder of my daughter-in-law. It is imperative that I speak to you.'

'How did you get this number, Mrs Verge?' Brock saw the others prick up their ears at the name.

'I have many friends, Chief Inspector, and this is urgent. I have important information which you must know before you go any further. We must meet this afternoon.'

'I'm afraid ...' Brock began, but the imperious voice cut him off.

'I am confined to a wheelchair, so it would be convenient if you were to come to me. I live in Chelsea. When can you get here?'

'Can you give me some idea of the information you have, Mrs Verge?'

'Not on the telephone.'

'Very well.' He checked his watch. 'I can get to you at five. What's the address?'

As he drove them back to Battle, Suzanne said, 'I'd hoped you might have stayed over with us tonight, David.'

It was the first time she had said it openly in front of the children, and Brock felt she was making a point.

'Sorry. I'd have liked that, but I've got a lot to do.'

'He's got to get on with catching Charles Verge,' Stewart chipped in.

'I'll visit again soon,' Brock added. 'I promise.'

3

Madelaine Verge occupied the ground floor of a discreet Edwardian brick residential block in a leafy back street. There were unobtrusive indications that the resident was wheelchair-bound in the ramped approach to the front door where steps had once been, and the key-hole at waist height. Brock spoke into the intercom and she opened the door, a frail but belligerent grey-haired woman sitting bolt upright in the chair as if challenging comment. Inside the hallway it was clear that the whole interior had been gutted and remodelled to a light and spacious open plan.

She led him through into the lounge area, then wheeled about and peered at him intently for a moment through bright, alert eyes, as if trying to assess whether he was worthy of the task he'd been given. Then she invited him to sit, on a modern stainless-steel and black leather chair.

'Would you like a drink, Chief Inspector? Whisky?'

The voice was less strident than on the phone, but still forceful.

'I'd better not, Mrs Verge. I'm driving.'

'A little one, surely. I know I could do with one.' She didn't wait for a reply, but glided over to a built-in cabinet and took out a bottle and glasses, holding them carefully in arthritically twisted fingers.

'Ice?'

'Just water, thanks. Shall I get it?'

'You can bring the glasses through, if you like.' She handed them to him, then led the way to the rear of the house where a galley kitchen was laid out with a view over a small, lush garden.

'Charles designed everything here himself especially for my needs.' She waved at the low benchtops and cupboards, the specially positioned power points, the lever-action taps. 'He thought of everything.'

She dribbled water into the glasses and Brock carried them back to the lounge area. Although the spaces were designed to the same minimalist principles that he had seen in the crime-scene pictures of Verge's bedroom, here the walls were covered by framed photographs. He stopped to examine them.

'That was the one compromise I insisted on. Of course Charles wanted absolutely bare walls, but I said I must hang my photographs, so in the end he had to settle for designing the stainless-steel frames.' She chuckled affectionately at the memory.

All of the pictures seemed to be of Charles, either alone or with other important people. In one he was accepting a medal from the President of the Royal Institute of British Architects, in another shaking the hand of President Clinton.

'Many of these are other world-famous architects.' She emphasised *other*. 'There he is with Kenzo Tange and the Emperor of Japan in Tokyo. There with Peter Eisenman in New York, and there with Frank Gehry in Bilbao. Over here he's receiving the Erick Schelling Prize in Architecture. He was going to get the Pritzker, you know, if not this year then the next. I'm quite certain of it.'

The photographs recorded Verge ageing, from slender youthfulness to a more powerful middle age. In the most recent picture, taken on a rooftop with a group of Arabs, he seemed to have lost weight.

Miki Norinaga didn't appear anywhere, but there was one extraneous figure, a thin man with glossy black hair shown in a grainy black-and-white enlargement running in a singlet and shorts on a racing track.

'My husband, Alberto, Charles's father. That's him running for Spain in the 1948 Olympics in London. That's how I met him. One day I was sitting in the tube with a girlfriend, and there were these two very charming young men sitting opposite us, with running shoes tied round their necks. We got chatting, and they said they were going to run in the Olympics. That's the way it was then, so informal and casual. The athletes simply got on a bus or a tube with their kit and turned up for their event. We fell in love straight away. By the time the games were over we were engaged. We got married three months later in Barcelona and Charles was born in the following year. Alberto was an architect, too, you know. He was very progressive and becoming very well known in Spanish circles when he died suddenly eight years later.'

Brock felt he was being indulged, or perhaps indoctrinated into the Verge story by a very committed curator and archivist.

'You're obviously very proud of your son's achievements.'

'Oh, I am. I make no apology for that. He was an outstanding man. Posterity will confirm his talent. That's why this appalling lie must be laid to rest.'

'What lie is that?'

'That Charles murdered his wife.'

'Didn't he?'

'Of course not! The idea is quite preposterous. He was not a stupid man, Chief Inspector, and he did not lose control of himself. If he had had some dreadful quarrel with Miki, he simply would have walked out. The idea that he might have murdered her in this gruesome fashion and then run away is absolutely unbelievable to anyone who knew him. Apart from any moral scruples, he would never have acted so extravagantly against his own best interests. Believe me, I knew my son.'

She said this with a fervent insistence, but still as one presenting a purely rational argument.

'Then where is he now, Mrs Verge?'

'He is dead.'

'Dead?'

'Murdered, as surely as Miki was murdered. Indeed, that's *why* she was killed, to hide the fact of Charles's murder and make him appear the guilty party.'

She saw the frown on Brock's face and renewed her attack, leaning forward in her chair with frustration. 'It's perfectly simple; if you want to murder someone without drawing suspicion on yourself, you make him disappear and then kill his wife and make it look as if he did it and fled. It's the obvious conclusion, isn't it? The police always suspect the close family members first. The point is that *Charles* was the real target of the murderers, not Miki.'

'Murderers? More than one?'

'I would assume so. I imagine it was a professional job.' She said this scornfully, as if nothing but the best in the way of murderers would be good enough for her son.

'Instigated by whom?'

'By someone who stood to benefit greatly from his death. Chief Inspector, the work that Charles was involved in was not only wonderful architecture, it was also business on a very large scale. At the time of his disappearance he was the leading contender to design and build a new city for two million people in the province of Zhejiang in China. It would have meant enormous contracts, not only for his practice and that of other consultants, but also for British construction and engineering companies. Of course, when Charles disappeared the Chinese went elsewhere. They appointed an American firm.'

'And you're suggesting that the Americans murdered your son?' Brock had to make an effort not to sound incredulous.

'Why not? They can be very ruthless, the Americans, where business is concerned. But it may not be them. There were probably half a dozen other major projects coming Charles's way that someone would have killed for, either for money or prestige. The point is that this is a far more plausible motive than the one your predecessor insisted on pursuing so single-mindedly. All along I have been trying to point this out to him, without the slightest success. Instead he has stubbornly focused on the idea of a lurid family scandal, like a salacious schoolboy.'

This was going too far. Brock was about to point out coolly that she might be assumed to have a vested interest in this other explanation, when he stopped himself. Did she really prefer to have her son dead in order to preserve his reputation? Looking at her tight-lipped intensity, at the hall-of-fame pictures covering the walls, he rather thought she did. The alternative was probably just too painful.

So, instead of challenging her, he simply said, 'I'm sure Superintendent Chivers would have looked carefully into your suspicions, and I shall certainly talk to him about them.'

She didn't look convinced. 'It happened on the Saturday, May the twelfth, I'm sure of it. I believe they were waiting for him in his apartment when he returned from America. Sandy Clarke, his partner in the practice, picked him up at the airport and brought him home, and he was never seen again. I think they had already killed Miki and set up the whole thing. When he arrived they killed or drugged him, then took him down in the private lift to his car in the basement and drove him away. The abandoned car and clothes on the coast were meant to look implausible. I mean, no one could imagine Charles killing himself in such a way — such bathos!'

'How would he have done it, Mrs Verge?' Brock asked quietly. She seemed about to protest at such a question, then changed her mind. She had thought about this, he could see.

'He had a beautiful glider,' she said. 'I don't suppose you know anything about gliders.'

'Actually I do. I used to fly them myself, at a club down in Kent.'

She cocked her head and offered him a little smile. 'How interesting. Superintendent Chivers had no idea what I was talking about. Charles was passionate about it. He used to take me up, you know, even after I was reduced to this ...' She slapped the arm of her chair. 'We shared the sense of liberation, of escape from the drudgery of gravity. You do know what I mean, don't you? To glide through great cities of cloud at dusk, to pass under the rim of a cumulus and rise into the vast dome ... He was inspired by the architecture of clouds, by the infinite possibilities of light and space and form.'

'Yes, I do know what you mean,' Brock said, hearing the phrases that had most probably come from Charles, and the almost sensual agitation in her voice. 'And you feel that's how he would have chosen to make an end of things?'

'Exactly! He would have taken off into the dying sun and flown out to sea and simply disappeared. I know he would — he almost told me as much once.'

'He discussed it with you, disappearing?'

'Not seriously. But like many creative people he was liable to periods of darkness. During one such time he told me that, if it came to it, that's how he would go, just vanish into the blue.'

'It would have required help, to launch the plane ...'

'No. It's a Stemme S10 Chrysalis, Chief Inspector. A self-launching sailplane, with a 93 horsepower four-stroke aircraft engine and conventional landing gear.' She rattled off the specifications as if any fool should know them.

'A powered glider?'

'Yes. He loved the independence that it gave him, the ability to take off unaided and fly out of trouble when the gliding currents let him down. It was a fine example of hybrid technology, he used to say, such as he was famous for in his architectural designs. He has a field near Aylesbury where he kept the plane, and he could take off and land there unaided. That's where he would have gone if he'd wanted to disappear. The Chrysalis has an engine range of 900 nautical miles at 120 knots …'

She turned her head to gaze out the window at the sky, her eyes unfocused as if she were picturing the pale cross of her son's plane far out across the North Sea.

'But the plane is still at Aylesbury?'

'Yes. And whoever set up that grubby little pantomime on the south coast, you can be sure it wasn't Charles. He had more *style* than that.'

'Was this the important information you wanted me to know?' Brock asked gently.

'I thought it was vital that you understood this right from the outset, before you become embroiled in all the detail. And I shall be going to stay with my grand-daughter tomorrow, in the country near Amersham, and I wanted to tell you before I went. She's pregnant, you know, with Charles's grandchild.'

'Ah yes.' Brock drained his glass and shifted in his seat, but Madelaine Verge was reluctant to let him go.

'She lives not far from the house that Charles built for me when he first came home from Harvard, where he did his master's degree. Briar Hill was the first building the Verge Practice built, and it launched his career. It received most wonderful publicity. He said later that it was the best thing he ever designed. I lived there for twenty years, until I lost my mobility, and then it was just impossible to cope with all the changes of level. Charles had recently divorced his first wife, Gail, and he wanted me to live in the city, near him, so he converted this flat for me.'

'His first wife is an architect too, isn't she?'

'Gail, yes. They began the Verge Practice together, but of course Charles was the real driving force. After Charlotte was born Gail took a less active role, but until the pressure of his work took its toll on their marriage, she was always very supportive of his talent.'

Unlike the second wife, Brock inferred. He got to his feet. 'I have a lot of work to do, Mrs Verge. I'd better go. But thank you for your information. I promise I shall look into it.'

She pushed herself forward with her right hand, her left still clutching her untouched whisky. 'I wanted you to understand how important this is, Chief Inspector. I have lost my son, but I cannot bury him, nor save his reputation. Only you can do that. I am helpless.'

Brock doubted that.

4

The two teams assembled at the appointed time, awkward in each other's company like players who were uncertain what the game was, let alone which side they were on. Brock opened the proceedings by outlining the new orders from above and inviting Chivers to take over the briefing. The superintendent glowered at the meeting, as if daring anyone to find fault with what he was about to say, then slowly lit a cigarette in defiance of the sign on the wall behind him. In a flat, monotonous voice he delivered a well-prepared summary of his four-month investigation, aided by photographs, diagrams, a world map and the police scene-of-crime video. The acoustics of the room in the basement of New Scotland Yard were poor, and several times a voice from the back of the room would pipe up, 'Sorry, chief, what was that last bit again?' and Chivers would clear his throat, raise his volume a little and repeat.

At the end there was silence, no one game to ask a question. Chivers lit up again. His grinding monotone seemed to have cast a spell on them all, and Brock noticed the deadened expressions on the faces of Chivers' team. Finally, Brock's inspector Bren Gurney asked for more information on the Barcelona connection. Verge had a number of relatives there from his father's family, and in addition he had done architectural work in the city, including an apartment building in the port area for athletes competing at the 1992 Olympics, and he had visited the city regularly. Of the relatives, one had been of particular interest, a cousin who had been a close boyhood friend of the fugitive. This man ran an engineering manufacturing business which exported a range of valves and pumps to various parts of Europe and Latin America, and in particular Argentina, where he owned a local sales and servicing company.

Relatives and other contacts had been interviewed by detectives of the Cuerpo General de Policía in Barcelona, the CGP, and by members of Chivers' team, but none admitted to contact with Verge since his disappearance. Phone calls and financial transactions between the families in Spain and England were being monitored, and between the cousin's businesses in Barcelona and Buenos Aires, so far without result.

There was one other possible link with Barcelona. On the same Monday morning that Miki Norinaga's body had been discovered in London, a holidaying English couple called McNeil had been strolling along the Passeig de Gràcia, the main avenue of Barcelona's fashionable Eixample district, when Mr McNeil noticed a man get out of a taxi and quickly cross the pavement in front of them, then enter an adjoining building. After a moment's thought he said to his wife that he thought he recognised the man as the famous architect Charles Verge. McNeil was a recently retired structural engineer, and although he had never met Verge in person, he had seen his picture many times in industry journals, and confidently picked him out later when shown photographs. He didn't realise the significance of his sighting until they returned to England a week later, when they discovered the papers full of the Verge scandal, and he phoned the police hotline. By that stage the police had already had dozens of reports of Verge from all over Europe, but they knew of the family connection with Barcelona and paid particular attention to McNeil's story. From maps and photographs supplied from Spain the couple identified the building on the Passeig de Gràcia, and its tenants were questioned by the CGP — paying particular attention to the staff of a travel agency on the first floor — but again there was no result.

Someone asked about Verge's state of mind at the time of the murder. The clients he had met in California in the week before the murder had been interviewed, as had the crew on the overnight flight back to London, and both could say no more than that he had seemed normal and not unduly stressed, and he certainly hadn't appeared drunk when he disembarked. He had been met at Heathrow by his business partner Sandy Clarke, who said they had talked about Verge's successful trip and about a presentation they were doing on the following Monday morning. Verge had been calm and in good spirits.

According to his friends and colleagues in London, his relationship with Miki had gone through a change in the previous year or so. He had worshipped her when they first married, but more recently there seemed to have been a cooling between them, and rumours of disagreements. However, there had been no public scenes, and no one believed that Miki Norinaga might have had a lover. Everyone appeared to find the idea of Verge committing a violent murder quite inexplicable.

'What you've got to understand,' Chivers said, 'is that they all think Charles Verge was the Archangel Gabriel. He might have been an egotistical bastard at times, but that was okay because archangels have a lot to put up with. The important thing was that he could mesmerise the big clients, come up with the big ideas, and pay them all big salaries. And if he did bump Miki off, well, she probably deserved it, didn't she, because archangels are always right. What they're all secretly hoping is that he will turn up any day now with a perfectly reasonable explanation and everything can go back to the way it was before the Fall.

'And they didn't like Miki. They won't come right out and say it, because they're all nice middle-class people who wouldn't speak ill of the dead, but it's pretty obvious. The men didn't like her because they thought she manipulated Verge into marriage when he was on the rebound from a divorce, and she promptly changed from being a lowly apprentice into someone who acted as if she was the boss herself. And the women didn't like her because she was aloof and didn't share in their gossip, and because she got off with the man they all secretly fancied.'

Kathy, who had been examining the crime-scene and autopsy photographs, asked, 'Were there any injuries apart from the stab wound?'

Chivers shook his head. 'Nothing. What of it?'

'If they got into an argument and he flew into a rage, you'd think there would have been some preliminary physical stuff, a shove, a slap. Going out to the kitchen and selecting a knife seems very deliberate, cold.'

'That was how he got angry, apparently,' Chivers said. 'He didn't rant and rave. One of his staff said he could kill with a look if someone stuffed up. Another said it felt like being verbally disembowelled. And the killing was very efficiently done. The medical examiner was full of admiration. One very powerful, clean, deep blow. We did get an opinion from a psychologist, who was interested in the fact that both the blade and the woman were Japanese. He suggested that there might have been something symbolic in the act.' Chivers snorted to indicate what he thought of that idea.

When the questions seemed to have come to an end, Brock said, 'I had a call yesterday from Verge's mother, Madelaine Verge. She wanted to tell me about her theory that Charles was murdered for commercial reasons, and that his wife was killed to put us off the scent.'

This caused a buzz of interest, silenced by Chivers' exasperated shake of the head.

'Crap. She started flogging that line as soon as it became obvious to everyone else what her darling boy had done. She tried to get the press to take an interest, but they soon discovered that she had nothing to back it up. One of the tabloids tried to run with it — *Distraught mother claims Verge victim of conspiracy* — that kind of thing, but couldn't make it work. We did look into it, but came up with nothing. Charles's staff thought the idea was ridiculous. We couldn't find anything more substantial than a mother's wishful thinking.'

Brock decided to leave it there. He thanked Chivers, then read out the list of names of members of the earlier team who would be transferring to the new investigation, including Chivers' exhibits officer, statement reader and action manager, and the liaison coordinator with overseas forces. He had agreed these beforehand with Chivers, but it was an uncomfortable moment nevertheless, and at the end of it Chivers got to his feet, ground his cigarette in a plastic cup, stiffly wished them good luck and left with those no longer required.

Only one of the newcomers was a woman, Kathy noticed. DS Linda Moffat, the overseas liaison coordinator, was a tall, dark-haired thirty-odd year-old, who presented confidently and economically when it came to her turn to describe what they'd been doing. She spoke of her contacts, the Alonsos and Garcías and Alejandros, as if they were all old friends, and when Brock asked about Barcelona she became quite lyrical.

'Captain Ramiro Alvarez and Lieutenant Jésus Mozas are our two CGP contacts. We've visited them twice and they've been over here once. Ramiro's a bit grim, but Jésus is lovely. The trouble is, both they and Buenos Aires seem to be going a bit cold on us. We think they've been told to be polite but not spend any more money. Super-intendent Chivers was thinking of going over there again soon to try to keep them involved, but I think he was waiting until we had something definite to follow up. He was planning to take me,' she added hopefully, then clamped her mouth tight when she noticed the smirks passing between the men.

It took the rest of the morning to work through the business and allocate jobs. Kathy observed the way Brock quietly brought the two halves of his team together, coaxing Chivers' people to reconsider what they had done, identifying the areas of old ground that would have to be gone over yet again. Though he appeared all method and rationality, for Brock the most important part of the process was encouraging something more intangible, an act of faith, a belief that he would simply be luckier than Chivers. Sharpe wanted to believe this and so did the remnants of Chivers' team, flagging now after four months without a result, and Brock needed their faith to bring the hunt back to life.

When they finally broke up, Brock asked Kathy if she would go with him to have a look at the crime scene and talk to Verge's colleagues. She was glad, because he hadn't said in the meeting what her role in the investigation would be and she was afraid of being sidelined because of the committee business, which she was already regretting. A preliminary meeting of the working party had been called for later that afternoon, and she knew she'd have to watch her time.

As she drove across Westminster Bridge she decided to ask Brock what she would be doing. He didn't reply at first, gazing out of the side window at the sunlight glinting on the great wheel of the London Eye. Finally he said, 'I want you to explain Verge to me, Kathy. Get me inside his head. I want to understand what he was thinking when he did it. What was in his mind as he drove down to the south coast? Maybe if we understand better how his journey began, we'll have a better chance of working out where he's ended up.'

Sounds all right, she thought, then began to wonder how it could be done. Get inside his head. She pondered this as she negotiated the South Bank traffic, slowing at roadworks under the railway bridge by London Bridge station, past Southwark Cathedral then across Tower Bridge Road and into Bermondsey. Just lately, with Leon, she'd begun to doubt if it was possible to get inside anyone else's head, especially a man's. They'd been living together for six months, but there were parts of his mind that were completely closed to her, she knew, just as there were parts of hers that she hadn't let him see. And if it was impossible with someone that close, how could you do it with a man who had vanished four months before?

As if he were reading her mind, Brock said, 'You might have a talk with his mother, and while you're doing it, imagine her as a man, and twenty years younger.'

Not a bad idea. Maybe she should do the same thing with Leon's mum, the tyrant of the Desais.

'And if that doesn't work, you might get some inspiration from this ...' Brock reached into his briefcase and pulled out the kids' scrapbook. 'Stewart and Miranda put it together. Quite a good effort, and a lot more lively than our files.'

Kathy smiled. She knew the children, abandoned by their mother to their grandmother's care, and she knew of their ambivalent attitude to Brock, seen sometimes as a heroic crime-fighter and other times as an intruder threatening the security of their home. She wondered if this project was an attempt by Stewart to come to terms with his grandmother's friend.

She turned off Jamaica Road into a maze of narrow streets that led towards the old brick warehouses lining the south bank of the river. Tyres drumming on granite cobbles, she slowed opposite a vertical plane of glass, shockingly naked among all this brick and stone, which she recognised from a picture in the Verge Practice brochure that Superintendent Chivers had circulated at the briefing. In the photograph, the half-dozen floors behind the glass had been filled with people, illuminated like mannequins in a department-store window or actors in some kind of experimental theatre, but now she could see no one.

A woman was waiting for them, introducing herself as Jennifer Mathieson, information manager, her red hair made more vivid by a black silk blouse and suit. As she led them to a glass lift in the central atrium, Kathy noticed that not only the structure of the building, but also all of its furniture and fittings — including the reception desk, stairs and tables — were made of glass and glittering stainless-steel rods.

'It was you who found the body, wasn't it, Ms Mathieson?' Brock asked as they glided upwards.

'That's right.' She sounded nonchalant, the shock and immediacy of her discovery long gone. 'I'll take you up to the apartment after you've seen Sandy Clarke.'

The lift sighed to a stop and she led the way to a glass-enclosed office to one side of the atrium with a view out over the river. The room was spartan and immaculately neat, a row of gold-embossed design award certificates forming a frieze along one wall. Clarke rose to his feet from behind his desk, shook hands gravely and they took their places on black leather swivel chairs arranged around a glass-topped table.

He was tall, careful and rather elegant in both dress and movements. He straightened his tie with fingers that were long and delicate, like a pianist's. 'Has there been some new development?' he asked, and it seemed to Kathy that the possibility worried him.

But as Brock explained the changes to the investigating team Clarke looked pained, as if at the thought of having to go through the whole thing again for their benefit. 'It all seems academic now,' he said, voice flat. 'You're not going to find him after all this time, are you?'

'You think he's found a secure bolthole?'

'I didn't say that. As I told your colleagues, I find this whole tragedy inexplicable. The idea of Charles committing murder and then running away just doesn't make any sort of sense to me. Both actions would be completely out of character.'

'Is there any other plausible explanation?'

'Well ...' Clarke sighed as if reluctant to go over old ground, and ran a smoothing hand over hair which was still thick, though flecked with grey. 'My only thought was that he must have disturbed an intruder when he went up to his flat that morning, someone who had already killed Miki, and then forced Charles to leave with him. But I accept that you've found no evidence of anything like that.'

Brock nodded. There had been no sign of a forced entry or a struggle. 'You were the last person to see him that Saturday morning, weren't you?'

'Yes. He'd been over in California for the previous three days on a project, and I picked him up at Heathrow after an overnight flight from Los Angeles. He was his usual self, energetic, wanting to know what had been going on, and he got me to make a detour on the way home to look at a site he was interested in. When we reached our offices I gave him a copy of a report we'd done for a presentation on the following Monday, so that he could brief himself over the weekend, and he took the private lift straight up to his apartment. I worked in the office for the rest of the morning, then went home, and I didn't see either him or Miki again.'

'What about Mrs Madelaine Verge's theory, about some kind of commercial sabotage?'

Clarke shook his head ruefully. 'I know she's convinced herself it's the only explanation, and I can't blame her for that, but it doesn't stack up. Oh, I'm not saying that some of our competitors wouldn't stoop to dirty tricks. A couple of years ago a large model of a competition entry of ours for a new parliament building in East Africa mysteriously caught fire the night before the presentation, and we were pretty sure it was no accident. But not this, not murder. Apart from anything else, the Americans who won the Wuxang City project didn't need to resort to anything like that. They won because they undercut our fee bid, that's all. They wanted it more than we did, and cut their fee below what we were prepared to contemplate.'

'What about other projects?'

'No, it's really not plausible. Knocking us out wouldn't necessarily guarantee that a particular competitor would get the job. It's not credible.'

'How long have you worked with Mr Verge, Mr Clarke?'

'Almost twenty-five years. I joined him in the early days, soon after he and his first wife, Gail, returned from America, when we worked from a couple of rooms in the house they'd bought in Fulham.'

'So you know him very well. How would you describe him?'

'Oh ... totally committed, passionate about his work, tremendous energy, inspirational, a great persuader, very imaginative ...' The adjectives trailed off.

Brock said, 'I heard someone describe him as an egotistical bastard.'

Clarke allowed himself a little smile. 'He would probably have accepted that, a necessary part of the job. You see, to arrive at a design concept with absolute clarity, and then to sustain it through the years of challenges and difficulties of getting it built, you need a certain single-mindedness, a confidence in your own judgement that might be interpreted as arrogance. And we all accept that. Anyone coming to work here knows that they have to do things the Verge way.'

'Yes, but in personal matters ... a passionate man, you said. Capable of a crime of passion?'

'Passionate about his work, I said. But he didn't allow his emotions to run away with him. He was much more deliberate. That's what I found so inexplicable.'

'And you didn't notice any changes in his behaviour in the months leading up to the murder?'

'I've thought a lot about that. I mentioned that I'd seen him taking pills a couple of times, but I understand his doctor wasn't prescribing anything, so they were probably just aspirin or vitamins or something. As for his manner, I thought he did seem more agitated lately, less inclined to concentrate, which I put down to overwork. And I was aware, the whole office was, of some undercurrent between him and Miki. More on her side, actually. She seemed less dependent on him, less willing to defer.'

'Ms Norinaga was strong-willed too, was she?'

'Oh yes.'

'How did that work, if he was so used to being number one?'

'At first she was his devoted disciple, hung on his every word. Then later, after they were married, he indulged her, encouraged her to express her own ideas.'

'Well, I suppose it was natural that she'd want to do that. She was an architect in her own right, wasn't she?'

'It was hardly the same,' Clarke retorted. 'Charles was im-measurably more experienced, and talented. I mean, Miki had only been out of architecture school for a few years.'

'Do you think he might have been losing his touch? I suppose architects can go off, like soccer players?'

'It doesn't usually work like that. Architecture is a long game, and architects tend to get better with age and experience. Frank Lloyd Wright designed one of his greatest masterpieces in his eighties. Charles wasn't even approaching his peak ...' Clarke paused as if struck by some thought.

'What's the matter?'

'It just occurred to me — Wright's second wife was murdered, too. Their servant went berserk with an axe, if I remember rightly, killed her and burned the house down.'

Brock sucked his mouth doubtfully. 'You're not suggesting a parallel?'

'No, no, of course not. Only ...' He shook his head. 'Goodness ...'

'What?'

'Well, Miki Norinaga was the niece of a client of ours in Japan — that was how she came to work for us here in the first place, as a young graduate. And Frank Lloyd Wright's second wife — I'm trying to remember this from history lectures and I'm not even sure if they ever married — anyway, she was the wife of one of his clients. Wright had this breakdown, burnt out when he turned forty, and he ran away with her to Europe. They told nobody, just took flight and disappeared. Then later, after they'd returned to America and he'd built this house, she was murdered ...'

Clarke took a deep breath and seemed to pull himself together. 'I'm sorry, this isn't relevant. What else can I tell you?'

Brock fished inside his suit pocket for his half-rim glasses, propped them on his nose and began to turn the pages of his notebook as if looking for something. Clarke waited for him with a frown.

'How was his sex life?'

Clarke looked startled. 'Frank Lloyd Wright's?'

'Charles Verge. Were there any difficulties in that area?'

Clarke's face darkened. 'I wouldn't know. We didn't talk about that sort of thing.'

'Really? Not even a hint? Is there any possibility she might have had a boyfriend?'

'No,' Clarke said flatly. 'I went through all this with the last people. We would have had some inkling if she had.'

'And you noticed nothing odd in his manner that Saturday morning?'

'I've gone over that hour in my mind a hundred times. He seemed absolutely normal, a bit tired from the flight, but untroubled.'

Brock seemed unhappy with this reply. 'From his photographs I got the impression that he'd lost a bit of weight recently, let his hair grow.'

'You're right. It's sometimes difficult to notice small changes when you see someone almost every day, but Denise, my wife, commented that he'd lost weight. She thought he was looking younger.'

'Was he drinking more?'

'I hadn't noticed … He certainly wasn't affected by drink that morning.'

Brock said nothing for a moment, studying his notes, then asked, 'So there was no sign, looking back, that anything was wrong?'

'Premeditated?' The word burst abruptly from Clarke, who seemed almost as surprised by it as the detectives. He flushed and added, 'Is that what you're thinking? That Charles planned it?'

It wasn't what Brock had meant, but he was intrigued by Clarke's response. 'Is that a possibility, would you say?'

Clarke shook his head firmly. 'No, I'm sure it isn't.' He swung his chair round to face the glass wall overlooking the river. 'How could it be?' He stared out at a gang of pigeons wheeling in the sky as if he would have liked to join them.

Honest men, Kathy thought, trained as boys to tell the truth, and despite a lifetime of contrary experience, can betray themselves in small ways. They begin fiddling with paperclips or suddenly avoid a questioner's eyes, as Clarke had just done. Curiously, she found it harder to spot the same signs in women.

Brock seemed to have had the same perception. He stared thoughtfully at Clarke for a moment, then turned to the information manager. 'What about you, Ms Mathieson? Did you notice any change in his manner?'

'Well, you're right about him losing weight. I think it was stress. And I did think he'd lost interest a bit lately. Do you remember the last awards night, Sandy? We were up against the other big London names — Foster, Rogers, Wilford — for the annual design awards, and that usually brought out the competitive side of Charles. But he seemed almost indifferent last time.'

Clarke shrugged and glanced at his watch. 'I'm rather pressed for time at present, Chief Inspector. Do you think I might hand you over to Jennifer to show you the flat, and Charles's office too, if you wish?'

'Just one more thing, Mr Clarke. I understand you were also the last person to see Ms Norinaga alive, on the Friday night?'

'Yes, that's right. We were working late on the presentation for the Chinese on the following Monday. The others finished about eight, but Miki and I went on till eleven.'

'That's late.'

'Yes, there was a lot to do to get everything ready so the media team could finish the video for Monday.'

'How was Ms Norinaga when you left her?'

'Tired, but quite cheerful. Excited about the project.'

'She didn't mention anyone coming to visit her that weekend?'

'No, she didn't say what her plans were.'

'And you didn't go up to her apartment that evening before you left?'

'No.'

Kathy knew that the autopsy hadn't been able to establish the time of death more closely than the twenty-four hours between the Friday and Saturday evenings.

Brock nodded, and he and Kathy got to their feet and followed Jennifer Mathieson, leaving Clarke contemplating the pigeons whirling outside his window.

'There are two penthouse apartments,' Mathieson explained as they waited for the lift. 'The idea was that the senior partners would live there and share a housekeeper and cook, but in the end only Charles moved in. Sandy and Denise couldn't face living on top of the shop, I suppose.'

'So the other flat was unoccupied at the time of the murder?'

'That's right. There were people working down on the office floors over that weekend, but this lift gives independent access to the penthouse floor from the street and the basement car park, where Charles kept his Landy.'

Kathy looked at the floors stacked like bookshelves around the atrium. There were people working at computers and drawing boards, a group clustered around a table, but not as many as she had expected.

When she commented on this, Mathieson lowered her voice and said, 'Our staff has shrunk by a third in the last four months. It's been a catastrophe.'

The lift arrived and they stepped in. When the doors closed she went on, voice normal again, 'In fact, I'm moving on myself. It became pretty clear in the months after Charles disappeared that things were going to change, with projects being cancelled and no new ones coming in. Sandy puts a brave face on it, but I'd be surprised if they're still in this building a year from now.'

There was little in the apartment to add to what they had already learned from the police video and still photographs of the crime scene, except that it could now be appreciated in the context of the whole building, with the same steel and glass detailing carried through into its bathrooms and kitchen and furnishings generally. It occurred to Kathy that the Japanese kitchen knives looked as if they could have come from this same kit of parts, so that it was almost as if Miki Norinaga had been killed with a splinter of the building itself. The only colourful element in the whole flat was a large painting in the living room. It was an abstract with geometric figures, squares and segments of circles, in vivid primary colours, and the contrast between it and the severe constraint of the rest of the interior hadn't been apparent on the video. The signature in the bottom corner meant nothing to Kathy, but those on the black outfits in Miki's wardrobe certainly did.

After they'd had a good look round, each taking notes, Jennifer Mathieson took them back to the lift and down to the level of Clarke's office, but this time she led them to the opposite side of the atrium, where Charles Verge had had his office. She opened the door with a key.

'Apart from his computer and his diary, which your people took away, everything is exactly as it was last May.'

There were a desk and chairs identical to those in Clarke's room, bookshelves, a drawing table and another low table on which a model stood. On the drawing table lay an open book, a roll of yellow tracing paper and a pencil abandoned on some rough sketches, as if Verge had only just stepped outside. Despite the similarity to Clarke's office, the atmosphere seemed quite different, more sombre and purposeful. There were no framed certificates on the walls, but just one etching, of what looked like some gigantic ancient crypt, with iron rings attached to huge stone piers. It was hung directly over the model, which was a large grey and white construction beneath a clear Perspex cover. Kathy looked back up at the etching, trying to work out if there was supposed to be a connection, when a voice behind her said, 'Piranesi, eighteenth century.'

She turned and saw Sandy Clarke at the door, observing her.

'He drew fantastical prison scenes, terrifying and sublime. And that …' Clarke pointed at the model, '… is Charles's last master-piece, the Home Office project; not quite so terrifying, perhaps, but possibly sublime.'

'It's a prison, isn't it?'

'Yes, a radically new kind. Designed not just to punish or rehabilitate, but to change the man. I paraphrase, I'm not altogether au fait with the theory, but that's the essence of it. The building, along with the regime, the training programs, the medications and so on, is designed to reconstruct personalities, to make new men.' He said this with a slight sceptical lift of the eyebrow. 'Charles was fascinated by the idea. No, more than that, obsessed with it. He even spent some time in gaol as part of his research.'

'Not new women?'

Clarke smiled. 'This one is just for men. I believe they represent the bigger problem and the more testing subjects.'

Brock had been listening to this in silence. Clarke's words reminded him of a report he'd read about a new Home Office program, a radical response to an ever-expanding and recalcitrant prison population. He hadn't realised it had been taken so far.

Clarke had a book in his hand, which he offered to Brock. 'If you want to know more about our work you should have a look at this.'

'Thanks.' Brock examined the glossy hardback, thick and square, titled *The Verge Practice: Complete Works and Projects, 1974–1999*.

He had been skimming another book lying open on Verge's drawing board. On one page was a set of plans, titled 'Ledoux, Prisons, Aix-en-Provence, 1787. Engravings from Ramée.' The plans were each a perfect square divided into four quarters, and looked remarkably similar to the basic arrangement of Verge's Home Office model. Turning the page he had come across a section underlined in pencil. He had read it, then taken notes.

'I know what you're thinking,' Clarke said. 'You're thinking how ironic it would be if Charles ended up as the first inmate of his own masterpiece. I think we've all had that thought.'

'You don't see him as a suicide then?'

Clarke shook his head firmly. 'No. Never.'

It wasn't until they were back in the car that Kathy realised that she was going to be late for her committee. Well, there was nothing to be done about that, and the Verge case was much more interesting anyway.

'Odd that Clarke should have thought I was implying some kind of premeditation on Verge's part,' Brock said. 'I hadn't meant that at all, but that was the way he took it.'

'Yes, I noticed that too. Almost as if he'd been expecting someone to raise it.'

'Or half believed it himself. What kind of man would that make Verge?'

'Cold-blooded, sick? But as everyone keeps telling us, killing her like that was so much against his own interests.'

'Self-destructive as well as obsessive ...' Brock pondered, pulling his notebook out of his pocket. 'Did you notice that book lying on his drawing table? There was a passage there that was underlined.' He searched through his notes. 'I hate it when people mark beautiful books like that,' he grumbled. 'Yes, here ... Sometime in the 1780s the architect Ledoux was doing research for a prison he was designing. He was studying all the latest theories of incarceration, and he paid a visit to a Doctor Tornotary, a scientist, anatomist and amateur criminologist, who collected the bodies of dead criminals for dissection. This is what he wrote:

He sat me down in the middle of a select collection of heads, ranged in order. 'You who are an artist, who have studied the conformation

43

of the human body and its relations to the brain and stomach,' he said, 'judge the characters, vices, and crimes of these humiliating remains of the dignity of man.' After having reflected, I assembled my thoughts: 'The first and the second,' I said, 'were assassins; the third died of anger.' This was enough. He ran to his records, leafed through them: 'Ah,' he cried, 'I am not indeed mad.'

'What do you make of that? Why did Verge mark that passage?'
'Perhaps I should put it to my committee.' Kathy checked her watch. A jam had formed around the roadworks at London Bridge.
'I think I'll have a talk to his doctor,' Brock said.

5

Kathy hurried into the room, forty minutes late. Everyone was sitting round a table studying documents, and they looked up and stared at her. For a moment she felt exactly as she had on the first day of primary school, when her mother had got lost on the way and they'd arrived long after the classes had started. Then a man at the head of the table got to his feet and offered his hand with a warm smile. 'You must be Kathy. I'm Desmond. Welcome. I've been appointed the chair of this working party.'

Desmond was West Indian and in police uniform, the twin stars of an inspector on his shoulders. He introduced her to the others, and she shook their hands in turn. There was one other person in uniform, Shazia, a woman constable wearing the new Hijab headdress for Muslim officers. Next to her was Rex, wearing a Sikh turban, then a young white man with cropped hair, narrow glasses and a cool, slightly myopic gaze. He was Nathan, apparently, and next to him was Jay, a young white woman, also with cropped hair and narrow glasses. Finally, Desmond introduced her to a man seated by his right hand, Robert; the oldest person in the room, Robert was a middle-aged administrative officer appointed to service the working party. He gave Kathy a small, incurious smile, as if he already knew all about her.

'I'm sorry about the short notice for the meeting,' Desmond went on. 'It's been sprung on all of us. Apparently time is short. I hope it didn't put you out too much.'

'No, I'm sorry I'm late. I've just been put on a new case and I got caught up.'

'I hope it's something interesting,' Shazia, the WPC, beamed enthusiastically.

'Yes, it is.' Kathy hesitated and they all looked at her expectantly. 'The Verge inquiry, actually.'

'Oh, how exciting! Has there been some new development?'

'No, just some changes in the team.'

'Well, at least they've put a woman on it,' Jay, the other woman, chipped in. 'The men wouldn't want to catch the bastard. They all believe his wife must have deserved it.'

Desmond coughed tactfully. 'Let's get back to business, shall we? Robert has prepared a package of material for each of us, and we've been scanning through that.' He indicated a plastic folder sitting at the remaining empty chair. Kathy took her place and opened the package, heart sinking at the thick wad of material within — agenda, terms of reference, summary of background, briefing papers, photocopies of press cuttings and statements ...

She paused at a page outlining the CVs of the members of the working party. Desmond was in the personnel department of the Metropolitan Police, and Shazia had recently joined the Race Hate Unit at Rotherhithe. Rex was a civilian member of a community policing committee, Nathan was a lawyer with a large private charity and Jay represented a body called Gay Victim Alliance. Looking at the six names, Kathy thought how careful someone had been with the selection. There were three men and three women, three white and three coloured, three police and three civilians. It was a masterpiece of balance; whatever happened, no one could accuse its convenors of bias, except perhaps in age, for they were all young.

'Let's turn to the agenda, shall we?' Desmond suggested. 'I've put the program as the first item, because that is the most critical thing at present. Our immediate deadline is the next meeting of the Joint Conference in three weeks. Each of the working parties will be expected to present an interim working paper at the conference, with some initial analysis and ideas ...'

There was a buzz of consternation round the table.

'Three weeks?' 'That's ridiculous!' 'Are you joking?'

'I know, I know,' Desmond said soothingly. 'It's just unfortunate how the timing has worked out. Believe me, I'm as concerned about it as you. As chair, I'll be the one who has to present our paper.'

Rex had been silent up to this point, but now he cleared his throat loudly and the murmur died away. Kathy noticed that he was resting his clenched fist on a newspaper folded to a large colour photograph. She recognised it because it had been in the paper she'd been reading on the tube into work that morning, a picture of the family of an Asian boy trampled by a police horse during a riot up north over the weekend.

'We cannot be steamrolled,' he said, in a deep, powerful voice that held everyone's attention, 'by some ridiculously short, artificial deadline, into producing half-baked ideas. I didn't agree to join this committee on those terms.'

'Yeah, that's right.' Jay nodded her cropped head vigorously.

'Of course, Rex, but I don't think ...' Desmond tried to calm things down, but the Sikh hadn't finished.

'There are a number of basic issues we have to address before we can even begin to think about producing statements. Such as the make-up of this committee.'

Kathy realised she wasn't the only one who'd been studying that. But how could he object to it?

Desmond clearly thought the same. 'Well, I wasn't involved in the selection process, Rex, but I must say, looking at who's here, that it seems extremely well balanced. I think Robert and whoever else was involved have done a pretty good job.'

'The fact that it's so evenly balanced makes the position of chair especially crucial. Presumably the chair has a casting vote, right?'

'The aim is to reach consensus, Rex. I would hope that we don't ever have to get to the stage of taking votes ...'

'All the same, the chair is important, symbolically and practically.' Rex was sitting very upright and still, not meeting their eyes, but staring down at the newspaper by his hand as he spoke. 'And right away we're giving the wrong message by having the committee chaired by a member of the police. I thought the whole point of this exercise was to listen to the community?'

'Yeah,' Jay agreed, watching Rex with interest.

'But the community just isn't going to give credibility to policies

47

coming from committees set up and chaired by the police, with a few token community reps to make them look respectable.'

Desmond took a deep breath. 'I wasn't involved in the decision-making process that led to my appointment as chair. Can you throw any light on the thinking behind that, Robert?'

Robert looked mildly surprised to be brought into the scrap, but he smiled benignly and said, 'Well, I rather think that the argument is that this whole exercise is being carried out by the Metropolitan Police in order to improve its performance and level of service to the community at large. So it is essentially a police process, informed by the highest possible level of input from community representatives, whose contributions will of course be absolutely crucial. The chair of each committee must have an understanding of the context within which new policies will be framed. In other words, the chairs must understand how the police service operates, and must be able to present the ideas of their committees in a way that the police hierarchy can understand and take on board.'

Rex suddenly rose to his feet, snatched up the newspaper report of the weekend riots and threw it onto the table in front of Robert. 'I think we all understand very well how the police service operates, thank you. And if the police hierarchy is so bloody stupid that they can't understand the words of ordinary members of the community without having them dressed up and interpreted, then I'm not inter-ested in having my name associated with this bit of whitewashing.'

He turned and marched out of the room.

The meeting sat in stunned silence for a moment, then Desmond got hurriedly to his feet and ran after the departed Rex. Robert looked shocked, unused, perhaps, to displays of naked anger in his usual line of work, or possibly contemplating a committee-selection disaster. Everyone else was silent, reluctant to speak out now in front of the bureaucrat. Robert must have sensed his isolation, and with an embarrassed little cough rose to his feet. 'Excuse me,' he murmured, and made for the door.

'Well,' Jay said, 'maybe this'll be more interesting than I expected.'

• • •

Brock's visit to Charles Verge's doctor was less contentious. The surgery was in a quiet cul-de-sac mews in Belgravia, and the doctor had a grave dignity to suit. 'I made a statement some months ago, Chief Inspector. I don't really see what I can add.'

'We're going back over some of the old ground just to make sure nothing was missed.'

'You're still no nearer to finding Charles, then? I really don't think I can throw any light on where you might look.'

And as Brock took the doctor back over his earlier statement, he tended to agree. Charles Verge had been his patient for over ten years, during which time he had seen his doctor two or three times each year, for an annual check-up and for other minor ailments — a recurring tennis elbow, some lower back pain, a couple of viral infections, and a spell of about a year following his divorce when he had been prescribed an anti-depressant. The only remotely unusual thing about the record was the fact that Verge hadn't seen his doctor at all in the twelve months leading up to his disappearance, a longer gap than any previously.

'I put that down to everything going well — with his marriage I mean.'

'You noticed a difference when he remarried?'

'Certainly. He seemed rejuvenated.'

'You were Ms Norinaga's doctor, too, weren't you?'

'Yes, since their marriage. The last time I saw her was a month before the tragedy.'

Brock consulted his notes. 'That was for a prescription for a contraceptive pill, wasn't it? Did she discuss her sex life with you?'

'Very little. She was a woman of few words, and it wasn't a language problem. She was very articulate and spoke English fluently. She was just very private.'

'There was no suggestion of any difficulties with her husband?'

'Not at all.'

'Tell me about this period when you prescribed anti-depressants for Mr Verge.'

The doctor consulted his file. 'It was seven years ago, around the time of his divorce. I do recall him saying that he had experienced periodic spells of what he called "despair" before, when he lost confidence in himself, but this instance was clearly related to the breakdown of his marriage.'

'I'm surprised. I mean, the picture I've been getting is of a man with supreme confidence in himself.'

'Mmm, he certainly gave that impression, but the marriage breakdown took its toll. His symptoms were classic — sleeplessness, lack of energy, poor appetite. I had him on Zoloft for fourteen months, moderate dose, then he came off it and the symptoms didn't recur.'

'And nothing more recently?'

'No.'

As he showed Brock out, the doctor seemed to feel a sudden surge of sympathy for the policeman with his rather weary stoop and disappointed frown. 'Haven't been much help, have I? But to be honest, you're not likely to catch him now, are you? He's probably sunning himself on some distant beach, and really, what good would be served by dragging him back here and going through all the trouble and expense of a trial and a gaol term, eh? He did a terrible thing, and he's lost everything as a result. He's no danger to anyone now.'

Brock guessed that a lot of people shared the doctor's opinion. Large sections of the press seemed to mask this view with only the barest of nods to notions of justice.

'I doubt if the victim's family feels that way, doctor. Thanks anyway for your help. Oh incidentally ...' a thought seemed to strike him, '... you wouldn't know if Charles Verge had a doctor in Barcelona, would you? He visited there quite frequently.'

'Sorry, no idea. But it's not likely that there's a medical explanation for any of this, is it?'

'No, you're probably right.'

Brock turned and strode away, taking a deep breath of the warm afternoon air and catching just a hint of the tang of turning leaves and approaching autumn.

When he got back to his office he opened the book that Clarke had given him on the work of the practice. It was obviously a high-quality production, printed on thick paper with a fine satin surface. The greater part consisted of beautifully printed photographs and plans, with a couple of introductory essays — the first, according to the dust jacket, an analysis of Verge's work by an internationally acclaimed author of numerous seminal works on architectural theory. If Brock had hoped for enlightenment from this he was quickly disappointed, for the text was, to him at least, largely incomprehensible.

He had always held that, if the giants of modern theory — Darwin, Marx and Freud — could write lucid prose, then so should everyone else, but he realised that he was in a minority. After struggling to comprehend the private meanings and convoluted phrasing of the first couple of paragraphs, he gave up and, like most other people he assumed, turned his attention to the pictures. The essay was peppered with little images — a Mongolian yurt, a Zeppelin airship, grain silos, a Japanese teahouse, a seashell, a glider — but what these had to do with Verge's philosophy of architecture Brock wasn't certain. He noticed a phrase that Madelaine Verge had used, 'hybrid architecture', which apparently had something to do with yin and yang and post-modernism and generally having the best of all possible worlds. He turned with relief to the photographs and plans of Verge's buildings. The sequence of plans was introduced by a quote from Le Corbusier, 'The plan is the generator', and although Brock found it impossible to interpret how they worked, for there was no lettering on them to identify the function of the rooms, he was struck by their abstract beauty, like densely worked cartoons or X-rays, some long and spiky, others gridded and square. The accompanying photographs were impossibly ravishing, like images from a fashion magazine or cookbook.

Leon was cooking when Kathy returned to her flat in Finchley that evening. He had been doing this a lot lately, and despite the resulting debris that made the small flat seem even more crowded, she'd encouraged it, although it made her feel bad, since she only provided takeaway pizza. Also, she wasn't sure of his motives. Sometimes she felt he was trying to prove that living so long with his parents hadn't left him incapable of looking after himself, but at other times she wondered if it was insurance, in case it didn't work out between them. His own explanation was that it was therapy, and tonight she could believe it. He'd had another sticky day, he said, his black hair flopping forward over his eyes, voice barely audible above the thump of the knife chopping the parsley. Two kids, pre-teen, found with some syringes under a pile of cardboard boxes that someone had set alight. With some alarm, Kathy realised that he was preparing roast chicken.

She was becoming convinced that he shouldn't be in the police force, at least not in the forensic area of laboratory liaison. His working hours revolved around the nasty end of the business, constantly confronted by the worst in life, a never-ending stream of crime scenes and their aftermath. Unrelieved by contact with living clients, he met only victims dehumanised by violent death, and she thought it was beginning to tell on him. He finished chopping and stood for a moment, as if wondering what to do next, looking forlorn and troubled and beautiful, and she was on the point of taking hold of him and telling him how much she loved him, when he suddenly shoved his hand inside the chicken carcass and began to scrape out the scraps of offal inside.

And she felt guilty, because he had had an escape plan and she had been one of the reasons he had abandoned it. As a laboratory liaison officer he couldn't rise above sergeant, so he had planned to go up to Liverpool University to do a master's in forensic psychology and move into a more open career path, perhaps in the private sector. Kathy had felt that she would lose him if he left, and had made it easier for him to stay than to go.

'You've got a lot of reading to do?' Leon nodded at the pile of documents she'd dropped on the table, and she told him about the first meeting of the Crime Strategy Working Party. After some hiatus Desmond had returned with Robert, but without Rex, and they had agreed to postpone the meeting until something could be worked out. Kathy tried to make it sound funny, but Leon didn't respond.

'The Asian kid is paralysed,' he said gloomily. 'The one who got kicked by the police horse. It was on the news. He'll likely be a quadriplegic. I shouldn't think this is a very good time to be starting up your committee.'

Kathy felt mildly deflated. 'Well, it would suit me if they forgot the whole thing.' She changed the subject. 'Did you call your mum today?'

He nodded, stuffing a whole lemon into the chicken. 'You can open that wine if you like.'

'How's your dad's tummy?'

'Okay. The doctor said he was pleased with the way it's going.'

'Good. I'm going to be out that way tomorrow. I thought I might call in on your mum.'

Leon looked at her in surprise.

'Just to see how she's coping. What do you think?'

'Fine ...' Leon looked extremely doubtful. 'Afternoon would probably be best. Do you want me to call her?'

'Don't worry, I'll do it once I know how my time is going. Do you want some help with that?'

'It's all under control.'

She thumbed reluctantly through the pile of her documents and, coming to the scrapbook that Brock had given her, pulled it out and opened the cover. Inside was the title, *Dossier on the Murder of Miki Norinaga and Disappearance of Charles Verge. Compiled by Stewart and Miranda Collins, aged 9 and 6, of 349A High Street, Battle, East Sussex.* She smiled to herself and began to turn the pages of cuttings.

Later, relaxed by the wine and a surprisingly competent meal, they lay together in the darkness in the large bed that almost filled the tiny bedroom, and into Kathy's mind returned the question Brock had asked and she had glibly deflected. Why had Charles Verge marked a passage describing an eighteenth-century architect identifying their crimes from the heads of dead criminals? She pictured the bizarre and macabre scene, and wondered how Verge might have interpreted it. Was he taken with the idea that somehow our worst acts were stamped on our faces? Or, if the faces preceded the acts, were we doomed to commit the crimes that our heredity or environment had conditioned us to? Or was it something to do with the idea of Verge's new prison, that you had to reconstruct the whole person, physically as well as spiritually, in order to free it from its criminal fate? She was on the point of drifting off, when the idea suddenly hit her. She blinked awake and sat up.

'He's changed his face,' she said.

'What? Who has?' Leon muttered.

'Charles Verge. He's had plastic surgery or something.'

'Very likely ...' Leon turned over and buried himself under the bedclothes.

She subsided back onto her pillow. Then another disturbing thought occurred to her. Just when had Verge marked the passage in the book?

6

First thing the next morning, Brock held another team meeting. In the grey light of day Kathy felt that her bright idea about Verge was blindingly obvious and hardly worth passing on. In any case, Brock was taking a different tangent.

One of the experts who had provided support to Chivers' team was a financial specialist from SO6, the Fraud Squad, and he had joined them that morning as Brock quizzed them on the details of their investigation of possible sources of funds for Verge on the run. As they explained where the trip-wires had been set up to warn of any of his close family or friends providing financial help, it became apparent that there was one possible major gap, the Verge Practice itself, whose income and assets represented the largest legitimate source of funds for the fugitive. The problem was that the firm was involved in so many financial transactions, large and small, with suppliers, consultants, contractors and sub-contractors in many different parts of the world, that it was impossible to monitor them all in detail. Superintendent Chivers had restricted checks to the most likely channels — Verge's company credit card and cheque book accounts — but that wouldn't help if he were getting assistance from someone inside the firm.

'What sort of person, Tony?' Brock asked the Fraud Squad man, who, in a black suit and with a pale expressionless face, looked as if he wouldn't have been out of place in a convention of undertakers.

'Almost anyone, sir,' he said with an air of regret. 'The ones able to authorise larger payments would be the most obvious — his partners, the finance manager, accountants, people like that. But anyone who knew the accounting system could probably slip something through to a dummy account if they put their mind to it. The girl who looks after the stationery, the bloke who approves the travelling expenses or maintains the computers.'

'He's got a lot of loyal staff there he might have contacted, chief,' Bren observed. 'And it's not as if they'd really be stealing from the firm. I mean, it is his money, after all.'

'How would we set about looking?' Brock asked.

Tony said, 'If they were sensible, it could be hard to detect. They could use a number of small creditors to avoid being conspicuous, and change the names every few months. We should get every payment verified by at least two people, and we might look for coincidences or anomalies. Maybe payments to several different people but all to the same bank branch, or with the same VAT number. An added complication is that the firm does a lot of foreign business. With their overseas projects, VP often forms one-off partnerships with locals to manage the contracts, and these could provide a way of getting money overseas.'

They discussed it for a while, until Brock, becoming impatient with the technicalities, finally said, 'Tony, I want you to brief Bren and a small team on how to make a start — where they should look, what they should collect, what questions they should ask. Bren, get a warrant before you go, and threaten them with Tony's heavy mob if they seem to be hiding anything. Make your presence felt, Bren. Make it very obvious what we're doing. If anyone there is in touch with Verge, we want to get them worried.'

There were reports of extensive roadwork delays on the A40, so Kathy headed north-west instead, picking up the M1 until it reached the M25 and the open country beyond Watford, where she turned off the main roads into hedge-lined lanes. There was an abrupt release from the pressure of heavy traffic, a sudden transition from the sprawling reach of the great conurbation into a rural landscape bathed in pure September sunshine, and she felt immediately cheerful. When she wound down the window the car filled with smells of wood smoke and damp silage. She came to a small village and stopped at the twisted crossroads in the centre to check her route. A thatched pub, its timbers painted black, stood silent across the way, and a bright scarlet tractor drove past, a dog in the cabin with a russet-faced farmer.

She came at last to a white gate bearing the name 'Orchard Cottage', and parked on the grass shoulder. When she stood at the gate she was presented with a little tableau, a rustic scene from a Pre-Raphaelite painting perhaps, except for the glint of chrome on Madelaine Verge's wheelchair. Beside her a young woman was reaching up into an apple tree for fruit to fill the basket that Madelaine cradled on her lap. The young woman was pregnant, the swell of her belly obvious beneath an ankle-length smock, and her cheeks were as rosy as the pippins she was plucking. Her hair was long, straight and black, and Kathy thought she could recognise something of her father in her Latin features, unlike the older woman whose silver hair had once been fair and whose complexion looked as if it were rarely exposed to sunlight. They were set against a backdrop of a simple brick-and-tile agricultural worker's cottage, wreathed in roses, and they turned their heads to stare at the newcomer as the hinges of the white gate creaked.

They both frowned when Kathy introduced herself. The young woman, Verge's daughter Charlotte, appeared frankly hostile, while her grandmother seemed at first put out that they had not sent someone more important. She quickly recovered herself and seemed prepared to make the best of it. 'Do come in,' she said graciously. 'We were about to have a cup of coffee.'

They sat in the sun at a wooden table in the back garden, also planted with gnarled apple trees. 'We have so many apples this year. We must give you some to take away with you,' Madelaine Verge, Lady Bountiful, observed, while her grand-daughter kept silent, resting a hand on her stomach. Kathy felt a little twist, quickly suppressed, of envy or regret.

'This is a beautiful spot,' she said. 'DCI Brock said that you used to live near here, Mrs Verge.'

'That's right. Just over that next rise. Charles built a house for me there, twenty-five years ago. His very first masterpiece. Are you interested in architecture, Sergeant?'

It was a polite inquiry, not expecting much.

'I'm fairly ignorant about it,' Kathy said honestly, and caught a small scornful snort from Charlotte. 'But you can't help being affected by it, can you? And I suppose if you were married to one architect, and had a famous son for another, you couldn't help becoming an expert.'

Madelaine smiled. 'That's very true. It becomes part of the air one breathes.'

'And have you followed the family tradition, Charlotte?' Kathy asked.

The young woman turned to glare at Kathy, taking so long to reply that her grandmother broke in, 'In a way. Charlotte is a graphic designer. A very good one. She runs her business from here, designing people's web pages. She's *extremely* successful.'

Charlotte winced at this grandmotherly endorsement, and got awkwardly to her feet. 'I'll fetch the coffee,' she muttered angrily.

'You must excuse Charlotte,' Madelaine said confidingly as she disappeared into the cottage. 'This has been a very emotional year for her. She feels the loss of her father keenly — they were very close, his only child. And then she'd split up with her partner just a short while before that, and now she's preparing to be a sole parent. All very trying.'

'Yes. Of course.' Kathy felt a familiar sense of viewing lives from the outside, as if through a lens, deciphering connections and relationships that would probably be irrelevant to her purpose.

'Do you have children, Sergeant?'

'No.' Kathy was aware of being probed, while Mrs Verge made up her mind whether it would be more productive to groom or attack her.

'Perhaps you're wise. They are a blessing, of course, but also a heartache.'

Especially if they go around stabbing people, Kathy thought. There was something odd about all this, something she was missing. 'But this seems a wonderful refuge for Charlotte,' she said. 'Is it just a coincidence that it's so close to where you used to live?'

'Not exactly. Charlotte was born a couple of years after Charles built Briar Hill for me, and when she was a child she had so many happy memories of staying with me there that when her relationship broke down she decided to get out of London and come to live in the area. Charles helped her financially, and now when I come to stay with her we go for drives and catch sight of the house again, and remember those happy days. Someone else owns Briar Hill now, of course. Charles sold it to a Spanish artist, a friend of his, on the condition that she promise to change nothing.'

Not only odd but a little spooky, Kathy thought, as if his mother and his daughter had decided together to live in the past, before all of this unpleasantness had happened. 'I can understand her resenting me for invading her privacy here to question you about her father.'

'She does rather regard the police as the enemy, I'm afraid. She thinks you believe the worst of her father, but I tell her that we must try to do everything we can to help you come to the truth of the matter, that Charles is the real victim in all this.' There was such a calm certainty in the way she said this that Kathy was impressed, despite her conviction that the woman was deluding herself. 'So how can I help you? And may I say that I was most impressed by your Mr Brock. Much more intelligent than the last fellow. I feel more confident now that we can make some progress at last.' She smiled.

Grooming then, Kathy thought. 'I've brought a copy of your earlier statements, Mrs Verge, and I'd like to go through some of the points you raised there, but mainly I'd like to get to understand Charles better, as a person.' Madelaine Verge beamed. Nothing would delight her more, her only regret being that most of the photograph albums were in her London flat, a fact for which Kathy was silently grateful.

When Charlotte returned they were deep in conversation about Charles's boyhood, his sense of mischief, his stubbornness, his enthusiasm for competitive sports, his oddly inconsistent school results until he suddenly blossomed just in time to get decent A-levels. Charlotte poured the coffee then said that she had work to do.

'Before you go, dear,' her grandmother said, 'would you please fetch me the family album in my room?'

'It must have been difficult for you, bringing him up on your own, Madelaine,' Kathy said, the intimacies of Charles's childhood having brought them to first-name terms.

'I always felt that I had his father, Alberto, at my shoulder, guiding me. He was a very special man, an Olympic athlete and a very gifted architect. I never made any attempt to guide Charles into his father's footsteps, but Alberto was always there as a shining example, and I was thrilled when Charles announced that he would become an architect, too. And it soon became obvious that the gift had been passed down, undiminished.'

Charlotte returned with an old photograph album, then disappeared again. It contained pictures from Charles's childhood, mostly bland and remote, but there was one that caught Kathy's attention for its strangeness. In it, the small boy was standing encased in some kind of tall, thin construction which Kathy couldn't make out. It looked something like a giant condom or a syringe, daubed with spots and surmounted by a crown, his face peering out from a hole cut in the middle.

'Oh, that's a favourite of mine,' Madelaine chuckled. 'He won first prize.'

Kathy looked perplexed.

'A fancy-dress competition! He went as the Empire State Building.'

Kathy got it now. The spots were windows, and the crown formed the famous silhouette. It was hard to make out what little Charles was thinking, but he didn't look happy.

Madelaine went on to talk about the early years of his practice, when Charles had returned from graduate school in America with a young fellow-graduate as his wife and had put out his shingle in London, penniless but filled with confidence. She then glowingly related the critical success of Briar Hill, its publication in *Architectural Design* and *Casabella*, and the triumphs of the middle years.

'The break-up with his first wife must have been hard, with her having been so much a part of all that,' Kathy said, trying to move the story forward.

Madelaine Verge took a deep breath, as if reluctant to come to that episode, then turned her head sharply at the sound of feet on gravel. 'Ah, George!' she cried as a man came round the corner of the cottage, carrying a garden fork and hoe. 'Did you get the plants you wanted?'

'Most of 'em, Mrs V. They were out of onions.' He lifted his cap to the women, squinting suspiciously at Kathy. He was a stocky figure, of late middle age, with a deeply lined face and wisps of fair hair across his pate, dressed in old clothes for garden work. He replaced his cap, picked up his tools and moved towards a freshly dug bed on the far side of the small lawn. As he turned away Kathy saw that the left side of his face was badly scarred.

'George is one of Charles's projects,' Madelaine whispered, leaning towards Kathy. 'He was in prison at the time Charles was doing research for the Marchdale project — are you familiar with that? Yes, well, Charles learned a great deal from George about prison life, so much so that he engaged him as a consultant and then, when he was released, Charles took him on as a general handyman to look after my little garden in town and to get this place into shape for Charlotte. It really was a mess when he bought it for her, but within a few months George had repaired the roof, knocked out a wall, put in a new kitchen and bathroom, redecorated, and now he's reorganising the garden.'

'Very handy.'

'And very honest and loyal. We trust him absolutely, despite his past. He is a real vindication of Charles's faith in him.'

'What happened to his face?'

'The story is that he had a pan of chip fat spilled on him when he was young. He has had a very tragic life.'

'We were talking about Charles's divorce.'

'Oh … yes.' Her voice hardened. 'Well, I think the truth of the matter is that Charles simply outgrew Gail. The split was inevitable, really.'

'Outgrew her?'

'In professional terms. Oh, Gail was very supportive in the early days, very clever with designing the details, Charles used to say. But as the practice grew, it really became far too demanding for Gail's abilities. She had to take a back seat, and I'm afraid that had its effect on their personal relationship. Charles was very sad about it, of course.'

'He had a breakdown?' Kathy ventured.

'No, no, that's putting it far too strongly. It was a setback, yes, and at a sensitive time for Charlotte, at sixteen. Gail … well, I'm probably biased, but she let a lot of people down, walking out like that.'

'But then Charles met Miki Norinaga.'

Silence for a moment, then the elderly woman said primly, 'Not immediately. There was an interval of a couple of years.'

'That must have been difficult for Charlotte too, her being not much younger than her new stepmother.'

Madelaine Verge turned a stern eye on Kathy. 'If you're trying to suggest some kind of family crisis arising from Charles's second marriage, you're quite wrong. Charlotte was starting at university, she had a new life of her own to focus on.'

'I get the impression that you didn't like Charles's choice much, Madelaine.'

The other woman seemed about to make some frosty remark, but then she raised her twisted hands in a gesture of resignation and sighed. 'Miki was an arrogant and manipulative young woman. But Charles fell for her, and there was nothing that I or anyone else could say to dissuade him.'

'Others tried, did they?'

'His colleagues were concerned. Sandy Clarke had the un-enviable task of voicing their reservations to Charles, but he swept them aside.' Then she added wistfully, 'He always had the courage of his convictions, my Charles.'

'Mr Clarke said that Miki became much more assertive as time went on. Do you think that Charles had begun to have second thoughts?'

Madelaine Verge sighed, as if weary at being dragged from the golden memories of her son's youth to the sordid complications of the present. 'He said nothing to me. And no matter how difficult his wife might have been, he would never, never have resorted to anything so grotesque and stupid as murdering her like that. And that really is the nub, isn't it, Kathy? You must see that. That's why you must come round to my point of view.'

'I have to tell you that from the information we've got, your idea about the American competitors just doesn't seem plausible.'

'You're direct, Kathy. I like that. Superintendent Chivers was always so tactful in dismissing my ideas that he ended up being patronising and offensive. I didn't say it was the Americans necess-arily, just that it must be somebody like that; a rival, a resentful enemy.'

'Charles was obviously a strong personality. Did he have enemies as resentful as that?'

'Clearly he did, and it's up to you to find them.'

Kathy asked if she could have a few words with Charlotte before she left. She found the young woman in a small room fitted out as an office, working at a computer.

'Hello, Charlotte,' Kathy said. 'Can I have a word?' The other woman grunted but didn't shift her attention from the screen. While she waited, Kathy looked around the room at the shelves of computer manuals and files, some rather impressive glossy computer printouts pinned to the wall, a calendar, and a framed lithograph which caught her attention. The geometric figures, three red squares on a fading yellow background, reminded her of the large painting in the Verges' apartment, and she thought she recognised the small black signature at the bottom. She asked Charlotte if it was the same artist.

'Yes,' Charlotte muttered, still not turning from the computer, and then, reluctantly, added a name, which Kathy thought was Ruth Diaz until she examined the signature more closely and realised it was Luz Diaz.

'Your grandmother mentioned that you have a Spanish artist as a neighbour, at Briar Hill.'

Charlotte finally turned away from her work and looked at Kathy with a resentful glare. 'Yes, it's her. She gave me that as a house-warming present, when I moved in.'

'She's a friend of your father?'

'That's right. You'd know all this if you'd read your own reports. She was *interviewed* ...' she gave the word a bitter emphasis, '... like everyone else. No wonder no one wants to know us any more. No one except the press, that is.'

'I'm sorry, it must have been very difficult for you.'

'There's several Charles Verge websites, have you seen them? All the latest sightings from around the world, the latest sick theories. He was in a three-way relationship with Miki and a lover of hers, did you know that? All three of them were heavily into cocaine, apparently, or LSD. That's where they got their ideas for buildings from. Or he was inspired by Jack the Ripper, and he's still stalking the East End with a carving knife.'

She turned away with a sigh. 'Just go away, will you? We don't want you here.'

Kathy had had enough of being dismissed by Charlotte. 'Well, I can understand that. But it won't go away until we discover the truth. You do appreciate that, don't you? There will never be any resolution to this until we find your father. Your child will grow up in the shadow of what he did, just as surely as you're living in it now. When she goes to school, when she applies for a job, people will go on whispering about her.'

Charlotte had gone pale and motionless.

Kathy went on remorselessly, voice low so that Madelaine wouldn't hear. 'In the end, you'll have to make up your mind about whether you can live with that, Charlotte. Hard as it may be to face this, you're going to have to help us find your father, so that your child can be free of what he did.'

'Get out ...' Charlotte's voice was a low hiss. 'Get out, you fucking bitch.'

Kathy's face was flushed as she returned to her car and drove off. She felt guilty, annoyed with herself. Maybe she would have been less brutal if Charlotte hadn't been quite so complacently pregnant, so obviously fecund.

On the outskirts of the village she pulled in to the roadside and made a call on her mobile to Scotland Yard. She got herself put through to the team's data manager and asked her to check the name. 'L-U-Z D-I-A-Z, pronounced "Looth Dee-ath".' She heard the rattling of a keyboard at the other end, a pause and then, 'Yes, here she is. Born 18.01.53, unmarried, Spanish citizen, two home addresses, one in Barcelona, Spain, the other in Buckinghamshire, England. She was identified as a possible person of interest on June 14 last and interviewed on July 20 by two officers of the Spanish CGP, and again in London by DI Heron and DS Moffat on August 17.'

There was a pause as the officer scanned the reports, giving Kathy a summary of the main points. 'Says she's been a friend of Charles Verge since 1993, when he bought one of her paintings ... They met from time to time when he was visiting Barcelona ... She claims not to know his relatives there, and she denies ever having a closer relationship with Verge.'

'We haven't spoken to her again since the seventeenth of August?'

'Don't think so ... hang on ... no, but both we and the Spanish police did checks on her telephone contacts and bank accounts through May, June and July. Nothing suspicious. And the Spanish police did a search of her Barcelona apartment in July, without result.'

'What about her purchase of the house in Buckinghamshire from Verge?'

'Yes, it's here. Contracts exchanged just over a year ago. All quite legit.'

Kathy considered all this. Luz Diaz was one of hundreds of friends, colleagues and acquaintances who had been checked, and it sounded as if the degree of interest in her had been appropriate. They had discovered nothing incriminating in her behaviour. The only thing that marked her out from all the rest was the fact that she had bought a house from him, which now happened to be close to the daughter he was expected to contact. And, perhaps, that she was single, close to him in age, commuting between Barcelona and Bucks, and artistic. Kathy wondered if she was attractive.

'Do we have a phone number for her?'

'Sure.'

Kathy rang off and dialled the number. After some time there was a reply. 'Allo?'

'Ms Diaz?'

'Yes.'

'My name is Detective Sergeant Kathy Kolla from the Metropolitan Police. We're updating our files on the Charles Verge inquiry, and I'd like to have a talk to you if I could.'

There was a deep sigh from the other end. 'I've told you everything I can. I don't know what else I can say.' The voice sounded husky, a smoker's voice, Kathy thought.

'It won't take long.'

Another sigh. 'Well … hang on, I'll get my diary.'

'Actually, I'm in the neighbourhood now, if that would be convenient.'

'Now? I'm in the middle of working.'

'It would get it over.'

'Oh … I suppose I could break for ten minutes. No more, okay?'

Kathy listened to her instructions on how to find the house and set off again. She passed into a wood and came abruptly upon a harvester filling the narrow lane. She slowed to a crawl behind it. Rooks shrieked down from the treetops and she felt a sense of unreality, as if this were all some kind of rural theme park and she a participant in a fairytale. Little Red Riding Hood, perhaps, on her way to her grandmother's cottage. The machine turned in to a field and she accelerated away.

She turned in to a gravelled driveway that threaded between tall beech trees and stopped in a clearing. Ahead lay a flagged path leading towards an opening in a white wall that sliced across the top of the slope. She reached it and stepped through onto a terrace, catching her breath at the sudden revelation of a panorama of rolling fields and copses, and in the distance hills that Kathy assumed must be the Chilterns. She realised that the white wall was a cunningly placed barrier between the enclosed woods and the broad view that lay on this side of the ridge, the doorway like Alice's space-warping looking glass.

The rectangle of a swimming pool was cut into the terrace in front of her, and to her right a horizontal roof plane hovered over what she took to be a bathers' pavilion. To her left, a second roof sheltered a larger pavilion enclosed by a glass wall, one panel of which was open, a woman standing motionless there, watching her.

Luz Diaz was wearing a paint-streaked pair of workmen's overalls and yellow plastic gloves. Her black hair was cut in a short bob, neat and compact like her figure. She gazed at Kathy with intent dark eyes for a moment, then stepped back and began to peel off the gloves.

Kathy followed her into the lobby of the house. One wall was made of polished stone, and chrome-plated columns of cruciform cross-section supported the floating roof. In front of them the floor was cut away to reveal levels below, and Kathy realised that the terrace was the roof of the house, built into the side of the hill. It was like a prototype, she thought, for the Thameside offices, with tiers of floors and double-height spaces facing a spectacular outlook. As they descended a spiralling steel staircase, Kathy could understand why Madelaine Verge, wheelchair-bound, could no longer live here.

'This is stunning,' she said.

Luz Diaz said nothing, leading her through an intermediate level that obviously served as her studio. Decorators' drop cloths were spread over the polished timber floor, in the centre of which stood a large, almost-bare canvas on an easel. Ms Diaz threw the gloves to one side and picked up a packet of cigarettes, not bothering to offer them to Kathy. She held the cigarette between the fingers of a cupped hand, almost a fist, which she brought to her mouth to draw on. Her hands were large, Kathy noticed, more like she would have expected a sculptor's to be.

'Sit,' she said, breathing smoke.

Kathy sat, but Luz Diaz did not, instead examining Kathy, feet apart, cigarette-wielding fist cocked, like a bullfighter assessing her next move.

'Thanks for seeing me at such short notice, Ms Diaz,' Kathy began.

'You say you were in the neighbourhood?' the other woman said suspiciously.

'Yes.'

'To see Charlotte Verge?'

'And her grandmother, yes.'

'Madelaine is here? Why did you see them? Has something happened?' The English was good but strongly accented, and Kathy had to attune to it and the smoker's timbre.

'As I said on the phone, we're updating our files on the inquiry.'

'I read in the paper this morning. There is a new detective in charge, yes?'

'DCI Brock, yes.'

'And you work for him?'

'Yes.'

'Why is this?' Diaz demanded. 'What has happened?'

'Look, won't you sit down, Ms Diaz? This isn't a formal interview. I just want to keep our paperwork up to date.'

'About me?' She frowned, ignoring the suggestion to sit, pacing now without taking her eyes off Kathy, as if sizing up some object she might be about to paint, or lunge at.

Kathy felt uncomfortably at a disadvantage. This was why it was better to get them to come to the station, she thought. 'Has anything happened during the past month that we should know about?'

'Happened? Like what?'

'Has Charles Verge tried to contact you?'

Diaz waved her smoking fist dismissively. 'Of course not.'

'It would be natural, wouldn't it? You were good friends, and you live close to his daughter.'

The other woman turned away, her mouth a tight line of exasperation. 'This is how you think. I came here to work in peace. I don't like to think that you are watching me. Maybe I should go back to Barcelona until this is all over.'

'You were good friends, weren't you?'

'You mean, were we lovers, is that it? That's what those cops in Barcelona went on about. It's the only kind of relationship between a man and a woman they understand.' She took an angry suck at her cigarette.

'So what was your relationship, exactly?'

'We were both professionals, and we admired each other's work.' She finally took a seat, as if reconciling herself to having to talk. 'I first met him at the opening of a show I had in a gallery in Barcelona. He was knowledgeable about contemporary painting and had definite opinions. He was very generous in his praise of my work and bought a small painting. Then he contacted me a week later to say that he wanted to recommend me to a client of his to do a big canvas, bigger than I had ever done in my life, for the lobby of a new building he was doing. He said my work and his would go together very well. I was flattered. The commission fell through, actually, but we became friends and when he was in Barcelona he would often come to my exhibitions or my studio.'

'So you've known him since the time of his first marriage.'

'Yes, about ten years. It has been a difficult period in his life, a time of change. He was very successful, sure, but first there was the divorce, then his affair with Miki. With me he enjoyed to talk. We had rapport. People said we looked like brother and sister together, and maybe that was it — we were both single children, you see.'

She shrugged and stubbed out the cigarette.

'How did you come to buy this house?'

'I explained all this to the other officers, in London. They checked the paperwork, didn't they? It was just chance, really. The house had been empty for several years since Madelaine moved out, but Charles couldn't bear to sell it because of what new owners might do to it. He brought me to see it one day when I was in London, the spring before last, and I fell in love with it. I had inherited some money at the time, and I had been looking for a new house and studio, and I thought how perfect this would be. The great window faces north, you see? The light is perfect for painting, and I needed somewhere where I could spend time away from the distractions of my scruffy little place in Barcelona. And he was right about his architecture and my painting being made for each other. Here they could be one. So I told him that if he would sell it to me, I would promise to change nothing.'

'When did you last see him?'

'He was in Barcelona in early April, we met briefly.'

'What did he talk about?'

'Mainly about his daughter. He had just heard that she was to have a baby, and he was very happy about this, but also worried about her not having a partner to help her. Charlotte had recently split up from the father, and then she discovered that she was pregnant.'

'Was Charles angry about that?'

'Angry? No. He thought the man was lazy, that Charlotte was well rid of him. But he wanted to help her. They had just found this cottage for her, near here. He said he hoped I wouldn't mind having her as a neighbour. I said of course not.'

'Did he talk about anything else?'

'About his work, I think. Yes, his prison.' She arched an eyebrow, catching the small crease in the corner of Kathy's mouth. 'You think that's amusing?'

' No. A bit ironic, that's all. It's an unusual project, isn't it?'

'Charles was very bound up in it ...' Now Luz allowed herself a tight smile. 'Yes, full of irony, I know. But he was really passionate about it. He said no other well-known architect would do such a project. They all want to design what he called safe public buildings — prestigious art galleries, museums, universities. No one had the courage to face such an uncomfortable subject as a prison. But he said that it is the father and mother of all buildings, because it does absolutely what other buildings do only in part. A prison is the building that most fully controls the lives of the people inside it, so the very best architects should design it.'

'Someone in his office said that he had the idea that his building could fundamentally change people. They said he was obsessed with it.'

Luz Diaz looked thoughtfully at Kathy. 'Did they say that? Were they laughing at him, do you think?'

'No, I don't think so.'

'Do they miss him? Or do they hate him for what he's supposed to have done?'

'I think they're just trying to weather the storm caused by it.'

'Yes, of course. We're all trying to do that ...' She said it wistfully, looking out through the large window as if she might catch sight of the missing man somewhere out there in the sunlit fields.

'You sound as if it affected you a great deal.'

The woman looked back sharply at Kathy. 'Not me, no. I meant the others. Although I miss him now, more than I would have expected.'

Kathy watched her reach for another cigarette. Her fingers looked pink and inflamed, as if she were allergic to something in the paint. 'Are you quite sure you haven't heard from him, Ms Diaz?'

Luz snapped the flame off and took a deep breath. 'Quite sure. And I'm quite sure I never shall.'

'Why?'

'Because his mother is right. He is dead.'

'How can you be certain?'

'I feel it. I know it. I am absolutely sure that he didn't murder his wife. And whoever did has made quite certain that you will never find him. You're wasting your time looking. Charles Verge doesn't exist any more.'

Luz Diaz got to her feet and looked at her watch. 'I said ten minutes. I've given you twenty. Now I must work.' She rammed the cigarette into her mouth and reached for the yellow gloves.

7

The idea of fronting up to another strong woman didn't appeal to Kathy, but she knew that Leon would have phoned his mother to warn her she might be calling. She rang the Barnet number and when Ghita Desai answered she heard the guarded tone in her voice.

'Yes, dear, Leon said you might call to see us. Is everything all right?'

'Yes, yes. I'm just going to be over your way, so I thought I'd say hello. But only if it's convenient.'

'Of course. Morarji may be resting. His operation, you know. But that doesn't matter.'

Kathy arrived armed with a bunch of flowers at the Desai house, its semi-detached neatness enhanced by some recently fitted double-glazing.

Ghita answered the door immediately, as if she'd watched Kathy's approach from behind the net curtains. 'How are you, dear?' She offered Kathy a cheek. Both she and her husband had the coal-dark eyes that Kathy found so disconcertingly attractive in Leon, but in their sagging faces the eyes gave an impression of deep fatigue, as if recovering from a very long period of watchfulness. Ghita peered at Kathy now through those dark eyes like someone conducting a physical.

'Are you sure everything's all right? There is nothing wrong?'

It was the unexpected visit, the rarity of direct contact, and suddenly Kathy realised that Ghita assumed she had come to deliver some momentous message concerning herself. 'Leon and I have decided to get married', perhaps, or more likely, 'You're going to become grandparents'. Yes, that was it. Ghita thought she was pregnant and had come alone to spill the awful beans. Because Kathy also saw, from the sombre expression on Ghita's face, the way she held herself braced, that such news would not be welcome. Not from her.

'No, everything's fine. Absolutely. How is Morarji?'

The brow between Ghita's dark eye sockets creased in a tiny frown of doubt, then eased. 'He's much better, really. But he gets tired. He's just having a little nap. You don't mind, do you?'

'Of course not,' Kathy said, wondering if he'd been packed off so that Ghita could have this out with her alone, woman to woman, without any fudging from Morarji, who liked her. 'These are for you.' She handed over the flowers and followed Ghita through to the living room. There was a smell of baking and air-freshener.

'Sit down, dear, while I put them in water and pop the kettle on.'

Kathy had never been left alone in this room before. Ghita was an immaculate housewife and every surface gleamed. She noticed a small perfume dispenser plugged into an electrical socket. There were embroidered linen protectors on the arms and backs of the brocade suite. On the mantelpiece were mementos of their days in East Africa, from where they'd been expelled, and above them a rank of framed family photographs, Leon conspicuous.

'And how is Leon?' Ghita bustled back in.

'He's fine. He's taken quite an interest in cooking lately. He's getting really very good at it.'

'Cooking?' Ghita looked appalled for a moment, until she managed to smooth the expression away. 'Well, I'm sure that will come in handy. And his work?'

'He's working too hard.'

'Ah,' Ghita shook her head. 'That job.'

'The trouble is he's so good at it. He's in demand.'

'He would be good at whatever he set his mind to. It's a mistake.'

'You mean forensic liaison?'

'I mean the police!' she said with sudden passion. 'It was always wrong for Leon, always.'

Kathy hadn't realised the depth of Ghita's opposition to Leon's work, and as she went on about the pay and hours, the dreadful

71

experiences, and compared them to what a cousin of his in IT was getting in the City, Kathy thought of Charles Verge's mother, equally dedicated to her only son. Both mothers had brought them up in some isolation, Madelaine as a widow, Ghita as a refugee, which had probably lent a certain intensity to their relationships with their sons.

'That was why I told him to go for the Liverpool course, as a way out, into the private sector.'

So Ghita had encouraged that, which Kathy hadn't realised. She felt as if she were seeing his mother for the first time, as if all their previous encounters had been so wrapped up in courtesies that nothing at all had been communicated.

Ghita obviously sensed she was getting onto dangerous ground, and moved onto a neutral topic. Were they planning a holiday this year? Time went so fast, the year was nearly over, and they hadn't managed to get away. When Morarji felt a little stronger they might try to have a break, somewhere warm …

She was interrupted by a movement at the door and the voice of her husband. 'Talking about me?' Naturally short and plump like his wife, Morarji Desai had lost weight, Kathy saw, and the dressing gown seemed to swamp him. But the good humour was as bright in his eyes as ever as he advanced across the room to kiss Kathy's cheek, ignoring Ghita who was immediately on her feet and objecting to his being out of bed.

'Ghita worries too much,' he said with a wink.

'Well, somebody has to,' she snapped back.

'It's a division of labour, you see, Kathy. She does all the worrying and I do all the fooling around. Very efficient. We're both experts in our own fields.'

It was true, and when Kathy tried to place Leon between these two poles she had to conclude that he was closer to the mother's. Morarji sat down with a chuckle while his wife went to fetch the tea. 'She wasn't giving you a hard time, was she?' he asked, voice lowered.

'No, no. We were just talking about Leon.'

'Of course, what else? But how about you? He tells us you're working on the Verge mystery now. What an exciting life you lead, eh? I have my own theories on what happened, you know …'

But Morarji never had the chance to expound them, for his wife returned with the tea and abruptly changed the subject. 'Leon told me to ask you to please pick up his computer and take it back with you.'

The computer question had been discussed before and always put off. On the one hand it would be very handy in the flat, especially for email and the web, but on the other it was bulky and would be difficult to fit in, and Leon seemed reluctant to make the decision to shift it out of his old home. His mother, too, seemed unhappy about letting it go.

'Morarji has been using it, but I don't know how Leon's managed without it,' she said doubtfully. 'He's very attached to it. It was our birthday present to him last year.'

'I've been telling him we should get a laptop,' Kathy said.

'That would be very wasteful,' Ghita said disapprovingly, 'when he already has such a good machine.'

'But if Morarji is using it ...'

'Oh nonsense. He only plays around on the web.'

It was obvious that Ghita was quite out of sorts about the whole business and, despite her husband's attempts to make amusing conversation, the rest of Kathy's visit was a subdued affair, made more painful by the labour of dismantling the computer in Leon's old bedroom and carting it down to the car. As she drove back towards Finchley, Kathy thought of Brock's suggestion that she imagine the mother as twenty years younger and male, but couldn't see Leon, or didn't want to.

He helped her carry the computer up to the flat on the fourteenth floor, and it was immediately apparent that it was going to be a problem. The flat was just too small, and there was nowhere to put it. In the end it had to be set up on one end of the table they used for eating and writing. The place was becoming impossibly cluttered, and despite her best efforts, Kathy felt herself showing her irritation.

'We'll have to get a bigger place,' she said, hearing the edginess in her voice. 'This is getting ridiculous.'

'Don't worry. We'll manage.'

Kathy caught herself angrily thinking of his mother's words: *somebody's got to do the worrying*. 'What's that stuff over there?' She pointed accusingly at a pile of bound documents spilled untidily beside the sofa.

'All the forensic material on the Verge case. Brock sent it over to me. Wants me to review it and find if they missed anything.' He sounded exhausted and defeated by the prospect. 'I haven't got the time, Kathy. Look at it. I'm up to here at work, and I've got my first university assignment due next week.'

This was why he needed the computer, of course, Kathy thought, and immediately her anger drained away. She went over and put her arm around him. 'Sorry, love. I'd forgotten about that. Can I help with the Verge files? You were involved at the beginning, weren't you?'

'Only for the first couple of weeks, then they moved me on to other cases.'

'Well, why don't you go through the technical stuff and I'll check the procedures. I know the drill.' As she said it she thought guiltily of the briefing documents for the Crime Strategy Working Party that lay in her briefcase, unread.

He shook his head. 'No, I'll have to do it …' But over dinner he conceded that it might just be possible for her to help.

They settled themselves with coffee at opposite ends of the sofa, the reports piled between them, and began to work through them in silence. At midnight Kathy rubbed her eyes, yawning, and realised she had reread the same paragraph three times and still hadn't made sense of it.

'I think I've had it,' she said. 'This stuff is so boring. What does this mean?'

She handed him the passage.

He squinted at it, eyes heavy. 'It means that the following traces weren't matched.'

'Well, why don't they just say that?' She took the document back and turned to a schedule on an earlier page. 'There's quite a number of them, fingerprints and DNA. So that means they weren't matched to either Miki or Charles Verge?'

'What date was that?'

She checked the report. 'June the fourth. That's a long time after the murder, isn't it? Three weeks.'

'They identified Verge's prints early on, but they had trouble

74

verifying his DNA. They had to get matches from his mother and daughter. They weren't a hundred per cent sure they had him till the end of May.'

'Well, if these samples weren't his or Miki's, whose were they?'

'The Verges did quite a bit of entertaining before he went off to the States, including a number of visitors from abroad. We weren't able to track them all down. There's a report on that somewhere, with a list of all the people who gave samples and were eliminated, including people like the cleaner and the two who discovered the body.'

Kathy turned pages until she found the list. 'Oh yes, there's over a dozen. What am I supposed to do with this?'

'Well, you could cross-check that list with the schedule of traces found in the apartment and make sure they're all accounted for, then see that any marked "check and refer" were properly followed up.'

She groaned. It would take ages, and this was just one small section. 'Brock shouldn't have put this on you, Leon. He should have a team of drones going through it.' The briefing documents for the Crime Strategy Working Party surely couldn't be more tedious than this, or more pointless, for they all knew that the forensic evidence had been singularly unhelpful.

'Come on,' Leon said, getting wearily to his feet. 'Let's go to bed.'

But an hour later Kathy was still awake, lying motionless at Leon's side while her brain, overtired and unable to shut down, nagged at the events of the day. She thought about the relationship between ambitious, protective mothers and their sons, and wondered if the sons then went on to become ambitious, protective fathers to their daughters. She thought about Charlotte Verge, named after her father, and tried to imagine what sort of a mother she, in her turn, would become.

Finally she decided that she would have to get up and occupy her brain for a while if she were ever to get to sleep. She slipped on a dressing gown and went back to the living room, depressingly untidy and crowded after their evening's work. Which would be more soporific, she wondered, the forensic or the committee papers? She remembered that the scene-of-crime reports had numbered the rooms in the Verge apartment on a computer-generated plan, and that the numbering went into double figures. That was the kind of place she and Leon needed. She opened the file and found the plan, trying to imagine how it would feel to live in such a place, then turned to the section of forensic schedules. If I get to the end of this section, she thought, I will at least have achieved something tonight. She took it over to the table, pushed the computer as far as it would go towards the window, and sat down.

Actually, it looked as if someone else had already checked the lists as Leon had suggested. On the photocopied pages there were pencilled ticks against most of the 'check and refer' items, a few of them circled. Trace number sixty-two, for example, was circled, but to find out what it was she had to refer to another schedule. She swore softly. This was so complicated. Why didn't they keep it simple? She established that trace sixty-two was a DNA sample taken from a pillowcase found in room seven, presumably a bedroom. She checked the plan and found that seven was in fact the utility room, and from a description of that room and its contents found that the pillowcase was one of a pair found in the washing machine, with a load of clothes. There had been laundry powder in the machine, but it hadn't been switched on. The second pillowcase had also yielded a trace, number sixty-three, but when she checked it against the original schedule she found that it had been ticked by the unknown checker, not circled. Why? she wondered sleepily.

Like the rooms and the traces, the people who had been identified from the DNA and other evidence in the apartment had also been given numbers. Trace number sixty-three, Kathy discovered, was a smear of lipstick which had been found on the second pillowcase and which had been positively identified as belonging to individual number one, who, from another schedule, turned out to be the victim, Miki Norinaga.

Kathy found her attention wandering. The repetition of numbers and lists was mesmerising and she began to think she might return to bed. She turned back to the circled trace, number sixty-two, and began to follow its trail; room number seven, the washing machine, the first pillowcase, a DNA trace this time, and finally the matching individual, number four. She turned to the list of people and read the name, to her surprise, of Charles Verge's partner, Sandy Clarke. Both he and Jennifer Mathieson had been automatically asked for fingerprints and DNA samples in order to eliminate any they may have inadvertently left in the flat when they discovered the body. And now here he was, apparently laying his sweaty brow on a pillow beside Miki Norinaga, who hadn't removed her lipstick. Kathy felt a jolt of excitement.

She began to search for any other traces attributed to individual number four. They had found his fingerprints on the bedroom door, she discovered, and that was all; not a hint of DNA anywhere else. She racked her brain for an innocent explanation for the pillow traces, but couldn't think of one. Sandy Clarke surely must have been Miki Norinaga's lover.

But why hadn't they heard about this before? Kathy had been there when Brock had asked Clarke if Miki might have been having an affair, and she had heard him dismiss the idea. There had been no hint of it in the briefings they'd had, or in any document she'd seen. Had the information simply been overlooked, lost in all the mountains of data? If so, the person who should have checked and referred would be in very deep shit. She gave a little shudder at the thought of Superintendent Chivers' reaction. Whoever it was would be crucified. She turned the pages to the end of the report. On the final page was a heading 'Action', and the words, 'Refer identified items to LO, DS Desai'. The unknown penciller had underlined the words twice.

Kathy sat for some time staring out of the window, trying to think this through. She gazed unseeing at the chains of streetlights twinkling dimly into the distant darkness. There was probably some unremarkable explanation. Leon was meticulous and methodical and surely wouldn't have overlooked anything like this. No doubt he'd asked for a further check of such an odd and isolated trace from individual four, and they'd discovered that it had been mixed up. Much more likely that it had belonged to individual two, Charles Verge. Somewhere further on in the piles of reports this would be recorded. Hopefully. She began to flick through the document pile for some sign of it, without success. Or maybe Leon was off the case when the referral was made, and the data had been lost by the laboratory liaison officer who took over from him.

His jacket was on the back of the other chair, and she knew he kept a small appointments diary in the inside pocket. She reached over for it and turned the pages back to the fourth of June. There was a note that read, 'K @ Bramshill all week', and she remembered that that was the week she'd been away on a course at the staff college. There were other notes for that and the following days; times and places of appointments, several marked 'PO'. Post office? It was impossible to tell whether they related to the Verge inquiry or other cases.

As she returned the diary to the jacket pocket another horrible thought occurred to her. She had complained to Leon that Brock should have got someone else to do this drudgery. Perhaps he already had. Perhaps the penciller had been working for Brock, and had informed him of the circled items that had never been followed up. Was this Brock's way of giving Leon a chance to redeem or hang himself?

She checked her watch. One thirty-five. She picked up the report and opened the bedroom door, hearing the rhythmic sigh of Leon's breathing. 'Sorry, lover,' she murmured, and stroked his shoulder. He came awake slowly, blinking, as if she'd pulled him out of a deep, dark hole.

When she explained what the time was and that she'd found something that couldn't wait till morning, he stared at her in disbelief, struggling to follow her words.

'A pillow?'

'Two pillowslips, Leon. Miki on one and Clarke on the other. And they weren't sleeping.'

'How do you mean?' Leon was rubbing his face, trying to clear his head.

'She had lipstick on.'

'What about the sheets?'

'They must have been washed in the previous load, don't you think? And this must have happened not long before the murder; well, within twenty-four hours, surely? Someone loaded the machine and then was distracted and didn't start it up.'

Leon shook his head. 'This is new? How come this hasn't come out before now?'

'Exactly.' The decisive way she said this made him sit up. She handed him the last page of the report.

'Oh.' He stared at the incriminating words, then finally said, 'I'm sure I've never seen this. I think I was off the case by then. What date was it?'

'June the fourth. That was the start of the week I spent at Bramshill.'

'Oh yes …' He covered his eyes with his fingers and rubbed. 'I remember.'

'Do you want your diary, to see what case you were working on then?'

He shook his head. Now the fingers of his other hand were beating a little rhythm on the pages of the report. 'No need, I remember that week. I'd definitely moved to another team by then.'

'Good. Do you know who took your place?'

Leon lifted his pale fingertips from the report to his face and wiped his mouth. 'Er … a guy called Oakley, Paul Oakley. We met up a few times to hand over.'

PO, Kathy thought. Not post office. 'Well, that's fine. He'll have to explain what happened.'

'He's left the Met now, gone abroad. That's what I heard.'

'Still, it's not your problem.' Kathy switched off the light and got back into bed, thoroughly relieved; yet, strangely, Leon didn't seem to be. And there was something else. The Bramshill course had been about advanced interview techniques, and one of the days had been devoted to stress indicators, the little mannerisms that people betray when they hide the truth. Leon's gestures might have been taken straight from the training videos.

He said, 'You're sure there's no reference to this later on in the reports? I mean, it might have been cleared up somehow.'

'Yes, I thought of that, and I looked.' Kathy was feeling drowsy now. 'But I couldn't find anything.'

'I'd better check too.' He sounded wide awake. She felt his weight shift as he got up, and she pulled the duvet up to her ear and drifted away.

In the morning, she was surprised to find him still at work at the table in the living room. He hadn't been able to find any further reference to the guilty pillowcase.

8

Leon was waiting for Brock as soon as he arrived at Queen Anne's
Gate. Kathy stayed out of the way as they disappeared into Brock's
office, Leon lugging the forensic files. After half an hour she and the
rest of the available team were called together.

Leon looked grey and preoccupied, Kathy thought, while Brock
appeared almost pleased in a grim sort of way, as he did when
presented with some unexpected new evidence of human frailty.

He spoke to DS Moffat first, the woman who had come to
them from Chivers' team. 'You remember your LO back in June,
Linda? Paul Oakley?'

She nodded. 'Yes, I remember Paul. He didn't stay long. Left the
force three or four weeks later. Got a better offer, I think.'

'Right, well Leon has come upon a piece of forensic evidence
that appears to have been overlooked, maybe due to the changes in
LO around that time. We'll have to do some more checking, but if
it stands up it suggests that Miki Norinaga and Sandy Clarke were
lovers. Has that idea ever come up before?'

People shook their heads, interested.

'I don't need to speculate on where that might take us. At the
least it'd mean that Clarke has lied to us, at the most he might be
involved in some way with the murder itself. Now I don't propose
to face him with this just yet. I want to find out as much as we can
about him first.'

He began to spell out what they should do. The forensic evidence would be thoroughly reviewed again; the team investigating

the financial affairs of the Verge Practice would focus their attention on transactions authorised by Clarke; the security video tapes harvested from the building and the surrounding streets would be pored over once more for possible sightings of Clarke on the weekend of the murder.

'What else?' Brock concluded.

Suggestions and counter-suggestions were offered and recorded on a whiteboard. The mood was becoming buoyant, Kathy sensed, as if everyone had been waiting for something like this, a fresh angle, a crack in the story that so far had led them nowhere. Miki's infidelity, if it were true, might provide a motive for her murder, though Kathy doubted if it would help them track down Verge. But Brock seemed the most confident of all, beaming encouragement as they discussed options, in stark contrast to Leon at his side, silent and dejected. He's taking it all too personally, she thought, and wanted to reassure and comfort him.

'Kathy?' Brock's voice cut across her thoughts. 'Any ideas?'

'Jennifer Mathieson,' she replied. 'So far she's given us the loyal PR story, but she's been working there for nearly ten years. She must have a pretty good idea of what goes on inside that place. And she's leaving them soon, so maybe we can get her to be a bit more frank.'

'Good idea. See if you can talk to her today, will you?'

Kathy nodded, aware that she was supposed to be with her committee all day from ten o'clock that morning. She checked her watch and groaned. She was going to be late again.

The issue that day for the Crime Strategy Working Party was sexual orientation. Before lunch there were to be briefings and discussion papers presented by members of the Lesbian, Gay, Bisexual, Transgender Advisory Group, followed in the afternoon by the formation of focus groups to consider the issues from the point of view of victims, perpetrators and police. By four o'clock each of these groups had presented long lists of objectives, strategies and targets, using felt-tip pens on large sheets of paper. Kathy felt she had become allergic to lists and their mind-numbing effect, although the other members of the committee seemed remarkably enthusiastic.

Finally, when the facilitators, experts and activists had gone, Desmond called the committee members together for a short meeting. Kathy, itching to get away to meet Jennifer Mathieson, was interested to see that Rex, the objector at the previous meeting, had rejoined the group and was now sitting at Desmond's left hand, with the administrator, Robert, on his right.

'Well, I think we've had a very productive day,' Desmond began. 'There are just a couple of pieces of committee business that I thought we should get out of the way before we break up. The first is that I'm pleased to report that we've sorted out the problem which Rex raised at our last meeting. The compromise we've worked out is that Rex will be appointed as deputy chair to the committee, to take the chair if I'm not available, and he will also have a casting vote in the event of a stalemate. Okay, then the next item ...'

'Hang on, Desmond,' Jay interrupted. She scratched purple nails through her short hair and frowned doubtfully through her lozenge glasses. 'Just go through that again, will you?'

Desmond patiently repeated himself, and added an explanation. 'Rex's point, which I believe you supported, Jay, was that it would send out the wrong signals to have a police chair. Well, this seems to be the best way to overcome that difficulty without compromising the original terms of appointment.'

'Are you offering this as a proposal for discussion?' Jay persisted.

'Well, no. It's already been approved, actually.'

'I see, by the boys' club, presumably.'

'Sorry?'

'Desmond, have you understood nothing of what was said this morning?' Jay was speaking softly, but it was clear that she was angry. 'The whole point of this exercise is to help the police reach out to the disadvantaged and under-represented, right? Am I right?'

'Of course.'

'And what is the greatest single source of disadvantage and under-representation? It's not sexual orientation, it's not even race — it is gender. Men commit crimes and women are their victims ...' She rode right over Desmond's attempt to modify this generalisation, and continued, 'And now the boys' club has decided to rig this committee so that two men will have the same voting rights as the whole of the rest of us put together!'

'No, no, these are only casting votes we're talking about, Jay,' Desmond said soothingly. 'I firmly intend that it will never come to that sort of situation …'

'Look at you guys.' Jay pointed at the three men sitting together across the table. 'The men set the agenda, run the meeting and write the minutes. The women are window-dressing, as usual. Well, what do the other women say? Shazia?'

Shazia pursed her lips, hesitated, then said carefully, 'I do agree with Jay, actually. It seems an unnecessary destabilisation of the original balance of the committee. And if the situation will never arise, why introduce it?'

'Right,' Jay agreed fiercely. 'Kathy?'

Kathy felt the eyes of the committee on her. The sensation was remarkably similar to the feeling she'd had in her first confrontation with an armed assailant — that she was about to be mugged for no very good reason.

'I think it might have been better for the committee to have worked this out together,' she offered, 'rather than be presented with a solution. After all, if we can't work through this sort of difficulty, how can we be expected to make recommendations to anyone else?'

This seemed to defuse the situation a little. Several people nodded grudgingly, but Rex, who hadn't yet spoken, decided to land the killer punch.

'Well, the fact is that this solution has been approved by senior management, and it really doesn't matter how it was arrived at. And if you want to press the matter, Jay, we can put it to a vote, and you will lose, with or without my casting vote.'

'No she won't.' Nathan, the sixth member of the committee, spoke up. 'I agree with her, and that would give a vote of four to two. I don't see any point in belonging to this committee if it's going to be run this way. I'd like to propose that Desmond stand down as chair so that we can have an election. I personally would be in favour of a female chair.'

This caused some excitement. Kathy wondered if Rex and Jay had each been planning their coups right from the beginning, waiting for the right moment to press their claims to be chair. She couldn't imagine why anyone would have such an ambition. She tried to visualise them making the presentation to the Joint Conference in two weeks, and decided that both of them, in their different ways, would love it; the public exposure, the press interviews and photographs. As for herself, she couldn't think of anything worse.

Robert, the bureaucrat, face expressionless, said nothing as the arguments ricocheted around the table. But when it began to look as if Desmond might agree to vacate the chair in the interests of peace, sounding rather keen to hand it over to someone else, Robert leaned over and murmured in his ear. Desmond listened, then nodded reluctantly and called the meeting to order.

'Look, I think we're all a bit tired after a demanding day. I suggest we adjourn now and meet again in the morning to continue the discussion in a calmer frame of mind. Can I just say that Robert advises me that the position of chair is not negotiable, unfortunately, so I suggest we work from that as a given.'

There was an angry response to this from Jay, then several people said they had appointments in the morning that they couldn't break. The next meeting was finally arranged for lunchtime on the following day, sandwiches to be provided by the Met. As she made her way to the door, Kathy was stopped by Jay, who also had a hand on Shazia's arm.

'Can you hang on for a bit, Kathy? We need to talk.'

'I'm sorry, Jay. I've got another appointment.' She looked at her watch. 'I'm late.'

'This is important, Kathy. This whole committee is becoming dysfunctional.'

Kathy eventually bought her freedom by giving Jay her mobile phone number, then hurried away.

When Kathy had phoned Jennifer Mathieson earlier that day, asking for an informal meeting, off the record, the Verge Practice's information manager had been happy enough to agree, provided it was somewhere the other people in the firm wouldn't see them. 'I don't want to be accused of leaking the gossip of the sinking ship,' she'd laughed.

'That's good,' Kathy had said. 'It's the gossip I'm after.'

The wine bar was in the City, not far from the offices of the property development company Jennifer was due to start work for the following week.

'I wouldn't have agreed to this if I hadn't been leaving VP,' she said, as they sat down at a quiet table with glasses of chardonnay. 'I'd have felt disloyal.'

'Are you saying you were holding stuff back before?'

Jennifer pursed her lips, looking disappointed. 'You're not trying to trap me, are you?'

'No, of course not,' Kathy said quickly, annoyed with herself for sounding like a prosecutor. She realised that the last twenty-four hours had left her tired and tense. 'Sorry if I sounded like that. I just wanted to chat really.'

'That's okay. I don't think I deliberately misled anyone, but it's difficult to keep a sense of balance when you're being questioned by police in a murder investigation, you know what I mean? At first I clammed up and just said yes or no. But then I felt this odd compulsion to talk, like a confession or something, about everything, and I had to stop myself and make myself remember that loyalty to the firm came first. Now I don't care.'

Kathy raised her glass. 'Cheers.'

'Salud.'

'Spanish?'

'It's what Charles used to say. Good luck to him. I hope he's drinking something cool like this on some exotic beach right now.' She sipped at her drink. 'I suppose I'm doing what he did, getting out, and I'm just realising that it feels pretty good. I've been with them for nearly ten years now, my first really responsible job, and I'd forgotten how intense it is in there. Where I'm going they work hard too, but they're so much more relaxed. They don't worry every decision to death. If they like the look of something but it costs a lot, that's fine. They don't care if it's not the height of good taste, or consistent with what they did last year, or cutting edge.'

Cutting edge. Kathy pictured the Japanese carving knife, like a small Samurai sword, with which Charles Verge had murdered his wife. Jennifer ran a hand through her hair. It was cut short, in a crisp, rather severe bob.

'I'm going to let this grow out,' she said, 'and I'm going to get some new clothes that aren't necessarily black, and maybe I'll have a baby instead of a coronary. So, what gossip were you interested in?'

'Anything that could help us with motive. What was she doing that caused her to end up dead? Could it have been an affair?'

Jennifer shook her head slowly. 'There hasn't been a whisper of anything like that. I suppose if she was very discreet, visiting some secret lover far away from the office, we may not know about it. She didn't share intimacies with us.'

'How about someone in the firm?'

'Not a chance. Oh, when she first came there were plenty of young guys who thought she was really cool and just about the neatest style accessory for an ambitious young architect you could imagine. But once Charles showed an interest that all stopped dead. It would have seemed sacrilegious, I suppose.'

'How about Sandy Clarke?'

'Sandy?' Jennifer looked at Kathy with surprise, then a grin spread over her face. 'It's a nice thought, but no. Mind you, I do remember him flirting with her when she first arrived, but Sandy flirts with everyone.'

'Does he?'

'Well, I'd call it flirting; he'd probably say it's just being agreeable. Whatever, he likes to make women feel good, and like him.'

'And go to bed with him?'

Something occurred to Jennifer, some memory that caused her expression to soften, but whatever it was she apparently decided not to share it with Kathy. 'Yes,' she said. 'That happens. But nothing serious or dangerous. Nothing that need disturb his perfect family.'

'It's perfect, is it?'

'Oh God, yes. Wife's family are old county, a mansion in the Cotswolds. He has a married daughter and two sons, both at Oxford, and they live in this fabulous house on the edge of Greenwich Park. He was a navy flier for a couple of years when he was young, helicopters, and he's still got some of that dash. Well, you've met him.'

'And he still pulls the girls.'

'Just as a diversion. He can be very amusing and charming, quite different to Charles.'

'Charles being the fiery and dangerous one?'

'Fiery, sometimes, and intense. Dangerous? Well, if Miki was having an affair he'd have been angry and jealous, certainly, but he wouldn't have done *that*.'

'So why did he?'

'Opinion is divided. Among my staff, the secretaries and bookkeepers, the reason is that he just flipped, because all designers are basically a bit obsessive and demented, aren't they? Among the architects the feeling is a) he didn't do it and it's all a terrible mistake, or b) she drove him to it.'

'How did she do that, if it wasn't with a lover?'

'It's to do with their work. Their lives are so bound up in their work that it would have to be that. Deep down they all care more about how to detail the next staircase than whether their wives are being screwed.' She laughed and drained her glass. 'Mmm, that's quite nice, isn't it?'

'Have another,' Kathy said.

'Thanks. Does this make me a paid informant? A snout? A grass?' She laughed again, enjoying herself.

Kathy signalled to a waiter. 'Go on, then, how did the work drive him to it?'

Jennifer frowned as if trying to work out how to explain. 'This is not spelled out exactly. It's more like an undercurrent of belief or superstition that you pick up from time to time in the drawing office. And in a way it is sexual, but not as straightforward as a lover.

'Did you notice the gender distribution at VP? Basically, there's a divide. The admin staff are mostly female, while the architects are almost entirely male. I don't know why it is. I've watched them recruiting and interviewing, and I never detected any bias, but not many women designers apply to work there, and those that come usually don't last. Maybe all architects' offices are like that, I don't know; but you'd think it would be a good profession for a woman, wouldn't you? I've wondered if maybe there's some kind of suppressed aggression or competitiveness at VP that puts women off. Anyway, whatever the reason, that's the general rule. But there are exceptions, like Miki, and before her Charles's first wife, Gail.

'I knew Gail Verge. I joined the firm the year before she left. I used to watch the way she and Charles worked together. Each evening, after the bulk of the staff had gone home, the two of them would tour the drawing office, going from board to board, or computer to computer. They would examine what each person was working on, and Charles would make notes and sketches on a pad of white paper he carried around with him, then he'd tear the page off and leave it for the designer to look at next day.

'But the thing I noticed as I watched them was that it was almost always Gail who took the lead. She'd stare at the work for a while in silence, then point at something and they'd have a discussion. Then Charles would nod his agreement and do one of his famous little spiky black sketches to show the guy what he had to do.'

The second glass of wine arrived and Jennifer paused while Kathy paid.

'I assume you'll get expenses to cover this, will you? The prices are scandalous here.'

'Don't worry,' Kathy said, trying to sound nonchalant. 'So you think Gail was the better architect?'

'I'm not sure. Maybe she was a more perceptive critic. Maybe her judgement was better. I think that must be very important for them, don't you? I mean it's one thing to be very creative and come up with lots of bright ideas, but it's also important to be able to decide between them and pick the winner. She was a deeper thinker than Charles, and had a lighter touch. I think that they complemented each other's strengths. Maybe you should talk to her, she might give you a different angle on Charles. I've got her number here.' She gave it to Kathy.

'Anyway, she must have decided she'd had enough of living in the shadow of Superman and she walked out, and suddenly Charles was on his own. And it showed; maybe not to the clients on the outside, but to Charles's hot shot designers. There were whispers in the office that he'd lost his touch. At first we put it down to depression over Gail leaving him, but then it began to seem more than that, as if some kind of magic had left with her. The projects kept rolling in, bigger and bigger, and the discipline of the practice and its talent kept the show going, but something was missing. The rave reviews in the international magazines became more cautious and people began to say that VP was becoming mainstream.

'Then Miki came along, and Charles came to life again, and everybody was hoping that she would be another Gail, a fresh young queen to rejuvenate the tired old king. I mean, she could draw like an angel and she looked the part, as if she'd sprung fully formed from one of his sharpest buildings, and although she was so young she had confidence and authority.'

'I thought people didn't like her.'

'On a personal level, that's true. She was arrogant and ambitious and cold. But that didn't matter. The point was that she might restore Charles's magic touch, turn the good back into the brilliant.'

'Did it work?'

'No. After they were married Charles began to give her more and more freedom in their design work together. It seemed okay, people were encouraged. Then came disaster. There's this building that nobody in the firm ever mentions now, the Labuan Assembly. Fortunately it's a long way away and almost nobody goes there, but those that have all agree that it's an absolute pig — out of scale, clunky and derivative. And it was Miki's.'

'But what about Sandy Clarke? Where does he fit into this?'

'Sandy is the one who manages the teams who develop the production drawings for the buildings after Charles and his people have worked out the concept designs. You could say that Sandy's talent is to bring Charles's designs to life as faithfully as possible. When he realised what people were saying about the Labuan Assembly building, he persuaded Charles to keep the architectural press away. Effectively he buried it.'

'How did Miki feel about that?'

'She was furious, but Charles knew in his heart that Sandy was right. After that he insisted on making all the major design decisions alone.'

'How did that affect their relationship?'

Jennifer shrugged. 'That was the end of the honeymoon. Things got tense.'

'What about the Home Office project, Marchdale Prison? Who designed that?'

'Charles, one hundred per cent. I would say that Marchdale is Charles's attempt to wipe out the shame of Labuan, his demonstration that he can still do it like in the old days. He was obsessive about it and took control of every decision, doing little sketches at night for the draughtsmen like he used to do with Gail. Mind you, to hear Miki talk about it sometimes, you'd have thought it was all hers.'

'Are you suggesting that as a motive for murder? Professional jealousy?'

'No. Everyone at VP knew whose work it really was. But if you were to look at their personal relationship as a reflection of their working relationship, you'd have to say that when he killed her she was already dead for him.'

'You mean, she'd outlived her usefulness? That's a pretty horrible idea.'

'Yeah. It's not a motive exactly, but when you're looking for the thing that finally put the knife into her heart, you have to bear that background in mind.'

9

That Wednesday evening Kathy sensed that something had changed between herself and Leon, although the feeling was so indefinite that she hesitated to make an issue of it. She had returned to the flat to find him working on his university assignment on his computer, the rest of the table covered in textbooks and notes. He'd apologised stiffly, as if they were two strangers temporarily sharing a railway compartment and sensitive to territorial rights, and had begun to clear things away. She said it didn't matter and tried to make conversation about their day, but he didn't join in, pointedly returning his attention to the screen. Then her mobile phone rang, and she became locked in an interminable and one-sided conversation with Jay about the importance of having a woman chair for the committee, and of the women members acting as a caucus.

Later she went out to buy takeaway for them both, which they ate in silence. Eventually she said, 'You're not angry with me are you, Leon?'

'Why should I be?' he said, not meeting her eye.

'I don't know. Because I spotted the mix-up with Clarke's DNA?'

'No, of course not. I just ... I've just got to concentrate on this work, okay?'

'Yes, of course. I can't help, can I?'

Suddenly he sagged as if he'd been punctured, the anger or frustration or whatever had been simmering inside him gone. 'No, thanks. I'm sorry, Kathy.'

'What for?'

He took a deep breath. 'For everything,' he said, and wouldn't elaborate.

Later that night, across the other side of town, Brock turned restlessly in his bed, sleep eluding him. He had always enjoyed the luxury of lying alone in a wide bed, the freedom to stretch and turn without disturbance, but lately this feeling had been replaced by an uneasy sense of loss and isolation. To take his mind off this he forced himself to recall the pages of the Verge scrapbook which Suzanne's grandchildren had given him. He could picture most of them quite clearly, the images of success and scandal. As he finally slid towards slumber his brain focused on one of them, a colour magazine photograph of Charles Verge standing beside the nose of his silver glider, dressed in black leather jacket and jeans. In Brock's torpid imagination the picture seemed to come to life, Verge breaking into a smile and walking jauntily out of frame, to reveal behind him in the shadowy space of the aircraft's cockpit a second figure, a dark outline only, handling the controls.

Kathy woke to find herself alone in bed, the smell of toast and coffee coming from the other room. She found Leon propped against the door of the kitchenette, flicking through a paper he must have gone out to buy. The computer was alive and he looked as if he'd been up for some time.

'Hi,' he said, not looking up from the page. 'Want some coffee? Your horoscope says you're going to be doing some travelling.'

Kathy wasn't sure, but she thought she detected a note of hopefulness in his voice.

They were making progress. She could sense it in the animated murmuring around the room as they waited for Brock to start the team meeting the following morning. As they each gave their reports it was apparent that everyone had something to offer, some suggestive little bit of fresh information, though where it all led Kathy still couldn't make out.

First it was reported that Sandy Clarke had been asked for a new DNA swab, and this request had apparently been met with something like panic. 'Went white as a sheet,' the officer said with satisfaction. 'Then demanded to know why, and when I said routine elimination he wouldn't believe me, then said he'd refuse and call his lawyer, then finally apologised and did the doings. Something to hide, I reckon.'

Kathy described her conversation with Jennifer Mathieson, and her assessment of Clarke's attitude to women. 'But she reckons that they couldn't have been having an affair without the office inquisition getting wind of it, so either they were very discreet, or it had only just started.'

It had not been possible to identify Clarke's car on the tapes retained from security cameras in the streets near his offices for Saturday the twelfth of May. Statements made by his staff had confirmed that he was present throughout the day, supervising the team preparing for the presentation to the Chinese on the following Monday, although it was also said that Clarke had been absent for extended periods during the morning; he was mainly in his own office, according to his statement, working on correspondence and other paperwork. It would have been quite possible for him to have gone up to the Verge apartment during this time, or even to have left the building, if he had avoided the routes covered by the cameras.

But it was the group working under Tony, the Fraud Squad officer, who had the most intriguing material to offer. Tony stroked his notes with loving fingers and eased his neck a little in his stiff white shirt collar, with his customary air of an undertaker presenting his estimate of funeral expenses. 'We haven't been able to get access to his personal accounts as yet, chief. We should progress that today, with any luck. But a couple of things have come up that may be of interest.'

He cleared his throat, for theatrical effect Kathy guessed, as if he were about to offer a special on the oak casket.

'We ran his name through the accounts we have had access to, and came up with two payments from him of ten thousand quid each, to the account of Verge's daughter Charlotte, in July and August of this year.'

'Mmm …' Brock scratched his beard ruminatively. 'Under-standable. Helping out the daughter of his old partner. She's had extra expenses lately with the new house, and a baby on the way.'

'True enough. Or the money might be intended for Charles. But it does raise the whole interesting question of who's entitled to what out of the Verge Practice. Talking to the accountants, it appears that on May the twelfth ownership of the firm was shared between the three equity partners, Charles Verge and Miki Norinaga and Sandy Clarke, in the ratio 45:25:30. Now only one of them is left.'

'What about Charles and Miki's successors?'

'The firm had an insurance policy to cover the sudden death of a partner. But Miki left everything to Charles, assuming he outlived her, and so Charles now theoretically owns over two-thirds of the business. If he were to turn up dead, his estate — principally his daughter Charlotte — would have his share paid out by the insurance company. But he hasn't been declared dead, so his assets are in limbo. Either way, dead or alive, Sandy Clarke effectively controls the firm one hundred per cent.'

Brock shrugged doubtfully. 'By all accounts business has been terrible since the murder. If you're suggesting Clarke had a financial motive to murder his partners, it hasn't turned out to be a very smart move.'

'Maybe that wasn't the motive, chief.' Tony's face took on a look of cunning. 'Maybe he had no choice.'

'How do you mean?'

'The accountants are only now getting around to finalising the books for the last financial year, and they've come across something interesting. In the twelve months leading up to last May, the Verge Practice made a series of payments to a company that nobody seems to know anything about: Turnstile Quality Systems Limited. The thing that alerted the accountants was the size and number of the payments, sixteen in all, amounting to a couple of million quid. When the accountants asked the bookkeeper at VP she knew nothing about the payments, which had been authorised directly by Sandy Clarke and not entered into the monthly accounts.'

'What does that mean, Tony?'

'Well, this only came up yesterday evening, so we haven't had time to do a proper check on Turnstile Quality Systems yet, but when we tried to phone them the number didn't work, so I took a drive out to their address, in an industrial estate in Neasden, number 27 Poplar Lane. It turns out that the last building on Poplar Lane is number 25, and nobody around there has ever heard of this company. The accountants wanted to take it up with Clarke, of course, but I told them to hold off until they get the all clear from us. The possibility is that he was using a dummy company to siphon money out of his own firm.'

'A couple of million? Surely someone would have noticed?'

'VP authorised well over a billion in payments to contractors last year, chief, and their own profits were very healthy. The invoices were VAT exempt, apparently, so there was no discrepancy in the VAT returns. They were bound to surface eventually, of course, but by then Sandy Clarke was the only partner left to worry about it.'

They discussed what they should do next, Brock allocated tasks and the meeting broke up. As she was leaving, Kathy found that she had a text message on her phone, postponing the committee meeting until the following Monday. Her first reaction was relief that she would have time to work with the team on the Verge case, but then irritation as she realised that all the important jobs had now been allocated. She hurried over to Brock and explained the situation.

'Oh, that's good, Kathy,' he said, sounding preoccupied and not overjoyed. She felt marginal, hanging around on the edges. 'And how is the committee going? I haven't had a chance to talk to you.'

'Pretty hopeless. Apart from a day's workshop on gay rights, we've spent the whole time quarrelling about who should be chair.'

'Maybe you should step in and take over.' He smiled at the idea. 'Yes, why not? This may be your opportunity.'

'I'd rather quit and work on the case full time. Is there anything interesting I can do today?'

'Interesting? Well …' he consulted the sheaf of papers on his clipboard, '… there's a lot that needs doing. There's a list of car numbers from the CCTV cameras needs checking …' He caught the look that crossed her face and stopped. 'Or … well, how do you fancy a trip up to Peterborough? That's where the couple live who thought they saw Verge in Barcelona on the Monday after the murder. We haven't reinterviewed them yet. It's always possible they may remember something else.'

A very long shot, Kathy thought, but better that than another list. So the horoscope in the paper had been right. She hid her disappointment and took the details. After a couple of phone calls she had set up meetings with the couple and made for the door, passing Tony and his fraud team. DI Bren Gurney was with them, chuckling at a joke someone had cracked. He looked alert and cheerful in the unfamiliar company of the Fraud Squad officers, and Kathy thought, that's where I should be, I've worked with SO6 before, then told herself not to be petty. She took the tube to Finchley to pick up her little red Renault and headed for the Great North Road.

Weaving among the trucks thundering north out of London on the A1 motorway, Kathy experienced a familiar sense of anticipation, of heading towards a foreign country, the one to which she and her mother had moved after her father died — the strange and intimidating Socialist Republic of South Yorkshire where, after her mother, too, had passed away, she had been taken in by her aunt and uncle. She thought guiltily that it was some time since she'd been up to see them, elderly now and frail in their little Sheffield terrace house. From Peterborough she'd be halfway there; she considered continuing north after she'd seen the McNeils, then dismissed the idea.

She followed the directions Audrey McNeil had given her, turning off the A1 at the first Peterborough sign and coming to an area of new detached houses on the outskirts of the city. From the welcome that Mrs McNeil gave her, she got the impression that the excitement caused by their possible sighting of the runaway had been thoroughly appreciated. Both women were prepared with documentation; Kathy with a file of the earlier interview transcripts and the plans and photographs supplied by the Barcelona police, and Audrey McNeil with her own collection of holiday snapshots, city guides and souvenirs.

'It's a wonderful city, so exciting, so much to see,' Audrey enthused. She was in her early sixties, Kathy guessed, hair silvering and eyes sharp. 'Wonderful buildings, the street life, the food ... Well, to be honest I think tapas is overrated, and Peter says I do a better paella than any of the restaurants we tried, but anyway ...' She poured tea as she rattled on. 'I have a Barcelona bridge partner now. We get on like a house on fire. Play practically every day. A grandmother like me, and the same age.'

It seemed Audrey spent much of her days, and nights too, playing bridge on the internet. She handed Kathy her pictures of Barcelona, describing each in turn and eventually coming to the only one that seemed relevant.

'Now this is the Casa Milà, which is on the same street where Peter saw Charles Verge, the Passeig de Gràcia. You see the sculpted shape of the balconies, almost like it's made of clay, or bones? It was designed by Gaudí, the famous Barcelona architect, who was run over by a tram. Peter is a great fan of Gaudí. He took pictures of all his buildings, including the great church of the Sagrada Família of course, dozens of them.' She turned to another packet but Kathy stopped her and guided her attention back to the Casa Milà.

'That was taken from right outside the building?'

'Yes. Peter was insistent that we cross the street to try to get further back, to get the whole building in, but the trees got in the way and he didn't take that shot in the end. So we crossed back over again and continued down to a café near the metro station, and it was on our way there that we saw him.'

Kathy unfolded her plans and got Audrey to trace the route. 'We worked out that it must have been this block here that we saw him, going into the entrance on the corner, there.'

'Okay, now in your earlier statement it's Peter who really describes the figure you saw, and you agree with him. I wondered if you could try to picture the scene again now and tell me what you saw.'

'Well, the trouble is that I took no notice until Peter said something like, "Oh, look at that chap over there, it's the famous architect Charles Verge", and then I looked and just caught a fleeting glimpse of him as he disappeared into the shadow of the entrance. I wouldn't remember it at all if Peter hadn't gone on about how important he was, and I got a bit irritated because frankly I'd never heard of him, not then. Now, of course, everyone has.'

'All the same,' Kathy persisted, sure she was wasting her time, 'could you close your eyes and picture the scene, and just replay it in your mind? Don't say anything, just try to visualise it, then tell me what you see.'

Audrey closed her eyes and sat motionless for a moment. Her lips pursed as if recalling the memory of her irritation with her husband, then her face relaxed a little and she made a gesture with her hand, as if tracing a movement in front of her. She opened her eyes and shrugged.

'Not much help, I'm afraid. I got a glimpse of someone dressed in black, that's all.'

'Black jacket?'

'Yes, I suppose so. Peter said afterwards it was a black leather jacket.'

'Forget about what Peter said, Audrey. I just want your impressions.'

'Well he was probably right. I think it may have been a bit shiny in the sunlight, just before he disappeared inside the building. And black trousers and black hair.'

'Length of hair?'

'I'm not sure.'

'Just now, when you had your eyes closed, you moved your right hand to the right, as if you were following his movement. Is that what you were doing?'

'Yes.'

'Only, if you were walking down the Passeig de Gràcia here …' Kathy pointed to the map, '… on the same side as the Casa Milà, surely he would have passed in front of you going from right to left, from the kerb to the building, that way, yes?'

Audrey frowned in thought. 'I suppose so. Well … maybe he did. I don't know.' Her irritation was surfacing again. 'You've got to realise that I didn't take much notice at the time. I mean, if Peter had said it was Elton John or Fergie or someone interesting I'd have paid attention, and anyway, it was a whole week later that we realised it might be important and had to think back. I mean, our whole time in Barcelona was packed with interesting sights, and this was just one little incident, over in a flash.'

'Of course,' Kathy said, conciliatory. 'Police hope for the impossible from eyewitnesses.' It was quite obvious that Audrey McNeil could tell her nothing new. 'So Gaudí's church is impressive, is it?'

'Actually, it's very weird,' Audrey said, and opened the packet of photographs.

. . .

After a decent interval Kathy said she would have to go to keep her appointment with Mr McNeil. He had officially retired from his structural engineering practice, Audrey had said, but still went in one day a week, to the irritation of his partners. Kathy followed her directions to the city centre and found the offices in a neat Georgian terrace not far from Peterborough's cathedral. The place was very different from the Verge Practice's glossy building. A receptionist and a couple of other staff were packed into a series of small rooms along with a purposeful jumble of hard hats, surveying equipment and computers.

'Audrey any help?' her husband inquired, lifting a pile of files to the floor so that he could sit on the other side of the desk.

'Oh, it's always useful to hear it direct, rather than just reading it from files,' Kathy lied.

'Nothing, eh?' he beamed smugly, and in that smile Kathy thought she might have seen the source of his wife's irritation. 'Well, I doubt if I can add anything new either, but fire away.'

Kathy got him to repeat his account, then said, 'So you saw him get out of a taxi over to your right, then walk across in front of you from right to left.'

'That's it, yes. I was concentrating on his face, trying to decide if it really was him. He looked younger than the photos I'd seen in the magazines, and his hair was a bit longer, but when your people showed me the most recent picture they had of him, I knew he was the one.'

'It's just that Audrey seemed to feel that she saw him go into a doorway to her right, not her left.'

'Well, that doesn't surprise me.' The grin spread over his face again. 'Do you know that it's now been scientifically proven that the only thing women can do that men can't is have babies, and the only thing that men can do that women can't is read maps.' He chuckled. 'If I'm ever forced to get Audrey to map-read for me in the car and she says, "Turn left here", I turn right, because I know that's what she means. You get my drift? Don't get me wrong, Audrey can be sharp as a tack, but she gets right and left mixed up. And she hardly had time to register him. But she did notice his hair, come to think of it. Did she mention that? I was telling her how he was England's leading architect and she got a bit cross with me going on about him and said something like, "Well, that's as maybe, but he needs to wash his hair. It's greasy." I'd forgotten that until now. But it's not surprising, is it? I mean, if he'd been on the run for forty-eight hours?'

Kathy went through the maps and photographs in her file with him, but he had nothing new to add. In fact, she had the impression from his answers, too quick and too confident, that he was determined to be absolutely consistent with what he'd said before. As she made to go he tried to interest her in visiting Peterborough Cathedral, a few minutes' walk away. 'The only remaining early example of a painted wooden ceiling in a major Romanesque church,' he enthused. She said she had to be getting back to London, but he insisted on walking her past the west front of the cathedral in a roundabout way back to her car, and explaining the theory that the odd spacing of the great arches was derived from musical intervals described in the *Boethius de Musica*, a work familiar to all educated men in the twelfth century, apparently. Kathy was careful not to get him started on Gaudí's church in Barcelona.

On the road back to London she thought about the McNeils' statements, wondering what she could report to Brock. Despite Peter McNeil's confidence, she wasn't convinced that the man he'd seen was Charles Verge. She'd never been to Barcelona, but she guessed that it must contain thousands of shortish men with black hair who looked a bit like the missing man. The building that McNeil had seen Verge going into had yielded nothing, and there had been differences in the recollections of husband and wife.

Driving south now, the sun was in Kathy's eyes, glittering from the glass and metalwork of oncoming vehicles. She recalled Audrey's comment that the leather jacket had appeared shiny in the sunlit street, just before it disappeared into the shadows of the doorway. Presumably the sunlight had also picked out his greasy hair, which she'd forgotten noticing. But that couldn't be right.

She turned off into the forecourt of a filling station and took the street plan of the Passeig de Gràcia from her file. As she'd thought, it ran almost due north-south, with the Casa Milà, the metro station and the assumed sighting of Verge on the east side. But it had been about ten-thirty in the morning, and surely the east side of the street would have been in shadow, the west side sunlit? Yes, she remembered the photograph of the Casa Milà, the façade in shade. And Audrey had thought that the man had walked across the footpath from left to right, as would have been the case if they'd been walking southward down the west side, not the east. It was as if the two McNeils had been describing completely different incidents, on opposite sides of the street. Which was about par for eyewitnesses.

She reported this to Brock when she returned. He shrugged as if he'd expected no more. 'This is how it is with taking over an old case, Kathy,' he grumbled. 'Faded memories, second-hand accounts. But at least the Clarke lead seems to be bearing fruit. That was a fortunate discovery, the forensic report on the pillow. Leon tells me you were helping him when he found it.'

Kathy nodded, still uncertain exactly what Leon had said. 'Is someone in trouble for missing it the first time?'

'Hard to say. It was probably just one of those things that happen when there's a turnover of people. The important thing is we've got it now.'

'And Clarke has been up to something?'

'There are several things I'd be very interested to hear his explanation about. I think we should be ready to speak to him quite soon.'

Dusk was falling, shop windows throwing bright pools of light across darkening pavements as Kathy drove south across the river to keep the appointment she had made with Gail Lewis. The architect had asked her to come to an address in Clapham, where she would be working all that afternoon and evening. It was a shopfront, Kathy discovered, with a sign reading 'South London Housing Aid'. Inside a woman was working at a word processor on a desk in the middle of the room. She looked up and smiled at Kathy as the doorbell tinkled, then looked beyond her to someone passing by on the street outside and gave a wave. There were posters and leaflets on the walls, with information on housing cooperatives and housing associations in the London area.

It was very hot in the office, and the woman's black skin glistened with perspiration. 'Hello, how can I help you?' she asked, seeming oblivious to the sounds of a violent argument going on beyond the partition behind her.

Kathy asked for Gail Lewis and the woman put her head round a door in the partition and said something. The noise died for a few moments, then started up again as a woman came through the door and shook Kathy's hand.

'Let's go upstairs.'

They climbed a steep staircase to a small bare room with a drawing board and T-square set out on a table, and Gail Lewis offered Kathy a seat.

'Is this your office?' Kathy asked, puzzled.

'No. I visit once a week to offer advice and work on new projects with some of the people who come here.'

She was a slight woman with grey hair cut short, wearing a shirt and jeans. From the brief file entry Kathy knew that she was the same age as Verge, fifty-two, and had met him in the master's program at Harvard he'd attended after completing his degree in England. An American, she still had a distinct New England accent, although Kathy assumed she had now spent as much of her life in the UK as in the USA.

Kathy was about to speak again when the sound of argument suddenly billowed up from below.

The architect's mouth tightened. 'Look, this isn't a very good time. And I really don't see how I can help you.'

'As I said on the phone, I just wanted to talk to you about your former husband.'

'Yes, but what exactly?'

The woman was impatient, and Kathy felt the pressure rising from below. 'I'd like to understand him better.'

'Understand what? He's fifty-two years old. You want me to summarise that in a sentence?'

'You were married to him for twenty years …'

'Well, maybe I didn't understand him either. Maybe that's why we split up. Look, I haven't seen him in eight years. Talk to the people who've known him recently — his mother, Sandy Clarke, his people at work …'

'Yes, I'm doing that.' Kathy felt that she wasn't getting anywhere. 'Was he ever violent to you?'

'Only with his tongue, which was bad enough.'

'Do you believe he could murder someone?'

'Yes, if he put his mind to it.'

'But that makes it sound deliberate. Everyone points out how disastrous this has been for him, that it must have been impulsive.'

For a moment Kathy felt that the other woman might have said something, but there was a sudden turmoil from below and she jumped to her feet.

'I'm sorry, I can't help you. I have to get down there and sort things out.' And then she was disappearing down the staircase. Kathy shrugged and took a last look around at the threadbare room with its peeling wallpaper, and thought about how different this was from the Verge Practice offices.

10

A brisk north-easterly breeze gusted up the long slope of Greenwich Park, ruffling the hair of the little boy in the pushchair. Despite the wind the morning was mild, the sun glinting through a silvery sky and casting a shimmer of light on the surface of the river and the glassy towers of Canary Wharf beyond. Sandy Clarke stooped and lifted the child, setting him on his feet. Like a mechanised toy, the little legs immediately began pumping and the toddler hurtled off across the grass.

Clarke had surprised both his wife and himself when he had announced over breakfast that he wouldn't be going in to the office that day. He added that he had paperwork he could do better in the peace of home, but that was fiction. In truth, it was simply an impulse, something to do with the claustrophobic atmosphere in the office and his inability to sleep these nights. And something, too, about the day itself, mild yet misty as if on a cusp between summer and winter, the past and the future, very like that other turning point, in May, when everything had changed forever.

When their daughter had arrived with their grandson later in the morning he had insisted on taking the child to the park, and now, watching him chasing tiny butterflies caught in the breeze, he found himself overwhelmed by a terrible sense of loss. The force of it made his eyes momentarily water and filled him with a desire to flee, not to some other place but to another time, twenty years before, when he had walked another child, his daughter, on this same grassy hillside. He had been cocky then, confident and strong. Now he felt like an impostor, as limp and undeserving as the used condom lying by his foot. They had worked on small buildings in those days, houses and office conversions, projects for which you could hold every detail in your mind. Now they tendered for whole cities. What madness was that, to imagine that you could design a whole city? All you made was a shell, an imitation of a real place. Had Charles felt that too, that their lives had insidiously progressed from the tangible and real to the grandiose and fake? For a moment Clarke was certain that he had, that Charles's tragedy — all their tragedies — boiled down to that.

But all lives have a trajectory, he thought, an axis running inevitably onward, regardless of our doubts. The thought of axes, of intention and certainty, was comforting, and appropriate, too, in this place criss-crossed by organising lines. His eye strayed down to the great central axis of symmetry of the Queen's House and Wren's Naval College, so firm and bold. It continued, he knew, back up the hill to the south, and along Le Notre's formal avenue to the gates of the park and then out across Blackheath to the spire of All Saints, and it also continued northward, aligning across the river to the distant Hawksmoor church of St Anne's in Limehouse, hidden now by the modern piles on the Isle of Dogs. And even this grand four-mile-long axis paled into insignificance alongside the greatest axis of them all, the invisible meridian running through the Old Royal Observatory up there on the hill, the axis of zero longitude encircling the whole globe.

Clarke's distracted musings on axes and life were interrupted by a figure approaching across the grass, striding as straight and purposeful as if following some invisible axis of its own; a bulky figure, hands thrust into the pockets of a black coat flapping in the breeze. Clarke recognised the cropped white hair and beard and braced himself. 'Deliver me, Lord,' he breathed in prayer, 'from eternal death on that dreadful day ...'

'Morning!' Brock hailed him as he came in range. 'Beautiful day.'

They strolled across the slope, following the trail of the little boy. Clarke felt a great calm descend on him, and when the policeman didn't seem inclined to broach the reason for his being there, Clarke saw no need to prevaricate.

'You've come about the DNA test, I take it?'

'Yes indeed.'

'It was positive, was it?' He took a deep breath, picking up the scent of distant chimneys. 'I didn't doubt it.'

'Why didn't you tell us before?'

Clarke bridled. The arrogance of these people was without limit, poking into everyone's lives, requiring everything to be confessed. 'It was and is none of your damn business, that's why!'

The detective looked mildly puzzled. 'When exactly did she tell Mr Verge?'

That stopped Clarke in his tracks. He felt the blood drain from his face. 'Dear God … She told Charles? She swore …' He tried to think clearly. 'But of course, she's told you too, I suppose.' How absurd that he hadn't realised that all along.

The policeman was looking distinctly unsettled now. He gazed at Clarke beneath lowered brows and said finally, 'Look, Mr Clarke, let's make a clean breast of it, eh? What have you got to tell me?'

Clarke gave a bitter laugh. 'You want a confession, do you? I should have thought that was hardly necessary if you've got the tests, and she's told you anyway.' But the anger faded quickly. What was the point? 'Very well, for the record, I acknowledge that I am the father of Charlotte Verge's child.'

'Blimey.' Bren Gurney sat down beside Kathy who was watching the interview on the CCTV screen. 'He was poking Verge's wife *and* his daughter? We'd better check out his old mum, make sure Clarke wasn't going for the triple crown.'

Brock was letting Clarke find his own pace. Since agreeing to make a formal statement the architect had behaved as if the act of confession had brought some relief. The question of a DNA test to confirm the parentage of Charlotte's unborn child had apparently been preying on his mind for some time, and when the police had asked for a second DNA sample he had assumed that it was for this reason.

'It was a farce, really. A farce that turned into a nightmare. I've never been caught out this way before. That it should happen at this stage, and with Charles's daughter …' He lifted his hands in a

106

gesture of appeal to Brock, man to man. Brock looked up from the report of the DNA test in which he seemed to be more interested, and nodded sympathetically.

'Charles and I had been invited to an architectural conference in Atlanta, last February. Charlotte had recently split up with her boyfriend of three years standing and was in the depths of despair, so at the last minute Charles invited her along. We'd been there a couple of days when some crisis blew up on the Marchdale Prison project and Charles had to fly back to London. I'd delivered my paper by that stage, and was getting a bit bored with the conference. The next morning I took Charlotte to see the Coca-Cola museum, and while we were there I mentioned that, in my opinion, the most beautiful city in the United States was Charleston in South Carolina. She'd never been there, and on an impulse we decided to go. I hired a car and we set off. That night we stayed in this rather seedy little motel, and I felt like Humbert Humbert with Lolita. It wasn't a very pleasant feeling.

'That was the farcical bit, and it lasted for one night only. The nightmare began a couple of months later when Charlotte told me that she was pregnant and I was the father. I was appalled, but she seemed rather ... well, pleased. She insisted that she would have the baby and that my name would be kept out of it.'

'This must have been a couple of weeks before Miki Norinaga was murdered?'

'That's right. After Charles disappeared, I contacted her again and said that I wanted to help her financially. She didn't seem particularly concerned, but I sent her some money anyway.

'Now look,' Clarke sat up straighter in his chair and glared at Brock, 'I've been completely open with you. But as far as I'm concerned this is a private matter between Charlotte and me. My wife doesn't know and ...' He faltered. 'I *assume* my wife doesn't know. Good God, Charlotte hasn't told her, too, has she? I can't imagine what could have possessed her to tell her father. Are you sure about that? And what has this got to do with your inquiries? Surely you're not suggesting that this has some bearing on what happened on the twelfth of May?'

The other person in the interview room was Tony, the financial expert, who, like Brock, seemed more interested in his papers than in what Clarke had to say. They were photocopied account statements and computer printouts, some of whose items Tony would tick as his eye ran down the sheets. But now, as Clarke ended on a somewhat plaintive note, he lifted his head and looked questioningly at Brock.

Brock cleared his throat as Clarke waited for a reply. 'I think we've been at cross-purposes, Mr Clarke. When I asked when *she* had told Mr Verge, I wasn't referring to Charlotte. You jumped to that conclusion. As far as I'm aware, Charlotte Verge has told no one of your involvement with her. She certainly hasn't spoken to me.'

Clarke rocked back, stunned. 'What! Then who ...?'

'It was your involvement with Miki Norinaga that I was interested in. That's what the DNA tests were for.'

'Oh Christ.' Clarke rolled his head back and stared up at the ceiling. 'So you know about that.' His voice was a whisper. 'I didn't think ... I have no reason to believe that she told Charles,' he said, but without conviction. 'It was a miserable affair. It meant nothing. She was being manipulative.'

'Poor bloke,' Kathy in the next room murmured. 'All these women keep taking advantage of him.'

'Yeah,' Bren agreed. 'Shocking. And them half his age.'

'You'd better tell me about it,' Brock said mildly.

'Oh ...' Clarke sounded weary now, resigned. 'It began a couple of months before that weekend in May. I'd given her a lift home from some function we'd been at. Charles was away. She started talking about the time when she'd first joined VP, and she accused me of flirting with her then. She was being playful, but I knew from past experience that when Miki acted coy she was up to something and you should watch out, so I didn't respond. Then she asked me if Charles had discussed his impotence with me. I was shocked and embarrassed. She said she needed to talk to someone, so I went up to the flat with her, and that evening we became lovers.

'It wasn't like any other relationship I'd had. It was brutally functional, and I sensed that I was simply being recruited to her side for some looming battle with Charles. I tried to avoid it happening again, but she demanded periodic sex, like a tax, or tribute.'

'What about that Friday evening, the eleventh of May, before Charles returned from America?'

'Yes. We'd been preparing for the presentation we had on the Monday to a delegation of Chinese ...'

'Yes, you told us about that.'

'Right. When we packed up for the night she demanded I go up to the apartment, to have a drink before I went home. It was about eight-thirty or so. I was tired, she mixed a pretty strong vodka tonic, and we talked for a while, then went to bed.'

'Did she talk about Charles?'

'Yes. She referred to him a couple of times with contempt, and I got the impression that things between them were coming to a head. As I said, I was dog-tired, and after we had sex I fell asleep for a short time and she had to wake me up. I felt terrible, had a shower and went home.'

'Did she change the sheets after you got up?'

'I don't know. I suppose she might have.'

'And the next day?'

'It was as I've described. I picked Charles up at the airport the next morning and we looked at a site he was interested in on the way back. I dropped him off at the private lift to the flat, and didn't see him or Miki again until we discovered her body on the Monday. I went home about five p.m.'

'The statements of the people you were working with suggest that there were extended periods when you weren't with them. You could have gone up to the apartment during that day.'

'I could have done but I didn't. I spent quite a bit of time alone in my office, dealing with correspondence and so on.'

Brock frowned, head bowed, as if profoundly disappointed. He glanced up at Tony, who gave a slight shake of his head.

'It's true,' Clarke insisted.

'No, it won't do. Here you are working alongside Miki Norinaga for, what, five years? Then she seduces you and within a couple of months she's murdered, possibly on the night that you last share her bed, according to the medical evidence.'

'No!'

'And at the same time her husband disappears,' Brock pressed on, voice hard now, 'and you've made it quite clear that he had very good reason to hate you, his closest business partner, who had seduced both his wife and his daughter. Is that how it was, Mr Clarke? Did

Charles learn what you'd been up to when he returned that Saturday morning, and call you up to the apartment to confront you? What happened then?'

'No! No!' Sandy Clarke was on his feet now, his chair crashing back onto the floor. 'This is insane. I won't say another word, not a word. I want to leave now.'

Brock looked coldly at him for a moment, then said, 'I'll repeat that I'm not satisfied with your account, Mr Clarke. Before you rush off you might like to consider how it will look if you refuse to cooperate at this point.' Then, voice becoming milder, he added, 'I'll suspend this interview now and we'll leave you alone with a cup of tea to collect your thoughts. Maybe you'd like to call a legal advisor?'

Brock and Tony gathered up their papers and left the room. On their screen Kathy and Bren watched Clarke stare blankly at the closed door. For a moment it looked as if he would storm after them, but then he shook his head in a gesture of despair or disbelief, and began to pace up and down.

'What do you think?' Brock came into the observation room, Tony in his wake.

'He sounds plausible,' Kathy suggested, 'but he's the type that would.' She looked at his clothes, expensive understated casuals — windcheater, slacks and leather loafers. He had come to a halt in the middle of the interview room, hands in pockets, head bowed, deep in thought.

'I'd like you to talk to Charlotte Verge again, Kathy,' Brock said. 'See what her version is. The timing of her announcement to Clarke about the baby sounds significant, so close to the murder. Maybe she did say something to her father or stepmother. But be discreet. Take a copy of the transcript of this interview with you. You might find some discrepancies.'

On the screen Clarke looked up as an officer came into the room with a cup of tea. As he left again, Clarke sat down at the table, took out a diary and began to make notes.

'Tony, I can see you're anxious to get on to the money matters,' Brock went on. 'We'll do that next, if he decides to cooperate.'

A tray of polystyrene cups of tea was brought for the watchers, who waited in silence as the figure in the room tapped a silver pen in agitation against the pages of his diary, kneading his forehead with his other hand as if to squeeze memories out of his brain. Finally, he got to his feet and strode over to the door, where he spoke to the officer who stood outside. A moment later this man put his head around the door of the observation room.

'He's ready to talk to you again, sir.'

'Good.' Brock and Tony picked up their files and made for the door.

'I suppose,' Clarke began, when they were seated again around the interview table, 'that panicking people is part of your technique, is it? Throwing wild accusations at them and seeing what they let slip.' He was calm again, in control of himself, determined not to be fazed. 'The problem with that is it can just create confusion. I've been going over that evening in my mind again, the last time I saw Miki, that Friday night, and I don't think I've really made clear to you what it was like.'

He waited for Brock to challenge him, but the DCI only nodded in a vague sort of way, as if not greatly interested.

Clarke drew a small circle in the margin of his diary with his silver pen, then drew a straight line through it. 'You see, her whole manner that evening was odd, out of character. When she insisted I go up to the apartment for a drink after we'd finished our work, I felt there was something in the wind, something involving Charles, presumably, that was preoccupying her. I assumed she wanted my support in some scheme or other, but she seemed to have difficulty getting to the point. She talked about the past, before she arrived on the scene, about Charles's relationship with his first wife, Gail, but I couldn't make out where she was heading. At one point she made some cryptic remark about having married the wrong partner, but I didn't really follow. And then, when she started to get amorous, I thought to myself that she was just trying to soften me up so she could share this big confidence, whatever it was, about Charles, and all I could think was how grotesque it was, because amorous seduction just wasn't her style at all.'

Clarke paused, looking questioningly at Brock, who still said nothing.

'Well, don't you see? I think she knew that there was this big row brewing with Charles, when he got back from the States, and she'd been hoping to get some sort of ammunition or support from me. But when it came to the point, she just couldn't bring herself to confide in me.'

He fell silent, the tip of the silver pen hovering over the page.

'Hmm. That's it, is it, Mr Clarke?' Brock said at last. 'Nothing else you'd like to tell us?'

'No, that's it.' Clarke snapped the diary shut and slipped it and the pen into his jacket pocket.

'Only we'd like to move on to other matters now. Tony?'

Tony cleared his throat and leaned forward, tracing his finger across an item on the page in front of him. 'Ahem, yes,' he began softly, diffidently even, as if broaching a delicate subject. 'I'd like to ask you about a payment made to a company called Turnstile Quality Systems Limited, or TQS, on the first of March of last year, in the sum of twenty-three thousand, one hundred and eighteen pounds and sixty-five pence.'

Clarke looked at him in astonishment for a moment, then turned to Brock. 'Are you serious? What is this?'

'Quite serious, Mr Clarke,' Tony said.

Clarke turned his gaze back to his lugubrious interrogator and gave a little snort of amusement. 'You sound like a quantity surveyor,' he said. 'How the hell should I know?'

'Well, you did authorise the payment, Mr Clarke, and nobody else seems to know anything about this company.'

'What?' Clarke shook his head, becoming annoyed. 'What was the name again?'

'Turnstile Quality Systems.'

'Doesn't ring a bell.'

Tony turned the page and ran his finger down the next. 'In the following month, sixteenth of April last year, you authorised a second payment to TQS, £86,453.27p. Do you remember that one?'

'No,' Clarke's voice was insistent, 'I don't.'

'Or a third in May, larger again — £156,978.50p.'

'No! They're obviously a contractor of some kind. Stage payments on a contract. The name means nothing to me, but someone must know. What contract number is it set against? What does it say on the payment certificates?'

'Well, that's the thing, Mr Clarke. There were no job certificates issued for these payments, no contract number quoted, and the funds were drawn from the Verge Practice working account, on your signature.'

'What?' Clarke looked startled.

'That's a quarter of a million pounds in just over three months, and the payments went on, right up to April of this year, a grand total of £1,932,786.90p drawn from Verge Practice funds in favour of a company that nobody knows anything about.'

Clarke frowned, thinking. 'I ... I don't know. We invest working capital and surplus income in various ways — property, funds, cash management accounts, I don't know. And last year was a very strong year. Surely the accountants, our bookkeepers ...?'

'They know nothing about it.'

'That's impossible. No, look, you've made a mistake. What are you suggesting, anyway?'

'Does the name Kraus mean anything to you, Mr Clarke?'

Brock, who, despite appearances, was watching Sandy Clarke closely at this point, saw the man become very still. There was silence for a long moment.

'Kraus? How do you spell that?'

'K-R-A-U-S. Martin Kraus.'

'No,' Clarke sounded offhand. 'I don't think so. Why?'

'He's listed as the sole director of Turnstile Quality Systems.'

Clarke withdrew his diary and pen from his pocket again and wrote the names in the inside cover of the book. 'Doesn't mean a thing, I'm afraid. But I'll check through my address book and email directory if you like, just to make sure.'

'Good idea,' Brock said, not mentioning that they had already done that.

11

The front door of the cottage swung open before Kathy's hand had touched the brass horse-head knocker, her approach betrayed by the sound of her feet crunching up the gravel path. Charlotte Verge stared intently at her visitor, then stepped forward across the threshold into the sunlight, followed by a rich whiff of cooking. She was wearing no make-up, her elfin features childlike, and Kathy recalled Clarke's reference to her as Lolita.

'What did you mean on the phone,' she demanded in a whisper, 'that you wanted to see me in private? What's it about?'

'It's about Sandy, Charlotte. Sandy Clarke.'

The dark eyes widened as she stared fixedly at Kathy, then blinked as her grandmother's voice called from inside the house, 'Who is it, Charlotte?'

The young woman frowned at Kathy, indicating for her to go inside. Madelaine Verge was seated in her wheelchair at the kitchen table, a knife in her hand, skinning tomatoes.

'Ah, Sergeant, what a nice surprise.' She wiped her hands on a towel and propelled herself across the room.

'That smells good.'

'We're making romesco sauce for our dinner tonight. It's a Catalan speciality. My mother-in-law taught me when I lived in Spain with Charles's father.'

'I'll have to get the recipe.' Kathy thought guiltily about the pizzas they'd been living off recently. Maybe that was why Leon was so down, still in withdrawal from his mother's cooking.

'Of course. And what brings you here? Is there news?'

'I'm afraid not, Mrs Verge. I just have to ask Charlotte a few questions.'

'Charlotte? Well, if you must.' Madelaine Verge looked displeased, but began to move forward as if to lead them into the sitting room.

'She wants to see me alone, Gran,' Charlotte said. 'It's because she didn't interview me properly the last time. It's not important.'

Kathy was surprised by the effortless way Charlotte told her lie. She raised the transcript of Clarke's interview that she was carrying as if it were some official document that spoke for itself. 'Just some paperwork to tidy up, Mrs Verge.'

Madelaine seemed reluctant to accept this, but Charlotte went on, 'We'll go outside. I could do with some fresh air.'

She led the way to the sitting room, and through the French window onto a brick-paved terrace overlooking the back garden. 'What about Sandy?' she asked quietly.

'He's told us that he's the father of your child.'

'What?' Her voice rose in a suppressed yelp. 'Why would he do that?'

'He misunderstood something we said to him. He thought we already knew. He assumed you'd told us.'

Charlotte looked horrified. 'No! You tricked him, didn't you? You told him lies about me.'

'It wasn't like that. It was an innocent mistake. We told him you hadn't said anything to us. But it is true, isn't it? He is the father?'

Charlotte looked away, towards the vegetable patch in front of which the handyman, George, was on his hands and knees, painstakingly positioning bricks on a bed of sand to form a new path. After a moment she turned back to Kathy. Her lips were pouted like those of a stubborn child.

'No one must know, you understand?' she said fiercely. 'Sandy was a fool to tell you. I don't know what got into his stupid head.' She was trembling and clutching her hands across her front as if to hold herself physically together. Then suddenly she froze, her eyes looking past Kathy to something behind her and low down. Kathy turned and made out Madelaine Verge's foot just visible through the bottom pane of the French window.

'Come on,' Charlotte muttered, and took off diagonally across the lawn, Kathy hurrying after. When they reached the line of apple trees Charlotte stopped and turned to look back. The gardener got stiffly to his feet and gave her a little wave, then wiped his brow with his handkerchief.

'He's making a path to the end of the vegetable patch, where he's going to build a sandpit for my kid. He's got it all worked out. Sometimes I wish he'd just bloody well piss off and leave us alone. He's so bossy in his quiet way.'

Him and Gran both, Kathy thought. Between the two of them Charlotte was pretty well chaperoned.

'Can't you tell him to go away?'

'It's not as simple as that. He feels he owes it to Dad to do what he can for me. He was in prison …'

'Yes, your grandmother told me the story. Are you his only client?'

'He does Gran's and Luz's gardens, too. I don't know about anybody else. I should be grateful. I'm hopeless at practical stuff like that, and when the baby comes …' She took a deep breath. 'In a funny sort of way it's a relief to be able to talk about the baby with somebody who knows the truth. But please, for Christ's sake, you mustn't let it get out. If Gran heard she'd die. And if it got back to my dad … wherever he is.'

An interesting thought, Kathy reflected. Would he come back to punish his partner?

'How did it happen?'

'None of your business, is it?' the young woman said bitterly.

'No. It was only if you wanted to talk …'

They walked a few paces along the row of gnarled old pippins, then Charlotte stopped again. 'What did he tell you?'

'He said you were in Atlanta together and your dad had to fly home suddenly. He said the two of you decided to drive to Charleston, and stayed there overnight in a motel …'

'A crummy little place, but he thought it had a tacky charm. I wondered if he just wanted to make sure we wouldn't bump into anyone he knew.'

'Did he rape you, Charlotte?

Colour rose up her pale throat. She clenched her jaw. 'It was't like that. I suppose I encouraged him.'

Why? Kathy wondered. It was hard to believe that Charlotte would find 'Uncle Sandy', the long-time family friend, physically attractive, though you could never tell. Was she punishing her father perhaps, for marrying a woman not much older than herself?

'After I split with my last boyfriend I decided I wanted a baby, but not a man to go with it. I thought he would do as well as anyone. Only, when it came to the point ...'

'But he insisted.'

'Something like that. It was gross, if you want to know. The first time he was so excited he came all over the front of me, before we'd managed to get undressed. After that I was so shocked I didn't argue. But it worked, didn't it?' She ran a hand across her belly. 'I got my baby.'

'And you told no one else but him?'

'No one.'

'Is it possible that he might have told someone?'

'It's not likely. When I told him he nearly had a fit. He was petrified that Denise, his wife, might get wind of it. He was so grateful when I said I didn't want anything from him that he actually wept.' She curled her lip with contempt.

'Why did you bother to tell him?'

'Just in case anything happened to me, and the baby needed someone to look out for it.'

'But surely your father ... I mean this was *before* your father disappeared, wasn't it?'

Charlotte shrugged. 'Yes.'

'Just for the record, Charlotte, could you give me the dates this happened?' Kathy turned the pages of Clarke's statement to check what he had said.

'Is that what he said to you? Can I have a look?'

'Sorry, no.'

'It's not right, having my private life being photocopied and passed around and I'm not allowed to read it. Anyway, I don't see why he'd lie. We went to Charleston on the sixteenth of February. That's when the baby was conceived, but I told the doctor it was the end of January, when I was still going out with my old boyfriend. That's where the birth date of the twentieth of October comes from, but the baby'll arrive a few weeks late, I dare say. Why, does it matter?' She suddenly glowered at Kathy. 'You think Dad will try to make contact when the baby arrives, don't you? That's what you're really interested in. You made that perfectly plain the last time.'

'I'm sorry, I know you're in an impossible position in all this. But if he does make contact ...'

'I won't tell you!'

Kathy nodded. 'I understand.'

As they walked slowly back towards the house Kathy said, 'Sandy mentioned that, on the night before Miki was murdered, he felt that she and your dad were going through some kind of crisis. Were you aware of anything like that?'

She said nothing at first, then spoke softly, as if the handyman or her grandmother might overhear. 'Yes. I don't mean to say he'd kill her, but I thought things were coming to a head between them. It had got so she didn't even pretend to be civil to me, and I could see how it hurt him. But if it had come to anything physical, she'd have been the first to go for a knife.'

She nodded absently at George, who was getting to his feet. His face was gleaming with sweat and bright red except for the burns on the left side, marbled pale.

'Getting warm now,' he grunted.

'Don't overdo it, George. Stop and have a cool drink. There's some beer in the fridge.'

'Reckon I will have a bottle, once I've finished this bit here.' He nodded to Kathy and returned to his labours.

They found Madelaine Verge busy in the kitchen.

'Ah,' she smiled at them. 'This is for you, Sergeant.' She handed Kathy a written recipe together with a plastic container of red sauce. 'We've got plenty, so here's some for you to try. You can add some wine if you like, and simmer it for a while to reduce it a bit more. Get some nice seafood to cook with it.'

'That's really very kind of you, Mrs Verge. I must find a supermarket, I'm out of just about everything.'

'Try the new superstore this side of Amersham. It's on your way back. Their seafood is excellent.' She gave directions as she ushered Kathy towards the front door. 'And please do call in whenever you're in the area.' Then her voice dropped suddenly and she grabbed Kathy's wrist tight. 'You're sure there are no new developments?

Tell DCI Brock that I demand to be kept in the picture, all right?'

Kathy disengaged her wrist. 'I'll tell him.'

The old lady's wrinkled face reverted to smiles as Charlotte came into earshot. 'Bye bye. I do so hope you enjoy the romesco.'

12

There was a sting in Madelaine Verge's bounty, Kathy discovered later, though she could hardly blame her for it. She had spotted the superstore on the road back to the A41, just as she'd been directed, and had driven in to the huge car park, relatively quiet at this time on a Friday afternoon. She filled a trolley with groceries, returned to the car and swore. A side window was smashed, chunks of glass scattered over the tarmac and the seat inside. Looking in she saw that her CD player had been roughly levered out of its housing in the dashboard leaving an ugly gaping hole with wires trailing. Her sunglasses were also gone, and, looking over the back seat, so was her briefcase. They'd left her coat and an umbrella.

'Damn.'

She felt the crude intrusion like a jolt, and part of her brain observed herself in the role of victim, passing through the stages of disbelief and outrage. She looked around at the peaceful rows of late-model suburban cars, a roof rack on one, a dog in another, warming in the autumn sun, and saw no sign of violence. Then she noticed the car parked on the other side of hers, like hers an older model without an alarm, and saw that it too had been violated, its glass scattered like icy tears across the blacktop.

It's nothing, she told herself. It happens all the time, to everyone, at random. Nobody hurt, no harm done, just a bloody pest. She loaded her groceries into the boot and walked back towards the building, looking between the cars as she walked. There was no sign of her briefcase. It was scuffed and worthless, and they would chuck it once they realised it held nothing of value, no electronic organiser, no mobile phone — but probably miles away.

And it was just then that her phone, fortunately stowed in her shoulder bag, began to chirp like a hungry chick in its nest. Of all the people she least wanted to hear from at that moment, Robert the committee administrative officer was certainly one.

'I'm sorry, who?' she queried, trying to think who the hell he was.

'Serving the Crime Strategy Working Party,' he reminded her.

'Oh, oh, of course. Sorry.'

'We're wondering if you could attend a special meeting, Kathy.'

She groaned inwardly. 'Oh, I suppose so, yes. When were you thinking …?'

'Now, actually.'

'I'm in darkest Bucks at the moment, Robert,' she heard herself snap. 'And my car's just been broken into.'

'Oh dear,' he said blithely. 'Is it driveable?'

'I assume so.' The ignition switch hadn't looked as if it had been tampered with. Why would they want to steal a vehicle like that, after all? 'It's just the window that's been smashed and some stuff taken.'

'Suppose I get a secure parking spot for you in the basement here. Will that help?'

Kathy was impressed. Anyone who could command a parking place beneath headquarters building was to be respected.

'Just give my name. In an hour?'

Kathy continued into the hypermarket and found the manager's office, where she reported her break-in to a pink-faced youth. As he painstakingly recorded the details in a book, she speculated that it might be his mates who were doing the cars.

'Have there been others?' she asked.

'Erm … I don't think it's company policy to give out that kind of information.'

'I'm a police officer.' She showed her ID.

'Oh … Yeah, one or two.'

'I couldn't see any cameras out there.'

'Only at the doors of the building,' he said.

'What's your local cop shop?'

She took a note of the phone number and gave him her card.

'I have to go back to London now. Tell them to ring me if they need to talk to me.'

Within the hour Kathy was shown up to a private office, the door of which bore Robert's name. He was expansive and quietly authoritative, quite unlike the reticent figure she'd seen in the committee meetings. She took the seat he indicated and accepted a cup of coffee.

'Neither of us has time to waste, Kathy,' he said, 'so I'll come to the point. We're becoming rather concerned about the lack of progress of the CSWP. I don't need to tell you that it has been less than productive so far. Now it may be that our choice of some of the members was unwise, but we can't do anything about that now.'

Kathy was surprised by his frankness and wondered uneasily where this was leading.

'The crucial point seems to be the chairmanship. It's become clear, I think, that Desmond's position as chair has become untenable. Would you agree?'

'I thought that wasn't negotiable.'

'There may be a way around it that would satisfy everyone, at least sufficiently to allow us to move forward. I've been canvassing opinion, and I'd like to run this past you.'

'Fine.'

'We'd like you to take on the chair.'

'Me?'

'It seems there is no other solution which the whole committee would support, and from our point of view it is crucial that the chair is a member of the service.' He sat back and beamed at her. 'So there we are.'

Kathy realised that her sense of confrontation was rather greater than it had been when faced with her robbed car. 'That's very gratifying ...'

Robert nodded. 'It won't be easy, but you'll have our full support.'

Kathy wondered about his continual references to 'we' and 'our'. Did he mean himself or was there a whole hierarchy of senior management involved?

'And I do appreciate the honour, but I'm heavily involved in a very important case right now ...'

'The Verge case, yes I know, but there are many others working on that. We're sure you can be spared. Given the time that's been lost already, the CSWP is going to rely on some intensive work by its chair, especially in the next few weeks leading up to the conference.'

The conference! A mild panic attack gripped Kathy at the thought of presenting the committee's spurious findings to five hundred senior police and community figures.

'The fact is, Robert, that I just don't think I'm cut out for that kind of thing. I haven't had any real experience. I don't speak well in that sort of setting ...'

Robert chuckled and shook his head. 'We think otherwise.'

Who the hell is 'we'? Kathy thought. Does it include Brock? She recalled his throwaway remark about this being her big chance.

'We have every confidence that you can handle it splendidly. And it will be a tremendous opportunity for you to *shine*, Kathy. To be *noticed*.'

That's exactly what I'm terrified of, she thought. 'Have you spoken about this to DCI Brock?'

Robert consulted a list. 'Brock ... Brock ... no. Should I?'

'He's SIO on the Verge case. I think he may feel he needs me there.'

'Indispensable are we, Kathy?' Robert smiled indulgently.

'Well, no, but ...'

'DCI Brock will fall in with our requirements, I have no doubt. This is a crucial matter, Kathy. I don't think I need to emphasise that, do I?'

'No, of course not. Can I have the weekend to think about it?'

Robert looked disappointed, as if she'd failed a test. 'What's there to think about, Kathy? Will it help to clarify your thoughts if I tell you that the Deputy Assistant Commissioner has agreed to the change, and wants a quick resolution?'

Oh thanks, Kathy thought. In other words, it's an order.

She hurried out of New Scotland Yard, leaving her car in the basement. They can keep it for another hour or two, she thought, looking at the cars exiting from the ramp, senior staff going home for the weekend. Her little wounded Renault had looked particularly pathetic down there among the BMWs.

Brock's secretary, Dot, nodded her through as soon as she appeared. 'He was trying to reach you, Kathy.'

'I was in a meeting. I turned my phone off. Was it about the committee I'm on?'

'No idea. Go on through.'

He was hunched forward in front of a video machine, Bren Gurney at his side. He looked up as she came in and jabbed the remote at the screen. 'Kathy! Just the person. Come in and look at this.'

'Dot says you were trying to reach me.'

'Mm. How did you get on with Charlotte?'

'Okay. I'm pretty sure she hasn't told anyone about Clarke being the father, and she was convinced he wouldn't have either. He's terrified his wife will find out.'

'Yes, well, things have moved forward. An hour after he left us he came back with a lawyer in tow, wanting to make a new statement. Grab a seat and watch.'

As they waited for the tape to rewind, Kathy added, 'It's possible that Clarke raped Charlotte. She was equivocal, but I think that's what it amounts to.'

Bren said, 'Maybe he forced himself on Miki, too.'

'That's what I wondered,' Kathy said. 'His description of how they came to be lovers sounded odd, sort of mechanical.'

'Yeah,' Bren agreed. 'Also, you've got to wonder about the relationship between Clarke and Verge. Why was Clarke deflowering his partner's nearest and dearest? Weren't there any other willing women around the place? Was his real motive to punish Verge?'

'Interesting,' Brock murmured. 'Here we go. Watch this.'

The screen cleared to show four men sitting around the table: Brock and the Fraud Squad officer, Tony, and Sandy Clarke and his solicitor. After Brock's caution and introductions, it was the solicitor who spoke. He was aiming to sound confident, Kathy thought, but somehow it wasn't coming off, as if he were still wrestling in his mind with the implications of what his client had told him. He understood that a reward had been offered for information on the whereabouts of Charles Verge, and he wished to put a proposition to the police on behalf of his client. First, he wanted to remind the police that his client had an unblemished record, and that the catastrophic events of May had caused great damage to him personally and to his employees. In light of this, he was willing to offer certain information to the police which might assist them with their inquiries, and he was willing to waive any claim to reward moneys to which the information might give rise, on condition that he be offered immunity from prosecution for failing to bring this information forward earlier.

'What a load of crap,' Bren breathed.

On screen Brock evidently agreed with this view, though he framed his refusal slightly more politely.

The solicitor began to say that he would have to consult with his client, but Clarke cut across him. 'It's all right. I'll say my piece.' He turned to Brock. 'You asked me if the name Martin Kraus meant anything to me. It does, or at least M. Kraus does.'

Perhaps it was the lighting in the interview room or the quality of the tape, but to Kathy it seemed as if Clarke's whole face had stretched tighter across his bone structure in the few hours since she'd last watched him from the observation room. His voice, too, seemed harsher and more strained in pitch.

'On the morning of Saturday the twelfth of May, a couple of hours after we'd got back from the airport, I had a phone call in my office from Charles.'

'That's Charles Verge, your business partner?' Brock asked, for the record.

'Yes. He sounded rather breathless, as if he was in a rush. He said that something had come up and he had to go out on an urgent matter. He didn't explain what it was or where he was going, but he said he had a favour to ask me. He needed some funds transferred right away to the account of an acquaintance, and he didn't have time to see to it himself. It was a family matter, personal, and he didn't want it to go through the firm's accounts. He wondered if I could see to it for him from my own funds, and he would square it with me when he saw me for the Wuxang City presentation on the following Monday. He was apologetic because the amount was quite large for such short notice, thirty thousand sterling. I assured him it wasn't a problem. He said it was a sensitive matter and he'd be grateful if I would keep it completely to myself. He had left the details of the account to be credited in a note on the desk in his office.'

'Did you understand him to be phoning you from his apartment in the Verge Practice building?'

'I got the impression he'd already left there, on his way elsewhere, and that was why he couldn't give me the details over the phone.'

'All right, go on.'

'I went into his office and found the note with the details of the account he wanted credited. During the course of the day I made arrangements over the phone to transfer thirty thousand pounds from my personal cash management account to that account. I remember that it was at a Barclays branch, in Barcelona. I don't have a note of the account number any more, but my bank must have a record. I had forgotten the name of the recipient until you mentioned it this afternoon. It was M. Kraus.'

On screen Brock was leaning forward to say something to Tony, who was shaking his head.

Brock said, 'Yes, well, we'll get you to obtain those details from your bank for us, Mr Clarke. Go on.'

'That's basically it. At the time I didn't attach any particular significance to it. I expected to see Charles on the Monday. When he didn't come to the presentation and then we found Miki's body, the shock drove the business out of my mind for a while. It was only later that day, when I was actually being interviewed by the police, that I remembered it. I was talking about something else, and it suddenly hit me in mid-sentence that perhaps the thirty thousand Charles had asked for was for himself, to help him disappear. I had to decide right there, in the middle of talking about something else, whether to mention this. I remembered how insistent he had been that I tell no one about it, and I decided to err on the side of loyalty to my friend and say nothing until I had had a chance to think it through. Once I'd made that decision, of course, it became impossible to go back on it without making myself appear to be involved. I'm sorry. I suppose I assumed you'd find out where he was without my help anyway. I realise now I should have said something.'

Very glib, Kathy thought.

'You're suggesting that Martin Kraus is an alias for Charles Verge?' Brock asked on screen.

'I've no idea. Maybe it's the name of an intermediary, someone who can pass the money on to him.'

'And what about the payments to Martin Kraus's company, Turnstile Quality Systems, that we asked you about earlier?'

'I know nothing about those. That's the truth. I acknowledge that it looks like my signature on the cheques, but I have no recollection of writing them, and I can't believe I could have done so on such a frequent basis and for such amounts without remembering. The whole process was irregular. Why were the invoices not processed in the normal way through the office?'

'Indeed. They were addressed directly to you.'

'But I never saw them!'

'You're suggesting fraud?'

'Well, what else can I suggest?'

'By your partner, Charles Verge?'

Clarke pursed his lips in frustration and fell silent. At last he said, voice weary, 'It doesn't make sense. If Charles wanted to draw large sums from the firm he only had to discuss it with his partners, Miki and me. We could have come to some arrangement, restructured the capital so he could liquidate some of his share against future earnings. But he never said a word, not to me anyway.'

'But the fact remains that, according to you, Charles knew Martin Kraus, the nominal beneficiary of these payments.'

'Yes. But it just doesn't make sense,' he repeated. 'I mean, it was bound to come out, wasn't it? I'm surprised the accountants haven't picked this up before now.'

'They say,' Tony broke in, 'that's because it was done by someone at a high level in the firm. Someone who could bypass the normal processes.'

'Well, it wasn't me.'

'Have you anything else you want to tell us, Mr Clarke?' Brock asked.

'There is something else, yes. When I decided to keep quiet about the thirty thousand, it also led me to, well, sanitise my account of Charles's recent behaviour, out of the same sense of loyalty.

The fact is that I was becoming increasingly concerned about his mental and physical state.'

'In what way?'

'It's hard to specify a precise event, more a gradual change. Something was going badly wrong with his marriage. I can't say exactly what, and I've learned over the years that it's unwise to interfere, but there was a certain tension that developed, and quite heated arguments about design directions, almost violent and sometimes embarrassingly public. Miki increasingly adopted the pose of an injured prima donna, while Charles sank into a kind of angry despair.

'I tried several times to suggest that he see his doctor for help, but he shrugged me off. He threw himself into the Marchdale Prison project as if it were a life raft, but he was so manic about it that that alarmed me too. He became more and more moody and erratic. It got to the point where I was nervous about him dealing with our clients on his own.'

Clarke reached for a jug on the table and poured himself some water. It was hard to see on the video, but there was the sound of a slight rattle of glass against glass as if his hand were unsteady. He drank deeply, then blew out his cheeks. It was a gesture of relief, Kathy guessed, as if he'd reached that stage in an interview where the subject has got the main business off his chest. Now he gets chatty, she thought, happy to offer cooperation just to get out the door.

'You said you were concerned about his physical state, too?'

'Well, he changed, looked different. Sort of puffy around the face, and grey from lack of sleep. He began to dress carelessly, as if he wasn't bothered any more how he looked. Most unlike him. Towards the end he seemed to find no pleasure in anything. Well, except Charlotte's …' His voice tailed off into a bout of coughing, and his face became red.

'Charlotte's child, yes,' Brock said drily.

'No, I mean, as if he really didn't belong any more, not following the details at meetings, forgetting appointments, driving his secretary mad.'

'Any signs of violent behaviour?'

'Anger, yes. Especially towards Miki.'

'Did she ever talk to you about their deteriorating relationship?'

'Not directly. Sometimes, when they were having a quarrel over some point of design, she would try to draw me in on her side, talking as if it was common knowledge between us that Charles's judgement was becoming unreliable. I found it acutely uncomfortable.'

'But she didn't mention threats or violence towards her?'

'No.'

'And on the evening of the eleventh of May, Miki didn't say anything specific about his return?'

'I told you, I had a feeling that there was something she wanted to tell me, but she never got it out. Just that reference to having married the wrong partner, as if she'd discovered that Charles was flawed in some way.'

Brock leaned forward with the remote and stopped the tape. 'There's a bit more but nothing new. What do you think?'

'I think Clarke is good at presenting facts to his advantage. He realised he had no choice but to tell you more about Martin Kraus, and to shift the blame onto Verge, who can't speak for himself.'

'We're checking what we can at the moment, phone and bank records, passport and immigration, but it's the first solid lead we've had. Depending on what Barclays can tell us, I'm thinking that I may send Tony over to follow the money trail at that end, with Linda Moffat as interpreter of course.'

'Lucky them,' Kathy said automatically.

'And I'm thinking that if we really can establish a link to Barcelona, then the McNeils' supposed sighting becomes particularly important. If they did see Verge, on the run, what was he doing there, who was he meeting? If it wasn't the travel agent, who was it?'

'Yes,' Kathy said doubtfully. 'I wish I could be more confident about them.'

'You think they're mistaken?'

'I think, between them, they may be confused about exactly where they saw him, even which side of the street. And if there's doubt about *where* they saw him, there's got to be doubt about *who* they saw.'

'Then we've got to eliminate that doubt, one way or the other. Which means taking them over there and walking them up and down that street until they stop being confused. And for that they'll need a chaperone, a detective to jog their memories and follow up anything that looks promising.' He looked at her, raising an eyebrow.

'Me? Oh … well, that would be great, but …' She thought bitterly of her meeting with Robert, and explained to Brock, 'I've just agreed to take on the chair of that bloody committee I'm on. I've been told it will require a full-time commitment for two or three weeks.'

'What?' Brock looked annoyed. 'Why the hell did you do that? You didn't talk to me about it.'

She didn't remind him that he'd suggested it to her earlier. 'I didn't have much choice. It was put to me that I had to agree on the spot. I said they should discuss it with you, but he said it wasn't necessary and that it had already been approved at DAC level.'

Brock's face darkened. 'Who said this?'

'The admin guy who services the committee. Robert.'

'Damn cheek!' He gave a low growl, like an old bear contemplating an unruly pup. 'Have you got this character's number?'

Kathy handed it to him.

'You might step out of the room, would you, Kathy? You too, Bren.'

'I've got things to do,' Bren said, getting to his feet.

Kathy closed the door carefully behind her and went out to chat with Dot. After a couple of minutes they stopped in mid-sentence at the sound of Brock's bellowed voice, muffled through the heavy door. Dot smiled. 'That's good. I haven't heard him do that for a while. He'll feel much better afterwards. I've been a bit worried lately that his friend might be mellowing him. What do you think?'

His friend. Kathy knew Dot was referring to Suzanne and assumed that she was about to be pumped. 'I haven't noticed it,' she said tactfully.

'You don't think she's trying to get him to leave the force?'

Kathy was saved from answering by Brock's face at the door. 'All sorted. You've got leave of absence from the committee until next Thursday, when you take up your position there full time. Okay? You'd better get on to the McNeils and persuade them to leave with you tomorrow.'

In the event the McNeils, who jumped at the chance of an expenses-paid trip to Barcelona, couldn't leave until the day after,

Sunday. While Dot started booking flights and hotel rooms, Kathy spoke again with Brock.

'Just make sure they understand about the subsistence rate,' Brock said. 'We're not paying for their bloody bar bills.' Then he added, 'Maybe you should get Leon to go with you.' He said it diffidently, and Kathy wasn't sure if it was a serious suggestion or just a probe.

'He's up to his ears in an assignment for his uni course. I doubt if he could afford the time.'

'Ah yes.'

'To be honest, it'll probably be a relief for both of us for me to get out of the way for a few days. The flat's a bit crowded since he moved his computer and books in.' The words came out without thought, and it was only when they were spoken that Kathy wondered with a small shock whether she really would be relieved to leave him.

'It's not a big flat, is it? Must be a bit tight for two.'

'Yes. We're thinking about finding somewhere bigger,' Kathy said, puzzling over Brock's tone, as if he were looking at the question from a completely different point of view, one which Kathy wasn't aware of. She decided to change the subject. 'On my way back from seeing Charlotte this afternoon, I stopped at a supermarket and had my car broken into. They took my briefcase, among other things, with the transcript of Clarke's interview.'

'Would anyone be able to identify him?'

'I don't think so. I didn't have the cover sheet, with the names.'

'Better send a report to the local boys, make sure they take it seriously. Was there much damage?'

'The side window was smashed. I'll get it fixed while I'm away.'

Brock nodded. 'Keep your eyes open over there. You never know, someone may have missed something. That's really why I want you to go. You speak some Spanish, don't you?'

'Very little. I started learning it last year.'

'I wish I was going too.' Brock looked regretfully around his office, at the files piled on his desk and the table by the window and spilling over the floor. 'Maybe if you find something you'll have to call me over.'

'I'll do my best.' Kathy grinned and headed for the door.

13

Kathy accepted the small plastic container of orange juice and stretched her legs as far as she could under the seat in front. The other two seats in the row beside her were occupied by the McNeils, who were discussing something offered in the in-flight magazine. DI Tony Heron and DS Linda Moffat were several rows ahead, having checked in together before Kathy and the McNeils had arrived at the airport. In fact it now seemed to Kathy, although she hadn't noticed anything previously, that Tony and Linda might have something going between them, or else were taking advantage of the trip to get something started. She had seemed positively flirtatious towards her Fraud Squad colleague when they had all eventually met up, while he had miraculously shed his funereal aspect and was transformed in a lightweight bomber jacket and navy T-shirt, and even, Kathy suspected, a touch of gel in his hair. Linda, too, was dressed for leisure rather than work, with white cotton slacks, a bright orange top, espadrilles and a pair of dark glasses propped optimistically on top of her head. The McNeils had also come in their Mediterranean holiday gear and Kathy, who had packed on the basis that this was a serious business trip, felt, in her black suit, as if she'd turned up at the wrong party.

But that didn't matter. She tilted the seat back, tuned the headphones to a jazz channel and closed her eyes. This was an unlooked-for break, a welcome change from the routine and familiar. Leon could take over the whole flat while he finished his assignment, and she wouldn't have to feel guilty about making a noise or spilling things on his precious papers, as she had with Madelaine Verge's romesco sauce on the Friday night when she'd told him about the trip. The coincidence of the Spanish food and the visit to Barcelona had made Kathy feel awkward, as if he might think she had been secretly planning to go away without him, but he had been pleased for her, and, as expected, turned down her suggestion that he come along.

'Next time,' he had said, and set about wiping the sauce from his textbook with paper towels. He had a sad air about him, which Kathy put down to a touch of the martyrs.

A steward offered drinks. Audrey McNeil and Kathy both asked for glasses of wine, Peter McNeil a scotch. Down the aisle Kathy saw Tony and Linda being handed glasses of champagne, and she smiled.

Peter had his Barcelona guidebook open and he and his wife began to give Kathy a briefing on the city. The hotel where they would be staying, on Linda's recommendation, was very conveniently located, they explained. Just off the Plaça de Catalunya, it was not far from the Passeig de Gràcia, where they thought they had seen Charles Verge, and only a short taxi, bus or metro ride to the Palau de Justicia, if that was where Kathy was heading. And from the point of view of sightseeing, it was also very handy to La Rambla and the Gothic Quarter. Peter explained all this with the complacent superiority of the seasoned traveller, interrupted from time to time by his wife's chirpy elaborations, delivered very fast before Peter could cut her off.

The original plan had been for the McNeils to stay just one night, flying home again on the Monday evening after spending the morning with Kathy on the Passeig de Gràcia, but they had arranged to extend their stay by another day — principally, it transpired, to allow Audrey to meet her internet bridge partner on the Tuesday morning. 'We've arranged to meet at a café opposite the cathedral. I have to brandish my copy of *Fifty Favourite Bridge Problems.*' She reached into her handbag to show Kathy the book. 'I'm really looking forward to it. It's so strange to meet her in the flesh after getting to know her so well as my partner in cyberspace.' She said the last word with relish, perhaps to make some point with her husband, who snorted indulgently and took a pull at his whisky. 'Fine building, the cathedral,' he said.

'Yes, Audrey showed me your photos,' Kathy replied.

'Oh no, that was Gaudí's church, the Sagrada Família,' Audrey corrected her with a smile and an unspoken undertone, *do get it right, dear,* so that Kathy felt obliged to repeat it.

'The Sagrada Família, right.'

'The cathedral is in the Gothic Quarter,' Peter said, 'not far from our hotel.' He pointed it out on the street map. 'It was started in 1298, but wasn't finished until 1913, to the plans of the original French architect. That's a construction period of six hundred and fifteen years. And our clients tell us we're too slow!' He had a good chuckle at this.

'Peter wanted to be an architect originally, didn't you, dear?'

Her husband's nose screwed up, in disapproval, Kathy thought, as if Audrey had betrayed some shameful weakness on his part. 'I suggested the idea to my father, who told me not to be daft. "Architects are all poofters in yellow ties," he said. Well, maybe they did wear yellow ties in those days, I don't know, but anyway, I took his advice and became an engineer, like him.'

'I always wondered about your father's sexuality,' Audrey said thoughtfully.

For a moment Kathy thought there might be a small domestic, but the prospect of the trip seemed to have mellowed Peter, who let the comment pass.

The plane descended over a brown landscape, and Kathy had the first inkling that they were coming to a place that had had a very different summer from their own, long and hot and dry.

Linda had said that 'Jeez', as she called Lieutenant Jesús Mozas, would most probably meet them in the arrivals hall, but when they reached it there was no sign of him, and after hanging around for ten minutes they decided to take two taxis into the city. When they stepped out of the building they were momentarily stunned by dazzling sunlight and heat, and as they drove down the motorway towards the city, Kathy had a sense of disconnection from the autumnal reality they had left behind.

She was impressed with Linda's choice of hotel when they arrived. An elaborately uniformed man hurried across the footpath to collect their bags, and the reception area was cool and impressively furnished with what looked like antique pieces. When the second taxi arrived, Linda was handed a note — from Jeez, she announced — apologising for not meeting them and saying that he and Captain Alvarez would come to the hotel for them at nine the next morning.

'That's too bad,' Linda smirked in Tony's direction. 'And you were hoping we could get down to work right away.' From the way Tony grinned back, this was clearly a private joke.

Kathy's room had a little balcony overlooking the street, one end of which ran into the wide Plaça de Catalunya, in which she could make out numbers of pedestrians promenading now that the afternoon heat was dissipating. After a shower, she went down to meet the others in the foyer. They walked out to the Plaça and from there into La Rambla, the tree-lined pedestrian avenue leading down to the port. The place was thronged with evening strollers now, sedately eyeing each other and the various attractions along the way. Mime artists lined one side of the route like statues, motionless until a coin was thrown into their pot, when they would jerk into life, bowing or gesticulating in character to their patron. There was Julius Caesar in full uniform, sprayed from head to toe in silver paint, and further along a terracotta-coloured Sitting Bull, and General MacArthur, complete with corncob pipe, in khaki.

Linda and Tony walked a few paces ahead of the others, at first turning back from time to time to point something out, but soon absorbed in their own conversation. They reached a stall with caged birds and she made a face of mock annoyance at some remark of his and punched him on the upper arm, then pulled him closer to her to examine the cages.

'They work together a lot, do they?' Audrey asked Kathy cautiously.

'They've been working on this case for a few months now, I suppose. Seem to get on well, don't they?'

Audrey gave a little smile. 'The spell of foreign travel. I used to discourage Peter from going away without me, though I'm sure there's no need now.'

Kathy glanced back at Peter, who had been distracted by a tarot reader sitting beneath one of the broad trees that lined the avenue, telling the fortune of an old man.

'Are you married, dear?'

'No.'

'Ah well. Plenty of time.' Kathy felt herself being scrutinised. 'Maybe you'll meet a nice Spaniard while we're here. They like blondes, I'm told.'

'Like Charles Verge's mother. She bumped into a Spaniard on the London tube and that was that. She came back to Barcelona with him and had Charles. I dare say they used to stroll along here fifty years ago.'

'Is she still alive?'

'Yes.'

'Poor woman. To think this tragedy was lying in wait for them all this time.' They walked a little way in silence, then Audrey McNeil added, 'I do hope you aren't expecting too much from us, Kathy. I mean, bringing us here will probably turn out to have been a complete waste of time.'

'Don't worry, they won't ask for the airfares back,' Kathy said, and they had a laugh, but all the same, she understood the woman's sense of being there under false pretences because she felt exactly the same. If anything came of the trip it would almost certainly be due to Linda and Tony.

They continued down the Rambla to the Columbus monument, and beyond that onto the pedestrian boardwalk and across to the new waterfront Maremàgnum, where Linda chose a small restaurant for them to eat at. She ordered plates of tapas and a couple of bottles of cava and they sat and watched the daylight dying on the water and the families taking a last turn of the quay before heading for home.

After breakfast the following morning, they gathered in the foyer to wait for the two officers of the CGP. Peter McNeil passed the time studying the city map, Audrey some postcards from the hotel desk, and Tony and Linda each other. The two Spaniards arrived promptly in separate cars. They wore plain clothes, Captain Alvarez in a sober suit, Lieutenant 'Jeez' Mozas in a leather jacket and jeans. Linda and Jeez greeted each other like old buddies, while Alvarez, whose expression was as tightly controlled as the little moustache drawn like a ruled ink line on his upper lip, stood back, shaking hands formally when introduced by Linda to the others. Kathy had the distinct impression that he was displeased by their visit, and especially by the McNeils. After the introductions he asked the couple in slow, stilted English if they would please leave the police officers to discuss matters among themselves for a few minutes. Obviously impressed by the man's gravity, they quickly got to their feet and left. The others sat in a circle in the lobby's armchairs, surrounded by the suitcases of departing guests, and spoke together quietly.

Jeez, whose English was more fluent and colloquial than his colleague's, led the discussion. 'Okay, the captain suggests that Linda and Tony and I go meet some guys in our commercial section who can help with your questions. We have an appointment at eleven with the manager of the bank. Captain Alvarez will accompany you, Kathy. You have anything special in mind?'

Kathy addressed herself to Alvarez, trying to gauge his reaction as she spoke. It wasn't easy, as he kept his face expressionless. 'I wondered if we could borrow one of your people to stand in as Charles Verge. One point seven metres, seventy kilograms, age about fifty, straight black hair, clean shaven ...'

'We know what he looks like,' Alvarez said drily.

'Of course. Wearing a black leather jacket, black trousers and shoes.'

Alvarez glanced at Jeez and gave a barely perceptible nod.

'Not a problem,' Jeez said. 'Give us an hour?'

'Ideally, I'd like to walk them down the street at around ten-thirty, at the same time on the same day of the week as when they think they saw him.'

'What are you wanting from these people, exactly?' Alvarez asked.

'There seems to be a discrepancy in their recollections of what they saw. We just want to be quite certain.'

The captain looked puzzled. Linda began to translate Kathy's words, but he cut her off. 'After such a long time? You have made a mistake?' His eyes narrowed accusingly. 'We sent photographs, plans.'

'They were very helpful. But my chief wanted them to come in person.'

Alvarez shook his head slowly, whether at the waste of his time or the incompetence of the British police Kathy wasn't sure, then he said something very fast and low to his lieutenant in what Linda later said was not Spanish but Catalan. Jeez nodded. 'Captain Alvarez will return for you and the English couple at ten-fifteen.'

'I understand the street isn't far away. We could walk up and meet him there.'

Again Alvarez said something in Catalan and Jeez translated. 'Captain Alvarez will pick you up here, at the hotel, at ten-fifteen exactly.'

'Whatever you say.'

An hour later, the captain was precisely on time. He arrived in a patrol car, followed closely by a taxi carrying a single passenger in a black leather jacket. Kathy and the McNeils bundled into the back of the patrol car that swept off into the Plaça de Catalunya, circling it to its far corner where the broad boulevard of the Passeig de Gràcia began. After six blocks it pulled over and Alvarez got out, followed by the others.

'This is the place,' he said, gesturing towards the building in front of them.

This wasn't how Kathy had wanted to play it, but she held her tongue. The McNeils looked around, trying to orientate themselves, obviously intimidated by Alvarez's manner. Kathy recognised some of the buildings from the photographs the CGP had sent them, and immediately realised that her fancy theory about sunlight and shadows was wrong. Now, in September, the sun would be at a similar angle to that morning in May, and she saw that the entrance Peter McNeil had identified was in full sun, even though it was on the east side of the street. The reason was the peculiar layout of the Eixample district, of which the Passeig de Gràcia was one of the principal streets. The quarter had been laid out as a model of town planning in the nineteenth century. The blocks were square, but with the added refinement that their corners were sliced off on the diagonal, so that where four blocks met, their corners created the effect of a small diagonal square at the crossing of the streets. The result was that, although the main east street façade of the Passeig was in shadow, the south-facing corners on both sides of the street were sunlit.

As they stood there the taxi drew into the kerb and the rear door opened. The passenger got out, pretended to pay the cab driver, and strode across the pavement in front of them towards the corner doorway, disappearing into the shadows inside.

'Okay?' Alvarez said, sounding ready to pack up and drive them to the airport.

'Well …' Peter McNeil frowned, still trying to get his bearings. 'Let me see. Yes, I suppose this must be the place …'

'Well, it doesn't feel right to me,' his wife said.

'What's wrong, Audrey?' Kathy prompted.

'I don't know … Are you sure the sun's in the same place? Only it's practically shining into our eyes, so you could hardly make out that man's face.'

Captain Alvarez's mouth tightened. This obviously wasn't what he wanted to hear, and Peter wasn't best pleased either. 'Oh yes you could, Audrey. At least, I could.'

'My eyesight's every bit as good as yours, Peter. And anyway, he went up some steps at the entrance to the building. I remember that now.'

'You didn't mention that before,' Kathy said.

'No, it's just come back to me. The building looked like this one, the same warm stone colour, but there were a few steps.'

'You're quite sure? Peter?'

He shrugged, dubious. 'I was only thinking about recognising his face. I didn't pay much attention to the building.'

Kathy turned to the Spaniard. 'Captain, they're agreed that they saw the person somewhere between the Casa Milà and the metro station. Could I suggest that we walk the whole of that route, just as they did?'

Alvarez frowned and asked her to say it again. She did, more slowly, and he shook his head. 'Is this necessary? It is long ago. They don't remember.'

He relented, however, and called his man back from the building entrance and gave him new instructions. They turned and walked the three blocks north until they were standing in front of the undulating façade of Gaudì's apartment building.

'Right,' Kathy said, 'I recognise this from your photograph. So from here you said you crossed the street to try to get a better picture.'

They crossed over, and the taxi, which had kerb-crawled behind them, did a U-turn and followed. They walked a block south, and then Kathy pointed to a corner entrance, with three steps leading into the shadowed interior.

'Yes, that's the sort of thing,' Audrey said.

'But it's on the wrong side,' Peter objected. 'It's to our right. He crossed from right to left. I'm quite sure of that.'

'I'm not,' his wife said stubbornly. They stood in irritated silence, glaring at each other, while the stream of well-dressed shoppers with expensive-looking carrier bags parted around them. Kathy sensed Alvarez reaching the end of his patience.

'Well, let's try something,' she said, sounding just a little desperate, she thought. She waved the taxi forward and pointed to the kerb just in front of them. It moved to the spot and the passenger got out and began his mime once more.

'Okay, we're moving forward, and you notice him, Peter. You're looking at something else, Audrey.'

'Yes, I can remember being attracted by the bright summer fashions in that window over there, but they're muted now, for autumn.'

'As he pays the taxi we walk on, past him, and he begins to cross the footpath behind us. You look back over your shoulder, Peter, because you think you've recognised him, then you tell Audrey who you think it is. Audrey turns and sees him disappear up the steps into the building. You're both right, you see — at first he was moving across from left to right, then when you were looking back he was going from right to left.'

'Ingenious,' Peter conceded, 'but I don't know ...'

'You could be right, Kathy.'

'And when you turned to look at him, the sun was behind you.'

'I don't believe we could have got it so completely wrong,' Peter protested.

Alvarez evidently agreed. He was shaking his head in disbelief. Kathy hurriedly said, 'Okay, let's keep going.'

She took a note of the address of the corner entrance, Passeig de Gràcia 83, and they continued along the route the McNeils had taken, crossing back to the east side of the Passeig, past the place where they had begun, and on to the entrance to the metro. Along the way they examined five more corner entrances as possibilities, but none had steps.

'So it really comes down to how positive you are about those steps, Audrey,' Kathy said.

'Oh Lord,' she sighed and closed her eyes, trying to focus on the mental image. 'I was quite certain when it first struck me, but the more I try to visualise it, the harder it gets.'

Captain Alvarez was examining his wristwatch pointedly and Kathy said, 'I think that's as much as we can do. Thank you for your help, Captain.'

'That's it?'

'Yes. Oh, there is one thing. Do you think you could get me a list of the businesses who use that entrance over there.' She pointed back across the street to the entrance with the steps, and checked the address from her notebook, 'Passeig de Gràcia 83'.

He seemed about to object, but then thought better of it and called to his officer in the taxi and gave him instructions. 'Now I take you to your friends.'

Kathy thanked him but said that she wanted to spend more time with the McNeils, who were looking bewildered. Alvarez gave her a card and pointed to the address, then turned and marched off to his car further up the street.

'He wasn't very friendly,' Audrey said. 'Did we upset him?'

'Don't worry about him. Let's have a cup of coffee.' She led them to a café, where they gradually relaxed. 'It felt like we were sitting an exam,' Peter said, 'and getting the questions wrong.'

When they'd finished their coffees, Kathy took them back up the Passeig to the Casa Milà, and walked them over the route again. Although they were now at ease and chatting freely, nothing new emerged. As they passed number eighty-three, the policeman in the black leather jacket emerged from the doorway into the sunlight, stuffing his notebook into his pocket, and headed away. Out of curiosity, Kathy went over to the entrance and mounted the steps. Inside, a directory board listed the occupants, but Kathy wasn't able to make out what businesses they carried on, and after a moment she gave up and they continued on their way back to the metro station. There she thanked the McNeils and told them their time was now their own. They were apologetic about not having been more help, and waved goodbye as Kathy hailed a cab.

• • •

As Kathy had expected, Linda and Tony's time had been much more productive. The bank had been able to provide several useful pieces of information, beginning with an address for their client, Martin Kraus, in an apartment block in the northern part of the city. They had gone with a carload of local cops to the address only to discover that the flat number didn't exist.

'Yet the bank forwarded monthly statements to that address over a six-month period,' Tony explained to Kathy. He was animated and so taken up with the chase that, Kathy noticed, he was able to keep his eyes off Linda for whole minutes at a time. 'I reckon he's done the same thing as he did with Turnstile Quality Systems in Neasden. There he got the Post Office to divert TQS mail to a business-accommodation bureau, where they held it for collection. They deal with hundreds of mail-drop customers, most of them dodgy, and couldn't give a description of whoever picked up the mail. Jeez's lads are checking that line now.'

'Did the bank manager ever meet Kraus?'

'He doesn't believe so, and there was no note of a meeting in the file. The account was opened by an assistant manager who's since moved to Madrid. They're trying to track him down, and a copper is talking to the rest of the staff at the moment, with a picture of Verge. The other thing that's really interesting is the history of the account. It was opened in October of last year. I've spoken to London, to get them to check if Verge was over here then.'

He passed Kathy a photocopy of the form that Kraus had completed to open his account, and pointed to a line under the address he had given. 'See that? He gave his nationality as Spanish, and provided identification documents of some kind. Jeez is checking on that as well.'

Tony turned to Linda. 'You got those other sheets, Lind?'

Lind? Kathy suppressed a grimace.

Linda shot him a smile, 'Yeah, here you go.'

Tony passed one of them to Kathy. 'This is a summary of the account history. It was opened on the fourth of October last year with a deposit of two hundred and fifty thousand pesetas, which is about a thousand sterling. There were no deposits or withdrawals until the twelfth of May this year, when forty-eight thousand euros were deposited — that's Clarke's thirty thousand quid sent over from England. Then on the fifteenth of May the account was closed, the whole balance transferred to an account in another bank.'

'Do we know where?'

'Yes.' Tony sounded sad. 'It's the same one that TQS transferred the payments they received from the Verge Practice to. It's offshore, and so far we haven't been able to track that money any further.'

Linda patted the back of his hand. 'Never mind, Tony.' She grinned at Kathy. 'He's really pissed off about that account, aren't you?'

'Yeah.'

'So what do we do now?' Kathy asked.

'Wait for Jeez and his lads to come up with something,' Linda said. 'I think we should get lunch.'

But by the end of the afternoon, after some long and un-productive hours spent waiting around in the CGP offices, they were no wiser. Only London had come up with anything definite, confirming that both Charles Verge and Sandy Clarke had been in Barcelona on the fourth of October the previous year, for a meeting with city officials to discuss the possibility of a new project there.

While they waited, Kathy thought she might at least check what the CGP had found out about Luz Diaz, and asked to see her file. It arrived just as they were leaving for the evening, and Kathy was allowed to take it with her.

14

That evening Kathy ate alone. There had been no sign of the McNeils at the hotel, and when Linda and Tony had half-heartedly suggested that she join them for the evening she had tactfully declined, saying that she wanted to look for a pair of shoes, then have an early night. Linda had suggested some places nearby and Kathy had left them to it. She did in fact buy a pair of sandals in a street off the Plaça de Catalunya, and had then strolled for a while through the narrow winding streets of the Gothic Quarter before emerging onto the Rambla. It was still early by Spanish standards, and she was able to get a table on a first-floor balcony overlooking the street. She sat, sipping a glass of chilled white *ranci* wine and watching the passing stream of people in the street below.

For a moment she thought she spotted Audrey McNeil's auburn hair among the crowd, but before she could be sure the figure was hidden behind a bookstall. Sitting there on her own, she realised that she enjoyed being the one uncoupled person in their party, and that she didn't envy the others their companionable state. She had a man of her own to go home to, of course, and she was lucky that, even after living in a confined space with him for six months, he could still make her knees go weak with a look or a touch. She thought of Tony and Linda, whose knees looked to be in a permanent state of weakness, and, at the other end of the relationship scale, of Audrey and Peter, who knew each other so well by now that they could anticipate their partner's every thought and word before it was formed. She dreaded getting to that stage with Leon, and wondered if that was a bad sign.

For her, orphaned in her teens, the idea of Leon still living with his parents at thirty-two had seemed weird, and it had seemed a big enough step to get him to move in with her. But what happened next? Somewhere she had read that, for unmarried couples living together, making a commitment before X months was too soon, and after Y months was too late, but she couldn't remember the numbers. Was six months too short or too long? Neither of them had raised the subject of marriage, let alone children. For a moment she imagined returning to London and finding that Leon, feeling lost in her absence, now wanted to commit, and she realised with a little twinge of guilt that the idea made her feel uncomfortable. Why was that? Was it just the congestion at home, easily fixed up by getting somewhere bigger? Or was it something else? Fear, perhaps, of suffocation or of being betrayed.

The waiter appeared with her starter, *amanida catalana*, the local antipasto. Oh well, she thought, how many people got it right anyway? What the hell were Brock and Suzanne doing, living at opposite ends of the county? She smiled to herself and lifted her glass in a silent toast to the old man. Maybe this was why they got on so well, sharing the same maladjustments.

Five hundred miles to the north, Sandy Clarke was also sitting alone, nursing a drink and contemplating the mysteries of human relationships. He was in the kitchen of his home, his laptop open in front of him on the pine table, the cursor blinking on a half-composed email. He had a large brandy in his hand, the third of the evening. After a strained interview with the police that morning, Denise, his wife of twenty-four years, had gone to stay with her parents for an indefinite period. Not knowing exactly what she had learned, or suspected, from her meeting with DCI Brock, Sandy had found it impossible to remonstrate with her. He'd wanted to tell her that nothing he had done had any bearing on their relationship, which he had always regarded as rock solid, mainly due to her utter dependability; nonetheless, he dreaded being asked to explain exactly what it was he had done. So he had said nothing and Denise had said nothing, and in silence she had gone.

The curious thing was that he felt almost relieved, as if some enormous responsibility had been lifted from his shoulders. In fact, the very greatest responsibility, for Denise, he now came to realise, had occupied a place so absolutely central to his life over the past twenty-four years that her removal made the other countless responsibilities — to his children and parents, to the firm, to clients and employees, to the old couple who maintained the investment villas in Greece, to the sports club of which he was president and the committee on design education of which he was chair, to the collector of taxes and the deliverer of newspapers — all seem somehow erased and meaningless, as if they had only existed in terms of that twenty-four-year life and if that were taken away then none of them counted any more.

This fantasy — for he knew it was only that, but what an unexpectedly beguiling fantasy it was! — gave him a literal sense of weightlessness, as in a recurrent childhood dream when he had floated down his suburban street in his pyjamas. He hadn't recalled that dream in forty-five years, and yet he could see it now as vividly as when it was fresh. He smiled, thinking of the small boy who had had the dream, a stranger now, yet somehow living deep inside him still.

He wondered whether Charles had had dreams like that, and immediately, at the thought of Charles, the sense of weightlessness vanished. Oh Charles, he thought sadly, I am so sorry. Too late, of course, but still, so very sorry.

15

Breakfast was available in the basement of the hotel, in a series of linked, windowless cellar rooms, one of which was filled by a long table bearing large quantities of eggs and cheeses, cold meats and fruits, cereals and breads, juices and hot drinks. Kathy filled her plate and made her way to a vacant dining table. Despite the generous portions of *amanida* and *canelons* the previous evening, she found herself hungry again. As she passed a low archway she heard Audrey McNeil's voice calling her. 'Kathy? Over here.'

She obediently joined them at their table, and they swapped information on what they'd done the previous day. Kathy noticed the copy of *Fifty Favourite Bridge Problems* tucked in Audrey's bag.

'I'm sorry you haven't had much luck so far,' the woman said. 'And we weren't any help.'

'I didn't really expect I'd be able to achieve much. I just resent sitting around in an office all day when I could be out exploring the place.'

Linda ambled by at that moment. She looked sleepy and extremely contented. 'Oh, hi,' she purred. 'We're back there. How are you this morning?'

It was agreed they were all fine, though probably not as fine as Linda.

'When are you meeting Jeez again?' Kathy asked.

'We thought we'd get a cab around ten.' She yawned expansively. 'There's no real hurry, until they come up with something. If I were you, I'd take the morning off. Have a look around Barcelona, for God's sake. What can you do in that dreadful office?'

'Good idea,' Peter McNeil piped up. 'Tell you what, I'll come with you, while Audrey's off meeting her Spanish grandmother bridge fiend.'

'Yeah,' Linda agreed. 'Take a city tour on the Bus Turístic. You can catch it just up the street, in the Plaça de Catalunya.'

'I know the place,' Peter said, 'and the kiosk where you get the tickets.'

Kathy didn't fancy being stuck with Peter McNeil all morning, but couldn't think of any polite way of saying so. 'Oh, great. But don't you want to go with Audrey?'

'Good Lord, no,' Audrey said. 'I don't want him hanging around when I meet Juanita.'

Twenty minutes later Kathy and Peter stood at the bus stop, clutching their tickets and complimentary guidebooks. They had debated which of two city circuits they should take, the red or the blue. Peter preferred the red, because it included the Sagrada Família, but Kathy, trying to ease her conscience at skipping work, said they should try to see as many places as possible that Charles Verge had been involved with. This meant the blue circuit, since it included the sports facilities for the 1992 Olympics on the hill of Montjuïc, including a small kiosk that the Verge Practice had designed there, as well as the new apartments of the athletes' village at Vila Olímpica on the waterfront.

'You can call it research,' Peter suggested conspiratorially. 'Getting into the *mind-set* of the murderer.'

The amateur sleuth, Kathy thought. At least he hadn't suggested that they might look for *clues*. Yet she had to revise her scornful judgement less than an hour later, when they reached the entrance to the Montjuïc site.

The idea with the Bus Turístic was that you could get off at any of the designated stops, then rejoin the tour on a later bus following the same circuit. They had stayed on for the first three stops, but then Peter suggested getting off at the Plaça d'Espanya, at the foot of Montjuïc and at the monumental entrance to the group of buildings constructed for the International Exhibition of 1929.

'There's something here that Verge would have loved,' Peter said. 'And from here we can walk up the hill to the Olympic buildings.' They set off up the formal avenue and came to the foot of a series of terraces and fountains lying in front of the Palau Nacional. 'This way,' he said, leading Kathy away from the main axis towards a grove of trees. They rounded the corner of one of the buildings and Kathy came to an abrupt halt.

'What's the matter?' Peter inquired. 'You look as if you've seen a ghost.'

'Not a ghost, a ghost house,' Kathy said, staring at the single-storey building lying in front of them, uncannily like the top floor of Briar Hill, the house that Charles Verge had built for his mother in Buckinghamshire. There was the terrace, the hovering roof planes, the glass pavilion that at Briar Hill enclosed the entry and stairs to the lower levels. 'Is this what you brought me to see?'

'Yes. I remember reading an article by Verge in which he said that his favourite architect, and the greatest influence on him, was Mies van der Rohe. Well, this would be just about his most famous building, the German pavilion for the 1929 Exhibition. It's one of the classic masterpieces of modern architecture, and it doesn't look the least bit dated, does it? I mean, it could have been designed yesterday, wouldn't you say?'

'So Verge would have seen this when he was a boy growing up in Barcelona? His father, the architect, would have brought him here, surely?'

Peter laughed. 'Well, no. After the exhibition they demolished the pavilion, and it was only rebuilt here in 1986, on the centenary of van der Rohe's birth. But Verge would have known the building from photographs. Every architecture student in the world would know it.'

They walked on to the open terrace of the building, now known as the Pavelló Mies van der Rohe, while Kathy tried to come to terms with the strange sensation of having been here already, but on an English hillside, as if the polished stone and glass structure were capable of floating from place to place like a magic carpet. The smaller glass enclosure now contained a visitors' shop, and as they went inside Kathy half expected to see the artist Luz Diaz standing waiting for her. Instead, there was a young woman behind the counter, wearing one of the black T-shirts on sale, with Mies's famous slogan, 'Less is more', in white lettering across the chest.

All the gifts and souvenirs in the glass cases were of elegant design, and among them Kathy spotted a silver pen that looked identical to the one that Sandy Clarke had used. It wasn't particularly expensive, either, and she thought she might buy it for Leon. As she was studying it, Peter suddenly appeared at her elbow, his eyes bright with some new discovery.

'I've found something,' he whispered excitedly in her ear. 'A *clue!*' Then, seeing the look that crossed Kathy's face, he added, 'No, really. Come and look!'

'Hang on.' Kathy replaced the pen and followed Peter to a corner of the room, where a book lay open on a table.

'Visitors' book,' he hissed, as if a sudden noise might frighten it away. He took her arm and led her to it, then turned the pages back to the month of May. 'There!' he cried triumphantly.

And there, indeed, it was. Kathy recognised the black, spiky architectural script even before she focused on the words. There was no date, but the entries before and after were both dated the fourteenth of May. The message read, *To the New Era!*, and in the space for name and address was written simply *Carlos*.

'My God,' Kathy whispered, catching Peter's mood of shocked elation.

'That was the day we saw him,' Peter breathed. 'He must have come here. Like a pilgrim to the shrine, to pay his respects, or gain strength perhaps. What do you think?'

It seemed a rather fanciful idea, but not more fanciful than the fact of that spiky script sitting there in public view all this time.

'Excuse me.' Kathy turned to the woman behind the counter. 'This entry here ...'

The woman came over and looked. 'Oh, that was a phrase that Mies used, "the New Era". It was the title of a famous speech he gave in 1930, the year after this building was built.'

'You wouldn't happen to remember the person who wrote this, I suppose?'

'When was it? Last May? Oh no, I couldn't possibly remember.'

Kathy reached into her bag for the photograph of Charles Verge and handed it to her. 'Would you remember this man coming here?'

'Hm, he looks familiar ... Oh, of course! It's Charles Verge, isn't it?'

'You recognise him?'

'Certainly. I'm an architecture student. We all know his work, and since May ...' She stopped and stared again at the entry in the visitors' book. 'Oh, Carlos!'

'Yes.'

'He was here?' Her face lit up with excitement. 'Wait until I tell the others!'

'No! Look, I'm a police officer, from London.' Kathy dug in her bag again for her ID. 'It's very important that we keep quiet about this, okay? What's your name? Please?'

The girl looked disappointed, but also captivated. 'Clara.'

'Well look, Clara, there are some very heavy detectives here with the CGP who will be very upset with you if this gets out. Understand?'

Clara made a face, then shrugged. 'Okay. I don't know how I'll be able to keep it to myself, but I'll do my best.'

'Anyway, it may not be him. We'll need to borrow this book for a while to do some tests. I'll give you a receipt and the names and telephone number of the local police you should contact if you remember anything.'

'What do I tell the boss when he notices the book is missing?'

'Tell him the police confiscated it and he should ring Lieutenant Mozas if he wants more information.'

Clara gave her a plastic bag for the book and called them a cab. Kathy thanked her and the girl said as they left, 'You know, I hope you don't catch him,' and gave them a broad grin.

Kathy dropped Peter at the hotel on her way to the police offices. As they shook hands on the pavement there was a cry from Audrey McNeil, hurrying towards them, looking flustered. It seemed that the meeting with her bridge partner had been something of a disappointment, not to say a shock, for 'Juanita' the grandmother had turned out to be a forty-year-old, childless, male butcher, who had taken a great deal of shaking off. He had been unapologetic about his deception, apparently, and became quite plaintive when Audrey said she would never play bridge with him again.

'The shocking thing, when I think about it,' she said, 'is how convincing he was as a grandmother. I remember all our little exchanges of news about our children and grandchildren, and he was so *plausible*. I thought I knew Juanita so well! I can still hardly believe she doesn't exist.'

'Well, maybe you should think about becoming someone else,' Peter said, clearly enjoying this. 'Become a biker or a lion-tamer or something. Wouldn't be hard for you.' He winked at Kathy, who was getting back into the taxi.

It seemed that the only progress that Linda and Tony had to report was that Kathy's list of the occupants of Passeig de Gràcia 83 had been left for her attention. They were twitchy with impatience at the delays. 'Jeez says that there's been some panic over an ETA bomb threat or something, but reading between the lines, I think he's embarrassed. My guess is that Alvarez is making us wait.'

'But why? What's his problem? He was pretty unhelpful with me yesterday.'

'Yeah, well, it was Dick Chivers' fault really. When he was over here a couple of months ago, Superintendent Chivers got a bit stroppy, acting as if these guys were working for us. Jeez says that at one point the super made Alvarez look bad in front of his superiors, and he hasn't forgiven him. If he's found out anything he's probably holding onto it to see what glory he can earn for himself before he passes it on to us.'

'Well, I've got something that might help us.' She described her visit to the Pavelló and showed them the entry in the visitors' book.

'Wow!' As Linda craned forward to look, Tony leaned over her shoulder, unconsciously stroking her arm. 'That is his writing, isn't it?'

'Looks like it.'

'Have you checked the rest of the book?'

'Not yet.'

Linda turned the pages back. 'Let's start at the beginning.'

While the two of them pored over the entries, Kathy examined the list that Alvarez's officer had left for her. The information was sparse, confined to a single sheet. Thankfully, she saw that the business descriptions had been translated into English. The building contained a lawyer, a financial consultant, medical consulting rooms, an accountant, a media company of some kind, two stockbrokers and an insurance broker. Almost any of them might have been of use to Charles Verge, Kathy guessed.

'Is anyone around?' she asked.

Linda looked up. Tony's hand was now stroking her neck. She caught Kathy's look of amusement and shrugged his hand away. 'Jeez left his extension number if we need him.' She handed it to Kathy who dialled and asked Lieutenant Mozas if someone could help her with the list. He came in after a few minutes with Alvarez's detective in tow.

'How can we help?' He gave Kathy a smile that was almost too big to be sincere, as if he felt compelled to compensate for his captain's offhandedness.

'I wondered if you had any more information on these companies?'

Jeez translated to the other man who seemed to have no English, then turned back with the answer. 'No criminal connections that we know of.'

'Okay, but what else? The lawyer, for instance?'

Again there was some discussion in Spanish or Catalan. The other policeman consulted a notebook, then Jeez said, 'Family law.'

'Well, that doesn't sound likely. What about the financial people? Could they have any connections with the UK?'

'That would take a lot of investigation,' Jeez said doubtfully. 'There's no one shady there that we know of.'

Kathy persisted. 'What kind of doctors are in the consulting rooms?'

More discussion and studying of notes. 'There are three doctors on the nameplate; an endocrinologist, an orthopaedist, and a third man who's retired.'

'Do we know what he did?'

Jeez shook his head.

Kathy thought about the list, then spoke to Tony, telling him about Passeig de Gràcia 83. 'It's probably a wild goose chase, but five of these businesses are in the field of finance.'

'Yeah.' Tony rubbed his nose thoughtfully. 'Why don't we send their names back to London, check if they've done any transactions with the UK recently. At least it would look as if we're doing something. They're probably thinking we're sunning ourselves on the Costa Brava for all the activity they've seen.'

Jeez got to his feet and asked if there was anything else he could do. Afterwards Kathy recalled that she had very nearly thanked him and let him go, but instead she said, 'Could we find out what the third doctor did, and also whether the lawyer ever had any of the Vergés family as clients?' She saw the look on Jeez's face and added, 'I'm sorry, Jeez. I'd do it myself if I could.'

'No sweat.' He smiled graciously. 'We'll do it right away.'

An hour later he found her in the corridor by the water cooler. She had stepped out for a drink and to get out of the stuffy atmosphere in the office. Burly cops with guns and combat boots strolled by, eyeing the unfamiliar blonde.

'Okay, the information you wanted. The lawyer says he's never acted for the Vergés family and has never met Charles Verge or his cousins. The doctor was a reconstructive surgeon.'

'Reconstructive?'

'Plastic.' The immobility of Jeez's features was more telling than any expression would have been. 'A pioneer of ...' he peered at his notes, '... closed rhinoplastic procedures, whatever they are.'

'Well ...'

'You know we checked out all the plastic surgery clinics in Barcelona for Superintendent Chivers, don't you?'

'I didn't know that, but ...'

'This man retired four years ago, on his seventieth birthday.'

'I'd like to talk to him.'

'I don't think that would be worthwhile. He's too old, he doesn't work at Passeig de Gràcia 83 any more and, also, he's known to us.'

'Known to you? You mean he's a crook?'

'Quite the opposite. He was awarded a police medal for his work on two of our men who were badly hurt by a bomb. He is very highly regarded by the CGP, especially by Captain Alvarez, whose men were the victims.'

'I see. I'd still like to talk to him. Will you come with me?'

'Only if Captain Alvarez approves.'

'Well, I'll speak to him.'

'He isn't here.'

'Jeez ...' He was being obstructive, she realised, his embarrassment only making him more stubborn. 'We can reach him on the bloody phone, can't we?'

Jeez clenched the muscles of his jaw, then said, 'I've already spoken to him, Kathy. He's busy and doesn't want to talk about it just now. He'll discuss it later. Maybe tomorrow.'

'*Maybe* tomorrow?'

'That's what he said.'

'Jeez,' Kathy heard herself speaking slowly and deliberately, holding back her irritation, 'did he specifically say that I wasn't to speak to this man?'

'Not specifically.'

'Okay, I'll go with Linda. Please give me the name and address.'

'No, Kathy. Captain Alvarez would be very annoyed.'

His face had become quite red, and Kathy realised that this wasn't his fault. She breathed deeply and said, 'Yes, of course. I'm sorry. Let's forget about it.' She threw the plastic cup into the bin and turned back to the office door.

'I'm sorry, Kathy,' he called after her, an edge of relief in his voice. 'We should have something for you on Martin Kraus soon, I think.'

She closed the door firmly behind her and said to Linda, 'Any idea what closed rhinoplastic procedures are?'

'Nose jobs,' Linda replied. 'My Mum's had one.'

'Fancy getting out for a while?'

They began by going to Passeig de Gràcia 83. The day had become hot, and the time was two o'clock, when most of Catalonia closes down for a couple of hours, thinning out the traffic on the boulevard. In the vestibule they found a polished brass plate with the names of the three doctors. Beside it was a modern directory board with removable letters identifying two of the doctors as being located on the third floor. The missing name was Dr Javier Lizancos.

Taking a small lift to the third floor, they found the door of the consulting rooms locked, but the buzzer eventually roused a young woman. She opened the door a few inches and said drowsily in Catalan that they were closed. Linda replied in Spanish that they were police, and needed some information. The girl switched to Spanish to explain that she was on her own and couldn't help.

Eventually the exchange got them into the small reception area inside.

'We need to get in touch with Dr Lizancos,' Linda said, offering her Captain Alvarez's card.

'He doesn't come in here very often now.' The girl studied the card unhappily. She hardly looked old enough to be out of school. 'Could you wait until the receptionist comes back?'

'We haven't got time. Do you know where we can find Dr Lizancos?'

'At home, I suppose.'

'Right.' Linda turned her notebook to a fresh page and handed it to the girl. 'Just write the address down here.'

'I don't know ...'

'Don't worry, it's just routine. Then we'll get out of your way.'

That seemed to make up the girl's mind. She took an address book from the drawer of the reception desk and found the entry. Linda handed her a pen.

'And the phone number too, please.'

The girl wrote down an address and two phone numbers and handed the notebook back. While she had been writing Kathy had opened the appointments book that lay on the desk, and had turned the pages to the fourteenth of May. She looked through the entries but nothing caught her eye, nor on the following days.

Linda pointed the page out to the girl and said, 'Can you tell if Dr Lizancos was here on that day?'

She shrugged, her eye scanning the scribbled names. 'There are no appointments for him.'

Linda thanked the girl, retrieved Captain Alvarez's card, and they left. 'This is much better than sitting around in that office,' she said as they got into the lift. 'Tony's been getting a bit ...'

Kathy waited for the word.

'... Who was it who said that men are animals with a dozen hands?' Linda concluded.

They emerged into the sunshine laughing, and hailed a cab. The taxi driver had to consult a directory to find the street. 'By the Hospital de la Santa Creu i de Sant Pau,' he finally told Linda.

'Eixample,' she explained to Kathy. 'Shouldn't be too far.'

The driver pointed out the Sagrada Família church along the

way, driving slowly past the queues of tourists waiting beneath the skeletal structure of the Passion façade.

'Peter McNeil was keen to get me here,' Kathy said. 'I'll have to tell him I saw it.'

The taxi turned in to the Avinguda de Gaudí, which cuts diagonally through the chamfered grid blocks of the Eixample district, and at its end the driver pointed to the eccentric neo-Gothic pinnacled pavilions of the hospital, explaining something to Linda.

'He says the guy who designed it was a bit crazy. He hated the grid of the city streets, and turned the whole hospital complex onto the diagonal, to face down the avenue towards Gaudí's church.'

The taxi driver said something more and Linda translated. 'He wanted every ward to be a little independent building surrounded by trees and fresh air, so he put all the connecting corridors and service areas underground.'

'Everyone seems determined to give me architecture lessons,' Kathy murmured.

The taxi stopped in a narrow street, shady with dense trees, the house hidden behind an old brick wall. They asked the driver to wait, and opened a creaking wrought-iron front gate. Inside was a garden, almost overwhelmed by foliage. They passed around an elaborate fountain and were confronted by an extraordinary ornate villa, in a style very similar to the hospital they had just passed. Built in red brick and tiles with stone trim, it was embellished with ornate Gothic arches, pinnacles and spires like a miniature gingerbread castle. The heavily studded timber front door stood open, and beside it a twisted wrought-iron bell handle was suspended on the wall. Linda tugged at it and they waited, staring into the impenetrable darkness of the interior.

After some time they heard a shuffling of feet from inside, and a small hunched figure lurched into the light. It was an elderly woman, dressed entirely in black, who eyed them suspiciously in turn. Linda wished her good afternoon and asked if they could see Dr Lizancos.

The woman peered at her and finally said something.

'She wants to know if we're American missionaries,' Linda said. 'And if we are we can fuck off.' She spoke some more, and Kathy recognised the word *policia*. She wished she'd got further with her Spanish lessons.

The woman still didn't seem inclined to be helpful, until Linda mentioned Captain Alvarez, then she barked something and shuffled away into the darkness, her black clothing rendering her instantly invisible.

'His wife?' Kathy asked.

'Housekeeper, I think. Probably came with the house.'

They stood in a pool of brilliant sunlight, growing hot as they waited, until at last the old woman returned and gestured for them to come in. Blinded by the sudden transition into darkness, they found themselves shuffling like her to avoid crashing into furniture. They followed the sound of her feet into a room very dimly lit from tall, shuttered windows. Her footsteps stopped and so did they. There was silence for a moment, then a bank of shutters jerked open with a rattle, throwing a shaft of light across the figure of a thin, erect man standing directly in front of them.

Perhaps it was the association with the first letters of the doctor's name, but Kathy was immediately struck by the image of a lizard. The head, clad in brown leathery skin, jutted out of a dark green silk cravat, and hands like lizard's claws hung from the cuffs of a white shirt. There was a tremor in the right hand as it rose and gestured towards some high-backed chairs, carved from black wood in a Gothic style. When they sat, he stared at them for a moment before taking a chair facing them. His movements were stiff, his hand trembling. He said something in Spanish and Linda replied.

'You are English?' he then said, in a very proper English, as if he'd learned it from listening to recordings of Noel Coward.

'Yes, sir,' Kathy said, offering him her card. 'From London.'

'But I don't understand.' The hooded lizard eyes drooped as he studied it briefly. 'Maria said you are with Captain Alvarez.'

'Captain Alvarez is helping us with a case.'

'A medical matter?'

'No ...'

'Then I don't understand how I can help you. Perhaps I should speak to Captain Alvarez.'

'We are trying to trace a man who went missing in May of this year, Dr Lizancos. We have received a report that he was seen going into Passeig de Gràcia 83 on the morning of the fourteenth of May, so we're talking to the people who work in that building.'

'Ah.' The lizard head nodded with understanding. 'But as you see, I am now retired. I very rarely go to the consulting rooms.' The slit of his mouth stretched a little in a smile. 'But how curious. They send two *lady* policemen from London. This missing person is not dangerous?' He gave a dry cackle.

Neither woman smiled back. Kathy said, 'Is it possible you were at Passeig de Gràcia 83 on the fourteenth of May, doctor?'

'I don't think so.'

'Could you check your diary?'

'I no longer have need of a diary,' he replied, the smile gone.

'Do you know a Barcelona family by the name of Vergés, by any chance?'

'I can't recall anyone of that name.'

Kathy handed him the photograph of Charles Verge. 'Have you ever seen this man?'

He studied it for quite a long time, then handed it back. 'I'm afraid not.'

'You must have an address book ...' Kathy began, but he snapped across her sentence.

'If such a book existed, I should not consider showing it to the police without official authorisation at the highest level. Perhaps I will telephone Captain Alvarez.'

Kathy realised that he had sensed that this was the way to get rid of them. 'I don't think we need to bother you further, doctor,' she said reluctantly, and they all got to their feet.

Linda suddenly gushed, 'This is just an amazing house.'

The old man eyed her. 'Do you know anything of Catalan Modernismo?' he asked in a superior tone.

'Very little,' Linda replied, and Kathy thought, but I'm sure we're about to learn.

'Did you notice the Hospital de la Santa Creu i de Sant Pau near here? Yes? This is by the same architect, Domènech i Montaner — in my opinion the greatest Catalan architect after Antoni Gaudí. It was designed as the house for the hospital superintendent.'

If Charles Verge had ever met this man, Kathy wondered what they would have made of each other's architectural tastes, for it was difficult to imagine anything less like the spare van der Rohe pavilion Verge had so admired.

'Well, it is remarkable.' Their eyes had become accustomed to the light and they could make out a massive stone fireplace at the end of the room and another extravagant fountain in the courtyard outside like the one in the front garden.

Lizancos gave a rasping chuckle. 'You won't see this in London, eh?'

'Oh, goodness no! And did you work at the hospital, doctor?' Linda beamed him a big, warm smile.

'I worked in many hospitals, and I had a private clinic. Ah, I see what you mean — the superintendent's house. No, it was sold by the Sant Pau many years before I bought it. It's too big for me now, of course. I should sell and go live in a little apartment.'

No, Kathy thought, you belong together, you and the house and Maria.

'That would be a shame,' Linda said, oozing sexy charm. 'You must have been a wonderful surgeon. The CGP have told us about your brilliant work with their men. Don't you miss it?'

'I'm too old.' He held up a hand to show them the tremor.

'Oh, I don't believe that.'

The lizard couldn't altogether resist the warmth of that lovely smile. Despite himself, Kathy could see, he wanted to stretch out and bask in it. 'Ah well, *hacer de la necesidad virtud.* You know that saying?'

'Make a virtue of necessity.'

'Your Spanish is good.'

'I know one too. *La mujer y el vidrio siempre están en peligro.*'

'Ah!' Lizancos' face creased in a leer. Linda giggled and spun round, knocking a glass figurine from the table at her elbow. As it spun towards the edge of the table Lizancos' hand flashed forward and caught it cleanly.

'Oh! I'm so sorry.'

Lizancos scowled with irritation, the spell broken. 'Maria will see you out,' he snapped, replacing the ornament carefully on the table.

'You did that deliberately,' Kathy said, when they were back in the taxi, heading for the city centre again.

'Yeah, I wanted to test his reactions. I didn't go for that shaky hand crap.'

'You thought he was faking it, too? I noticed the trembling stopped when I mentioned the Vergés.'

'Yeah, and when he held Verge's picture his hand was steady as a rock.'

'What did you say to him just before you knocked the figurine?'

'A woman and glass are always in danger. It's a saying. Lapped it up, didn't he? So, what do we do now?'

'I'd like to check out the private clinic that he mentioned. See if he really has retired.'

'You think he may have done a nose job on Charles Verge?' Linda asked.

'It's a possibility. I didn't like the way he answered my questions. Do you think he really doesn't keep a diary?'

'Probably summons up his appointments by black magic. Will Jeez help us?'

'Probably not.'

'That'll make things difficult. I could try talking nicely to him. He fancies me.'

'Does he?'

'Yeah, he told me. And I told him I don't go out with married men. Currently he's pissed off with me, because I've been going around with Tony, who is married.'

Given time, Kathy thought, they'd probably manage to alienate the whole Spanish police force. 'Maybe we shouldn't involve Jeez.'

Linda stared out of the cab window as they came again to the Sagrada Família, its spires rising above the incomplete structure like remnants of some lost and arcane culture. Then she began to thumb through her notebook. 'The girl gave us two phone numbers for Lizancos. Here ... They're both 93 numbers, which is the Barcelona region. The first one starts 93 487, which I'm pretty sure is a city number. They're usually in the 93 200s, 300s or 400s, so that's probably his spooky home. The other one starts 93 894, and I'd guess that must be outside the city. We might try that one.'

She fished her mobile phone out of her bag and pressed in the numbers. After a moment she began a rapid conversation, taking notes as she spoke. She said 'Muchas gracias,' rang off and sat back. 'It's a fitness club, called Apollo-Sitges, and it's in Sitges, which is about twenty miles down the coast. When I asked if Dr Lizancos was there she got cagey and asked who wanted to know. I said I was from his consulting rooms at Passeig de Gràcia 83, and the woman became more friendly. Dr Lizancos isn't there today, she said, but they are expecting him first thing in the morning. It sounded as if he goes there regularly.'

'A fitness club? Why there? There must be others a lot closer.'

'Maybe it has other attractions,' Linda said thoughtfully. 'They call Sitges the gay capital of Spain. Maybe Doctor Creepy has some special interest down there.'

16

Jeez greeted them in the corridor as they made their way to the office they had been given. He seemed in a good mood.

'Ah, ladies! Did you have a good lunch? While you were having the long lunch, we were working hard, as always, and we have results!'

'Well, that's wonderful, Jeez.' Linda switched on her heat-lamp smile.

'Yes indeed. A photograph of your Martin Kraus, no less! London will be pleased, yes?'

'Ecstatic.'

'Tony will show you, Kathy. I just want to have a word with Linda.'

'Oh, sure.' The two women exchanged a look and Kathy left them to it.

Tony was seated at his desk, shirt-sleeved, tie pulled open, looking as if he needed a good, long sleep. 'Oh, hi, Kathy. Linda with you?'

'She'll be along in a bit.' Kathy thought she noticed the slightest hint of relief in Tony's expression, as if fatigue might be winning over passion. 'You got something?'

'Oh yeah. Our pals have got us something at last.' He gathered up a sheaf of papers and began sorting through them, a sly look on his face, as if he wanted to hoard the revelations he was privy to. He began with a couple of photocopied documents.

'Seems our Martin Kraus was born in Barcelona in 1949, same year as Charles Verge.' He waved one of the sheets. 'Birth certificate.

Then he died, aged two and a half. He's buried in the Sant Roc cemetery.' He handed the second piece of paper to Kathy. 'Death certificate.'

'Right.' Kathy ran her eyes over the pages. 'When did the resurrection happen?'

'Early last year someone applied for a copy of the birth certificate, and shortly afterwards Mr Kraus applied for a passport ...' Tony clutched the next sheet as if he didn't want to hand it over.

'So we have his photo,' Kathy prompted.

'Exactly.' Tony beamed smugly and slowly handed it across. Kathy was aware of him watching her expression closely as her eyes focused on the picture of Sandy Clarke.

'Well, well. What do you make of that?'

Tony sat back in his chair, pressing his fingertips together as if in prayer. He seemed disappointed with Kathy's lack of reaction. 'A couple of possibilities come to mind.'

'Go on.'

'Theory one, and most likely in my opinion, it was a tax avoidance scheme, and probably all three partners were in on it. Excess profits are paid to a phantom debtor, Turnstile Quality Systems, registered offshore and with an imaginary proprietor.'

'Why was Clarke's photo used?'

'So that he could provide identification to open and access bank accounts on behalf of his partners. One of them had to, and Clarke was the one who authorised most contract payments.'

'Was he in Barcelona on the fourth of October when the Barclays account was opened?'

'Must have been.'

'What's the other option?'

'Theory two, the other two partners weren't aware of it. That means it was some kind of scam that Clarke was pulling alone.'

Kathy thought about this. 'But Verge knew about Martin Kraus and the Barclays account in Barcelona, didn't he?'

'So Clarke says.'

'You're suggesting that it was Clarke, not Verge, who closed the account on the fifteenth of May, and withdrew his own money that he'd transferred from London?'

'In theory two, who else could have?'

'Then Clarke would have had to come to Barcelona on the fifteenth of May.'

'Not necessarily. The transfer of funds was instructed electronically.'

'But why would Clarke pretend to send money to Verge, if he didn't?'

'Yes, interesting question. To make it look as if Martin Kraus was really Charles Verge, presumably, who conveniently isn't around to deny it.'

'Has this been sent to Brock?' Kathy asked.

'As we speak. It'll be interesting to hear what Mr Clarke has to say for himself, yeah?'

At that moment the door flew open and Linda marched in. She looked slightly flushed, her eyes bright. 'Well! So what's been happening?' she cried.

Later she caught up with Kathy at the water cooler. 'I've agreed to go out clubbing with Jeez tonight,' she said in a dramatic whisper.

'What about Tony?'

'He's got a lot of work to catch up on with this Clarke business. He wants a quiet night in his hotel room.'

'And what about your principles?' Kathy persisted.

Linda grinned. 'It's for the sake of the investigation. I'll persuade Jeez to do a check on that fitness club.'

'Good idea,' Kathy said. She didn't add that she'd already taken her own steps in that direction, having arranged a hire car for the following morning.

'Jeez has to have dinner at home, so he can't pick me up till ten. Why don't we eat together tonight, if you're not doing anything else?'

'Yes, I'd like that.'

They met in the lobby of the hotel at six-thirty and wandered out to the Plaça and then south through the old town and into the narrow winding streets of the Barri Gòtic, the Gothic Quarter, around the cathedral. Linda led them to a bar with outdoor tables where she ordered sangria and tapas.

Kathy looked around her at the evening sun glowing on ancient stonework, smart young couples parading across the square, kids roller-skating, old folks lined up on benches, the men conversing together on one, the women on another. 'This is magic,' she said.

The waiter brought a glass jug of cool pink liquid, and warned them about the children who stole handbags through the low hedge at their backs.

'I feel guilty,' Kathy went on. 'I just phoned my bloke at home, and he sounded cheesed off, and here I am swanning around enjoying myself, sipping exotic drinks in foreign parts.'

'Oh, we did try to do some work today,' Linda said, lazily eyeing three young men wandering by.

'Didn't amount to much really though, did it? Not after the stuff that Jeez got on Clarke — a dubious entry in a visitors' book and a creepy old man.' As she spoke, Kathy realised just how much she had wanted at least one of those leads to amount to something.

Linda laughed. 'You don't have to feel guilty, for God's sake. What else could you have done?'

'I don't know. I feel frustrated all the same. I've hired a car to drive down to Sitges tomorrow, but it seems pointless now. Don't fancy a drive down the coast, do you?'

'I'll have to stay here in case Tony needs an interpreter to talk to the bank people again. But you should go and see a bit more while you're here. You can get there and back in plenty of time to pick us up for the flight home. Tell them you want to return the car to the airport.' She raised her glass. 'Cheers. Are you married to this bloke, then?'

'Leon? No, we've been living together for six months now.'

'Sounds serious.'

'Sometimes it feels like no time at all; other times it feels like he's been there for ever.'

'I always seem to lose interest before then. How old are you?'

'Thirty-four.'

'Me too.'

Kathy imagined a checklist of basic questions in Linda's mind. It would be simpler if they all just carried cards of essential life data they could exchange. What stereotype are you? She'd be asking if Kathy wanted children next.

'Does he want kids?'

'We haven't discussed it.'

'Really?' Linda raised her eyebrows as if that were *very* significant.

'What?'

'I've found that usually comes up in month three or four, which is probably why I drop them at the end of month two.'

Kathy smiled. 'So you don't want kids?'

'My family was so utterly *nuclear*, so *solid*, that I think it put me off the whole idea. How about yours?'

Here we go, Kathy thought. 'I lost both my parents when I was in my teens.'

'Oh dear. But that didn't make you want to found a new dynasty?'

'The opposite, really. I suppose I got nervous of forming attachments, in case I lost them, too.'

'Ah, yes, of course.' Linda sipped thoughtfully at her drink.

That's enough of the amateur psychology, Kathy thought. The tapas arrived, the sun slipped below the rooftops and they changed the subject.

When they had finished their drinks and tapas they moved on to a small restaurant hidden in a back street of the old quarter, where Linda told Kathy she should try black rice, the most famous rice dish of Catalonia. And it was after this, strolling back towards the hotel, that Kathy's phone rang. She pulled it out of her bag and recognised Brock's voice.

'Kathy? How are you?'

'Great. Did you get my fax?'

'The entry in the visitors' book? Yes, thanks. Very ingenious. I'm glad to see you haven't lost your imagination.'

He sounded grim and preoccupied, and not greatly impressed by her discovery. 'Can they analyse the handwriting from the fax, or do you need the original?'

'You haven't seen my fax to you this afternoon? I sent it to the CGP number.'

'No.'

'Ah, well, you might want to get hold of it. It should make interesting reading.'

'Okay. Is it about Clarke?'

'Yes.'

'I'll go and pick it up now. We've also tracked down a retired plastic surgeon who may have been in the building that the McNeils now think they saw Charles Verge disappear into. I may need you to talk nicely to Captain Alvarez to get him to do a proper check on the man. He's reluctant …'

'Read my fax,' Brock said enigmatically. 'You're flying back tomorrow? Fine. See you soon.' He rang off.

When the passport photograph of Martin Kraus had arrived from Barcelona, Brock had immediately obtained a warrant and taken a couple of cars to the house near Greenwich Common. According to Sandy Clarke's secretary he hadn't been into the office that day. Apparently he had done this a couple of times lately, taken paperwork home to deal with in peace. Then she had added, hesitantly and with the proviso that she hoped the Chief Inspector would treat this as confidential, that he may not know about Mr Clarke's wife leaving him. He had told her the previous day, and he'd obviously been very upset and had said he might take the next day or two off.

Bees were humming among the hollyhocks that Denise Clarke had grown in the small cottage garden at the front of the house, a protective buffer against the city whose fumes nevertheless seemed to hang around the place. The house was silent and no one answered the doorbell. They went around to the back, where an officer broke a windowpane in the back door and so gained entry to the kitchen. A bottle of brandy, almost empty, stood on the scrubbed pine table next to an empty glass and a medication packet, also empty. A small ormolu vase of roses stood nearby, its petals fallen in a ring around its base. There was also a laptop computer on the table, power on but asleep, its light winking.

The smell of city traffic was as strong inside the house as out, as if they were stuck in the middle of a rush-hour jam instead of a leafy backstreet. Brock called out Clarke's name, but his words sank into muffling silence. 'Okay,' he said to the men at his back, and they moved forward to search the house. As he made towards the living room, Brock passed an alcove in one wall of the kitchen, beside the Aga, and he noticed that the traffic smell was especially strong here. Drawing on latex gloves, he went into the alcove and found a small laundry room and beyond it a door. When he opened it he was met by a nauseating gust of saturated exhaust fumes. There was no window, but in the dim light he could make out the dark shape of a car. He shut the door quickly against the stench and called for assistance.

The ignition was on, they discovered after they had opened the garage door to dispel the fumes, but the vehicle had long since stalled or run out of petrol, and the engine was cold. One end of a hosepipe had been neatly taped to the exhaust, the other to the rear passenger-side window, which was cracked open a couple of inches. Sandy Clarke sat slumped in the driver's seat which had been tilted back, his head cradled by the seat's headrest and his mouth open, so that he looked rather as if he was in the dentist's chair, waiting for the drill. The medical examiner would later discover that the larger muscle groups of the chest and thighs were locked in rigor, while the smaller ones in the face and hands were not. On this basis, and a rectal temperature of 13°C, he suggested an approximate time of death twenty-four hours earlier.

When Brock returned to the kitchen he had one of the team, who had more computer skills than he did, bring the machine to life. The man tapped a key and the screen flickered awake to reveal text, headed with the words, in capitals, 'A CONFESSION'. Afterwards they determined that the document had been saved at seven thirty-six p.m. on the previous day, Monday the seventeenth of September, and a copy of it was found on a disk in the shirt pocket of the dead man. It was this document that formed the bulk of the message that Brock had faxed to Kathy a couple of hours later, while she was exchanging personal insights with Linda over a glass of sangria in the square below the cathedral of Barcelona.

17

A CONFESSION

I, Andrew Christopher Clarke, being of sound mind (sound enough at least to recognise the inevitable when it stares me in the face), confess to the murder of Charles Verge and Miki Norinaga on the morning of 12 May.

It will be impossible for innocent people (more innocent than me) to appreciate the relief that I feel on finally putting those words down. I am not made of the stuff that successful murderers must be built of. For four months I have lived with my guilt, have risen after each sleepless night to the horror of it, have felt it grow inside me, hour by hour, fed by the innocence of everyone around me, and especially of my dear wife Denise, whose disgust I regret most bitterly of all, whose forgiveness I now know I shall never have.

Lately I have felt this guilt to be so heavy that it must surely be stamped on my features, visible to the detectives who know of such things and who have been grinding their way with such agonising slowness towards me. I feel them coming closer now, and to them I offer this explanation.

It will be apparent to most people who have been familiar with the Verge Practice over the past couple of years that relations have not been harmonious between the partners. After the debacle of the Labuan Assembly project (I'm sure someone will explain that one to you, Chief Inspector), it became increasingly clear to me that the partnership had lost its way so badly that it risked collapsing altogether. An architectural firm such as ours, which operates in the stratosphere of international practice, relies absolutely upon its reputation for high-quality innovative design. That is what our clients buy from us, and if the magic touch fails us, then our viability is punctured as fatally as a high-altitude balloon. Charles had that magic touch. When his devotion to Miki, indulging her ridiculous pretensions to great talent, crippled his gift, I saw the writing on the wall. I tried to reason with Charles, tried to tell him that Miki was destroying us, but he wouldn't listen. Then I said that I wanted to withdraw from the practice, but he wouldn't hear of it, and said that he wouldn't agree to me pulling out my share of the firm's capital. He believed the Marchdale Prison project would triumphantly restore our reputation. Good God, a prison of all things! I shuddered to think how the architectural press would savage him for it. There would be no mercy for a second Labuan.

Knowing how stubborn they both were, I could see that they would go on fighting each other until the balloon finally smashed to the ground, its goodwill and assets totally spent. I began to contemplate the need for a parachute.

Around the beginning of last year I got in touch with a private investigator who had expertise in company fraud on an international scale, and a reputation for discretion. He assured me that he could create the fictitious entities necessary for me to remove as much as possible of my own share of the capital of the practice over a period of time and without immediate detection. My aim was to reveal to Charles and Miki what I had done once the funds were safely out of their reach, and to resign forthwith, without further claim on the practice assets. I felt sure that, to avoid scandal, they would accept the situation as a fait accompli. I was, after all, only taking what was mine. They could then go on to destroy themselves and the Verge Practice to their hearts' content.

I instructed the investigator (whose identity I have no wish to betray) to proceed with the creation of a company called Turnstile Quality Systems Limited and its sole director Martin Kraus. He advised that there would be certain advantages in having Kraus as a foreign national, and I enjoyed the irony of having him born in Barcelona, like Charles.

All went according to plan until May of this year. By then I had transferred a significant amount of money to TQS and was looking forward to completing the arrangements by July, when I would sever my connections with the Verge Practice, well before the completion of the Marchdale Prison, when I anticipated that things would start to go from bad to worse, as far as our reputation and the value of our assets were concerned. But then I had the disastrous encounter with Miki Norinaga on the evening of 11 May.

My account to you of what happened that evening, Chief Inspector, was true as far as it went (I could hardly avoid confessing to having sex with her in the light of your DNA evidence). However, there was more to it than I explained. As I told you, she caught me at a vulnerable time. I was tired, and annoyed with Charles for having gone abroad at such a critical time in the competition for the Wuxang City project. Miki, on the other hand, was keyed up, energetic and decisive, and her seduction of me was almost rapacious. Afterwards, when she explained what was going on, I realised that it was also very calculated. She told me that Charles had been unable to have satisfactory sex with her for months, and that in every other respect their personal and professional relationship had deteriorated to the point that she no longer felt able to continue. She said that she believed Charles was a spent force, both as a man and as an architect, and that it was necessary for the design control of the practice to pass to her. She wanted Charles effectively to retire from an active role, and she wanted my support if he refused to agree.

I was astonished at her boldness. Here was a young woman just half a dozen years out of architecture school bidding to take control of one of the world's leading practices. I wanted to laugh in her face and tell her that, in my opinion, the problem with the Verge Practice was her, not Charles. But I was cautious, knowing how vindictive she could be to people who crossed her, and so I simply argued that, with or without my support, Charles would never agree to stand down from the firm he had created.

She sensed my equivocation, I suppose, no doubt as she had anticipated, for we had never been natural allies in the past. Her manner became harder and more threatening. She had heard a rumour, she said, from someone who had been to the Atlanta conference, that after Charles had left for home I had taken his daughter on a trip, and when we returned we had what her informant described as a 'sheepish look'. And then, in no time, Miki went on, Charlotte was pregnant.

Maybe my shock at her veiled accusation betrayed my guilt. At any rate, she ignored my denials and began to speculate about how Charles would react to the news that his old friend and partner had seduced both his wife and his daughter. Her ruthlessness was very disturbing. Although I was almost twice her age, I felt like an innocent compared to her. I tried to prevaricate, saying I needed time to think things over, but she wasn't having any of that. She wanted me to be there in the apartment the next morning, waiting with her to confront Charles as soon as he arrived back from the States, no doubt frayed after the overnight flight. I had no choice but to agree.

It was only when I returned to my office to collect my things and go home that the full implications of all this came home to me. If open warfare for control of the practice broke out between Charles and Miki, they would each demand my support against the other, and they would both regard my attempts over the previous year to disengage myself financially as a form of treachery. The man who had set up the bogus identities for me had warned me that there were tax implications to what I was doing, and that I would be in trouble with the Inland Revenue if they got to hear of it. If Miki made good her threat to tell Charles about my sleeping with her and Charlotte, I could hardly expect him to go easy on me. I would be faced with personal and public disgrace.

Over the next hour I did the hardest thinking I have ever done in my life. Whichever way I looked at the problem, there seemed only one inescapable outcome. There was no way now that either Charles or I could manage Miki. She was a law unto herself, and would destroy us both, therefore she would have to be eliminated. It was a shocking thought, but unavoidable.

For a while I thought of trying to stage some kind of fatal accident for Miki, but my imagination failed me. I had so little time, and the longer I delayed going home the more suspicious my movements afterwards must seem. I cursed Charles for having married the damn woman and creating this impossible situation. He should be the one to deal with her, not me. And even as I framed that thought, another followed. Why not? Perhaps he will.

It had the force of utter conviction, as when, at the end of a long and draining design session, one simple, clear idea emerges as being the surprising but inevitable solution. Charles would return the next morning, quarrel with Miki and murder her, then disappear, his flight demonstrating his guilt. All of my problems would vanish along with him. The thought of doing such a thing to Charles made me feel physically sick; but then, I had already betrayed him twice, and all of this was his fault, really.

As I was turning this over in my mind, distracting myself from the horror of it by concentrating on the details of what would have to be done to make it work, a terrifying thing happened. My mobile phone rang, and when I answered it, Charles spoke to me. I literally jumped in my seat, as if he must have been listening in on my terrible thoughts. He was at LAX, he said, waiting for his flight home, and he wanted to check on the progress of the Wuxang presentation. I managed to frame some reply, and then an idea struck me. I said there were some other things that we needed to discuss urgently, and I suggested picking him up at Heathrow so that we could talk about them on the way back. That was the first irrevocable step that I took. If he'd said no, that he would be too tired after the flight and to leave it until later in the day, perhaps I would have done no more. But Charles was indefatigable, of course.

I couldn't sleep that night, rehearsing the details in my mind. The next morning I rose early, packed some things that I would need into the car, and left without disturbing my wife. I got to the office and went straight up to Charles and Miki's apartment. Miki had been asleep, and asked me why I was so early. I said there was something we needed to discuss urgently, and she returned to the bedroom to get dressed. I went to the kitchen, took a carving knife, and followed her into her room. She was naked and smiled at me, flirtatious, asking what I wanted. I pushed her back onto the bed and drove the knife into her heart.

I had tried to anticipate the messiness of a stabbing murder, and was wearing old clothes that I would later discard far away. I had worn gloves since leaving the car, and tried very hard to avoid leaving traces. I took one of Charles's handkerchiefs from a drawer, stained it with Miki's blood and took it away with me in a plastic bag. When I returned to my car in the basement car park I changed into fresh clothes and shoes, and set off for Heathrow.

A year or so ago, we carried out a feasibility study for the Department for Transport, Local Government and the Regions into the possible uses of vacant government land in and around London. There is an amazing number of such pockets of unused land — inaccessible former British Rail yards, redundant Ministry of Defence sites, surplus storage depots — which the government was keen to sell off if some kind of viable use could be dreamed up for them. When I collected Charles from his flight, I told him that we had now been approached at short notice to do a full master plan for one of those sites, provided we could submit a preliminary report by Tuesday. I said I wanted to take him to the site in question to bounce a few ideas off him, and would then get the work under way. When we got there I was thankful to see that the place was as derelict and overgrown as when I had last visited it. We got out of the car to have a look round, and I then bounced off him not ideas, but a sizeable lump of concrete. He crumpled without a murmur. Nearby, I found a sheltered spot of soft ground and used the pick and shovel I had brought to dig a grave for him. I removed his outer clothing and buried him. I then returned to the office, had a good wash and made myself visible in the drawing studios before retiring to my office.

For the rest of that day I set about fabricating Charles's trail. It struck me as fortuitous that we had opened a bank account in Barcelona for Martin Kraus. I transferred money into it, as I described to you, as a kind of insurance in case TQS and Martin Kraus came to light, as of course they eventually did, hoping to make it appear that they were Charles's invention. That afternoon I took a bag with Charles's clothes, his bloodied handkerchief and a suicide note I had written for him, and drove down to the south coast in his car, leaving it on a meter which would, I hoped, guarantee its discovery on the Monday. I then caught a train back to London. I knew that the supposed suicide would probably not be believed, but that didn't matter so long as the hunt was for him, rather than for me.

In a way, that was the easy part, driven along by adrenaline. The difficult bit, as I soon discovered, was living with the knowledge of what I had done, and watching the investigation going on around me, waiting for some dreadful flaw to reveal itself. For instance, I found that I had mislaid one of my driving gloves, and was terrified that I might have left it in Charles's car. When the designer of a building makes a mistake he can always say to his client, as Frank Lloyd Wright famously did to one of his who complained that the roof was leaking, "Move your chair". When the designer of a murder makes a mistake, the result is deadly serious, as I have learned.

It became a terrible irony that I had been the one who had planned to break free of the Verge Practice, yet now I was the sole surviving partner, obliged to stay with the plummeting balloon for fear of betraying my part in events. After a couple of months of the investigation, I began to feel that I might indeed escape. Then they brought in the new team under DCI Brock, and the whole nightmare began again, from the beginning. And this time things began to unravel. After the interview last Friday, I realised that the game was up. Nothing could save me.

I've gone on too long. There is no point in delaying further.

Sandy Clarke

18

In her hotel room, Kathy read the fax for the third time. She felt cheated, and not only by Sandy Clarke. The McNeils, Dr Lizancos, Carlos with the black spiky writing, had all in their various, innocent ways embellished Clarke's false trail, even though Alvarez and Jeez had warned her against it. She'd cheated herself, that was the really annoying thing, because her idea had seemed more interesting.

And, just to compound her frustration, she discovered one further twist in the false trail before she turned in for the night. Sorting through her bag she found the slim file on Luz Diaz she had borrowed from the CGP. Reminding herself to return it before she left, she flicked through the pages. Though mostly in Spanish, it included the summary in English which had been sent to London following the interview that the Barcelona police had conducted with Luz on the twentieth of July. Two officers had visited her at the small studio apartment she rented. She had been cooperative and, they felt, credible. Afterwards they had spoken to her landlord, an elderly man living on the ground floor of the same block. He confirmed that she had lived there for six years, had paid her rent regularly and been a model tenant, quiet and extremely private. If she had any male visitors, he wasn't aware of it.

The only supporting documents that Kathy could understand were some copies of Luz's recent telephone bills. They were remarkable for their brevity. The artist had hardly used the phone at all. Some of the listed calls had been annotated with pencilled notes identifying the number — a taxi company, an art gallery, the airport. One was marked 'Sitges'. It began with the digits 93 894, just like Dr Lizancos's second number, and when Kathy checked her notebook she found it was the same. A year ago, Luz Diaz had made a call to the Apollo-Sitges Fitness Club. What did that mean?

Needing someone to talk it over with before she spoke to Brock, she phoned home, but got only the answering machine. When she tried Leon's mobile there was no response. She had a shower and went to bed.

The following morning she had her last big breakfast in the hotel cellar, then checked out and caught a cab across town to the car-hire office, where she picked up a little red Seat Cordo. Despite Clarke's revelations, she had decided to go ahead with her trip along the coast. There was nothing she could do to help Tony and Linda, and she was intrigued by the two references to the Apollo-Sitges Fitness Club.

She drove carefully through the city traffic, adjusting to driving on the other side of the road and trying to follow the route, drawn for her with a ballpoint line on a city map, towards the airport autovia. When she reached the A-16 she switched on the radio and picked up speed, opening the little car up to one hundred kilometres per hour, the sun shimmering off the roofs of industrial buildings and low-flying aircraft, and occasionally, in the distance, the glittering sheet of the sea.

Before long she reached the exit for Sitges Centro and turned off the highway towards the town, crossing under the railway line and continuing on through residential streets until she came to the seafront. After the density and bustle of Barcelona, the town had a pleasantly relaxed scale. Cream and pink hotels lined the front, overlooking colonnades of palm trees and the beaches beyond. Girls walked arm in arm along the boulevard, boys played beach volleyball or danced on windsurfers in the light breeze.

Kathy parked her car and strolled along the front. She thought she sensed an end-of-season mood, as if the bars and restaurants that lined the footpath had an air of fatigue after a long, hot summer. After a while she turned off into one of the narrow streets that ran up into the old town, passing shops selling sandals, straw hats and souvenirs, and climbing finally to the cluster of little museums and monuments on the point overlooking the Mediterranean. As she tried to take an interest in the odd collections of artworks and artefacts, she felt like a fraud, a tourist by default, extemporising until it was time to return to reality. She bought the most brightly coloured postcard she could find, ordered a short black at the next café she came to, and wrote a little message to Leon: 'One day we'll come here together.'

There was a payphone in the corner of the café, Kathy noticed, and on a shelf beneath it a well-thumbed directory. She went over and turned the pages to the As, jotting down the address for the Apollo-Sitges Fitness Club. The name was in English, she saw, presumably aiming at the tourist market. Perhaps Dr Lizancos was the owner, coming each week to check on his investment. The café owner gave her a stamp for the postcard, and unfolded a street map to show her where the Apollo-Sitges was located, in the newer area of the town to the west, and a couple of blocks back from the waterfront.

What with the big breakfasts, Kathy felt like some exercise. Why not? she thought. The worst that could happen was that she'd bump into Lizancos and he'd complain to Alvarez that she was harassing him. She walked back to her car, dug a T-shirt, track pants and trainers from her suitcase, and put them into a carrier bag.

The receptionist, a very muscular young man with hair as blonde as Kathy's and a name tag identifying him as 'Sigfried', eyed her navy suit trousers and white blouse, clearly wondering where she'd come from. 'Here on business?' he asked, in a strong German accent.

'Just passing through. A friend recommended you. Luz Diaz, from Barcelona. She's a member, I think. You know her?'

'I don't recognise the name. Are you interested in membership?'

'No, I don't think I'll be back for some time.'

'Okay. Just one session then, huh?'

'Thanks. I haven't brought a towel, though.'

'No problem.' He fetched one from a cupboard at his back, and led Kathy through to the gym. He pointed out the machines, the spa and the changing rooms in a bored voice, then left her to it. The place didn't seem very large, or very busy, with just a couple of men there labouring with weights. There was no sign of Dr Creepy, Kathy was pleased to see. Probably in a back office doing the books.

They clearly didn't have many female clients, for the women's changing room was tiny, with barely half a dozen lockers. Kathy put her clothes in one and returned to the gym to get started with stretching exercises and a spell on a treadmill. She stayed there an hour, working her way round the machines, and in that time the two men left and no one else arrived. At one point, when she was struggling with the preacher curl and regretting the big breakfasts, the German came in and began lifting weights at a bench in front of a large wall mirror. The trapezius and deltoid muscles of his neck and shoulders were massively developed beneath golden skin, and she wondered if he was working them for her benefit. Then the phone sounded from the front office and he strolled out, leaving her to herself once more.

Kathy got up from her machine, wondering what Luz Diaz's interest in this place had been. Was it the gym, or something else? Had Charles Verge ever been here? She picked up her towel and walked to the back of the room, where there was a door marked as a fire exit. It gave onto a short corridor with an escape door at the far end. There was one other door in the corridor, unmarked and on the opposite side to the gym, but when Kathy tried it she found it locked. She returned to the changing room, showered and left.

The gym was housed in a single-storey building whose stuccoed walls were washed terracotta. A laneway ran down one side of the building, and the wall onto the lane was windowless, punctuated only by a single door, part way along. This, Kathy realised as she was throwing her bag into the back of her car, must be the fire-exit door she had seen in the corridor at the back of the gym. What was odd about it was that there was at least as much building beyond the door as on this side of it. She relocked the car and made her way down the lane.

At the back of the building the lane turned into a yard, big enough for vehicles to manoeuvre. The back wall of the building, in the same terracotta render, contained a wide steel roller door, and beside it another door, also metal, with an intercom speaker mounted beside it.

Kathy was considering this when she heard the scrape of activity on the other side of the roller door. She stood motionless as a motor began to whine and the door began to rattle upwards. She saw the snout of a black Mercedes and beside it two pairs of legs. There was an absurd moment, which seemed to last much longer than its actual couple of seconds, when the people on both sides were aware of each other's presence without being able to see their faces. Then the door rose above shoulder level and Kathy found herself facing Dr Lizancos.

The lizard eyelids popped open as he recognised her, the leathery lips gawped apart. He appeared to be gripped by a panic attack. Then he whirled around and ran, while his companion, a middle-aged woman in a crisp white dress, stared after him in surprise. The door rumbled into life again and began to slide downwards. Kathy had a final impression of the woman's flat-heeled shoes turning away and her voice calling after Lizancos before the door hit the ground and the place reverted to silence.

Afterwards, driving back to Barcelona, Kathy wondered if she'd misjudged the old man. Perhaps he really was as respectable as he'd made out, not sinister at all. She imagined the effect on his elderly nerves of the door rising and her standing there motionless in the bright sunlight, like an avenging angel. Or maybe he had some other reason to be alarmed. What did he use the other half of the building for? Whatever it was required a location that was anonymous, windowless and secure. Maybe he had a laboratory in there, and was cooking up special pills for the clients of the gym.

When she arrived at the offices of the CGP she half expected to face a dressing down from Captain Alvarez, but it seemed there had been no complaint from Sitges, and everyone was relaxed and happy to see the case of the missing English celebrity resolved outside of Spanish jurisdiction. She returned the Diaz file, and Jeez helped them load their bags into the hire car, and shook their hands, lingering over Linda's.

Kathy asked Linda to direct her to Montjuïc on the way back to the airport, so that she could return the visitors' book to the Pavelló Mies van der Rohe. The same young woman was behind the counter and Kathy thanked her, explaining that the whole thing had been a mistake. The girl was disappointed, and Kathy, feeling mildly guilty about the whole absurd episode, asked to buy the silver pen she'd noticed before, as a souvenir for Leon. While the woman was wrapping it, Kathy admired the covers of the architectural books on display on the shelves. The images were gorgeous, with lustrous planes of colour basking beneath perfect skies, and entirely devoid of people. One in particular caught her eye, featuring an ornate skyline in brick and decorative glazed tiles. She thought it looked familiar, and when she checked the inside flap she saw that it was of part of the Hospital de la Santa Creu i de Sant Pau. The book was titled, in Spanish and English, *The Complete Works of Luis Domènech i Montaner*. She turned the pages and came to the hospital superintendent's house, now owned by Dr Lizancos. On impulse, and ignoring the formidable row of zeros on the price label on the back cover, Kathy handed the book to the girl. It would be fun to show Leon the pictures of the spooky house when she described her encounters with the strange pioneer of closed rhinoplasty.

There were long queues at the check-in counters at El Prat airport, and the flight to London was delayed for two hours. By the time they got to Heathrow it was late, dark, and raining. Kathy, Linda and Tony travelled into central London together on the tube as far as Leicester Square, where Kathy changed to the Northern line to Finchley. She felt tired and grubby as she finally struggled into the lift of her building. The palm-lined marine drive of Sitges already felt unreal and remote, and she longed to have a bath and curl up in bed with Leon. But when she opened the front door she found the flat in darkness, and when she switched on the lights she saw immediately that the table was bare, his computer gone.

Her first thought was that they had been robbed, but then she saw a note in Leon's handwriting propped against a small pile of unopened mail. It read, 'Kathy, had to leave. Sorry. Will talk when you get back. Love, L.' Then a PS scribbled underneath with a different pen, 'Sorry I didn't have time to get the car window fixed'.

It sounded rushed. Maybe his dad's had a relapse, she thought, and reached for the phone. As she waited for someone to answer, she realised how bleak the flat was without him there to welcome her home. Then she noticed his house key beside the pile of mail, and her heart stopped.

She heard his mother's voice. 'Hello?'

'Ghita? Hello, it's Kathy.'

'Oh yes. We were in bed, actually. We thought you might have phoned earlier.'

Why? 'My flight was delayed. Is something wrong? Is Morarji all right?'

'He's fine, thank you.'

'Leon's not here. I thought …'

'Everyone's all right. He wants to talk to you in person, face to face. But not tonight.'

Kathy's heart sank. This was sounding worse by the second. *Face to face.* 'But where is he?'

There was a delay before Ghita answered. 'He's here, actually.'

'Well, can I speak to him, please?'

'Not tonight, Kathy. He'll contact you tomorrow.' And the line went dead.

'The bitch!' Kathy breathed. She felt shocked and disturbingly vulnerable. What the hell was Leon playing at? Why wouldn't he talk to her? Or was that just a fabrication of his mother's? The thought offered a brief moment of comfort that quickly faded. They had been expecting her to ring, and Ghita had been appointed guardian of the phone. Nobody could get past Ghita. Kathy imagined a history of smitten teenage girls trying to phone the handsome Indian boy, and being blocked by Ghita. Was that all she was, the latest in a long line of Ghita's rejects? She felt angry now, and for a moment considered driving over there and storming their snug little semi. Then the anger turned cold, and she went to run a bath.

While it was filling the phone rang. She raced to pick it up. 'Hello?' She just stopped herself from adding, 'Leon?'

But it was Brock's voice on the other end. 'Ah, you're home, Kathy. Good. You got back safely then.' His voice sounded cautious and concerned, as if he had hardly expected her to get back in one piece.

'Yes. The flight was delayed. I've just got in.'

'You must be tired.'

'I am rather.'

'Well, I won't keep you. I just wanted to make sure everything was okay. It is okay?'

This wasn't like Brock, and Kathy had a sudden suspicion that he knew something, about Leon. For a moment she almost told him that he was gone, but then she bit it back and said only, 'Yes.'

'Good.' He didn't sound reassured. 'I'll see you tomorrow, then.' He hung up.

Kathy swore to herself and began to pull off her clothes.

19

Commander Sharpe stood at his window, gazing with satisfaction at the scaffolding on the roof of the Home Office building. 'Our friends are very content, Brock. Very content.'

'You've told them already?' Brock asked unhappily.

'Certainly.' Sharpe lifted his coffee cup to his mouth and sipped, then came and sat down to face Brock. 'Time is short. The Palace was on the point of calling the whole thing off. The Home Secretary is expecting questions in the House. There's no way we can keep quiet about this, you know.' Then he broke into a smile. 'Oh, I understand how you feel. You want to keep it all close to your chest until you've dotted every I and crossed every T.'

'Verge's body would help,' Brock said morosely.

'No sign yet?'

'We've got the list of sites they surveyed for the DTLR, and we're searching them as fast as we can, but so far nothing.'

'Hm. But there's no suggestion that the confession isn't genuine, surely?'

'I'd have preferred it in his handwriting, with his signature.'

Sharpe chuckled again. Clearly he was in a good mood, indulging the reluctant Brock. 'That's not how it works any more, is it? Pretty soon we'll all have lost the knack of handwriting — and of speech, too, I shouldn't wonder. Just communicate through keyboards. But you said in your report that only Clarke could have known many of the things he referred to.'

'Yes.' It was true. The affairs with Miki and Charlotte, the references to TQS and Kraus, the Barcelona bank account — no one else outside the police force knew of all of these.

'Details,' Sharpe insisted, 'like the bloodstained handkerchief found in Verge's car, and the single driving glove, neither of which we released to the press.'

All true. So why was he unhappy? Perhaps it was the confession itself, its form rather than its content. It wasn't like any suicide note he'd ever seen before. For one thing, it was long, longer than any other he'd come across — except one, a rambling twenty pages of invective and self-pity left behind by a city bankrupt. But that one had been tear-stained and almost incoherent in places, with sentence structure and spelling all over the place. Clarke's confession, on the other hand, was written in impeccable prose, even allowing for the computer's spelling and grammar checks. And it had been written fast; the computer recorded the document as having been created at six fifty-four p.m. and saved at seven thirty-six p.m., just forty-two minutes later. Two thousand six hundred and eighty-two words in forty-two minutes, which was some going. No doubt he'd been thinking about it for much longer, marshalling the ideas, composing the phrases. He probably had most of it memorised before he began. But he couldn't have been very drunk when he wrote it, just as he couldn't have been very drunk when he taped the hose so neatly to the car. Presumably he completed those preparations and then settled down with the brandy and sleeping pills that had been absorbed so plentifully into his bloodstream.

And then there was the tone of the confession; rather calculated, it seemed to Brock. Clarke had spoken about his feelings of horror and regret, but in such a very controlled way, like an observer rather than a participant. Brock sensed no real panic or terror, no blackness of despair. In fact, the tone seemed rather playful in places — the metaphor of the high-altitude balloon, for example — even tongue-in-cheek, 'I then bounced off him not ideas, but a sizeable lump of concrete'. Brock knew the whole thing by heart. Of course, a psychologist would provide a professional opinion.

'Maybe you just expected the hunt to take longer, be more difficult,' Sharpe suggested.

Brock conceded a nod. Yes, that might well be the case. He felt a little like someone brought in to break down an impregnable door, only to find that it crumples at the first assault.

'Maybe you feel frustrated that in the end he escaped us?'

That too. He had felt a surge of frustration when they discovered Clarke's body and he had realised, even before they reactivated the computer, what they might find there.

'But the point is, Brock, that the job is done — and brilliantly, too. This is a triumph for the service and for you personally. I have to confess that I doubted you could pull it off before the opening of Marchdale, but by God you did! And clearing Verge, too, that's the great thing. The Home Office aren't the only ones who'll be breathing big sighs of relief. The great architect's reputation is restored, his buildings are masterpieces once again, the judgement of his friends in high places is vindicated. All Verge's prestigious clients, all the august bodies that showered awards on him, all the people who had egg on their faces for having patronised a notorious murderer, will now be breaking out the champagne. Good grief, *we* should be breaking out the champagne!'

And that, Brock reflected, was perhaps the real reason for his misgivings, for Sharpe had made it quite plain at the start that any result that cleared Verge would be particularly welcome, and he had duly obliged. Was it perverse to feel uncomfortable when you fulfilled other people's fondest wishes?

Kathy, newly established as chair of the Crime Strategy Working Party, was also feeling uncomfortable. She had reported to Queen Anne's Gate that morning on autopilot, her feelings frozen as she waited for Leon to ring, and had been told to report immediately to Robert at New Scotland Yard. There she had sat through a two-hour briefing in which the administrator had told her exactly how the committee might be run, what outcomes she might expect, and how they might be achieved. At the end of it she thanked him mechanically and they proceeded to a meeting room where the rest of the committee were now assembled. She found them remarkably cooperative and eager, while she felt detached, suspended in limbo. At one point, Rex began to make difficulties about some procedural matter, but she cut him short and brought him into line hard. The others seemed impressed, Shazia sending her a covert smile and Jay a thumbs-up, but Kathy herself was oblivious.

Just as they broke for a sandwich lunch, her phone finally rang.

'Leon,' she acknowledged formally. Her voice sounded, to her own ears, as if she were still conducting the meeting, though she felt cold sweat beneath her shirt. 'What's going on?'

'I wondered if we could meet for a drink this evening?'

'Sure.' Her voice sounded ridiculously remote, and she mentally shook herself, trying to force her feelings to the surface. Hell, he needed to know how she felt! 'I missed you last night.'

'Yes, I'm sorry. I'll explain.'

'Where?' He would go for neutral ground, she guessed, where the other cops wouldn't be. She remembered the first time they'd had a drink together, in a pub south of the river, near the forensic science labs. He'd said he sometimes stayed there overnight when he was working late, and she had thought that he was married and looking for an affair.

But instead he suggested a pub tucked down a side street off Whitehall. It would be convenient for her to catch a train home afterwards on the Northern line, she realised. Maybe that was his reasoning.

The afternoon passed in a blur. At its conclusion, several of the group congratulated her on the way she'd run the meeting, and even Robert murmured a few approving words in his guarded way, yet she felt as if they were talking to someone else. She detached herself and caught the lift down to the ground-floor lobby where she surrendered her pass and stepped out into a cold, blustery evening. Wrapping her coat around her, she started walking towards Whitehall, the breeze whipping her fair hair round her ears. By the time she got to the pub she felt damp and wind-blown but refreshed, ready to face whatever was coming. She anticipated the worst, of course. What else could she think? It was probably Alex Nicholson, the forensic psychologist who had always fancied Leon and had tried to convince him to do a year's master's course with her up at Liverpool University. Yet now that she really confronted the possibility, Kathy found it hard to see Leon as a cheat. How boring, she thought, hardening herself, how disappointing. He would find it almost as painful to tell her as she would find it to listen, but she resolved she wouldn't make it easy for him. At least he hadn't just sent her an email.

It was four days since she had last seen him, and when she first caught sight of him, seated at a corner table in one of the little rooms that made up the pub, she felt a jolt of shock. It seemed so long since they had been together, and he was more beautiful than she remembered. It was as if, on the point of losing him, she was finally allowing herself to realise how she really felt about him. Then he looked up and saw her, his dark eyes widening anxiously as he rose to his feet.

He had bought two glasses of white wine for them, their usual these days. She almost told him she wanted something else, then caught herself in time. 'Hello, Leon.'

'Hi.' He looked exhausted, she thought, and for the first time she could see his father's dark rings of fatigue around the eyes. 'How was your trip?'

'It seems a long time ago now.'

'Yes.' He couldn't meet her eyes.

'Well, what's the story?'

Perhaps he'd prepared some gentle introduction, something with a touch of irony or self-deprecating humour maybe, but Kathy's cold question threw him off track.

'I'm sorry, Kathy. I really am. It's just that I've reached a point where I can't go on. It wouldn't be fair, to either of us ...' He saw the tightening of Kathy's mouth at this, and stopped. He looked as if he were trying to pick his way through a verbal minefield.

Kathy said quietly, 'Spit it out, Leon.'

He seemed to cut several preliminary paragraphs and said, 'It was that week you were at Bramshill, in June.'

The week when Sandy Clarke's DNA result had slipped through the cracks, Kathy remembered.

'Something happened,' he went on. 'I was forced to take a hard look at myself. Since then things haven't been the same, with us. I thought ... I hoped they could be. But while you were away this time it all blew up again ...'

Was that how it was? She couldn't remember things being

different when she returned from the course at Bramshill, apart from the usual mild strangeness after a period apart. A small glimmer of hope came to Kathy. 'This hasn't got anything to do with that forensic report that wasn't followed up, has it?'

'In a way,' he said gloomily. 'Yes.'

'You're not in trouble over that, are you? Oh God, darling, why didn't you say? You know I'd back you up.' She reached her hand across the table to his, but he drew back. 'Is it Brock?' she asked, mystified. 'Is he giving you a hard time?'

'Has he spoken to you?'

'Not about this, no, but I can talk to him. You know it wasn't your fault. It was that other bloke who took over from you, wasn't it? What was his name? The one who went abroad. Are they trying to blame you for his mistake?'

Leon shook his head. 'Paul Oakley, that was his name. He's back in the UK now, and Brock's spoken to him.'

'Well then ...'

'It isn't the forensic report that's the problem, Kathy. It's Paul.'

'He's the problem?' Leon was being frustratingly slow and halting in his explanation. She felt like shaking him, and had to force herself to be patient. She was supposed to be expert in interviewing techniques. She mentally checked off the stages of the formula for questioning suspects — prepare, engage, explain, account, closure and evaluation. Which one had they reached?

'He's gay, Kathy.'

'So?'

'While you were at Bramshill I had to brief him on the material for the Verge inquiry. We spent a fair bit of time together.'

Kathy recalled the entries in his diary, *PO*. 'Yes, so?'

'So he told me I was too.'

'What?' Kathy stared at him, then started to laugh, but Leon looked devastated. 'Leon, that is crazy. Of course you're not gay.'

'Yes, I am,' he said softly. 'I knew, all the time. I just didn't want to face up to it.'

Kathy blinked in disbelief, running through the possible things she could say, but Leon's obvious sincerity and conviction stopped her dead. 'Are you telling me you had an affair with this Paul Oakley?' The impossible words froze in her throat like ice cubes.

'No … He wants to, but I had to clear things up with you first.'

'Leon, this is nonsense. Some bloke appears, and out of the blue …'

'It wasn't out of the blue, Kathy. I told you, I've had these feelings before. I knew, as soon as he began talking about it, that he was right.'

Kathy sat back in her chair, speechless. She was aware of the murmur of normality from the tables around her intruding into the unreality of the thoughts going through her head, the phrases about outrage and betrayal and deceit. But she couldn't voice them, not yet. She wasn't prepared to move on to 'closure' and 'evaluation'.

Finally she broke the silence between them. 'Does your mum know?'

'No.' His voice was almost inaudible. 'I just said we were splitting up. I wanted to speak to you before I told them.'

I'd like to be a fly on that wall, Kathy thought, then corrected herself. No, actually she wanted nothing to do with it, any of it. She got abruptly to her feet and walked out. Her last image of him was sitting, head bowed, in front of two untouched glasses of white wine.

It probably wasn't a good way to leave, she reflected, as she walked blindly down dark, rain-swept streets. Too impulsive. But what was a good way?

She found herself on the Victoria Embankment, standing at a stone wall facing the dark river. It seemed unbelievable that she could have been living with him for six months and not have known, not have had some inkling. She remembered the conversation with Brock, when he had asked her to get inside Charles Verge's head; she had privately doubted if this was possible, because she sometimes felt that she had no idea what was going through Leon's head even though she was living with him. Well, you got that right, girl. You just didn't realise how ignorant you were. She began to laugh quietly to herself, the rain diluting her tears.

20

The following morning, Brock called a team meeting to wind up the Verge inquiry. As they sat waiting for him to appear, the others read the accounts in the morning papers, passing them round with the offhand shrugs of insiders who know the real story, for the information released to the press had been carefully pruned. A senior member of the Verge Practice, Andrew Christopher Clarke, had been found dead in circumstances that suggested suicide. Certain new information had come into the hands of the police, who were now satisfied that Charles Verge was not responsible for the murder of his wife Miki in May, and was himself a victim of her assailant. Police were continuing to search for his remains, but did not expect to lay charges against any other parties. An inquest would be held into the death of Clarke. The Home Office meanwhile confirmed that the official opening of Marchdale Prison, Charles Verge's last masterpiece, would take place as scheduled on the following Thursday.

The team debriefing should have been a buoyant occasion, marking the conclusion of a successful investigation, but it was clear as soon as Brock swept into the room that self-congratulation was not on the cards. For some reason that was not immediately apparent, the old man was grim. A hangover, some speculated, or maybe the mysterious lady friend they'd begun to hear rumours of was giving him a hard time.

In a rapid delivery which suggested that meandering from the point would not be tolerated, Brock outlined the main directions of their investigations and then invited each person in turn to summarise their progress. Bren began, describing the hunt for Charles Verge's body in the vacant government landholdings. He knew Brock's aversion to lists presented on overhead transparencies, and wisely kept the slides of the schedules and classifications of the sites in his file. Wisely, too, he decided to forego the PowerPoint presentation of site photographs on which he'd worked late into the previous evening, on the sensible assumption that, the way the old man was, the computer would undoubtedly screw up. Instead he concentrated on the core facts. The Verge Practice had looked at forty-six sites for the DTLR, covering a total of three hundred and fifty-two hectares, many of them overgrown and inaccessible, and including extensive derelict structures, several of which had collapsed or flooded basements. The police teams had so far eliminated fourteen of the sites. In the process they had lost two men due to muscle injuries and one dog with a damaged paw. They had discovered several animal corpses and one human, that of an abandoned baby in a carrycot. But no sign of Charles Verge.

'Thank you, Bren,' Brock said heavily. 'Is there anywhere you haven't been to yet that you were desperate to check?'

'Not really, chief.'

'Officially we go on looking. In reality, we stop as of now.'

'Right.' Bren sat down with relief.

They moved on to the money trail, the hunt for the assets of Martin Kraus and TQS Limited, which had gone cold somewhere between the Marshall Islands and Nauru. By now it was apparent that Brock, far from trying to wrap up the whole thing neatly, seemed more intent on goading them into self-criticism, prodding them into suggesting weaknesses in their approach and lines of inquiry that they may have missed along the way. Some time during the course of this the door opened and Leon Desai walked in. Kathy watched him, unblinking, as he gave a little nod of acknowledgement to Brock and slid into a seat at the back of the room. As he turned his head to scan the people present she dropped her eyes and stared unseeing at her notes.

By the time the report on financial matters was finished, Brock was drumming his fingers with impatience. 'Leon,' he called out, 'we need a little illumination in all this fog. Can you help us?'

'Yes, I think I can.' Leon rose to his feet with a ghost of a smile. The sound of his voice, soft and so familiar, made Kathy's insides shrivel. 'We've pretty well completed the forensic examinations relating to Clarke's death, and they're unambiguous.'

He summarised the autopsy results and the examination of the death scene. The fingerprint evidence in particular was overwhelming. He passed a book of photographs to Brock, showing ringed and numbered fingerprints in various locations in the dead man's house.

'The trail is very clear,' Leon said. 'The computer, the door to the garage, the doors and window of the car, the tape on the hose, the brandy bottle, the CD in the car player, all clearly printed.'

'Hell,' Brock growled. 'I asked for a little illumination, not a bloody searchlight. It's almost too blindingly clear. So there's absolutely no indication of anyone else being present?'

'No. There are some extraneous traces, but they're probably irrelevant.'

'Like?'

'There's a heel mark on the step down into the garage from the kitchen, not made by Clarke's shoe. Probably made at an earlier date. And there are some organic fibres adhering to the adhesive on the tape used to secure the hose to the exhaust pipe which we haven't been able to match.'

'Organic? What kind of organic?'

'We're not certain. Possibly fibres of leather.'

'Well, make sure, Leon. Make bloody sure.'

Leon frowned at the tone in Brock's voice. 'Yes, of course.' Then he added tentatively, 'And there's one negative result. Clarke's widow has confirmed that the driving glove left in Charles Verge's car did belong to her husband. It was a new pair, a birthday present from his grandson. Only they've run the tests on it again, everything they can think of, and they still can't find any traces on the inside. The lab people would argue it's never been worn.'

Brock stared at him, expression indecipherable. 'What's that supposed to mean?'

'I don't know.'

Tony from Fraud, bolder than the rest, piped up. 'What's the deal, chief? According to the press statements we're totally satisfied that the case is closed. Is there a doubt?'

'There's always a doubt,' Brock said balefully.

'But the confession, chief,' Tony persisted. 'No one knew all that about Clarke apart from Clarke himself — and us, of course.'

'Even so, I want your reports to spell out what we haven't done, as much as what we have, okay?'

'Fire insurance?'

'Something like that.'

When the meeting finally broke up, the word went out for a celebratory drink after work at the pub around the corner. Kathy overheard someone ask Leon if he'd be there, and his reply that no, he was tied up that evening. She went off to write up her report feeling bleak. It was Friday, and the void of a lonely weekend loomed ahead. It seemed incredible that it had been only last weekend that she'd flown to Barcelona. Between then and now, the whole world had changed. Then she began to feel angry with herself. Self-pity was a waste of time. There were lots of things she could do this weekend. Probably. She could get the car window repaired for a start. Then it occurred to her that Leon had left behind the door key to her flat, but not to her car. Was it a Freudian slip, she wondered? Was there some rebellious part of him that knew he was making a fool of himself and wanted her to know that?

Shortly before five p.m. Kathy was standing on a corner opposite the nondescript office block where he worked, near to the Forensic Science Laboratories. She hesitated, trying not to feel furtive. She asked herself, why not phone? Why not march across to reception and demand her key back? But she did neither. Soon a stream of people began to emerge from the building, Leon among them. She watched him turn to his left and pace away, yet still she held back. He seemed so self-contained. The thought of a scene made her feel sick. She began to follow, thinking, now I'm stalking him. If he turned around he'd recognise her pale blonde hair immediately, but he strode on, oblivious, until he came to a pub she remembered, where they'd had a drink once, long ago. He took the door with 'Saloon Bar' etched on its frosted glass panel, she the one marked 'Public Bar'.

It was busy with Friday night office drinkers, and she had to work her way through the crowd before she could see him. She had no sooner caught sight of him talking to a man standing at the bar, when he looked over and spotted her. She was aware of him staring at her, disbelieving, as she pushed through to where they stood.

'Hello, Leon.'

He looked angry and embarrassed. 'What are you doing here, Kathy?' he asked in a low voice.

'I needed to speak to you. Aren't you going to introduce me?'

The man standing at Leon's shoulder smiled. 'This isn't the amazing DS Kolla, is it, Leon?' He offered her his hand. 'Paul Oakley.'

She took it. It felt soft and moist in hers. She was disturbed by his appearance. Her immediate reaction was a kind of relief that he seemed so unimpressive, with a rather doughy complexion, plump features and eyes that were too small. How can Leon find him more attractive than me? she wondered.

Paul chuckled — a rather smug chuckle, she decided — and said, 'Well, let me get us all a drink. What's yours, Kathy?'

'Scotch,' she said, aware that she was talking through her teeth. 'With water.'

'Fine.' He turned to the bar, waving a twenty.

'Kathy, for Christ's sake …' Leon muttered under his breath.

'Sorry, but I had to see you.'

'Not here —'

'You've got my car keys.'

'What?' This threw him.

'You left the key to the flat, but not the car.'

'Oh God.' He began digging in his pockets. 'No, these are mine. Are you sure?'

'Positive.' She wanted to add, and what the hell do you see in him? But she didn't.

'Well … Oh, hang on, I put them in my jeans pocket to go down to the basement, but then I never went. They must still be there. Sorry. I'll drop them in to Queen Anne's Gate.'

So there had been no rebellious corner of his psyche sending an SOS.

Paul handed around the glasses. 'Well, cheers. I've heard so much about you, Kathy.'

'And I've heard almost nothing of you.'

'Is that right?' He shot a conspiratorial look at Leon, who was staring unhappily at his glass of chardonnay. 'Hasn't Leon told you about our plans?'

Was he talking about a wedding? Kathy felt nauseous.

Paul took a card from the top pocket of his suit jacket and handed it to her. She read: *Independent Forensic Services, Paul Oakley B.Sc., Managing Director.*

Cocky bastard, Kathy thought, then wished she'd thought of another word.

'What, is Leon joining you?' she asked.

'That's the plan.'

'Well, we're discussing it,' Leon said defensively.

Paul gave his chuckle. 'Leon's a great one for keeping things close to his chest, right, Kathy?' For an awful moment she thought he might be going to give Leon a cuddle. 'Big market, Kathy. Lots of opportunities.'

'Who are your clients?'

'We're just at the initial marketing stage, but potentially the whole range — commercial, defence counsels, coroner's court, even the Met, who knows?' He grinned.

Leon seemed to pull himself upright with an effort. 'Kathy,' he said softly. 'I'd like you to go now.'

She met his eye for an extended second or two, then nodded, downed her whisky in one gulp, managing not to choke, and turned on her heel.

That night she couldn't sleep. Twisting from side to side in her bed, she worked through the things she should or shouldn't have said, debated whether she should or should not have ever gone near that pub. The only positive thing was that she could now put a face to the man, but in some ways that only made it worse, more drab, more sordid.

She forced herself off this track by thinking about work. Distracted by Leon, she had been unable to finish her report for Brock, which now seemed pointless anyway, with her theories of Spanish plastic surgery disproved. Why was Brock so reluctant to close the case? Did he really think it possible that Clarke's suicide might have been staged? Who would have had a motive? No one in the Verge Practice, surely, for the scandalous death of the third senior partner would be the final blow to their chances of recovery.

Someone, then, with an interest in restoring Charles Verge's reputation, perhaps? The thought of Verge's mother and pregnant daughter trying to drag a comatose Clarke into his car to stage a suicide brought a grim smile. Or what about Charles Verge himself, lurking somewhere in the shadows?

But no, it made no sense. She remembered Tony's words to Brock: 'No one knew all that about Clarke apart from Clarke himself — and us, of course.' The idea of one of 'us' being responsible produced another flicker of a smile in the darkness, cut off by the sudden thought that it wasn't really funny. After all, if Kathy herself hadn't spotted the discrepancy in the forensic reports, Clarke would probably still be alive. Should she put that in her report to Brock? It certainly wouldn't do Paul Oakley any good, she thought maliciously, to underline the mistake he'd made on his last job with the Met, especially if he was now hoping to get work or a recommendation from them.

Maybe Paul Oakley murdered Clarke, she thought, aware that her mind was meandering into fantasy now, at the outer perimeter of sleep. Hard to see a motive, though. Oakley had done Clarke a good turn, after all, by overlooking the forensic test on the pillow. The oversight had been extraordinarily damaging to the investigation as it turned out, and almost inexplicable, given the checks in the system. But suppose he hadn't overlooked it — suppose he'd deliberately hidden it?

Kathy's eyes snapped open. Now that was an interesting idea. There had been a case the previous year, of a civilian scene of crime officer who had supposedly approached a thief with an offer to lose the fingerprints he'd found at the site of a robbery. Oakley had been on the point of leaving the force; suppose he'd seen the opportunity to make a bit of extra cash by offering to bury an embarrassing bit of evidence that placed Clarke in Miki Norinaga's bed? And when it finally came to light, what would Clarke's reaction be? Would he contact Oakley? Threaten him with exposure?

Kathy sighed and turned over again. It was nonsense, of course, but a satisfying fantasy. Maybe sleep would now be possible.

21

By eleven on Sunday morning, Suzanne Chambers had decided that enough was enough. Brock had arrived at lunchtime the day before, and it was soon clear that all was not well. Her grandchildren had picked up the signs quickly, and made themselves scarce after the first few threatening growls. She didn't regard him as a moody man, nor especially self-indulgent, though living on his own was bound to have its effect. So she put his current behaviour down to exhaustion after the climax of his big case, and lack of sleep compounded by an inevitable sense of anticlimax. Yet that night she was aware of him twisting and turning, sleepless in the bed beside her. Overtired, she thought, and tried not to be disappointed by his perfunctory and preoccupied gestures of affection.

Over Sunday breakfast things were no better. He brightened briefly over bacon and eggs, and produced a couple of comics that he'd bought for the kids and forgotten to give them when he'd arrived. But when Stewart, encouraged by this, asked him eagerly about the Verge case, he was met with an ominous silence. Suzanne didn't like the hurt look in the boy's eyes. Then later, when they were reading the Sunday papers together, he abruptly threw the pages aside and jumped to his feet, marching out into the back garden with a muttered comment about fresh air. She picked up the page that had apparently provoked this, and saw the articles on Charles Verge, detailing the triumphant restoration of his reputation, the excitement in architectural circles over the revolutionary design of his last great building, and the latest rumours about the death of his partner.

She looked out the window at Brock's back, his shoulders stooped as he poked disconsolately at the ashes of a camp fire the children had made the previous day, and was at a loss. There was nothing contentious about the articles. The police were not attacked. On the contrary, he himself was mentioned in positive terms. There was even a suggestion that if he had been in charge of the case from the beginning, it might have been resolved long ago. She put the paper down and followed him outside. A light south-easterly breeze was clearing the clouds from the sky, and sunlight was beginning to sparkle on the glossy leaves of an old rhododendron bush.

'I think it'll be fine by lunchtime,' she said. 'Shall we go to The Plough?'

He grunted a yes.

'On the condition that you talk to me in words of more than one syllable, and don't frighten the children.'

He turned to face her, a look of puzzlement on his face. 'Is it that obvious? Sorry.'

'What's the matter, David? No one's sick or anything, are they?'

'No, no. It's the case, that's all.'

'But it's a triumph for you, isn't it? Everyone says so. Your boss is pleased, isn't he? And the papers say the timing was perfect, saving everyone's face over the prison opening.'

'Yes.'

'Well then, will you tell me why you're so unhappy? Not now — at The Plough, when you've got a pint in your hand.'

He smiled and put an arm around her shoulders, and they walked back inside.

The principal attraction of The Plough was a menagerie of ancient animals — a horse, some mangy rabbits, a cantankerous goat and two peacocks — for which the landlord's aged mother had provided refuge in the back garden, possibly as an object lesson to her family on the care of the elderly. While the children renewed their acquaintance with the beasts, Brock and Suzanne took their drinks to a bench in a sunny corner.

'It's his body,' Brock said at last, wiping beer froth from his whiskers. 'We can't find Verge's body.'

Suzanne misunderstood. 'Yes, that must be upsetting for the family.'

'No, I don't mean that. I think …' He paused, as if hesitating to put his thoughts into words. 'I think there may not be one. I think the whole thing may be a sham.'

She was startled. 'Oh … But everyone is so sure. Did you read the interview with the Prince about the opening of the prison?'

'Yes. As you said, the timing was perfect. That's one of the things that worries me.'

Suzanne said nothing for a while, thinking. She understood about worriers, never satisfied unless there was some disaster to anticipate. She was a bit of one herself, though she'd never thought of Brock in quite those terms. 'You really think he might still be alive?'

'Yes.'

'But, David …' She stopped. The notion seemed preposterous. 'Have you discussed this with the others?'

'I can't. The case is closed. I can't start spreading rumour and doubt. I just hope I'm wrong, that's all.'

'You think he's that devious?'

'I thought that from the beginning. I had an image of a clever and devious man, evading his pursuers, and everything I learned about him seemed to confirm it. Now we're asked to believe that he was a helpless victim, duped and murdered by a colleague who struck me as fairly transparent.'

'You're not just disappointed that your reading of the situation was wrong?'

'There's that, I suppose.'

'And no one else has had any doubts?'

'Kathy thought she'd picked up some kind of a trail in Spain, but the suicide and confession of Verge's partner put an end to it. The problem is, you see, that to explain it the other way, you have to believe that Verge didn't just act impulsively last May. You have to accept that he was planning the whole thing for a year or more beforehand, setting up companies and milking funds from his own firm, constructing the whole damn story. And more than that, that he's probably been here all the time, in England, pulling the strings, while we combed the rest of the globe for him. And there's no motive for it. Why would he do such a thing? He was at the height of his success. Why would he deliberately blow it all away?'

'Apart from the lack of a body, what else is wrong?'

Brock shrugged with irritation. 'A confession that doesn't sound right, a trace at the suicide scene that doesn't match anything ... Nothing definite.'

Suzanne sat back, beginning to understand the scale of Brock's dilemma. 'What can you do?'

'I don't know.' He took a deep swallow of beer.

Suzanne sipped her wine thoughtfully. 'It depends on your reading of Verge, doesn't it? Whether he really was as cunning and manipulative as you imagine?'

'Yes. We've spoken to all the people close to him, but in the main they think he was a hero.'

'What about his wife?'

'She's dead ...'

'Didn't he have a first wife? Have you talked to her?'

'Kathy did. Didn't get anything. They'd had no contact for almost a decade.'

'She might have a more informed view of his deviousness. Most divorced women do.'

'It's a thought.' He turned it over in his mind. 'Yes, it is a thought.' He took her hand and gave it a squeeze. 'Thanks.'

'There's a price,' she said. 'The bar billiards machine was free when we came through. Stewart is looking rather bored with Dobbin and his mates. He'd be thrilled if you offered him a game.'

It was raining heavily on Monday morning when Kathy arrived at Queen Anne's Gate. The weather matched her mood after a difficult weekend. She had been to see two movies, neither of which she could now remember, and using her only recipe book had cooked herself an elaborate meal, which she had been unable to eat. It hadn't helped her sense of isolation when Linda Moffat had phoned on Saturday morning to ask if she and Leon would like to make up a foursome to a concert that night. Tony had won some tickets, apparently, and his wife was elsewhere. Kathy had said that they were already committed to something they couldn't get out of, and had wondered afterwards at her inability to tell the truth. And now she was faced with a whole week chairing the Crime Strategy Working Party.

Bren Gurney appeared from around a corner and gave her a weary grin. There were dark circles under his eyes.

'Baby keeping you awake?' she asked. His third girl was now three months old.

'Yeah. Little bugger.'

'You love it.' Then, on impulse, she added, 'Is Brock about?'

'Don't think so. I saw him half an hour ago, but he was heading off somewhere. Not in best of sorts. They sent him a couple of invitations to the opening of Marchdale Prison later this week, and he reckons he has to go. He asked me if I'd go with him, but I've got too many other things to do. I said I'd find somebody. What about you, could you go? It's on Thursday.'

It sounded like a good excuse to get out of at least one day on the committee. 'Yes, all right. Listen, maybe you can help with what I wanted to check with him. I haven't finished writing up my Verge report, and there's something I'm not sure about. You remember the bit about the missing forensic evidence on the pillow? I was the one who first spotted it, and I just wondered if that was finally cleared up, how it happened and everything.'

'Sure. Didn't Leon tell you?'

She began to frame some innocuous lie, then stopped herself. 'The truth is, we're not talking at the moment. He's moved out.'

'Oh, hell. Sorry about that, Kathy. I thought you two were all set.'

'Yeah, me too. Apparently not. But it wasn't his fault it was overlooked the first time, was it?'

'No, no. The lab ran an internal inquiry into how it happened. They were very pissed off, as you'd expect. But Leon was in the clear.'

'Right. So it was the other guy's fault, the other LO?'

'No, it was a clerk who stuffed up. A part-timer, only there three days a week. No continuity, of course. They got rid of her. The report's on my desk. Borrow it, if you're interested.'

'Great. I might do that. Thanks, Bren.'

'I'll tell Dot you'll go to Marchdale with the boss. She'll give you the details. Maybe you'd like to come over for a meal, see the baby?'

'Thanks, Bren. I appreciate it. Maybe when she's settled down a bit? I wouldn't want to give Deanne any extra work at the moment.' The truth was, she didn't think she could face babies right now.

'Sure.' He waved and continued on his way.

The wet Monday morning seemed to have affected the mood of the committee, too. They were fractious and uncooperative, niggling over trivial points. They were supposed to have prepared outline position papers for general discussion on policy relating to their particular areas of interest and expertise, but none of them had. Like recalcitrant schoolchildren, Kathy thought, surveying the sulky expressions around the table. Even Robert seemed sleepy and off-colour, hardly bothering to help her steer their discussions in more positive directions.

Finally, towards lunchtime, Kathy lost patience. Knowing that her voice sounded too angry, she declared that it was pointless to go on like this, and proposed that they pack it in until everyone was in a more constructive frame of mind.

Her outburst was met with a surprised and embarrassed silence, and Kathy felt herself blushing, not quite sure what to do next. Then Jay ran a hand through the bristle on her head, and adjusted her lozenge glasses, which appeared to be a shade of blue today. 'Yeah, well, that's right,' she said. 'I mean this whole thing is crap. We're not getting anywhere because we haven't even begun to address the fundamental problem.'

'Which is?' Robert blinked at her as if waking up. He seemed genuinely interested to know her opinion.

'The nature of the police, Robert. Ranks, uniforms, mind-set — they're an army. A *male* army, of occupation.'

This produced a stir of interest. The administrator smiled languidly and said, 'Oh, come on. Two of the three officers on this committee are women.'

'Yes, and there are women in the all-male rugby club, too. They clean the toilets and serve behind the bar. Sorry Kathy, Shazia, but it's true. The whole organisation is founded on a male model of domination and aggression. Until you deal with that, you're wasting your time. Look at this stuff.' She lifted her pile of the supporting documents, the effort making the tattoos on her biceps swell. 'Cosmetics. Public relations crap. Rape-denial.'

Everyone began talking at once, some laughing, others serious. Kathy caught Robert's eye. He was beaming at her, pink lips pursed with amusement as if to say, what an absolute fool, but what else can you expect? She suddenly found his complacency very irritating indeed.

As the voices died away she called the meeting to order and said, 'Jay's obviously made a point that we all find interesting. I happen to think that it's a very valid point of view and one we ought to consider seriously in our report.' She was aware of a choking sound from Robert. 'But we need these ideas set out in a coherent form. We need a report. We need all our reports, mine included. They don't have to be in fancy English. Dot points will do. Just something you can talk to and we can discuss. I think we should finish now so we can spend the rest of the day preparing them for circulation tomorrow morning. Come on, please,' she added, feeling a sudden panic at the thought that in a very few days she would be standing in front of five hundred sceptical faces mouthing whatever feeble platitudes her group could cobble together. 'Help me.'

As they left the room, Jay said to her, 'Thanks for the words of support. Did you mean them?'

'I think I'd need to know more about what exactly you mean.'

'How about lunch? I'll give you a run-down.'

Kathy hesitated and Jay added, 'It's okay, I identify as queer, but I'm not practising.'

'Oh,' Kathy said. 'Right.'

The wine bar was crowded, and they were lucky to find a small corner table to sit at with their turkey and avocado sandwiches. 'I think I need this,' Jay said, raising the glass of wine. 'I found it difficult to get my brain working this morning.'

'Until the end,' Kathy said with a smile.

'Well, I believed what I said. Most of the time we just trot out formulae we know everyone expects us to say, but this I believe. They're different from us, Kathy. We all know it, but we pretend it's otherwise. That Y chromosome does something to them. They think differently, feel differently.'

'You make them sound like aliens.'

'It's safest if we do think that. It's when we believe we understand them that we get into trouble.'

A few days ago Kathy would have dismissed this as nonsense, but now she wasn't so sure. She thought about Leon and the shock of realising that she had lived with a man for six months without detecting the most important thing going on inside his head. And about Sandy Clarke, whose secret life had, it seemed, been completely unknown to his wife of twenty-four years.

As Jay went on to explain her ideas about 'degendering and demilitarising the police force', as she put it, Kathy imagined what her colleagues would make of it. Total garbage, of course. But there was something excitingly radical and fresh about it, too, at least to her, and she determined that she'd put something of it into their final report, if only to give Robert palpitations.

Her mind drifted back to Jay's opening comments about men, and she pictured Paul Oakley at Leon's side in that pub. Did they understand each other? And how could she dislike Oakley so instantly, when she knew nothing about him? One look had been enough. Yet she'd been wrong about his incompetence, because she had wanted to believe it. The report on Bren's desk had been quite clear in blaming a female clerk, Debbie Langley, for the error. In transcribing the original report she had apparently omitted the crucial item, then discovered her mistake a week later and amended the computer file without informing anyone and without realising that the file had already passed through the system.

'Anyway, there's no point in pursuing it in our report,' Jay was saying. 'Your five hundred Chief Constables won't want to know.'

'No, but it might be nice to stir them up a bit.'

'Watch out, Kathy. Don't make yourself too conspicuous. You know when something goes wrong they all gang up and pin the blame on a woman.'

'True enough.' Kathy laughed, then thought, could that be what happened to the clerk, Debbie Langley? She finished her sandwich and said, 'Tell me, Jay, do you think a grown man, who was secretly gay, still living with his parents, could hide that fact from his mother? Don't you think she would know, deep down?'

Jay shrugged. 'Depends on her attitudes.'

'Traditional, I'd say.'

'Then, in my experience, she would probably be the first to know and the last to admit it to herself.'

Kathy wondered. 'Somebody else said to me recently what you just said about not understanding men. Charles Verge's first wife said she divorced him after twenty years because she couldn't understand him.'

'I think there was a bit more to it than that. Chalk and cheese.'

Kathy was surprised. Everyone seemed to have opinions about the Verges. 'How do you know?'

'A friend of mine knows Gail Lewis. She runs a homeless shelter, and Gail has done work for her. She reckons Gail is great, really caring and sincere, unlike Verge, big-noting himself in all the colour supplements. Mind you, she did wonder if they might be getting together again.'

'How come?'

'She saw them together one time, and they seemed to be very friendly.'

'That must have been a long time ago.'

'A year or two. My friend's been at the shelter for a couple of years now. Verge dropped Gail off there one night. His silver Ferrari drew a bit of attention in that neighbourhood, and my friend recognised him.'

Kathy was puzzled — that wasn't what Gail Lewis had told her. As she said goodbye to Jay the discrepancy troubled her, so she pulled out her phone and rang Brock's number.

Brock made his way around Regent's Park past Primrose Hill, eventually discovering the place tucked away in a back street of Camden Town, part of a terrace built of pale-yellow London stock bricks, blackened with age and the rain. There was a speaker by the front door, and a brass plate reading *Gail Lewis, Architect*. He pressed the buzzer and waited under his dripping umbrella. A male voice said, 'Yes?'

'Detective Chief Inspector Brock for Ms Lewis. I phoned.'

'One moment.'

Gail Lewis opened the door, regarding him with a searching curiosity in her grey eyes, and Brock, getting an impression of sharp intelligence, felt as if he should have prepared more thoroughly for his visit. They shook hands and she led him down a hallway running the length of the house to a room at the back — her office, she explained — which had been extended into an L-shaped area around the small, paved rear courtyard. It was more like a workshop than an office, Brock thought, with its air of purposeful activity. Modest and informal in atmosphere, it could hardly be more different to the Verge Practice's grandiose offices. It was physically different, too, the building and furniture made predominantly of pine rather than stainless steel. A man was sitting at a computer, a woman was building a balsa-wood model over by the windows. They both looked up and smiled at Brock as he passed, and he noticed how young they seemed; students, perhaps.

'If you don't mind we'll talk at my board,' Lewis said, leading the way between plan-chests and tables to the far corner. 'I'm expecting a call that I really need to take, and I'll want to refer to my drawings. Would you like a coffee?'

Brock said yes, and the young man called after them, 'I'll get it, Gail.'

They sat in her workstation, partly screened from the rest of the office by the tilt of her drawing board, to which a half-finished plan on tracing paper was taped. Wanting to get a better sense of the woman before he got down to business, and remembering the banks of machines in the Verge draughting studios, Brock said conversationally, 'You don't design on a computer, then?'

'I still prefer a pencil,' she said. 'At least for the early stages. I think better with a pencil in my hand.' She picked one up, clicking the lead forward, and took a notepad from the side table, as if she were about to interview him. 'I'm puzzled by why you should want to see me, Chief Inspector. You're in charge of the case, aren't you? I've seen your name in the papers.'

The case, as if there could be no question why he had come.

'That's right. You may have read that we're closing down the investigation, but we just want to make sure there are no loose ends.'

'One of your officers spoke to me not long ago. A woman, I can't remember her name.'

'Sergeant Kolla, yes. You were caught up in some other business at the time, I think, and she wasn't able to cover all the points she wanted to raise with you.'

'What do you want to ask me about?'

'I'm still puzzled by the relationship between your former husband and his partner, Sandy Clarke. I thought, having known them both over an extended period, you might be able to throw some light on it for me.'

Two little creases appeared between her brows as she considered this. 'The papers say that Sandy Clarke murdered Charles and Miki, and confessed to this in a suicide note.'

'That's right.'

'And you're quite satisfied that's true?'

'We are.' He saw her eyes narrow at something, his choice of 'we' rather than 'I', perhaps, sensing him distancing himself. 'There doesn't seem much room for doubt.'

'And now that the case is closed you decide to come to have a chat with someone who hasn't spoken to either of them for years.'

He was saved from responding to that by her phone. 'Excuse me.' She reached for it. 'Hello? Yes, put him on.'

Brock watched her straighten in her seat, heard her voice take on a brisk authority.

'Steven? Thanks for getting back to me ... Yes, it is important; it's about the bathroom tiles. I've spoken to the supplier and they'll be on site on Monday ... Yes, Monday. They're diverting another order for us, but there are no type EG30s, so we'll have to change some of the details ...'

She spread a drawing from the side table across her board and put on a pair of glasses. The young man appeared with mugs of coffee and biscuits, and Brock waited while Lewis went through the details and brought her call to an end. She finally put the phone down, smiling to herself as she took off her glasses. 'Got you,' she said, then glanced over at Brock. 'Sorry about that. He was hoping to use the missing tiles as an excuse for his delays. Where were we?'

'You were going to give me a portrait of Charles Verge and Sandy Clarke.'

'Actually I was going to ask you again why you're here. Are you having second thoughts?'

'The coroner will have to bring a finding on the death of Sandy Clarke. Until that's done, I'm open to any ideas, no matter how unlikely.'

'You haven't found Charles's body, have you?'

Brock felt transparent, rather as he imagined the builder at the other end of the phone must have felt. 'No.'

She regarded him gravely for a moment, then turned her attention to her coffee. 'While I was waiting for you to arrive

I remembered an essay I once read, about how architects could learn about problem-solving from the *great detective*.' She said the words with an ironic emphasis, and he wasn't sure if she was having a dig at him. 'It was about how they both have to cope with masses of pragmatic detail, but in order to do that they have to stand back from the detail and form an overall vision of the case, a theory or paradigm. That's why Sherlock Holmes sat at home playing the violin while others scurried around collecting boring facts. Are you here to collect facts or play the violin, Chief Inspector? Because if it's the first, I don't think I can help you.'

'I'm not sure I follow.'

She reached behind her to a shelf laden with heavy volumes bearing titles like *Specification, Standards* and *Timber Code*, and pulled down a thick manual. 'This is the design brief for a district library we're doing at the moment — not a big building.' She let it fall open and scanned the page. 'The Assistant Librarians require an office at twelve square metres per person, with four power points each, a carpet grade B on the floor, a lighting level of five hundred lux and sound reduction index of thirty-five decibels between rooms. There are over two hundred pages like that, of facts that make up the essence of the problem. But how do you generate a solution from facts like that? You can't just pile them all up, room after room, and hope they somehow sort themselves out. In any case, many of the facts contradict each other, or are open to interpretation, or will have changed before the building's finished. So you need something else, a big idea, that's somehow truer and tougher than the data, but is also faithful to it. Would you say your job is like that?'

'It sounds familiar.'

'The trouble is, your big idea may be wrong. I once did a house for a couple who were friends of ours. There were several unusual things about the brief — their interests, the site and so on — and I arrived quite quickly at what I thought was the right answer. They liked it, and we went ahead. But I knew something wasn't quite right. I'd got there too quickly, the whole thing had been too easy somehow, too glib. You know what I mean?'

Brock nodded. He knew exactly what she meant.

'One day, in an idle moment, I started doodling, and a different answer, the right answer, appeared on my board. It was too late to do anything about it, we were committed, and I couldn't say anything to the clients. The other scheme was built, and they were perfectly happy with it — but I knew, and I felt terrible, like a detective who'd sent the wrong man to the gallows. I had the same feeling when I read the reports about Sandy.'

She paused, setting her pencil down on the edge of the drawing board midway between them, almost as if offering it to him. 'You're worried you've got the wrong answer, aren't you? You think Charles is still alive.'

Brock didn't reply for a moment, and the sound of rain splashing outside the windows in the courtyard filled the silence. Then he said, 'What made you so sure, about Sandy?'

'Just what I knew about him. He was a very steady, calm, practical man. He had to be to stick with Charles all those years. Oh, I know he had a roving eye, but there was never any suggestion of coercion or violence. He had a kind of self-possession, rather old-fashioned, like Gary Cooper or someone, that appealed to women. I daresay Charles and Miki together might drive many people to distraction, but the idea of Sandy plotting a fiendish double murder is, well, unbelievable — to me, anyway.'

Brock reached for his coffee, then slid it away, feeling nauseous. It was as if his own doubts had found a voice in this woman, stern and unequivocal, and he felt obliged to challenge them. 'Did you part on bad terms from your ex-husband, Ms Lewis?' he asked, the words sounding pompous as he spoke them.

'You mean, am I prejudiced? Of course, we all are. But no, we didn't part on bad terms, not really. We just reached a point where I realised I had to leave him. You might say I left for professional reasons as much as personal ones, although the two were so mixed together. As we became more successful, I began to realise that we were after quite different things. For me, a good reputation was a means to being able to do good work, whereas for him the opposite was true — the quality of our work was a means to attract publicity and success. He was fanatical about publicity; I couldn't understand it. He'd lose sleep fuming over some mildly critical comment in a review of one of our buildings, while I'd be lying awake trying to work out how to detail a window. And as the projects got bigger and the clients more prestigious, the differences in what we wanted

211

became more difficult to reconcile. His ambition was like a steam-roller, and in the end I decided I had to step out of the way or be squashed. He felt terribly betrayed, of course, the way he did if one of his bright young designers decided to quit. It was an affront to his ego.'

'You make him sound insecure.'

'Does that surprise you? I suppose people have told you that he was so full of self-confidence, and that was true. He loved being with people, and drew energy and confidence from them, but on his own, in the middle of the night, he was as insecure as the rest of us — worse.' She nodded to herself, recalling something. 'I remember once, it was in New York, we went to an opening at a little gallery in SoHo. There was an exhibition of photorealist paintings, and one of them was a huge watercolour, about eight feet by five, of a hermit crab. It was a stunning image, of this soft little crawling thing pinned beneath an enormous florid shell, like a building it was dragging around on its back. Charles seemed mesmerised by it. Later I offered to buy it for him, but he was horrified at the idea, and eventually confessed that he saw himself as that little crab, forced to live inside the wrong body.'

'The wrong body?' Brock remembered the underlined passage about the criminals' heads in Verge's office. 'What did he mean by that?'

'I think he meant that he'd spent his whole life trying to be someone else, the person that his mother wanted him to be, maybe — his father the Olympian.'

The reference to the painting reminded Brock of something else, and he said, 'You were acquainted with a number of painters were you? I'm thinking of a Spanish artist, Luz Diaz, who bought the house you and Charles designed for his mother.'

'Briar Hill. Yes, I heard she was living there, but I've never met her. Charlotte told me about her in one of our conversations — we maintain a rather distant mother–daughter relationship by phone. She was always her father's daughter, and was very angry when I left Charles. I used to think …'

She stopped in mid-sentence, a startled look dawning on her face. 'I'm being very slow, aren't I? If you think it possible that Charles is still alive, that Sandy didn't kill him, then you also think that Charles may have staged Sandy's suicide — that he's here, in this country.' Her surprise turned to alarm. 'You think he's come back?'

'We haven't got anywhere near thinking that, Ms Lewis,' Brock said. 'As I said at the beginning, I'm just trying to cover every angle, for my own satisfaction. As far as the authorities are concerned, there's absolutely no doubt that your former husband is dead.'

But Gail Lewis wasn't reassured. As she reached forward for her pencil Brock saw a tremor in her hand. She fiercely clicked the lead.

'In any event,' he added, 'you've surely got nothing to be worried about.'

'You don't think so? Chief Inspector, if Charles has been crazy enough to slaughter his wife in May, and then come back to kill Sandy now, I don't think anyone connected with him can feel safe!'

Brock sipped his coffee thoughtfully, then said, 'You were talking just now about too much data. One of the problems in my line of work is false data, people who tell us lies. You lied to my sergeant, didn't you, Ms Lewis? You told her you hadn't seen Charles Verge in eight years.'

She looked startled, then guilty, her face turning pink. 'How did you …? Yes, you're right, I did lie. I felt bad about it afterwards, but I just wanted to get back to my meeting, and there was no point … I thought there was no point.'

'Tell me.'

The woman sighed, shaking her head. 'I bumped into Charles one evening about a year ago, at the opening of an exhibition. He was at his most charming, the champagne was flowing, and he suggested we have dinner together, for old time's sake. God knows why, but I agreed. He was a little drunk, and a little tired, and during the course of the meal he came out with all this stuff. His marriage was finished, Miki was a nightmare, Sandy was a shit, the partnership was doomed. The thing was, he was laughing all the time he said it, as if he was describing some ridiculous comedy he'd seen at the movies. He was quite witty, almost boasting about his disasters, and I laughed along with him. He said that he'd like to wipe the slate clean, do away with them all, and start afresh.'

'He said that, that he wanted to do away with them all?'

'Yes, something like that. I didn't think it meant anything, and forgot about it until Miki's murder. Then I decided I didn't want to remember what he'd said that evening. I didn't want anything more to do with the story of Charles Verge. Then I read that it was Sandy who had killed Miki and Charles. But if you're saying now that Charles may have engineered the whole thing ...'

'All the same, you're surely not in any danger.'

'Aren't I? I was one of the people who let him down, perhaps the most, in his eyes. And I remember something else he said that evening, when he dropped me off and said goodbye. He said that in a year's time we might meet up again, and I should remember what he'd said.'

There was no panic in her eyes, but certainly there was fear.

'But surely,' Brock felt himself being dragged into confidences that he didn't really want to share, 'in the unlikely event that Charles did kill Sandy Clarke, his purpose was much more deliberate than just getting even?'

'How do you mean?'

'The death of Sandy Clarke cleared Charles Verge's name, re-established his reputation.'

'His reputation ...' She thought about that, sipping absently at her coffee. 'Yes, you're right.'

And yet, Brock thought, that wasn't quite the whole story. Like Gail, he felt as if his thinking had been slow, unwilling to pursue the implications of a scenario he didn't want to believe. But if Verge, officially cleared and dead, was still alive, any program of vengeance would be open to him. He thought again of the suicide note on Clarke's computer. Whoever had written it had known that Clarke was the father of Charlotte's child. Did that betrayal pre-cipitate Clarke's death, and did it now put Charlotte herself at risk? Who else?

'I mean, he was a rational man, yes? Not unstable.' He tried to make it sound like a positive statement, rather than a plea.

Gail drew the shape of a cone on her pad, frowning. 'He had mood swings ... periods of depression. I don't think they were properly diagnosed then. Charlotte said he had one for a year after I left. Maybe he's had better help since then.'

Or none at all, Brock thought, and watched her add a small creature peering out from under the bottom edge of the conical shape, legs and eyes and one lopsided claw.

She looked up suddenly and said, 'It's funny you mentioning that Spanish woman just now, the artist. Charlotte told me about her buying Briar Hill at the time that Charles was buying the cottage nearby for her, and I thought it was an odd coincidence. Knowing that Charles and Miki's marriage was rocky, I wondered if there might be something going on between Charles and this other woman, almost as if he were establishing an alternative happy little family down in Bucks. Then there was Miki's murder, and Charles disappeared, and another thought came to me. In retrospect, it was almost as if Charles had set about taking care of everything before the tragedy happened — getting Charlotte settled, and establishing the Spanish woman nearby, like a kind of chaperone or proxy parent.'

'He's never contacted you, since May?'

'No, of course not.'

'You're absolutely certain of that? No unexplained silent phone calls, no indirect approaches? He would have needed help after it happened, and he might have thought of someone from the past, like you, who we wouldn't necessarily consider.'

'He wouldn't have come to me. And I haven't the faintest idea where he would have gone. I thought of Spain, like everyone else, but I don't know of any secret boltholes.'

'There was speculation that he might try to make contact when Charlotte has her baby. Do you think that's plausible?'

'I guess it's possible. He'd want to know, of course, but he wouldn't be stupid enough to make a direct approach. You think Charlotte might know how to send him a message? Or the Spanish woman? Or Madelaine, of course … Formidable Madelaine.' She thought for a moment, then said, 'Actually, if I'd been asked what would make him come back, it wouldn't have been Charlotte's baby.' She reached over to the table beside her and handed Brock a thick magazine. The front cover showed a dramatic glossy photograph of a building, so geometric and brilliantly coloured that at first glance it looked like an abstract graphic, two squares, red on the left side and blue, fretted with shadows, on the right. Beneath the name of the magazine was the issue's title, 'Il Carcere Nuovo'.

'Marchdale,' Gail said. ' "The New Prison". It came out last week, ahead of the opening, and before they knew about Charles's reinstatement. That didn't bother the Italians one bit. In fact, from the text you'd say that the fact that the architect was a famous murderer only increased the building's glamour. But they also give it a very detailed appraisal, and the conclusion is that it's brilliant.'

Opening the magazine, Brock found pages of dense text interspersed with plans and lush photographs. He wondered how they'd been able to conjure such blue skies, such beautiful raking shadows, in the fen country.

'I have a friend at the *Architectural Review* who tells me that their special issue is about to come out, equally glowing. It seems Marchdale really is Charles's masterpiece, and I can't imagine how he'll be able to stay away, especially now, with this sort of publicity.'

He thanked her for her time and she led him to the front door. The rain had stopped, a weak sun forcing through the cloud. As he walked back to his car, several streets away, he felt rather as if he'd been through a Turkish bath, like he sometimes did after a particularly probing conversation with Suzanne. The effect was both exhausting and rejuvenating. He wondered what story he could use to mobilise the security services and local police at Marchdale to be alert for a man who no longer existed.

22

Kathy tried the home number on file for the former laboratory clerk Debbie Langley. She wasn't expecting a reply in the middle of the day, but the phone was answered by Debbie's mother, with whom she apparently lived.

'Debbie gets home from work at six,' the mother said.

'Well, would it be convenient if I called tonight at, say, six-thirty?'

'I don't know,' the woman said defensively. 'Does she know you?'

'We've never met. I'm with the police. It's not a big matter, and it only indirectly affects Debbie, so it'd be easier me seeing her at home rather than asking her to come to a police station. It won't take long.'

Debbie's mother agreed, and Kathy put the phone down, feeling a squirm of guilt.

The house was a rather gloomy dark-red brick semi, not far from the local commuter rail station and shops. The paint on the garage door was peeling and the concrete path cracked. Debbie Langley opened the door looking worried. Her make-up was fresh, her cheeks flushed as if she'd rushed to get ready to face this unexpected complication to her day. From the back of the house came a smell of cooking and the sound of a child's voice. She closed the front door after Kathy and led the way into the front sitting room, the furnishings spotless but worn.

'Could you tell me what this is about?' she demanded anxiously, clutching her hands. Kathy had the impression of someone who had faced a fair bit of bad news lately and was bracing for another little smack from fate. 'It's not my car is it? Only I told Cheryl when I lent it to her that I'm not going to be responsible ...' She stopped, seeing Kathy smile and shake her head.

'No, it's nothing like that, Debbie. It's just a loose end I have to tie up on a case I'm on at the moment, and it's absolutely nothing for you to worry about.'

'Oh, good.' She drew a cautious breath of relief.

'It's in connection with your work at the laboratory.'

'But you know I don't work there any more, don't you? I'm on the clerical staff at the hospital now, full time. I was only part time at the lab, you see, and I really wanted full-time work. If it's about the same thing they came about before, about the internal review, well I thought I'd done everything needed.'

'Yes, it probably does overlap with that. When was it, that they spoke to you?'

'Oh, a week ago? Maybe more.'

'And what exactly did they ask you about?'

'He had a report he was writing, about tightening up procedures. He just wanted my signature.'

'Did you read the report?'

'Oh no, it was too long, and he was in a hurry.'

This sounded wrong. Kathy wondered what kind of inquiry they'd carried out. She herself had only seen the summary of conclusions, not the background documents.

'But he explained what was in the report?'

'Not really. He said he just needed to get everyone who'd worked there in the past twelve months to sign off on it, and frankly I wasn't bothered, now I don't work there any more.'

'Did he talk about last May, about some work the lab was doing then, on a case for us?'

'May? I don't think so. Which case was that?'

'The Verge case.'

'Oh, I remember that one! We were all fascinated. Well, everyone was. I remember telling Mum when I was typing up the forensic schedules, you know, about the bloodstains and that.' Debbie suddenly looked anxious again. 'That is all right, isn't it? I mean, we could talk about our work ...'

'No, it's fine. And did the man who saw you last week mention anything about your work on that case?'

'No, I'm sure he didn't.'

'He didn't say that was what the report was about?'

'Oh no. I mean, I wouldn't normally have signed something without reading it, but he was in a hurry, and since I knew him and everything ... Why? Is something wrong?'

'There's been a suggestion that someone made a mistake in the original forensic report for the Verge case, Debbie,' Kathy said carefully. 'I just thought he might have mentioned that to you, maybe asked you if you knew anything about it.'

'A mistake? Oh dear, was it serious?'

'It caused a bit of delay.'

'Well, it certainly wasn't me. I was always very careful, especially with the big cases. I was just a keyboard operator, you see, mainly transcribing reports. All those lists! It would have been easy to skip an item. Some of the girls would copy them by eye, but I had my own method to make sure I didn't make a mistake. If I couldn't transcribe electronically, I'd make a photocopy and strike out each item in turn after I'd entered it, to make sure I didn't miss any. It was slower, but it avoided errors.'

'And he didn't ask you about the Verge case, about this mistake?'

'No, he never mentioned it.' Then she added plaintively, 'I am very careful, you know. I've learned the hard way.'

'Okay.' Kathy got to her feet.

'That's all?'

'I think so. You say you knew this person who came to see you? Someone you'd worked with at the lab?'

'Yes. He was one of your people, one of the LOs.'

'Oh, really?' Kathy felt a surge of shock. 'Not an Indian guy?'

'No. It was Paul. Paul Oakley.'

On the way home Kathy stopped for a hamburger. She felt dirty, as if she'd been caught peeping through keyholes. Oakley had obviously engineered some kind of cover-up of his mistake back in May, so that his consulting opportunities wouldn't now be blocked. He had stabbed Debbie Langley in the back, and she didn't even know it. He must also have inveigled people still working in the lab to accept the 'confession' he'd tricked out of her. Maybe he'd persuaded

Leon to help. But it was all internal to the lab, none of Kathy's business. If Leon wanted to get involved, too bad. It was all too personal, too messy.

All the same, she found it hard to leave it alone. That night, lying awake, she decided that there was one last thing she could do, just to make sure it really was none of her business.

The Crime Strategy Working Party was scheduled to convene at ten the next morning. At nine Kathy was standing in the stark reception area of the Verge Practice offices. She asked for the personal secretary of Sandy Clarke, and gave her name and identification to the receptionist, who entered the details into the computer on her glass table.

Kathy remembered Clarke's secretary from her visit with Brock two weeks earlier. She introduced herself and followed her to the lift. Close to, her face seemed frozen, and Kathy recalled an article on botox injections she'd read in the paper, but the woman's eyes showed a glazed immobility, and Kathy decided she might be on sedatives.

'Had you worked with Mr Clarke for long?' she asked, and the woman, not shifting her gaze from the flicker of steel passing beyond the glass walls of the lift, gave a little sigh.

'Fifteen years.'

In her office she offered Kathy the desk diary she had kept for Clarke, and Kathy sat down and began to work through it, taking notes from time to time. As she worked she was aware of the other woman sitting motionless at her desk, watching. The phone didn't ring.

Eventually Kathy said, 'There are a number of entries where the names of the people aren't recorded, just their organisation. I suppose the receptionist downstairs will have a record of everyone who came?'

'Yes.' The woman blinked, and Kathy imagined a frozen brain behind the frozen face. Then she added, 'You can access that on my computer.' She swivelled in her seat and slowly brought the machine to life.

The firm had an awful lot of visitors, Kathy realised, seeing the names scrolling down the screen, and thinking of her ten o'clock meeting. She began giving the secretary dates and times, checking the column with the names of organisations. Eventually the woman seemed to realise the pattern.

'These are all visits by the police?'

'Yes. There's a mix-up in our records. I just have to check for our reports.'

'Oh.' She gave a sigh of deep disapproval and continued to the next entry.

At last, the minutes ticking away, they came to the twenty-third of May, a Wednesday, nine days after Miki Norinaga's body had been discovered. The name Sergeant Paul Oakley jumped out of the screen at Kathy with an almost physical impact. 'You remember this one?' she asked calmly.

The woman thought, then she checked the appointments in the desk diary. 'I don't remember him particularly, but I remember that morning, because the next appointment was with the Mayor, and Sandy kept him waiting.'

'According to the reception record, Sergeant Oakley arrived on time for his appointment, and left forty-three minutes later.'

'That's right, he overran his time. You see there ... the Mayor arrived ten minutes before your sergeant left, and Sandy kept him waiting ...'

Kathy thought she was going to say more, but when she looked at her face she saw tears welling out of her eyes and spilling down her cheeks. The woman just stared back at Kathy, saying nothing.

'I'm sorry,' Kathy said softly. 'But just let me be clear. Sergeant Oakley stayed talking to Mr Clarke in his office all that time, did he? He didn't go up to check the apartment again, or anything like that?'

After a long moment's silence Kathy didn't think she was going to get a reply. Then the stiff lips whispered, 'That's right.'

She was late for her meeting, but nobody seemed to mind. The mood had changed, and everyone was cooperative and enthusiastic. They had all prepared their presentations; some on laptops, others on alarmingly thick sheafs of paper. As the first presentation got under way, Kathy's heart sank. It seemed pretentious to her, and ridiculously remote from the reality of policing. Soon her attention began to drift, and she turned her mind to the problem of what she was going to do about Paul Oakley.

When the afternoon session finally came to an end, everyone except Kathy seemed highly satisfied by their efforts. Robert beamed smugly as he gathered up his papers, and even the reluctant Rex was full of good humour. Kathy hurried to the door, anxious to get back to the office, but she was intercepted again by Jay.

'Hi. That went really well, didn't it?'

'I suppose.'

Seeing Kathy turn to go, Jay added, 'There's something I wanted to ask you.'

'Can it wait, Jay? I need to get back to the office before people leave.'

'I'll come down with you.'

Kathy found herself alone in the lift with Jay, who went on, 'I'm going with some friends to a gig next Saturday, and I just wondered if you'd like to come along.'

'Oh.' Kathy was surprised. Suddenly she was being showered with invitations. Well, why not? 'Okay … fine.'

'You will? Great!' Jay seemed unexpectedly pleased. The lift doors opened at the ground floor. 'Fantastic. I'll let you have the details tomorrow. See you.' Jay grinned and waved goodbye as she surrendered her pass and hurried out into the street.

Kathy found Bren at his desk, head bowed over paper, thinning dome gleaming under the fluorescent lights. 'Hi, Kathy. How's it going? Look at this stuff. It's all been piling up while we were working on Verge. Now there's no escape. I'd much rather be out stomping around the countryside in wellies looking for stiffs. You're lucky to be tied up in that committee. Cushy number, yeah?'

'Swap.'

'Like that, is it?'

'Yes.' She hesitated, not wanting to add to his burdens, then said, 'I've got a bit of a problem, Bren. I wondered if I could talk it over with you.'

'Sure.' He waved a hand at a chair. 'Take a pew. I'm glad of the excuse. Want a coffee?'

Kathy said, 'I'll get it,' and went over to the pot brewing on top of a filing cabinet nearby while Bren sorted his papers into piles. 'It's to do with that business I asked you about yesterday.'

'The stuff-up with the lab? Yes, fire away.'

'Well ...' She sat down, handing his mug over, 'I followed it up. I went to see the clerk they said was responsible.'

'Did you?' He grinned. 'Blimey, you have got time on your hands. So what was the problem?'

Kathy accepted the rebuke with a shrug. 'Something about it bothered me. Anyway, when I spoke to her it turned out she didn't know a thing about it. She'd got a new job because she wanted full-time work, and the lab never questioned her. Instead, someone went to her house and got her to sign something she didn't even have a chance to read. They never mentioned the Verge case. She was set up.'

Bren frowned. 'That doesn't sound like the lab.'

'No, it doesn't, does it? And the thing is, the person who went to see her was one of ours, the LO who was implicated in the initial mistake, Paul Oakley.'

'Blimey, that smells.' He thought about this, then said, 'But if the lab accepted it ... I mean it's their business, isn't it? And Oakley's left the force now, hasn't he? Was the woman upset when you spoke to her? Did she want to complain?'

'No, not at all. She just wants a quiet life.'

'Well then, I don't see the problem, Kathy. These things happen.'

'I think there's more to it than that. This morning I went to the offices of the Verge Practice, to talk to Sandy Clarke's secretary.'

Bren looked puzzled. 'You have been busy.'

'Going through their records, I found that Sandy Clarke had a visit from Paul Oakley on the morning of the twenty-third of May.'

Bren's perplexity deepened. 'Yeah ...?'

'This was nine days after Miki's body was found, and two days after Oakley took over from Leon as LO on the case. It was also two days after the lab results on the pillow with Clarke's DNA were first recorded.'

'Okay. So Oakley wanted to familiarise himself with the scene.'

'No, he didn't go up to the apartment. He stayed in Clarke's office the whole time. The secretary remembers that they were so engrossed that Clarke kept the Mayor waiting for his next appointment.'

There was silence for a moment, then Bren said softly, 'What are you thinking, Kathy?'

'I don't know ...' Now it came to the point, she found she couldn't bring it out into the open.

'Come on. You've got a theory, haven't you?'

'Well ... it's just, the mistake, the cover-up. Like you said, both unlike the lab. And both involving the same officer who pays a private visit to the suspect at the critical time when the crucial information gets lost ...' Again she hesitated, hoping Bren would finish the train of thought for her, save her from actually putting it into words.

'Go on,' he said impassively.

'I thought about that case last year, the SOCO who tried to lose evidence for money.'

Bren said nothing at first, then under his breath, 'Hell.'

'What do you think?'

'I think you should talk to Brock.'

'I can't.' And this time she knew she couldn't put it into words, not all of it. 'Oakley is a good friend of Leon, and Leon himself might have got involved without realising it, and Leon and I have just split up, so it'd look as if I was stirring this up out of spite.'

'So you want me to take it on.'

She nodded.

'Well ... we can't just leave it, can we?'

'I appreciate it, Bren. I mean it. This has been really bothering me.'

'Don't worry. You can forget about it now.'

'Thanks. It's been weighing me down.'

And that was true, she realised, as she walked away. She literally did feel as if a weight had been lifted from her shoulders.

There was a stack of mail and papers waiting on her desk, too. She flicked through them, then froze at the sight of an envelope addressed to her in immaculate handwriting she knew very well. Leon's. A rush of possibilities came to her — he had made a terrible mistake, he couldn't live without her, he wanted to meet again. She almost got on the phone to tell Bren to forget what she'd said about Oakley, but instead she picked up the envelope, seeing it tremble in her hand. Inside was a standard form with the report of forensic tests carried out on her car. There was no accompanying letter, not even a signature.

She sat down with a deep breath and scanned the report, hardly taking it in. No fingerprints, no distinguishing MO. Some fabric traces had been found on the jagged edge of glass remaining in the window frame. Further action requested? Kathy ticked the 'NO' box and slipped the form into the file tray. She tore the envelope with its neat handwriting into a dozen small pieces and threw them into the bin.

23

Paul Oakley sounded delighted to get the call from Bren, requesting a meeting. 'I'll come to you, Bren,' he said. 'Any time it suits. Today? Not a problem. I'll be there.'

He was under the impression, so Bren soon realised, that the purpose of their meeting was to discuss ways in which his fledgling company, Independent Forensic Services, could assist the Met, and specifically the Serious Crime Branch.

'Leon put in a plug, did he, Bren? Well, what are mates for, eh? To be honest, there's a fortune to be made out there in what I call the badlands, you know, discreet testing of celebrities' fag ends for dodgy journos who want to know what diseases they've got, that sort of stuff. But that's not what we're interested in. With my background in the force, true forensic work is our forte.'

Bren let him talk without interruption, trying to assess the man. He'd had little contact with him before, and tried to keep an open mind, but Oakley's endless optimism and overenthusiastic sales pitch began to grate.

'... Rigorous support for rigorous police work has always been my passion, Bren, and I think we can honestly compete with the old hands and come up with a service of absolute dependability, integrity and, most important, attractive cost. You and I both know what a burden it is to your inquiries to know that each and every DNA test is costing your budget three hundred and twenty pounds. Suppose we could improve on that by, say, twenty per cent. That means twenty per cent more tests, maybe a twenty per cent better success rate.'

'Cost is important, sure,' Bren said, breaking into the flow. 'But reliability has got to be the most important thing.'

'Absolutely!'

'And there have been a few slip-ups in the past that have been both costly and embarrassing.'

'Sure, sure.' Oakley nodded his head vigorously.

'We're just cleaning up the end of the Verge inquiry, and that was badly compromised by a lab mistake. Well, you must know all about that. You were the LO at the time, weren't you?'

Oakley's smile didn't waver, but his eyes became a little brighter. 'Briefly, Bren, briefly. Then I left the force and went overseas.'

'Where did you go?'

'To the States. Caught up with a few contacts I'd made to get right up to speed with the latest developments over there before setting up our company. We explored a few possibilities — franchising, partnerships, etcetera — but in the end we decided to go independent. Best way.'

'Right. So you know all about the problem with the Verge evidence. What was it, a breakdown in supervision?'

'I'm not really acquainted with all the details, Bren. Leon told me a bit about it. He said it was all cleared up now, though. Is that right?'

'Seems so. Apparently a clerk called Langley made a simple error. Did you know her?'

Oakley shook his head slowly. 'Leon did mention the name. I suppose I must have bumped into her, but I can't really recall. You know, mistakes like that can be the result of size, Bren. The organisation gets too big, too unwieldy, and quality control suffers. Whereas with a small outfit like ours, there's more personal responsibility. Fascinating case though, the Verge murders. And you've cleared it all up magnificently — with a bit of help from DCI Brock, I dare say.' He chuckled. 'You must be delighted.'

'Yeah, it was interesting. Did you ever meet Sandy Clarke?'

'The killer? No, I don't believe I had that pleasure. Must have been a devious character.'

'Oh yes, there are a few of those around.' Bren glanced at his watch. 'Well now, have you any literature you can leave me, Paul? I'm afraid I'm due in a meeting.'

'Oh, can't I buy you lunch, Bren? Never mind, another time.

Here's our prospectus and some brochures to pass around to who-ever you see fit, okay?'

Bren showed him to the door, then went up to Brock's office.

'Chief,' he said, noting the ordnance survey map spread out over the old man's desk, Brock peering closely at it through his half-rims.

'Morning, Bren.' He straightened.

'The fens?' Bren asked, seeing the tracery of dead straight roads and waterways passing unswerving across the map.

'Yes. Marchdale.'

'Working out how to get there?'

'Something like that. What can I do you for?'

'I've got a bit of a problem. Something I need to pass by you, if you've got the time.'

They settled in the two old leather chairs that Brock had long ago installed each side of the fireplace, and Bren spelled it out.

'If Kathy got it right about the clerk and the Verge office records, then Oakley was lying through his teeth, no two ways about it.'

'Yes, I see. You say you spoke to Oakley alone? I suppose Kathy was caught up in her committee.'

'It's a little more complicated than that. I think she's worried that Oakley might have got Leon involved in this somehow.'

'In what, exactly?'

'Hard to say. I'll let her put you in the picture, chief, but I gather she and Leon aren't seeing eye to eye at the moment, and she'd rather be kept out of it.'

'Hm. Even if Oakley was responsible for the original slip-up, and has covered it up, it's still hardly a matter for us.'

'Kathy feels there's more to it. She thinks that the original forensic evidence against Clarke may have been deliberately hidden.' He saw Brock's eyebrow go up and added quickly, 'It's just a theory, but she thought it needed checking out.'

Brock got to his feet and went over to the window, and stared out at the damp morning. The top floors of the main Scotland Yard building were visible over the rooftops against the sky, and he visualised Commander Sharpe at one of those windows staring back down at him.

'I'll have a word with the director at the lab, Bren,' he said finally. 'Then we'll decide what to do.'

• • •

When the committee reconvened early that afternoon, after a shared lunch of sandwiches and orange juice provided by Robert's assiduous staff, Kathy was handed a note requesting that she report to DCI Brock as soon as she was free. She managed to bring the session to a close within an hour, and hurried back to Queen Anne's Gate, where she found Bren waiting with Brock in his office.

'Didn't think you'd get away so soon, Kathy,' Brock said. 'Come in, sit down. We've been talking about the Oakley business you asked Bren to follow up. He's had an informal interview with Oakley, and I've spoken to the director at the lab, and both seem to raise more questions than they answer. I understand you don't want to be involved in this for personal reasons, which is understandable, but I'd like to hear your comments all the same.'

Kathy, still a little out of breath, nodded. 'Yes, fine.'

'This is a copy of the statement that Debbie Langley signed when she was visited at home, ten days ago.'

He handed Kathy a single faxed sheet. The text stated that Debbie Langley freely admitted that it was possible, under the pressure of the workload during May of that year, that she was responsible for the error in transcription which had led to a piece of forensic evidence in the Verge investigation being overlooked. It was signed and dated by her, and as Kathy scanned past her signature to the familiar scrawl underneath, her heart gave a jolt. The statement had been witnessed by DS Leon Desai.

'I don't understand,' she said softly. 'I even asked Debbie if it might have been an Indian who came to speak to her, and she said no. She knew Oakley quite well from her days at the lab, she said. She was adamant that it was Oakley.'

'But he could hardly be the one to witness her statement,' Bren said. 'He doesn't work at the lab any more, and he was under suspicion himself. The question is, what's Leon playing at?'

'Well,' Brock said, 'we can check that easily enough. But then there's Oakley's conversation with Bren this morning. He denied knowing Debbie, and also said he'd never met Sandy Clarke.'

'Clarke's secretary was quite clear. Brock, I'm not imagining this …'

Brock raised a placatory hand. 'Of course not. Bren spoke to her again, and we have a signed statement and a hard copy of their record of visitors that day. He was definitely there. So, what's going on? Bren says you have a theory that Oakley may have deliberately hidden the evidence against Clarke.'

'It's a possibility, isn't it?'

'In order to blackmail Clarke?'

Kathy said nothing, hearing the scepticism in Brock's voice.

'Well, how do we find out? He's hardly going to admit it. Blackmail, perverting the course of justice on a major inquiry — he'd be looking at what, ten, fifteen?'

His question hung unanswered, until Kathy finally said, 'That's what bothers me. If he did do that, and then the evidence finally came out, and Clarke realised that he'd paid Oakley off for nothing, what would Clarke do?'

'Speak to Oakley?' Bren said. 'Threaten to report him?'

'It's the timing again,' Kathy said. 'Clarke died so soon after you confronted him with the DNA evidence, before you really had time to question him in depth. And there's the tidiness of the scene of Clarke's suicide, the neat fingerprints in all the right places. You'd expect an LO to at least get that right.'

Bren looked troubled. 'I think we're getting way ahead of ourselves. Oakley wouldn't have known enough to write Clarke's confession, would he?' He turned to appeal to Brock, who seemed absorbed in his own thoughts.

'He might if he'd had help,' Brock murmured eventually. 'If he'd seen the record of Clarke's interview with us, and spoken to someone who'd read the file. You're worried that Leon might be involved somehow, I take it, Kathy?'

'I think … I think he might want to help a former colleague, another LO. Innocently, I mean. I think Oakley could have used him, like with endorsing Debbie's statement.'

'Interesting.' Brock roused himself, glancing at his watch. 'I've got another meeting now, and we've asked Mr Oakley to come in to speak to Bren and myself at four. I'd like you to watch it on the closed circuit, Kathy. Let's talk again after that.'

As she and Bren made for the door, Brock called Kathy back. 'Bren mentioned that you and Leon are going through a bad patch, Kathy. I'm sorry. You okay?'

'Yes, I'm fine.'

'A temporary hiccup, I hope?'

She drew a deep breath. 'Doesn't look like it. But it has nothing to do with this. I don't want to see him compromised by someone like Oakley, that's all.'

Was that all? She found it hard to concentrate on anything in the hour before she went to the small monitoring room next to the interview room to await Oakley's arrival.

He was clearly very pleased to be asked back so soon. He shook hands vigorously with Brock, who thanked him for coming in.

'Very glad to, Chief Inspector. This is a follow-up to my meeting with DS Gurney, I take it?'

'In a way.'

'Excellent. As the lads at Quantico like to say, "Let's go drill some data".'

Kathy saw a scornful look cross Bren's face, and almost felt sorry for Oakley as he gushed on. But there was something deeply egotistical beneath the enthusiasm, she thought, something a little too clearly self-serving.

'Before we go any further, Mr Oakley,' Brock was saying, 'I want to make it clear that this is an official interview in connection with our investigations into the murder of Ms Miki Norinaga on the twelfth or thirteenth of May last. Just so there's no confusion, I shall caution you in the usual way, and emphasise that you're not obliged to answer our questions, though we will value your assistance.'

Oakley looked astonished, but recovered enough to give a puzzled smile and offer his full cooperation.

'Good. We're interested in a meeting you had with Sandy Clarke at the offices of the Verge Practice on the morning of May twenty-third, a couple of days after you took over as LO on the Verge inquiry.'

'Sandy Clarke?' The lines of perplexity on Oakley's face deepened, and he suddenly wrapped his arms around himself, clapping one hand over his mouth in an attitude of deep thought, which looked to Kathy more as if he were imitating the monkey that wasn't supposed to speak any evil. 'Sandy Clarke ... Are you sure?'

'Quite sure. Was there more than one meeting, perhaps?'

231

'What? Well, no. To tell the truth, I can't remember meeting him at all. I think I may have mentioned that to Bren yesterday.' His eyes narrowed cautiously now as he glanced at Bren sitting by Brock's side.

'There is a record of everyone who enters and leaves the Verge offices, and Mr Clarke's secretary is quite clear on the matter. Apparently you had so much to talk about that you overran your time, and Mr Clarke was late for an important appointment. You remember now? Maybe you have a pocket diary you could check?'

Oakley's hand began to move, then stopped. 'Well, if you say so, Chief Inspector, I suppose I must have met him. There was so much going on just then … Is it important? I suppose you're going back over all his contacts, are you? Now that he's been identified as the culprit?'

'The odd thing is that you kept no record of your meeting, apparently. In the files you left behind, at least.'

'Really? Well now, let me see …' He made a big show of reaching into the briefcase he had set at his feet, and coming up with an electronic personal organiser. 'May twenty-third?' There was silence as he tapped and scrolled and fiddled around. 'Oh, here we are. You know, you're right. I've got an appointment here for "V.P." at eleven a.m. Would that be it? Yes, I remember that week — chaos, it was. And I believe I do remember going to the Verge offices soon after I took over as LO. To orientate myself.'

'It was only four months ago. What did you and Mr Clarke talk about?'

'I couldn't say exactly. General stuff about the case, I suppose.'

There was a long silence, then Brock said in an undertone that Oakley might not even have been expected to hear, 'You disappoint me, Mr Oakley.'

Kathy couldn't see Brock's expression clearly on the small monitor, but she knew the impression Oakley would be registering, of withdrawal, of values being readjusted, of options reconsidered; all uncomfortable.

'Perhaps …' Oakley forced confidence into his voice. 'Perhaps if you told me what this was about … What you're after, exactly …'

But Brock ignored him and, as if suddenly bored, got to his feet and walked heavily over to the window, hands thrust deep into his pockets, and stared bleakly out at the rain.

Bren cleared his throat. 'This morning I asked you about another person you claimed you hadn't met — Debbie Langley.'

It was at this point, Kathy decided, that Oakley finally began to realise that none of this had anything to do with giving him business. He stiffened visibly, and she imagined the brain cells beginning to fire at panic speed.

'Do you still deny meeting Debbie Langley recently?' Bren barked. Oakley didn't reply. 'Let's save time,' Bren persisted. 'I have here a copy of a statement signed by her on September thirteenth, ten days ago. She says you got her to sign it. Did you?' Still Oakley said nothing. 'Did you pay her to sign this, Mr Oakley? Did you give her money?'

At the time, Kathy wasn't sure if this was a good approach — possibly, she admitted to herself, because it hadn't occurred to her. But it galvanised Oakley. His face went very pale and he found his voice.

'I understand now,' he said, voice shaking slightly with the effort of controlling himself. 'I understand what this is about now. You people … you always stick together, don't you? I know what this is about. It's that Kolla woman, isn't it? She's behind this, right? My God, hell hath no fury, eh?'

Despite the jolt at hearing her name, Kathy was struck by how anger had changed Oakley. No longer the supplicant salesman, he seemed stronger, more formidable, even to have a certain dignity. She wondered if she'd misjudged him.

He stuffed his personal organiser back into his briefcase, a slight fumble betraying his agitation, then he was on his feet.

'Where are you going, Mr Oakley?' Bren asked.

'I'm leaving,' he said, and added, in a parody of Brock, 'and *you* disappoint *me*, *Mr* Gurney.' He turned and swept out of the room. Kathy heard his footsteps thump past in the corridor outside.

'Well,' Brock was saying as she walked into the interview room, 'that was interesting. What did he mean by that, Kathy?'

She saw Bren deliberately turn his attention to his file.

'He obviously thinks I engineered this. He's a good friend of Leons. He must think I'm stirring things up to get at Leon or something.' It sounded feeble, but it wasn't up to her to spell out what was going on between Leon and Oakley.

'He seemed very emotional,' Brock said. 'Have you two met before?'

'Just the once, in the company of Leon. We exchanged a few sentences, that's all.'

'Hm. What did you make of him, Bren?'

'Well, he didn't need his gadget to tell him where he was on the twenty-third of May. He knew bloody well, and he remembers what he talked to Sandy Clarke about. The question is why he doesn't want to tell us about it.'

'Exactly. And if it were important, you'd think there would be some trace of it somewhere. Would Clarke have made a record of the meeting? A file note, or a word jotted on the back of Oakley's card? Would he have discussed it with someone at the office, or with his wife? And we'd better speak to Leon about his signature on this statement of Debbie Langley's, and anything else he cares to enlighten us on. But you can leave all that to us, Kathy. You can forget about it.'

If only, she thought, as she made her way back to her room, a feeling of foreboding growing in her.

She spotted him just as she reached the shelter of the canopy outside her block of flats. She was shaking the water off her umbrella when she saw him running through the rain towards her, the splash of his footsteps muffled in the downpour. The collar of his black raincoat was turned up, his black hair gleaming as he passed beneath a light.

'Kathy!'

'Hello, Leon.' Her heart sank as she took in the features of his face and remembered how beautiful he was.

'Kathy, you've got to stop this.' He was close, eyes bright and angry.

'What?'

'What you're doing. It's so stupid.'

'I'm not doing anything, Leon. Do you want to come in?'

'No! You went to see Debbie Langley, didn't you?'

She nodded.

'I wouldn't have believed you'd react this way. It's so incredibly vindictive! But there always was a hard streak in you.'

'Leon, I don't understand what's going on, and I don't understand

234

what Paul Oakley's been playing at, but I do think you should watch out. He's —'

'Don't you threaten me!' He stopped himself, as if remembering that he had to focus on one thing only, and not lose his temper. 'Look, for whatever reason, you've made something out of nothing. I'm telling you, you've got it all wrong. I want to ask you, please, stop this. Get Brock and Bren to drop it.'

'It's gone past that. Paul hasn't been truthful. He has to be straight with them.'

It was only when she was safely in the lift, her knees trembling, that she became aware of her unfortunate choice of word. She hoped Leon hadn't thought it deliberate. He would take it as further evidence of her hard streak, she supposed. As the lift rose slowly through the floors another thought occurred to her, that Leon had stood over her in the way she had seen other men behave, trying to intimidate a woman by physical and verbal pressure. She had never imagined he would have been capable of that.

Later that evening, as she was about to go to bed, the bottle of wine finished, the Leonard Cohen CD milked of every bleak meaning, she jumped at the sudden ring of the phone. At first there was silence on the line, and Kathy wondered if Paul Oakley might be turning his hand to menacing behaviour. Then she heard a woman's voice. 'That's you, is it, Kathy?'

She recognised Leon's mother, sounding hesitant but also vaguely put out, as if it were Kathy who'd made the call, and at an inconvenient time.

'Hello, Ghita.'

'Kathy, Leon has told us that you and he have, er, had a difference.'

'Yes.'

'Not irreconcilable, I hope?'

'I rather think it may be, Ghita.' And Kathy thought, she doesn't know, he hasn't told her.

'Oh … I'm sorry about that. We both would be, Morarji and I.'

Kathy was surprised. It was the first indication of approval Ghita had ever given her.

'Are you quite sure? There's nothing that we could do? Perhaps if you were to tell me what the problem was?'

'I really think you should ask Leon.'

'Only he seems so very unhappy. He hardly says a word, just stares into space. It's so unlike him.'

Kathy couldn't think of a word to say.

'Oh well. I just thought I would ask. If there is anything, you will tell me, won't you?'

'Yes. Thanks.'

Then, in a quite deliberate tone, Ghita said, 'We always hoped, you see, that you two would make a go of it,' and Kathy realised suddenly that Ghita did know, even though he hadn't told her, and that she had known for some time.

24

A watery sun was lifting the mist from the fens in pale curtains, revealing a country of unnerving flatness. From time to time Brock would ask Kathy to stop the car while he scanned the landscape with a pair of binoculars, and the silence, the eerie light and the limitless horizontality spread out around them like an alien sea.

Brock was preoccupied. He had told her to keep her eyes open during the visit, but hadn't said for what. At one of their stops they found themselves next to an abandoned World War Two airfield. He examined it carefully through the glasses, then raised them to the hazy sky, as if he half expected to see a silver glider overhead. He was the navigator, guiding them according to some scheme of his own on a circuitous journey along the grid of minor roads that criss-crossed the marshlands.

Then, at last, when Kathy was beginning to wonder if they were completely lost, they saw it. It seemed like a mirage — so abrupt, so totally unnatural, that she gave a little gasp and pulled the car into the verge. The image that came into her mind was of a gigantic Rubik's cube, sunk into the fen so that only its top layer glistened improbably over the sea of wild grasses.

Still Brock detoured, getting Kathy to circle the strange object while stopping periodically to peer at it and the surrounding countryside. During the course of this she realised that the building seemed to be made up of four large cubic elements, each in a vibrant primary colour, blue, green, yellow and red.

They came finally to the approach road, a ribbon of new concrete laid along the top of a dyke, aiming dead straight at the cleft between red and blue cubes. Brock recognised the view from the cover of Gail Lewis's architectural magazine, and, as if in acknowledgement of this, the sun finally broke through, bathing the coloured walls in a brilliant light, and the sky above crystallised into a limpid cobalt blue.

There was a minimum of disturbance to the natural landscape around the building, no fences and only the most discreet of signs and lighting bollards. Ribbons of the surrounding water and grasses ran across the car park and forecourt, right up to the building's base. The car park was already almost full, a small group of chauffeurs standing together in conversation beside a Rolls Royce. Kathy found a space and they walked across gravel towards the glass entrance between the cubes. Two men stood outside, watching the arrivals, and Brock went over to talk to them. Looking at the way they stood, hands clasped in front of them, Kathy guessed they might be armed, and when Brock returned she asked, 'We're not expecting trouble, are we?'

'No, no,' Brock replied, and led the way through the entrance.

Inside, men and women in black suits checked them in, gave them name tags and pointed the way to a broad ramp rising into the heart of the building between blue wall and red. They came to a hall in which a couple of hundred people stood about in conversation. Sunlight rippled over them from skylights in a coffered vault high overhead, and Kathy was reminded of a stripped-down version of the dungeon etching hanging in Charles Verge's office.

Brock headed for a table where cups of coffee were being dispensed. Kathy followed, registering the low roar of networking notables, in their expensive suits and high-ranking uniforms. She had a sickening feeling that the audience for her working-party speech would be very much like this.

After ten minutes Brock touched Kathy's arm and indicated a group emerging at the top of the ramp. Madelaine Verge was at the front, her wheelchair guided by a man Kathy barely recognised at first, being now clean-shaven and dressed in a smart suit. Behind them walked Charlotte and Luz Diaz, arm in arm.

'Who's the man?' Brock murmured.

'His name's George. He does the garden and odd jobs for Charlotte. For Luz, too, I think. I don't know his other name. He's an ex-con that Charles Verge came across when he was doing the research for this place, and took under his wing, apparently.'

Several people detached themselves from the crowd and hurried forward to greet the Verge family effusively, and when the royal party arrived shortly afterwards, Madelaine and Charlotte Verge were among the first to be introduced to the Prince, who talked to them animatedly for several minutes.

Chairs had been set out in the hall, facing a lectern and screen, and when everyone had settled a senior bureaucrat from the Home Office gave a welcoming speech and invited the guest of honour to perform the official opening. The Prince spoke of the urgent need for fresh thinking in the field of criminal rehabilitation, of his profound belief in the power of architecture to shape our lives, and of his hope that the brave experiment of Marchdale would stand as a beacon in a bleak social landscape. This was met with warm applause, and he continued with praise for the process of consultation and research which had gone into the whole project, and in particular the willingness of the architect to undergo a period in detention himself in order to experience prison life at first hand. It was only when he came to speak of the building itself that his enthusiasm seemed to falter. He referred to its ambitious scale and rigorous planning, but in guarded terms that suggested that, perhaps, the scale was just a little too overwhelming, the interpretation too ruthless, and that his briefing had failed to prepare him for the shock of all this unbridled modernism. Recovering, he proceeded to unveil a plaque and declare the building open.

The next speaker was a psychiatrist, the leader of the team of criminologists and Home Office experts which had compiled the initial brief, and had developed the concept with the design team. She described the theory and organisation of the complex so that those who wished to go on one of the conducted tours would appreciate what they were witnessing.

Using a plan projected onto a large screen, she pointed out the features with a cursor. Around the central administration core in which they were now located, prisoner facilities were arranged in four zones, each forming a square around its own central landscaped exercise area. The zones were easily identifiable, she explained, each being denoted by a thematic colour of the spectrum, from blue through green and yellow to red. This sequence marked the stages of the inmates' residency, from induction into blue to final rehabilitation and release from red. The progress through these four domains was to be governed by a system of education, therapy and incentive. The building's design formed an intrinsic part of this system, with every aspect contrived to reinforce the underlying program. She illustrated this with views of amenities, finishes, colour schemes, environmental controls, right down to the design of furniture and crockery, clothes and diet, in each of the four zones. The cumulative effect, she said, was of a progress from alienation to integration, from institutionalisation to independence. The building was a machine for the reconstruction of human consciousness.

This was met with polite but restrained applause. The woman's tone had been just a little too confident for such a sweeping and unproven claim, like the building itself perhaps. Half the audience, Kathy suspected, didn't believe a word of it. But Madelaine Verge clearly did, sitting upright in her chair with eyes bright. This was a vision worthy of the brilliant son now brilliantly vindicated. Did they give out posthumous knighthoods? Kathy wondered. Maybe they'd need to see a body first.

The speeches over, the guests were invited to attach themselves in groups of a dozen to one of the many black-suited men and women who were available to take them on a conducted tour. Brock and Kathy hung back, watching the lines of dignitaries file through the connecting doorway to Blue Square, like oversized children on a school outing, passing whispered jokes about doing time and not bending over in the showers.

'Ah, Chief Inspector!'

They turned at the sound of Madelaine Verge's voice, sharp as a warder's. Her chair was cutting through the crowd, the others in her party following in her wake. From the fierce look in her eye, Kathy thought they were about to be taken to task, but when she was close enough Mrs Verge took hold of Brock's right hand in both of hers and squeezed it hard.

'I am so very grateful to you. I felt certain, that first time we met, that you would bring an end to our nightmare, and you did. I told you then that my son was dead, do you remember? An innocent victim. No one but us believed it then ...' She gestured with her head to the group behind her, all staring intently at Brock as if to gauge his reaction. 'But you proved that we were right!'

Kathy was particularly struck by the look on George's face, tight-lipped, bright-eyed, as if suppressing some inner elation. She thought she could appreciate his feelings, the convict as an honoured guest at a party of police and prison bigwigs.

'It was a difficult thing for people to accept, Mrs Verge.' Brock spoke deliberately, without a trace of pleasure at her praise. 'Even today there are some who find it hard to believe that your son is not still alive.'

'What?' She released his hand. 'How can they possibly do that?' She jerked her head back angrily. 'Well, you must make it your job to persuade them that they're wrong, mustn't you!'

'We would all feel much happier if we could find his body.'

'Ah, yes.' Madelaine Verge's face recovered its composure. 'I have reconciled myself to the possibility that that may never happen. Do you know Sir Christopher Wren's epitaph in St Paul's? *Si monumentum requiris, circumspice.* "If you want a monument, look around you." That shall be my son's epitaph, Chief Inspector.' She lifted an arthritic hand in a wide arc. 'Look around you ...'

As she swept away, Kathy said to Brock, 'Is there really anyone who thinks he's still alive?'

He said nothing for a moment, staring after the departing group, then murmured, 'Yes, Kathy. I rather think there is.'

They joined the last departing group, and passed through the door into a narrow tunnel, walls, ceiling and floor coloured dark blue, which led abruptly into a lobby of dazzling white light. Kathy noticed that the comments and humorous asides quickly died away as they followed their guide through the quarters of Blue Square. It was so stark, so depersonalised, so minimal in its design, that it had a numbing effect on the brain. It took her a while to notice the most telling detail, the complete absence of any of the plethora of controls — plugs, sockets, switches, handles, taps — which are scattered over the walls of any normal room. Here, everything was operated remotely, by men with electronic controls. There was nothing on the smooth bare walls that an inmate could touch to make anything work, to cause a door to open, a toilet to flush, a light to glow.

By the time the party reached the courtyard at the centre of Blue Square, their minds had so adjusted to the purgative effects of all this visual absence that the foliage of the blue larches in the sunlight seemed extravagantly artificial. Conversations began to revive, if cautiously, when they had passed up the ramp to Green Square, where some muted colours were allowed. There was even a light switch or two. But it wasn't until Yellow Square that they were given a narrow glimpse of the outside world, the first time their eyes had been able to focus further than a few metres, and the sight of fens stretching to the distant horizon had a disturbingly agoraphobic effect.

When they finally reached Red Square, the whole group, both sceptics and believers, seemed to recover their spirits. Kathy saw it on the faces of other groups they met there, a sense of relief and of a return to normality. Here were armchairs, newspapers, coffee-making facilities and large picture windows, some of which actually opened to admit the boggy breeze. People were checking their watches, commenting that it had been only an hour, but felt like a lifetime.

On the way back, following a strung-out line of expensive motors across the fen, Brock's phone rang. He grunted into it, agreed to something and shoved it back in his pocket. 'Your friend Mr Oakley wants to speak to me again. With his solicitor this time.'

Kathy felt a knot of anxiety form in her gut.

Paul Oakley and his lawyer wore similar striped ties, as if they belonged to different houses of the same public school.

'Mr Oakley's purpose in requesting this interview is to clarify his statements to you yesterday and answer openly any further questions you may have. But before we begin, he has asked me to make three points.' The solicitor slipped on a pair of gold-framed glasses and consulted his notes. 'First, he feels he was unfairly treated yesterday in that he was allowed to believe the purpose of the meetings was an innocent business contact when in fact it was to gather information about him relating to a possible criminal matter.'

'He was cautioned,' Brock objected.

'But only at the second meeting. In his first meeting there was no indication of the real purpose, and he feels this amounted to deception and entrapment.'

'Go on.' Brock picked up a pen and began doodling, looking bored.

'Secondly, he believes this underhand treatment was inspired by one of your officers who has a personal grudge against my client, and that any suspicion of wrongdoing on his part is malicious, completely unjustified and grossly unfair. And thirdly, he would like it to be known that, if any of your officers denigrates his reputation to any third party, then I am instructed to seek legal redress against that officer.'

'His reputation?' Brock said softly. 'Your client told Sergeant Gurney and myself several very significant lies yesterday. What do you want us to say? That he's an honest man?'

Kathy examined Oakley's face on the screen, apparently unperturbed by this. He had been a copper, after all, and knew the importance of not getting riled.

'He was confused by your unexpected questions about matters in the past, and was provoked to speak without due consideration.'

'The past? He denied knowing a woman he went out of his way to visit just days ago.'

'Phil, may I?' Oakley broke in smoothly, talking to his solicitor as if wanting to borrow his partner on the dance floor.

'Be my guest, old chap.'

'Chief Inspector, I didn't tell you about visiting Ms Langley because I did that as part of an internal procedural review by the laboratories, and I didn't see, frankly, what business it was of yours. I still don't.'

'You weren't asked to assist that review, you got someone else to falsely witness the signature you obtained by deception from Ms Langley, and you lied to us about it. In fact, you behaved exactly like someone trying to cover up the fact that the original loss of important forensic information was your responsibility, not Ms Langley's.'

'Not true. The original mistake was Debbie's, there's no doubt in anyone's mind about that. Ask the other clerks at the lab, ask her supervisor. She was famous for her cock-ups. She was always getting flustered and distracted and losing her place. Look at the notes in her personnel file, the record of warnings and complaints. She was in the wrong job, and as soon as they decently could the lab got rid of her.'

Poor Debbie, Kathy thought, listening to Oakley's hatchet job. But it would be too easy to check for it not to be true, and, remembering the young woman wringing her hands in the front room of her mother's house, Kathy could see it all too clearly.

'But the lab didn't want to turn it into a major industrial relations issue. Debbie was gone, and everyone just wanted to move on. Someone at the lab told me that it would help to have some kind of statement from her, and I volunteered to have a word with her. We'd always got on well, and I was outside the loop, less threatening. Okay, I may have cut a corner or two getting her signature, but it was in everyone's interests, including hers. What was the point of rubbing her nose in it? No hurt feelings, no claims of wrongful dismissal, no problems.'

Oakley sat back, exchanging a look with his lawyer, who nodded at him as if to say, couldn't have put it better myself, old chap.

'Let's turn to your meeting with Sandy Clarke on the twenty-third of May,' Brock said. 'Why did you lie about that? Was that none of our business too?'

Oakley took his time. He put his hand to his mouth in the same gesture Kathy had seen him use the previous day, then stroked his chin and said, 'No, I genuinely didn't remember it.'

Liar, thought Kathy. Too smooth, too bland.

'There was so much going on that week, and, frankly, he didn't make that much of an impression on me.'

'But you remember now, do you?'

Oakley drew a desk diary from his briefcase. 'I checked my old work diary, and found a reference.' He opened it to a marked page and passed it across to Brock, who read the entry aloud.

'"Eleven a.m. S. Clarke, partner Verge, his request — purpose? Pen — he to advise Chivers." Would you interpret that for us?'

'Well, as far as I can. First of all, the meeting was at his request — he'd phoned me the previous day to arrange it. And at the end of the meeting I was still unclear what the purpose had been. He talked about the effects of the publicity on his business and the morale of staff, etcetera, but I told him that he should speak to Superintendent Chivers about all of that. Then he asked how long the forensic tests would take, and when they could have access to the apartment again, and I described our progress in general terms.

I seem to remember he asked about the DNA samples we'd taken from some of the staff, including him, and whether they'd be destroyed after the case was over. It was all rather vague, and I got a bit impatient, as I had things to do.'

'What's this reference to "Pen"?'

'Yes, he slipped that in at the end. I didn't really follow what he was saying at first. It seems that when he discovered the body he had a few minutes alone in the bedroom while the other person with him went to raise the alarm, and during this time he noticed a pair of his glasses and a pen of his lying in the room. He showed them to me, a silver pen and reading specs. He said he'd had no idea what they were doing there, and that either Verge or his wife must have picked them up by mistake. Anyway, he'd pocketed them, because there was no doubt they were his, and he wondered now if he'd done the wrong thing. I said he should tell Chivers, and he agreed. Then he asked if there were any other unexplained objects in the apartment that the police were interested in, and I said again that he should speak to Chivers, but I wasn't aware of any. He seemed, I don't know, over-anxious about the whole thing. I put it down to delayed shock.'

'Did you report this to Superintendent Chivers?'

'No, I left that to Clarke. There was too much else on the boil.'

'Your memory seems to have made a remarkable recovery, Mr Oakley. Anything else?'

'That's the lot.'

'Pity you didn't tell us all this yesterday.'

'Yes, well, like Phil said, if you'd gone about things differently, I might well have been able to. No hard feelings, eh?'

'One last thing. We'd like an account of your movements on the Monday before last, the seventeenth.'

'What?' Oakley looked shocked and his solicitor began to protest, but then Oakley stopped him, face grim. 'Doesn't matter, Phil. We'll give the gentlemen what they want.' He pulled his electronic diary out of his briefcase and began to tap. In the event, his alibi for the evening on which Sandy Clarke had died could hardly have been more solid. The previous evening, Sunday, he and a friend had flown to Dublin, where Oakley had grown up. They had stayed there two nights, returning on the Tuesday morning. The friend was a police officer, Sergeant Leon Desai.

245

· · ·

Another envelope with her name in the familiar handwriting was waiting for Kathy at her desk. She steeled herself and opened it this time with hardly a tremor. Another forensic report form. Two samples, identified by number and a brief description, were listed at the top of the sheet, and beneath, in someone else's handwriting, the words 'Positive match'.

This must have been meant for someone else, she thought, then recognised her car number in the description of one of the samples. She read the descriptions again, then a third time as realisation came. One was the trace of material found on the broken glass in her car window, smashed on the fourteenth of September, and the other was the leather fibres found on the adhesive tape attached to the hosepipe used to gas Sandy Clarke on the seventeenth of September. Fibres from the same source, a pair of gloves most likely, three days and twenty miles apart.

25

'I've just spoken to the local police,' Kathy said. 'They had nothing to tell me.'

'Take me through that day again,' Brock asked. On the desk in front of him he had the report sheet that Leon had sent to Kathy, together with the original forensic reports on Clarke's suicide and Kathy's car.

Kathy consulted her notebook. 'Friday the fourteenth, the day you interviewed Sandy Clarke, and he thought you'd discovered that he was the father of Charlotte's baby because of his DNA. You asked me to go out to Buckinghamshire to speak to Charlotte, to check his story. I phoned her to say I was coming, and drove out there in my own car, the Renault. I got there about two-thirty p.m., and stayed for half an hour. She was angry that Clarke had told us about Atlanta and the baby, and seemed keen to keep it a secret, but she confirmed his account. On my way back to London, I stopped at a new supermarket outside Amersham and did some grocery shopping. I suppose I was inside for about twenty minutes, and when I came out I found the side window smashed and things missing from my car — the CD player, sunglasses and my briefcase containing the transcript of Clarke's interview. I noticed that another car next to mine had been broken into as well. It was about the same age as mine, a blue Ford, and didn't have an alarm. I went back into the supermarket to report it to the manager, who admitted they'd had a few similar break-ins.'

She turned the page of her notebook. 'While I was in the car park

I got a phone call from Robert, the administrator for the committee I'm on, wanting me to meet him urgently at headquarters, so I didn't hang around to talk to the local cops. I left my details and returned to London.'

'What else was in your briefcase?'

'There was a small calculator … some notepaper, envelopes and stamps. The Clarke transcript was in a red plastic folder. There was a London A–Z. And I think there may have been the book that goes with my Spanish language tapes. I haven't seen it since. The local police said nothing's been recovered.' Something else niggled at the back of Kathy's mind, but she couldn't pin it down. Then she remembered. 'There was something else. The scrapbook you gave me to look at, Stewart and Miranda's. It was in my briefcase too.'

Brock looked up sharply.

'I'm sorry,' she said, thinking of all the work they had put into it.

He shrugged. 'Not your fault. I'll make it up to them. You must have been followed from Charlotte's house to the supermarket.'

'Yes.' Kathy looked glum. 'Though I can't imagine how they could have done it without me spotting them. The lanes are narrow and twisting around there, and they would have to have stayed close not to lose me. And as far as I can remember, there's nowhere near the cottage that they could have waited in a vehicle out of sight.'

'You didn't discuss going to the supermarket with Charlotte?'

'No, but her grandmother was there, Madelaine Verge. It was she who recommended it. She gave me some sauce she was making, and suggested I buy some fish to go with it. I told her I needed some groceries anyway, and she told me about the new supermarket.'

'And Charlotte heard this conversation?'

'I think so. Yes, I'd forgotten that. They both would have known I was going there.'

'But did they know about the Clarke transcript — assuming that's what the thief was after?'

'Charlotte certainly did. I referred to it while I was talking to her, and she wanted to read it. I said she couldn't. I don't think she would have told her grandmother about it. She seemed anxious to keep it secret.'

'Well, I don't believe that Madelaine Verge was capable of driving after you and breaking into your car, but I suppose it's just conceivable that Charlotte might. Or alternatively one or other of them could have contacted someone else who came after you. Sandy Clarke, perhaps. That would explain the same gloves being used in both places. Except that we never found the gloves at Clarke's house.'

'Why would he want to rob my car? He already knew what was on the transcript, and could ask for a copy any time he wanted.'

'He might have been after something else. Perhaps he thought you had the whole file on him. This was at a time when he knew he was under suspicion. Maybe Charlotte phoned him and said you'd just been there, brandishing a file on him, and he saw a chance to find out how much we knew or suspected.'

'We can check her phone records for that day.'

Brock lifted the phone and made a short call, then replaced the receiver and began turning the pages of the reports in front of him, reading them again. Finally he asked, 'What did you make of Oakley this afternoon?'

Kathy's mind filled with one thought, a thought she had been suppressing with considerable force since watching Oakley's interview — that Leon had gone to Dublin with him on the same day she had left for Spain, when he had been so desperate for time to finish his university assignment. The thought burned so brightly that she couldn't see past it to answer Brock's question. 'I ... I'm not sure.'

'Did he sound plausible, do you think?'

Yes, she thought, this time he had seemed plausible, and she sensed that Brock and Bren had felt that too, becoming less aggressive in their questioning. 'Some bits, certainly. The bits we can check.'

'Yes. How about the meeting he had with Clarke?'

Kathy forced herself to concentrate, wondering what Brock was leading to. 'That seemed inconclusive. I thought there must have been more to it than he was saying.'

'What did you make of the bit about Clarke's pen and glasses?'

'That didn't make much sense.'

'Can we believe Oakley?'

Kathy thought. 'Probably. I mean it doesn't do him any credit, does it? He should have reported it to Chivers.'

'Exactly. He probably thinks Clarke did tell Chivers, and that now we're wondering why he didn't report it himself, so he decided to come clean. But if Oakley is telling the truth about that, what does it mean?'

'I don't know. Why would Clarke mention it? It could only tend to place him at the scene and incriminate him.'

'And why didn't he refer to it in his confession, when he did mention his lost driving glove? Suppose he was genuinely mystified by it, and worried enough to try to pursue it. Imagine for a moment that he didn't kill Miki and Charles. He's called up to the bedroom, to the shocking scene of Miki's corpse. Then, while he's waiting for help to arrive, he notices things that belong to him. He thinks he must have left them there on the Friday night, and he doesn't want to have to explain what he was doing in her bedroom then, so he snatches them up and looks around desperately for anything else incriminating. But later, he becomes increasingly certain that he never had that pen and that pair of glasses with him on the Friday night. How had they got there? Had someone deliberately planted them?'

'The murderer,' Kathy said. 'Charles Verge.'

And catching the expression on Brock's face, she understood for the first time his odd detours around the fens of that morning, and his sense of expectancy when they reached Marchdale. 'You've been thinking this for some time, haven't you? You do think he's still alive.'

'Just a private doubt, Kathy. Let's keep it that way.'

'You've thought this all along?'

'I wasn't sure, but when I spoke to Gail Lewis she seemed to confirm my doubts. And then I became worried. If Verge really is the killer then she may be at risk too, and perhaps others. It depends how rational he is.'

'Did you really think he might show up at the Marchdale opening?'

'It seemed too good an idea to ignore. But perhaps he had other eyes and ears there to witness the event for him. Because, if he is here among us, I think it's a fair bet that he's got help, don't you?'

'And Oakley is in the clear?'

'I believe he is. Oh, if he'd been better at his job he might have picked up Debbie Langley's error, and he should have made a report of his meeting with Sandy Clarke. I'm sure Leon would have done. I doubt if it goes further than that.' Then he added, 'Leon did well to pick up this match between the two traces. Did you ask him to chase it up?'

'No, he must have done it off his own bat.' Neat Leon, efficient

Leon, badly needing to prove something, Kathy thought.

Brock said, 'Odd that he should be such good pals with Oakley. I'd have thought they'd be opposites, really. No?'

They were interrupted by Brock's phone. He listened for a moment, then thanked the caller and hung up. 'They've checked Charlotte's phone records. It wasn't used within an hour of your visit. We'll have to find out Clarke's movements that afternoon, but if it wasn't him, who else could it have been? Someone Charlotte could confide in, someone in the neighbourhood.'

'Someone like George ...' Kathy said softly.

'Who?'

'The gardener. We saw him at Marchdale, remember? Helping with Madelaine's wheelchair. He was working in the garden the day I spoke to Charlotte. He would have seen how upset she got — he might even have overheard some of what we said. He certainly seems to be devoted to her. She could have got him to follow me and steal the transcript.'

'And then kill Clarke?'

They both thought about that, chilled by the idea of Charlotte, fragile and pregnant, arranging the death of the father of her child. And for what reason? To stifle the scandal of the child's parentage? To restore her adored father's reputation? And they both made the same calculations — armed with the information in Clarke's transcript, the person who broke into Kathy's car had three days in which to concoct the suicide message, perhaps taken to Clarke's house as a typed letter on which they planned to plant his fingerprints and a scrawled signature, but instead transferred it to the convenient laptop. Would they both have gone to visit Clarke that evening, Charlotte to gain entry, drug Clarke and type the note, George to do the heavy work of arranging the death scene?

'What do we know about this George?'

'Almost nothing. He was there the first time I went to Orchard Cottage, and Madelaine Verge told me that he had been sort of adopted by Charles when he was doing the research for Marchdale. He was either an inmate or an ex-con, and Charles took him on as a handyman and gardener. I don't even know his surname.'

'I don't remember any reference to Dick Chivers' team interviewing him.'

'I suppose he wouldn't have seemed relevant. He's sort of invisible, in the background, doing odd jobs and the garden, keeping an eye on things. Charlotte spoke of him almost as if he were a kind of chaperone, like her grandmother, who seems to spend most of her time there now.'

Brock recalled Gail Lewis's comment about Verge appearing to have established a haven for his daughter in Buckinghamshire, 'an alternative happy little family' she'd called it. And now here was another player, George the handyman.

Kathy was thinking of the lizard doctor, Javier Lizancos, and his clinic behind the gym at Sitges. You automatically assumed, of course, that the purpose of plastic surgery was to restore, to beautify, to make younger, but presumably it could equally do the opposite, disfigure and age. And she also thought of the look of triumph on George's face that morning at the opening of the prison.

'This may sound a bit far-fetched,' she said, 'but George is the same height and build as Verge, wouldn't you say? I don't suppose it's possible ...' She hesitated to put the idea into words, sure that Brock would find it absurd. But she looked up and saw that he was nodding.

'Can't be difficult to find out,' he said.

Brock filled his lungs. 'Lavender, cows, autumn foliage. This is a real haven, Ms Verge. A bower.'

Charlotte wasn't impressed. She eyed him over the swell of her belly and said, 'What exactly did you want?'

She hadn't put on any electric lights, and the evening glow from the small window barely penetrated the shadows of the far corners of the room. Most of the wall surfaces were covered with shelves of books, with the tall volumes on art, design and architecture at the bottom. Brock raised his chin towards the novels packed up to the low ceiling.

'You're a great reader, I see. You obviously appreciate fiction.'

No response.

'You must excuse me,' Brock went on with a deep sigh. 'It's been a long day, and this armchair is very comfortable. Why we're here, yes. We're required to prepare a report for the coroner who'll be conducting the inquest into Sandy Clarke's death. We have to outline his life

in the days leading up to his death, and, as far as we can, any indications of his state of mind. We interviewed him on the morning of
Friday the fourteenth of September, but unfortunately we have very
little information about his movements after that time. His wife left
him alone at their Greenwich Park house on that Friday evening to
go to stay with her mother, and she didn't see him alive again. Nor
did any of his work colleagues or neighbours, as far as we've been able
to establish. Now, we know that you and your baby must have been
very much in his thoughts at that time, and we wondered if he had
been in contact with you at all over that weekend.'

'No.'

'You're quite sure? You may remember that Friday was the day
that Sergeant Kolla here came to speak to you about Mr Clarke's
claim that he was the father of your child.'

'Yes, of course I remember, and no, I didn't have any contact
with him at that time.'

'What about other people here? Is your grandmother still
with you?'

'She's in her room. She was very tired after the trip to Marchdale
this morning, and she's gone to bed early. I don't want you to disturb
her. She would have told me, anyway, if Sandy had called.'

'All right. Anyone else? Do you have a cleaning lady?'

'No.'

Kathy said, 'What about your gardener, Charlotte? Is he here at
the moment?'

'No. He drove us back from Marchdale, then left. But he
wouldn't know anything.'

'All the same, we might check. What's his name and address,
Ms Verge?'

She seemed on the point of refusing, but then relented with a
frown of irritation. 'George Todd, but there's no point to this. He
lives in the village.' She gave an address and phone number.

'Thanks. How long have you known him?'

'Since I moved in. The end of June.'

'Oh, I thought you came here before your father ... before he
disappeared.'

'He bought the cottage for me in March, but there was a lot
needed doing to it. George worked on it for about three months.'

'And did you see him during that time, while he was working on the house?'

'No, Dad said it was always a disaster for the client to visit their building while it was being refurbished. George contacted me at the end of June, when it was ready, and helped me move in.'

'So you didn't actually see George in person till the end of June?'

'That's right. What are you getting at?'

'It's not important.' Brock tucked his book back in his jacket pocket. 'Looks as if we disturbed you for nothing. Impressive ceremony this morning. Were you all pleased with how it went?'

Charlotte eased herself to her feet with difficulty. 'Except for what you said to Gran, about some people thinking my father is still alive.' She glared accusingly at Brock. 'What did you mean? You really upset her.'

'Oh, I'm sorry. I certainly didn't intend that. I was just making a general point, that she should be prepared for the fact that some people will never be satisfied until Mr Verge's body has been found, that's all.' He gave her a bland, sympathetic smile, and watched the frown of distrust deepen on the young woman's brow.

As they were walking down the front path, she called after them, 'Oh, and there's no point you trying to talk to George anyway. He's gone away.'

'Away?' Brock turned. 'Where to?'

'I don't know. He mentioned it when we got back from Marchdale. He said he was going away for a few days.'

There were lights on in the front room of the house, the end of a row of old brick terraces on the edge of the village. The woman who answered the door wiped her hands on her apron and looked at Brock's identification anxiously.

'Oh dear. George rents the attic room, but he's not here just now. Why?'

'We're anxious to talk to him. We understand he's gone away for a few days. Do you know where?'

'He didn't say. He's a private sort of person. He's not got into trouble again, has he? I know he's on parole, but he's never been the slightest bother to us.'

She agreed to take them up to his room, which confirmed her claim that George Todd was the cleanest tenant she'd ever had. Everything was spotless. The few clothes in the wardrobe, including the suit they'd seen him wearing that morning, were immaculately folded and creased. The kettle and toaster on top of a small food cupboard were spotless. The small fridge was empty, wiped clean. On a shelf stood an orderly row of books concerned with horticulture, looking as immaculate as when they'd left the shop. The room reminded Kathy of a prison cell, ready for inspection.

When they were back in the car, Brock said, 'This is making me feel very uneasy, Kathy, but let's not jump to conclusions too soon. We'll keep your theory to ourselves for the moment. We'd better get it right. I've a feeling no one's going to be happy about this.'

'One malicious wounding with intent to resist arrest, two woundings with intent to do grievous bodily harm, three aggravated assaults with intent to rob, sixty-seven convictions for theft, five for handling stolen goods.' Brock paused, scanning the piece of paper in his hand. They were all staring at an enlarged photograph of a tough, battered face, the left side covered by livid scar tissue. Kathy barely recognised the gardener or the man pushing Madelaine's wheelchair at the Marchdale opening.

'So approach with caution,' Brock continued. 'Aged fifty-five years, of which eighteen have been spent in gaol, twelve in category A prisons. George Todd is currently on parole. An alert was issued last night, but so far we have no idea of his current whereabouts. We believe he may have information relating to the Verge case, and we want to know his whereabouts on the afternoon of September fourteenth, when DS Kolla's car was broken into, and the evening of September seventeenth, when Sandy Clarke died. We are also looking for a pair of black leather gloves, traces of which have been found at both scenes. Apart from the rented room where he lives, we also have warrants to search the two places where he is known to work regularly as a gardener and handyman — Orchard Cottage, belonging to Ms Charlotte Verge, and Briar Hill, owned by Ms Luz Diaz — and also the house of Mrs Madelaine Verge in Chelsea, which Todd also visited. Apart from gloves, we are interested in tools that might have been used to break the car window, any written notes resembling Sandy Clarke's suicide statement, and anything which might belong to, or indicate recent contact with, Charles Verge.'

People looked puzzled. 'You mean recent as in before May twelfth, chief? When he died?'

'No, I mean since May twelfth. I mean like in the last few weeks.'

This produced a murmur of consternation. Brock's raised hand restored an expectant hush. 'The coroner will expect us to be thorough. In the absence of Verge's body, we'll be expected to be able to say categorically that he's left no recent traces, and these women are the people who would have been closest to him, the ones he'd most likely have tried to contact, if he'd still been alive.'

'We're to search the whole properties, sir? Not just the out-buildings where Todd might have kept his tools?'

'Everywhere, but do it tactfully. If they ask, explain that you're looking for something Todd might have hidden or mislaid. Don't tell them you're looking for traces of Verge — that'll only upset them.'

You can say that again, Kathy thought, picturing the reaction of the three women to this violation. It was as if Brock were planning to put his hand into a beehive. The team looked doubtful too, perhaps imagining trying to explain to Madelaine Verge that they were searching her underwear drawers for something that her gardener might have hidden or mislaid. For once Kathy was glad that she would be tied up all that day with her committee.

The Crime Strategy Working Party was going well under Kathy's chairmanship, so everyone agreed, and she could only assume it was one of those cases of something going right when you'd paid it no attention, because she'd hardly given it any serious thought since Leon had left. She sat through the rest of the day half listening to the others excitedly discussing institutionalised racism and homo-phobia, and wondered how she was going to get through another weekend, and how Brock and the rest of the team were making out. When Jay spoke to her in the lunchbreak about the arrangements for Saturday night, it took her a while to remember what the other woman was talking about.

'Do you know the pub on the corner of Old Compton Street? I thought we could all meet up there. What do you think?'

'Oh, fine. Yes, that would be fine.'

Jay lowered her voice, and looked sheepish. 'I know you're a copper and everything, but when you're off-duty, you're off-duty, right?'

'How do you mean?' But Kathy knew exactly what she meant.

'Well, some of my friends like ...' Jay stopped as Shazia, balancing a paper plate of sandwiches and a cup of orange juice, joined them. They didn't get a chance to finish the conversation, and afterwards Kathy wondered what she was getting herself into.

Brock rocked forward on the balls of his feet, absorbing the confrontation between stubble fields and hedgerows out there, and stainless steel and leather cushions in here. It was a platitude of modern architecture, he knew, but it still had the power to shock, the unmediated impact of room and landscape through a sheet of naked glass.

Luz Diaz stood with her back to him, arms folded, smoking angrily. 'I cannot believe that this is permitted in this country. It is worse than Franco.'

'I'm sorry, Ms Diaz. But the coroner ...'

'Fuck the coroner!' She spun around to face him. 'That's just an excuse. You know what I think? I think you enjoy breaking into people's houses and turning over their private things. I think you are no different from criminals.'

'Did you know that your gardener had an extensive criminal record?'

'George? Yes, of course I knew. Charles told me all about George, ages ago, before I even came here. He met him in prison, when he was working on the Marchdale project. Is that all you see? A man has a record, so that's it? Do you look beyond that? Do you know anything about him?'

'Tell me.'

'He was a model prisoner, doing a degree in horticulture with the Open University. No, he was *the* model prisoner, that is what the prison governor told Charles — the best, the most responsive prisoner he had ever met. And he had had a terrible life. Did you know that he witnessed his father murder his mother when he was five? Did you know that he was shockingly abused by the relatives who took him in, and then again when he was put into care?'

The blaze of anger in her eyes died a little as she took in Brock's look of concern. 'No, I didn't know that.'

'Well, you should do better research, Chief Inspector. George is probably the most trustworthy and honest man I know. What do you suspect him of doing?'

'I can't say at present. But your assessment of his character is very helpful.'

'You're just saying that to calm me down, yes?' But despite her words, Brock saw that her stabs at her cigarette were less violent. 'You believe that once a thief, always a thief, right?'

'I think it's very hard for any of us to change a pattern that's shaped our whole lives.'

Luz frowned at him. 'So you would say that once we have decided what we are going to do with our lives — you a policeman, Charles an architect, me a painter — that those things then lock us into their own patterns? You think after thirty years of thinking and acting in our different ways, we're so shaped by the experience that we simply can't change?'

'Something like that.'

She stared back at him as if trying to provoke him into saying more, then broke into a smile. 'But people do it all the time, don't they? And in your heart I bet you believe that you could still be anything you want. And George is the proof that you can be. He overcame his past and changed himself.'

Brock smiled back. 'We'll see, Ms Diaz. We'll see.' Then he added, 'Is that why George was important to Charles, because he was able to change himself, like a hermit crab throwing off its shell?'

Luz looked startled. 'Why do you say that? That was ...' She stopped herself and turned away, crushing her cigarette into a glass bowl. 'George was a resource, that's all. Charles paid him as a consultant, because he knew everything about prisons from the inside.'

'I see.' There was a thump from the floor below, a muffled curse, and Luz stiffened. 'If those bastards break anything ... I have jars of pigment down there from Venice. It's the only place in the world you can get it. You'd better tell them ...'

'Don't worry, they know their job. And is that why you left Barcelona, to change yourself? Or your painting, perhaps? Your colours are so bright and clear, the geometry so sharp — will that survive this damp English light?' He nodded out to the view, where evening mist was seeping out of the copses.

'I haven't experienced an English winter yet,' she said, lighting another cigarette. 'But perhaps it is the reason, yes. We all need a change of perspective from time to time. Something to make us think and feel in fresh ways. A change of palette ...'

Another dull thud sounded from below and Luz wheeled around and made for the spiral staircase. 'I'm going to see what those people are doing.'

Brock remained in the artist's studio, going over to a shelf of books. Most of them were gallery exhibition catalogues, many with pages marked by slips of paper. When he opened them he found illustrations of her work. They dated back over ten years, from private galleries in Barcelona, Madrid, San Francisco and New York.

George Todd's yellow motorbike was spotted early that afternoon, twenty-four hours after he had disappeared, parked outside a small holiday hotel in Bexhill, the place where Charles Verge had supposedly walked into the sea. Todd had apparently booked into the hotel the previous evening. Within half an hour he had been located in a pub less than a hundred yards away, and begun the journey back to London under escort.

Now he sat on the other side of the table, painstakingly rubbing his fingertips with a handkerchief. Brock could see no remaining traces of the ink, but still he rubbed and scoured.

'I thought you scanned them electronically now,' Todd said softly. 'What's the point, anyway? Did you think I were someone else?' A Yorkshire accent. He looked up from his scrubbing with a glint in his eye, as if relishing some private joke. 'Who did you reckon I was then, Charles Verge?'

Brock said nothing. The idea did seem far-fetched now, a clutching at straws.

It was hard not to stare at Todd. There was a fastidious intensity about his gestures, which contrasted oddly with the anarchy of his damaged features. Brock noted the creases down the arms of his shirt, the way he folded the handkerchief neatly before replacing it in his pocket. The crew that had searched his toolshed at Orchard Cottage had commented on how obsessively neat everything was, like in his rented room. Brock had seen it before, the model prisoners who responded to the order and discipline of prison that had been so absent from their early lives. More than one of the assessors in Todd's file had diagnosed an obsessive-compulsive personality disorder.

'What were you doing at Bexhill?'

'I wanted a few days' holiday. Decided to go down to the seaside.'

'To the place where Charles Verge was supposed to have disappeared.'

Another private smirk. 'Seemed as good a place as any.'

'When did you first meet Mr Verge?'

'Two, two and a half years ago.'

'That was at …' Brock consulted his notes.

'HMP Maidstone. He was doing research.'

'How did he come to meet you?'

'I was picked, by the governor, to talk to him about my experiences. We hit it off. I was able to put him right on a few things.'

Brock wondered if the two men had recognised something of themselves in the other. 'What sort of things?'

'He was interested in how people feel when they're inside, how their attitudes change over time, what makes them tick. Then later on, when he was working on his plans, we talked about them. I helped him design Marchdale.' The claim was made flatly, without bombast.

'Did he pay you for your help?'

'He insisted. He called me a consultant, and put money into an account for me, for when I got out. Don't worry, it were all declared. I paid tax on it.'

'And you got out last January? What did you do then?'

'He invited me to work for his family, as a general handyman and gardener. I got Orchard Cottage ready for Miss Charlotte, painting and wallpapering and repairs, and I do the gardens and other odds and ends for her, and for Mrs Madelaine Verge and Ms Diaz at Briar Hill. Ask them. I'm a good worker.'

Brock didn't doubt it, and moved on to Todd's whereabouts at the time of Kathy's car break-in and Clarke's suicide. He had been working in Charlotte's garden at the time of the first, he said, though whether she or her grandmother had seen him there all afternoon he couldn't say. As for the second, he thought he had been at home that evening, probably watching TV, but he couldn't be sure. The absence of a firm alibi didn't encourage Brock. None of the teams had found a pair of black gloves, or anything else incriminating.

It was six p.m. before Kathy returned to Queen Anne's Gate from her committee meeting. She passed Brock on the front steps. Clearly he was in a hurry, buttoning his coat against the chill with one hand, the other clutching a briefcase, a preoccupied frown on his face. He grunted hello, unsmiling, and marched off down the street in the direction of headquarters.

Bren was inside in the lobby, consulting the appointments book.

'What's up with the boss?' Kathy asked.

'Shit and fan have connected, Kathy. Phones have been melting, explanations demanded.'

'The searches?'

Bren nodded gloomily. 'Not a thing. No black leather gloves, no hidden messages, not even a trace of an illicit substance in Todd's medicine cabinet. You heard we found him, did you? Sitting in a pub at Bexhill having a quiet beer. Said he was having a seaside break.'

'Really?' Kathy was stunned, and realised how convinced she had become that Todd and Verge were the same man.

'And he's definitely who he says he is?'

'Sure. We took his prints and DNA, and had his parole officer in.'

'Does he have an alibi for the times on the fourteenth and seventeenth?'

'Convincingly vague. He runs a motorbike, by the way. Yellow Honda, with a black crash helmet. You don't remember seeing it in the supermarket car park, do you?'

Kathy thought. 'Sorry, no. And the women have complained?'

'Long and loud, in person and through legal representatives, and to higher authorities. Brock's just been called in to see Sharpe. Hell, it isn't as if we couldn't have seen it coming. What was in his mind, do you know, Kathy? It was almost as if he believed that Charles Verge was still alive.'

Kathy shook her head.

'I can just hear Sharpe telling him he's being obsessive. And it's true. Well, isn't it?'

'I don't know, Bren. I really don't.'

'And how certain is this match of the leather fibres?' Sharpe demanded.

'Ninety-seven per cent,' Brock replied.

'Ninety-seven per cent certain of what?' Sharpe insisted. 'That they're from the same glove, or from the same *type* of glove, or from a *similar* piece of black leather?'

'A piece of leather processed in the same way, using the same dye.'

'And that covers what percentage of the total number of leather items on sale in London?'

'I don't know.'

'There could be hundreds of matches for these samples, yes? Thousands maybe. One might be from a bag and the other from a glove, or the sleeve of a jacket, or a shoe. You see my point?'

'Yes, sir.'

'And you must have realised this, yet you persisted. Why?'

'I said when we met a week ago that I felt it was premature to close the investigation, sir, especially in the absence of a body.'

Sharpe's face hardened, his voice taking on a repetitive stress as if he were reciting an obvious truth or a nursery rhyme. 'And I made it quite plain to you that the case was over. I congratulated you on a brilliant result. I made it crystal clear that everyone was completely satisfied.' He reached for a file and slammed it down in front of Brock. It was open at a record of a meeting dated the twentieth of September. The wording was almost identical to what Sharpe had just said.

'You seem intent on shooting yourself in the foot, Brock. Almost obsessional about it. Why is that?' Sharpe stopped pacing and sat down. 'I've assured the three women that neither they nor their gardener will be disturbed again, and that the case is closed. You'll write to them yourself, today, and confirm this, and apologise for any inconvenience and distress. All right?'

'Yes, sir.' He felt ten years old again, in the headmaster's study, the only one of the Black Hand Gang to have been caught wiping boot polish on doorhandles on April Fool's Day.

'And I want a copy of the letters for my file.' Sharpe filled his lungs and relaxed slowly. 'Anyway, on a brighter note, your DS Kolla seems to be acquitting herself extremely well on the Working Party committee. Robert is very pleased with her, tells me she's taken it by the scruff of the neck and made it perform. Excellent leadership qualities, he says. Focused. Sound.'

Sound was Sharpe's favourite quality, Brock knew. He was in no doubt that his own soundness quotient had taken a dive.

'You might learn a thing or two from her, Brock.'

He stopped for a double scotch at a pub on the way back, a little place packed with office workers in no hurry to get home. They jostled and laughed too loudly at their own jokes, shouting their orders through the smoke to the girls behind the bar, and after ten minutes Brock felt a little better. He fought his way out onto the street and continued back to the annexe in Queen Anne's Gate. It occupied a four-storey brick terrace of what had once been indiviual houses, later connected by a warren of doors and corridors and converted to offices, most recently belonging to a publisher. In a few years it would change its use again, Brock thought, and no one would remember or care what he and his people had done here.

He stopped at an office on the second floor when he saw Kathy inside working at her computer. 'Sorry I was a bit abrupt earlier,' he said. 'Was in a bit of a hurry.'

'Bren said there was trouble.'

As she looked up from the screen Brock was struck by how dark the shadows around her eyes seemed, how hollow her cheeks. Or perhaps it was just the light. 'A call to order from above. The Verge case is closed. Drop it, forget it.'

'I'm sorry.'

'Oh, maybe they're right. We had our chance. Look, I've got some paperwork to clear up, but do you fancy a meal later on?'

'Yes, okay. That would be fine.'

After he'd gone she sat for a while thinking about the Verge case, then, inevitably, about Leon, then back to Verge. She thought of Brock's conviction that they'd got it wrong, his fear that Verge might strike again, and her absurd notion about Todd. It was so easy to see threats and shadows where none existed.

Her phone rang, Brock's voice, but sounding odd, asking her to come to his office. When she got there she was startled to see the blank, stunned look on his face.

'You all right?' she asked.

'Sit down.' He shook himself, ran a hand across his eyes. 'I just had a call from Suzanne. She happened to mention that the children had met up with someone we know, someone on the force, she assumed. Yesterday afternoon, they were coming home from school, and he met them outside the shop.'

Kathy visualised the children in their school uniforms outside the front of Suzanne's antiques shop and home on the High Street in Battle, wondering what this was leading to.

'He called them by their names, and said that he was a good friend of ours, and that he'd heard they were very interested in the Verge case. He said he'd heard they'd made their own dossier of the case, and it was a very good piece of work.'

Now Kathy understood. She felt a chill as she recalled the title page of the scrapbook that had been taken from her car, with the children's names, ages and address.

'Could they describe him?'

'Oldish man, funny accent, and he spoke to them in an odd way, with the left side of his face turned away.'

'Oh God.'

'It's a threat, Kathy, or a warning.'

'Yes.'

'That's what Todd was up to.'

'What can we do?' And that, Kathy realised, was the big question, the reason why Brock was immobilised instead of calling all hell down upon the head of George Todd.

'Sharpe won't let me act on this without some confirmation,' Brock said. 'I'll go down there now, and try to get something concrete from the kids. Maybe Sharpe will agree to an identification parade.' He said it without conviction. 'At the least I can get Suzanne to take them away somewhere safe for a while.'

For how long, she thought, and what then?

'I'm sorry, Brock. I feel this is my fault, with the scrapbook.'

'Nonsense, it was sheer bad luck. At least it confirms that Todd is tied up in this. If the worst comes to the worst, I'll take the bastard away for another little holiday, and beat the truth out of him.'

'What can I do?'

'Nothing. Absolutely nothing.' He got to his feet and began shoving documents into his briefcase. 'I'd better go.'

Kathy felt helpless. 'I'll see you on Monday. You won't do anything till then, will you?'

He smiled grimly. 'Don't worry. Have a good weekend.'

Later, sitting alone in her office, she came to a conclusion. She picked up her phone and rang the number of a twenty-four hour ticketing agency.

26

In view of the tools she was carrying, Kathy had checked her bag in at Heathrow, though she had brought little else. After retrieving it from the carousel at El Prat, she made for the car-rental desks on the ground floor and hired a little Seat like the one she'd had before. Thinking of her current bank balance, she decided not to pay extra for additional damage insurance. It was the last Saturday in September, the sky outside was pale blue, the temperature mild, and a fresh easterly breeze spiked the jet-engine fumes with the tang of salty sea air. She wound the window down and headed south. By two p.m. she was driving along the waterfront of Sitges.

It was only ten days since she'd been here, yet it seemed like another period of her life entirely, a time of innocence, of unforgivable naivety. There was the café where she had written the postcard to Leon, imagining that they would return here together, perhaps — who could tell? — on a honeymoon. And all the time that she had been playing the detective in Spain, thinking that she might find the answers that had eluded everyone else, she had been oblivious to the unravelling of her own life. On the very same Sunday that she had come to Barcelona, Leon had gone with Paul Oakley to Dublin. On the Tuesday, when she'd been looking for clues in the Mies van der Rohe Pavilion, he had returned to London, and on the Wednesday, while she was writing her postcard, he had been removing his stuff from her flat. She felt a sense of bitter satisfaction now at the cruel synchronicity, as if she'd deserved to be hurt, for being so unaware, so smug.

Not any more. This time, right or wrong, she would set the agenda. She turned the car and drove to the Apollo-Sitges Fitness Club.

It had an abandoned air, the front door closed, an empty Coke bottle standing on the front step. She rapped on the door and noticed a sign hanging behind its glass panel. Its printed letters announced that it was 'tancat', and beneath, in a felt pen scrawl, 'closed'. When she walked down the side lane to the rear yard she found an empty dustbin, and plastic bags blown against the foot of the roller door. She tried the intercom and found that it was dead.

Kathy returned to her car and drove back to the seafront. She had missed lunch and felt hungry. She took a seat at the Bar Chiringuito overlooking the beach and ordered sardines, bread and mineral water from an old man who bustled about as if run off his feet, although she was the only customer. Afterwards, she drove through the town until she found a cinema, and fell asleep watching a love story she couldn't follow.

Daylight was fading when she emerged from the theatre. The streetlights were lit, groups of young people strolling, window shopping, wearing jumpers or jackets against the cool evening breeze. When she got back to her car she pulled on her black tracksuit top with the hood, and packed her tools in a small backpack that she slipped under her seat. She took her time making her way back across town, letting the sky turn completely black, and parked a block away from the gym. It was a neighbourhood of small hotels, out of season now, and houses on narrow lots. Shrubs and trees spilled over the dividing walls, and there was a smell of pine resin in the night air. She met no pedestrians and almost no vehicles on the street as she approached the unlit building.

She pulled on latex gloves and used the rubbish bin in the yard at the end of the lane to haul herself up onto the parapet of the rear building. On the way up she examined the burglar-alarm box mounted over the side doorway, and thought it looked new. She crouched behind the parapet, catching her breath and getting her bearings. The sky was clear of cloud, and there was a pale light from a half moon as well as the reflected glow from streetlights.

It looked to her as if the building had been constructed in two stages. The gym at the front, facing the street, would have been the original part — once a garage, perhaps, or a workshop. It had a pitched roof spanning the width of the plot, and Kathy recalled the industrial steel trusses she had seen inside the gym. The rear half of the building looked more recent, and had a flat roof, on which Kathy was now squatting. Windowless, its natural light was provided by rows of square roof lights raised on kerbs above the granulated roof surface. As she moved forward to have a closer look at them, she caught sight of a lit window in a neighbouring building, the white light of a TV flickering soundlessly inside.

The roof lights looked strong and new and, Kathy guessed, alarmed. Their plastic surface was thick and translucent, so that when she shone her flashlight the beam couldn't penetrate to illuminate the interior below. Kathy imagined the filtered milky light that would come from them, as if the people beneath didn't want the sight of a cloud or the sound of a dog barking to disturb whatever they did down there.

She walked the length of the flat roofed section and came to the triangular gable of concrete blockwork that formed the back wall of the gym. There were roof lights in that section too, she recalled, remembering daylight in the gym, but there they were formed simply as panels of clear corrugated plastic inset into the metal roof sheeting. Peering over the edge of the gable she could make them out, paler rectangles in the dark sloping surface. She climbed onto the pitched roof and edged forward to the nearest one, crouching low so that her silhouette would stay below the ridgeline of the roof. Though she was reasonably fit, the unfamiliar movements and the strain of trying to do everything in total silence were having their effect. She was breathing heavily, her heart pounding, her fingers and ankles aching from trying to keep a grip on the corrugated metal roofing. As she eased her backpack off she imagined it sliding down the smooth pitch, and herself following it into the void.

She thought the larger screwdriver might do the job, and managed to force its blade under the edge of the plastic sheet. But the metal roof gave her no leverage, and she had to pull the two parts of the crowbar out of her bag, screw it together and lay it alongside the edge of the plastic to act as a fulcrum. She put all of her weight on the handle of the screwdriver, and felt the sheet begin to rise, then switched tools and used the jemmy to try to force it up.

There was a creak of protest from the restraining screws, then a sudden explosive bang as they gave and the plastic sheet jerked open. Kathy froze, feeling her arms trembling from the effort.

There were no shouts, no sounds of doors opening or dogs barking. She lay against the metal sheeting, letting her breathing return to more like normal, then carefully put the tools back into her bag and slipped it back over her shoulder. The ache in her ankles had spread up to her thighs now, from the tensing of her legs against the roof, and she thought she should have begun with stretching exercises, and how ridiculous it would be to pull a muscle breaking into a gym.

She lifted the edge of the plastic roof light sheet and squeezed her head and shoulders inside, looking for the winking red light of a movement detector. Nothing. She pointed a pocket torch into the darkness. The beam picked out a steel truss right in front of her, and in the dimmer distance a row of exercise bikes on the floor below, their handlebars erect like bulls' horns. It wasn't too far to the ground, she thought optimistically, perhaps twelve feet from the bottom chord of the truss, maybe only ten. She reached out to take hold of a vertical bar of the truss, and began to wriggle herself and her pack through the gap beneath the edge of the sheet, swinging one foot then the other onto the bottom chord, an inverted T in section and uncomfortable to stand on, but strong enough to take her weight. She pulled the roof sheet down behind her as well as she could, and stood clinging to the steelwork of the truss, feeling like Spiderwoman. Then she lowered herself to hang from the bottom bar and dropped to the floor.

She sprawled on all fours, but felt thankfully intact. Checking again for alarm sensors, she felt the guilt pangs of the novice burglar. The musty smells of the gym accused her; she was an intruder, an illegal, beyond the pale of decent bodybuilders. And looking around, her eyes growing accustomed to the dim light filtering down from the roof, she realised she wasn't going to be able to climb out the way she'd come in.

The door at the back of the gym hall was neither wired nor locked, and she found herself in the corridor that led to the fire exit in the external wall to the alley. That would have to be her way out. Across the corridor was the door to the rear half of the building.

She used the screwdriver and jemmy in combination again to try to force the lock. As she applied pressure she imagined the possibilities. The door might be bolted on the other side, it might be alarmed. As she gave a final jerk it sprang open with a crash and she tensed, waiting for the siren howl or clanging bell, but none came.

Her torch showed a short corridor ahead, with three identical doors on each side, each with a circular porthole window, and beneath that an empty slot for a name. She tried the first door on her left. It was empty, but the furniture and fittings it had once contained had left their traces. There were the imprints on the vinyl floor sheeting of four heavy casters where a bed had been, the scuff marks of a side chair, the blank rectangle of a bedside cabinet. On the walls were brackets and connections for a TV, a light, headphones and a call button.

Kathy continued to the end of the corridor, pushing open the door to a further suite of rooms. There was what had probably been an office, two storerooms with empty shelving, and a room that might have been an operating theatre, with mountings on the ceiling for heavy lights and a washbasin with extended lever taps such as a surgeon might operate with his elbows. Every fitting, every notice on the pin boards, every paper roll in the toilets, had been scrupulously removed, and from the smell of cleaning fluid in the stale air, every surface had been scrubbed.

She made her way back to the fire exit and pushed the bar. Still no alarms sounded. The night was cool and she could hear the faint murmur of surf and the moan of a siren. When she reached the street she noticed a blue lamp flashing above the front door of the gym, and realised she must have triggered a silent alarm. The siren's howl was louder now. She turned and jogged to her car, keeping to the shadows close to the garden walls. Once safely inside, she did a quick U-turn and headed back through the city to the highway beyond.

27

Plan B. When she got back to Barcelona, Kathy drove into the centre of the city and parked near the hotel where they had stayed ten days ago. She wondered about asking if they had a room, but she guessed it would be expensive and postponed a decision, though it was now gone ten p.m.

She approached the Plaça de Catalunya on foot along a narrow twisting lane, and, turning a corner, suddenly found her way blocked by a police car and a small knot of people. She recognised English accents. A man was saying loudly, '… all over me, then this other bloke offered to help. Next thing he'd taken my wallet …'

As she got closer Kathy saw that his shirt was covered in some brown liquid, and a foul smell hung in the air. A woman said, 'We were warned about this!'

The two cops, looking bored, made room for Kathy to get past.

'They looked so respectable,' the woman complained, and Kathy thought, yes, you just can't tell who's a thief these days.

'Hey!' A man's voice, calling after her. She turned and saw one of the policemen wave at her. He began to walk towards her. For a moment she thought of running, but instead gave him a smile. He looked stern and pointed at the pack slung over her right shoulder, then waved an admonishing finger. He made a gesture like someone snatching it, then mimed wearing it properly on her back, with both straps. She grinned and thanked him, and he gave her a wink. Clearly she was more interesting than the tiresome middle-aged tourists who were making such a fuss.

She found a place in a café overlooking the square. There were shiny aluminium tables and chairs spilling out across the broad pavement, the outdoor ones packed by under-thirties who were maintaining running conversations with the crowd passing by. Kathy chose a table in a corner inside, where the light was bright enough to study the book she had brought in her backpack, *The Complete Works of Luis Domènech i Montaner*.

She ordered a long black and turned to the plans of the house of the hospital superintendent of Sant Pau. It wasn't a large house, quite modest really in terms of the number of its rooms, but compensating in the extravagant flourishes of its details. She traced the route that she and Linda had taken through the house, from the front door through the hall to the main salon at the rear where they had met Dr Lizancos. From the plan she saw that there was also a dining room, kitchen and maid's room on the ground floor, and a staircase leading from the hall to the upper floor, containing three bedrooms. There was no cellar or any room indicated as an office or study, but there was one unidentified feature, a turret room at roof level, circular in plan and accessed by a spiral staircase rising from the top of the main stairs. The lizard's lair, Kathy thought. She memorised the plans and the intricately ornamented elevations, paid for her coffee and set off once again.

The street was deserted, the house in darkness when she reached the front gate. She eased it open cautiously, trying to remember if it had squeaked on her first visit, and then she was in the deep shadows of the overgrown garden, making her way carefully along a meandering path. The dark outline of the house rose above her, its pinnacles and gargoyles bristling against the night sky.

The path took her round to a small rear lawn. There were the windows of the salon, and above them those of the main bedroom, all in total darkness. Beyond the garden wall a motorbike spluttered, a horn blared, but within the shroud of the garden nothing stirred.

Kathy retraced her steps to the front of the house, visualising its layout. And there, in the far corner of the front elevation, almost obscured by a thick canopy of foliage, rose the turret, capped by a conical spire like that of a fairytale castle. As she worked her way closer, past an arbour and a waterless fountain, she saw that this side of the house was clad in a dense fabric of ivy. Gnarled and thick, it draped the wall like assault netting. A cat burglar couldn't have asked for better. Rapunzel, Rapunzel, Kathy breathed, let down your hair. She grasped two handfuls and tested her weight. The plant held it easily. She raised one arm higher and began to climb.

Halfway up she was able to stand on a ledge formed by a stone moulding to catch her breath before moving on to reach the main parapet, above which the turret rose skyward. She found that by standing on the lip of the parapet she could reach one of the turret's windows, a leaded framework of small diamond panes. She selected one and used her small screwdriver to bend back the lead until she could prise the glass free. She reached inside for the handle, opened the window and hauled herself inside.

It felt a little like being at the top of a lighthouse, with windows overlooking the city in all directions. Heavy drapes were bunched at intervals, and she slid these closed so that she could use her torch without attracting attention. A bench ran all the way around beneath the windowsills, interrupted only at the entrance from the head of the spiral stairs. Beneath the bench were cupboard doors, their dark green panelling picked out in scarlet. There was one office chair, incongruous in tubular steel among the medieval fitments. Even more incongruous was the video player. Kathy imagined Dr Lizancos sitting up here, a wizened Captain Nemo at the controls of his Gothic Nautilus.

She tried the cupboard doors; all were locked. Regretfully, she jammed the head of the larger screwdriver in the edge of one and levered it open, splintering the frame. Inside was a pile of old files. They looked like medical records, but were all in Spanish, which she couldn't decipher. The names of the patients, if that's what they were, seemed to come from all over Europe — German, English, Scandinavian. Dates were spread over the eighties and nineties.

The second and third cupboards yielded scores more files. Kathy was becoming concerned at the damage, and more importantly the noise her forced openings were making.

The videotapes were in the fourth cupboard. They were numbered. She picked the one which looked the newest and slid it into the player, pressing buttons. The screen came alive with lurid colour and she sat down.

At first she thought it was a pornographic film. The fat sausage of a man's penis lay slack between his open hairless thighs, in large close-up. Some fingers appeared from the side of the screen to lift it up. More fingers prodded the testicles. The fingers were covered with creamy coloured latex.

The fingers disappeared and there was a long pause, the penis lying limp, as if the camera were waiting for it to stand up and perform some sort of trick. Then the fingers reappeared, this time holding a gleaming scalpel. Both Kathy and the camera recoiled slightly.

'Oh my God …' she breathed, as the blade touched the flesh and soundlessly began to slice.

It was the most shocking thing she'd ever seen, but she couldn't drag her eyes away, watching the blade cut and cut until the whole organ came away.

She gave a violent jump as hands gripped her shoulders and the lights came on.

The hands moved down to her biceps, caressing almost, then squeezed so hard she gasped with pain. With no apparent effort they lifted her bodily out of the chair and swung her round to face Dr Lizancos. The old man was breathing heavily from the exertion of climbing the stairs. He gazed malevolently at Kathy from under his thick lids, then his eyes darted around the room. She saw his suspicion flare into anger as he spotted the broken cupboard doors. He stabbed at the video to switch it off. His mouth was a pale line, tight with fury. He barked something in Spanish or Catalan to the man who held Kathy, and she recognised a name, Sigfried, the bodybuilder at the gym. He grunted and increased the pressure of his grip. Kathy gasped, aware of her eyes watering, the feeling dying in her arms.

'How did you get in here, lady?' Sigfried murmured in her ear.

She nodded towards the curtain. 'The window, over there.'

Lizancos scurried over to draw back the curtain and examine the missing windowpane, then started examining the contents of Kathy's backpack, hauling out the housebreaking tools wrapped in a towel.

'How did you come to the house?' Sigfried asked.

'Taxi.'

Lizancos dropped the tools and came over to empty her pockets. He examined the contents of her wallet, her passport, then held up the Hertz key ring. He glared at her accusingly and the steel fingers squeezed so hard that she thought they must surely snap something.

She gasped. 'Ah … In the street outside … a block to the left. Red Seat.' The grip eased.

The lizard doctor slithered out of the room, and she heard his feet on the stairs. Sigfried said nothing as they waited, effortlessly maintaining his paralysing grip.

A little later Lizancos returned with a roll of surgical tape and a pair of scissors. He said something and she was pushed backwards into the chair, her arms stretched behind her. Lizancos cut a length of tape and strapped one wrist to the tubular frame, then repeated the process with the other wrist and both ankles. Then Lizancos gave Sigfried instructions and the bodybuilder nodded and left, turning his torso sideways to get the broad shoulders through the narrow doorway at the head of the stairs. Lizancos knelt in front of the broken cupboards to check the damage and their contents, tutting and muttering under his breath.

Sigfried was gone for ten minutes, and when he returned he was holding the copy of *The Complete Works of Luis Domènech i Montaner* that Kathy had left in the car. He spoke softly to Lizancos and handed him the book, and the old man raised his eyebrow and glanced at Kathy, with a hint of something like respect, she thought. Trying to seize the moment, she said, 'Look, I'm sorry for the intrusion, but you should be grateful I was so discreet. I need to know what Charles Verge looks like now, and where we can find him. Tell me that and you won't hear from us again. It's that simple.'

It was hard to tell if the doctor had understood her words, and she began to speak again, but he ignored her and said something to Sigfried, then turned and left.

There had been a look of resolution on the leathery old face, and Kathy had the feeling that she was running out of time. Sigfried was regarding her impassively, leaning casually against the bench, huge arms folded. She thought she should try to provoke him. Trying to sound unconcerned she said, 'You don't look the type to be into genital mutilation, Sigfried. Are you sure you know what Dr Frankenstein is getting you into?'

He gave a ghost of a smile and raised his index finger to his lips, indicating to her to shut up. A few minutes later Lizancos wheezed up the stairs again, carrying an old leather doctor's bag. He opened it on the bench in front of Kathy, while Sigfried positioned himself at her back. From the bag Lizancos began to extract a variety of things: disposable gloves, swabs, cotton wool, a stethoscope, and — Kathy stopped breathing — a metal box of what looked like surgical instruments. He fished around some more and produced a syringe in a sterile packet, and a small brown bottle. For some reason Kathy thought of the brown stain on the English tourist's shirt, and thought how fortunate he had been in his assault.

'You know I'm a police officer, don't you?' she tried. 'Captain Alvarez will be very angry if anything happens to me.'

They ignored her, Lizancos unpeeling the syringe and filling it from the brown bottle. He came to her side, bending to wipe her arm with cotton wool, and as he did so he hissed in her ear, 'I don't think so.' Then he jabbed the needle in.

Kathy began to protest. 'That is the most stupid . . .' But no more words came.

28

A gust of cool air on her left cheek. She didn't want to get out of bed and tried to turn over, but found she couldn't. Something was holding her down. There was a roar of noise, then silence. She opened her eyes, saw pale light and immediately felt a wave of nausea swell inside her. She closed her eyes quickly and it gradually subsided.

Someone was speaking, a man, insistent. Something touched her shoulder and she tried opening her eyes again. This time she made out a circle. She realised she was sitting, not lying, and simultaneously registered a steering wheel in front of her face. Struggling to free herself, whatever was holding her released abruptly, and she found herself rolling to her left. The nausea lurched in her stomach again, and she saw a polished black boot looming in front of her face. It began to move, but not fast enough. She vomited over it and a man cursed. Her vision blurred and she fell forward onto the ground.

After a while, she opened her eyes and saw that she was lying on bare earth by the side of a highway. Occasional cars and trucks were passing, engines roaring, headlights ablaze under a sky the pale grey of dawn or dusk. She sat up slowly and took in the flashing blue light on the car parked behind her Seat. One cop was crouching over his shoes, wiping them with a piece of newspaper, while the other looked inside her car. She noticed with a groan that the front of the Seat was caved in against a concrete post.

The cop straightened out of the car and replaced his cap. He said something to the other man and held up her passport in one hand;

in the other was an empty bottle. Brandy, Kathy guessed. They both looked down at her with disgust on their faces.

It was late morning before Captain Alvarez and Lieutenant Mozas made an appearance at the district police station where she had been taken. By that stage she had been given a breath test, a blood test, a medical examination, water, coffee and a bread roll. The young doctor had offered to pump out her stomach, but she had declined, although she still felt dazed and horribly sick. This wasn't surprising, he had suggested, with a blood alcohol reading of that magnitude. A woman officer had taken her to a washroom, where Kathy had tried clumsily to clean up her clothes. She had examined the arm where Lizancos had injected her and found only a faint red mark. Apart from that and the hangover, she seemed to be untouched.

Alvarez looked stiff and proper in a black double-breasted suit, hair brushed hard against his skull, as if he'd come straight from mass. Mozas, in jeans and sweater, might have been taking the family on a Sunday outing. Neither man seemed pleased to be there. Alvarez sat opposite her across the table, Mozas, disconcertingly out of her cone of vision, somewhere to her right.

'Why are you here, Sergeant Kolla?' Alvarez asked. He had the same look of distaste on his face as the highway patrol officers, and Kathy wondered if there was some particular taboo in Spain against drunk women. She thought they must have had enough British tourists pass through to get used to the idea by now. Probably the whole building despised her.

'I …' Her throat felt dry and clogged, and her first attempt to speak ended in a coughing fit that brought back the nausea. They waited with exaggerated patience while she took a sip of water and tried again. 'I had a free weekend,' she said hoarsely, 'so I thought I'd come back to Barcelona, as a tourist.'

'Are the drinks in London so expensive?' Alvarez sneered.

'It was a very cheap flight.'

'Who did you come with?'

'I came alone.'

'Where is your luggage?'

'In the car?'

The policeman lifted her backpack onto the table and emptied it in front of her. Towel, wash bag, sunglasses, change of shirt and underwear, and *The Complete Works of Luis Domènech i Montaner*. There was no sign of her tools.

'What is your hotel?'

'I never got around to finding one.'

'Where did you go last night?'

'I'm afraid I can't remember.'

'Yesterday afternoon?'

Kathy shrugged. 'Sorry, my mind's a blank. I don't even know where you found me.'

Alvarez's eyes and lips narrowed with irritation. 'Did Scotland Yard send you?'

'Absolutely not. They have no idea.'

Alvarez snorted, half turned in his chair and lit a cigarette. Mozas took this as his cue to edge his seat closer to Kathy's right side and say quietly, 'This is no good, Kathy, this "I don't remember" business.'

'But it's the truth, Jeez. I honestly cannot remember taking a single drink last night.'

'You think someone gave you something?' he offered sympathetically. 'It happens. An attractive young woman on her own, a man slips something in her coffee and she wakes up twelve hours later remembering nothing ...'

'Well, I suppose it's possible.'

'But you weren't raped.' His tone hardened abruptly. 'What would be the point, if your phantom did nothing?'

'He's your phantom, Jeez. I can't remember a thing.'

'Did you come here to meet someone, perhaps? Someone you met the last time you were here?'

'No. I just thought I'd take a stroll down La Rambla.'

'So you went to La Rambla?'

'I can't remember.'

Alvarez snapped something and both men got to their feet. Kathy was taken out to a cell. Her belt and shoelaces were removed and the door was locked. She examined the plastic cover on the mattress of the single bunk, then stretched out on it and tried to sleep.

She woke to the clang of the steel door. A uniformed man gave her a tray with a sandwich and cup of water, and left again. She found she was hungry.

When they took her back to the interview room she saw from the clock on the wall that it was now two-fifteen. Three hours had passed since the two detectives had spoken to her, and now here they were again. Kathy wondered what they'd been doing. They seemed to have accumulated some files of paperwork.

The younger man, with the better command of English, sat opposite her this time, with Alvarez, glowering, to the side.

'Do you feel a little better, Kathy?' Mozas inquired sympathetically.

'A bit, yes, thanks.'

'Good. And perhaps your memory has come back?'

'I'm afraid not.'

'Well, let's try to help it. Yesterday you got off the plane at El Prat and went to the Hertz desk. Do you remember that?'

'Vaguely.'

'It was five past one when you signed for the car. You got behind the wheel of a red Seat Cordo, and you drove out of the airport. Where did you go?'

Kathy shrugged.

'Into Barcelona?'

'I suppose so.'

'I don't think so, Kathy!' The detective gave a grin of triumph, and Kathy felt a little chill, wondering what they could know.

Mozas consulted his notes. 'You went to Sitges.'

'Did I?'

'Oh yes. And please don't say you can't remember.'

Kathy said nothing. She saw that Mozas was dying to tell her how he knew.

'How do you know that, Jeez?'

'You drove down on the A-16 autopista to Sitges. Your vehicle was filmed going through the Castelldefels toll booth at one twenty-two p.m.'

'Oh.'

'Did you go to Sitges the last time you were here, Kathy?' Mozas asked. 'You must remember that!' He grinned again, and Kathy recognised a trap.

'Well, yes, I did,' she said carefully. 'I drove down the coast one afternoon. It was very pleasant.'

'Any particular points of attraction? Places of interest?'

'I did a bit of sightseeing …'

'And you went to a fitness club, yes?'

'I believe I did, yes.'

Alvarez suddenly unleashed a stream of angry prose at Mozas, who stiffened, his playful manner evaporating. 'The captain says that you are full of shit, Kathy. He wants you to tell us the truth now, or he will hand this over to our bosses to take to the highest levels in Scotland Yard. We know you broke into the Apollo-Sitges Fitness Club yesterday evening …'

'No.'

'The alarm was recorded at eight twenty-three p.m., and your car was photographed again on the autopista at eight fifty-four p.m., returning to Barcelona.'

They've had help, Kathy thought. Lizancos has told them exactly where to look. What else has he told them?

'Why would I want to break into a fitness club? Are you accusing me of a robbery?'

'No, Kathy. In a way it's much more serious than that. The building is owned by Dr Javier Lizancos, as you well know. You've met Dr Lizancos, of course. You went to his home on the eighteenth of September, the day before you went to Sitges to visit his premises there.'

Kathy noticed that Captain Alvarez had picked up *The Complete Works of Luis Domènech i Montaner* and was pointedly turning the pages, studying the illustrations.

Mozas leaned towards Kathy across the table and lowered his voice. 'Is there someone you are in contact with here in Spain, Kathy? Another arm of the police services, perhaps? The Guàrdia Civil? It would be so much simpler if you would tell us. It would avoid misunderstandings.'

'No, really.'

Mozas looked put out. 'But you cannot even speak Spanish! You don't have Linda with you. What did you expect to achieve?'

'I just wanted a change of scenery for the weekend.'

Alvarez got to his feet and reached towards her, brandishing the book. For a moment Kathy thought he was going to hit her with it. Instead, he slammed it down on the table, open at the page illustrating the house of the superintendent of Sant Pau, and glared at her.

Mozas said, 'Dr Lizancos has reported an intruder in the grounds of his house in the Eixample district last night. This house, that you have the plans for in your bag. Fortunately he had a guest staying with him, the manager of his Sitges building, who had come to report on the break-in there. This man scared off the intruder, but he did take note of a car parked outside in the street. A red Cordo, with the same number as yours.'

Kathy felt thoroughly outclassed by the lizard doctor. She wondered what he had done with her tools. Was he holding them back, like a careful boxer reserving the big punch, or had he already planted them somewhere?

'Look, Jeez, I can't help you with this. There's obviously been an unfortunate series of coincidences, but I'm sure you don't have time to waste where no real harm has been done, and I don't think either of us would want an embarrassing international incident.'

'I'm not sure that can be avoided, Kathy. You see, from where we are sitting, it looks as if a member of the British police has been caught carrying out illegal acts against a Spanish citizen on Spanish soil. Dr Lizancos is a very distinguished man, highly regarded. He holds the police medal as well as many other honours. He is a personal friend of Captain Alvarez, who, incidentally, is very pissed off that you and Linda passed yourselves off as acting on his orders when you went to visit the doctor the first time.' Mozas paused, his stern expression softening a little. 'Is there someone you would like to contact for help, Kathy? Your superior? It doesn't seem fair that you should have to deal with this all alone.'

Kathy imagined Brock at the end of a pleasant Sunday lunch with Suzanne, and felt a sharp pang of longing for home. But ringing him would only seem to implicate him.

As if reading her thoughts, Mozas said, 'Mr Brock is your immediate boss, isn't he? But he's only a chief inspector. I think Captain Alvarez will want to go higher than that. Much higher. Do you really want to be crucified alone?'

Kathy felt sick.

• • •

They took her back to the cell and left her there for several more hours. Finally, Lieutenant Mozas came for her with a uniformed cop. The two of them chatted amiably in Catalan while Kathy was led out to the front counter of the police station. One by one her possessions were produced and signed for. Mozas looked at his watch and said something to the desk officer, who muttered and sped up the process, then they were leading her to a patrol car in the street outside. It was a balmy evening, with the glow of sunset on the tiled roofs.

'What's going on, Jeez?'

'You've got a plane to catch,' he said. 'You know, I never saw big guns move so fast, Kathy.' He laughed and consulted his notebook. 'Commander ... Deputy Assistant Commissioner ... Assistant Commissioner ... Deputy Commissioner ... back to Commander. Is that right? Such odd names. I thought commissioners were the people who check your ticket at the movies. Here's your orders, by the way.'

He handed her a copy of a fax with the Metropolitan Police letterhead. It read, 'DS K. Kolla is ordered to report for interview at the office of Commander D. Sharpe, Room 632, New Scotland Yard, at 0900 hrs on Monday 1 October.'

'Tomorrow morning,' Kathy murmured.

'Yeah. Tough.'

'What's the story?'

'You've been working too hard, and you've had some personal problems, yes? To do with a boyfriend? You've had a breakdown, something like that. Anything to keep that headline out of the paper.'

'What headline?'

'*Drunk lady cop arrested in Spain.*' Mozas laughed again. He seemed to be enjoying himself. 'Your drink-driving charge will stay on the record, in case you ever try to come back. You'll have to sort out the damage to the car with the hire company.'

Well, Kathy thought, at least I won't be giving the speech to the police conference on Wednesday.

'Boy, your clothes really stink of booze and stuff,' Mozas said. 'How's your hangover, by the way?'

'Terrible.'

'Get yourself a drink in the airport. It'll make you feel better. If there's time, that is.' He leaned forward and spoke to the driver, who flicked on the siren and pressed his foot to the floor. Mozas leaned closer to Kathy and lowered his voice. 'I got rid of your burglar's tools. I thought you'd want that.'

Kathy looked at him with surprise. 'Why did you do that?'

He shrugged. 'I thought you were in enough trouble without the physical evidence. Alvarez wouldn't have agreed to let you go if he'd seen those.'

'Thank you, Jeez. I appreciate it.'

'Lizancos and his gorilla set you up, didn't they?'

'Yes.'

'You know, you should have come to me in the first place, Kathy. I could have helped you.'

'I'd have got you into trouble, too.'

He shrugged. 'And now you've got yourself into a hole. I guess they'll kick you out.'

'Yes …' She saw the terminal building ahead, and suddenly felt quite calm and settled, for the first time that day. 'Unless I can come up with something really smart.'

'Like a miracle?' Mozas laughed. 'Good luck!'

29

Kathy stared out the window at the baggage-handling trucks circling the parked aircraft. Rain was streaming across the glass, making the picture blur and streak as if she were weeping. She sighed and got to her feet, joining the queue of passengers shuffling towards the exit.

There was a crowd waiting on the other side of the barrier. A group of children were waving frantically at a Spanish girl in front of Kathy, limousine drivers held up placards with names. In the confusion Kathy didn't immediately notice the dark figure standing off to the left, but when she was through the crush and into the open space of the arrivals hall, something made her turn to see Luz Diaz closing in on her.

'Hello, Sergeant Kolla,' the woman said. 'Welcome home.'

'Hello. You look as if you were expecting me.'

'Dr Lizancos phoned to tell me about your adventures in Barcelona.'

'You know him, of course.'

The woman gave a little nod.

'How did he know what plane I was on?'

Luz smiled. 'Captain Alvarez felt obliged to brief the doctor when they decided to let you go. I decided to come and meet you. There are some things we should discuss. My car is outside.'

Kathy hesitated. She met the woman's eyes and felt a return of the nausea that had disappeared during the flight. 'I don't think so. It's been a long day.'

She noticed Luz's eyes shift to a spot beyond her right shoulder, and turned to find George Todd standing there. He had his hands in the pockets of his leather jacket, and he was regarding Kathy with the closest attention.

'Even so, it's important that we talk before you meet with your superiors tomorrow morning, Kathy,' Luz said. 'It concerns Charles Verge. I take it you believe he's still alive?'

'Yes.'

'Dr Lizancos said you were very persistent. He said you wouldn't give up.'

'Clever old Dr Lizancos.'

'I can take you to Charles.'

'Why would you do that?'

'You do want to find him, don't you?'

'Yes.'

'Come on, then.' She linked her arm through Kathy's and led her towards the doors.

Later, as they headed north up the M25, Luz turned to Kathy in the passenger seat beside her and said, 'You are a very determined young woman, aren't you? Did you really do all that breaking and entering in Spain off your own bat, or did someone put you up to it? Chief Inspector Brock, perhaps? I always thought he might be hard to convince.'

Kathy didn't reply. She watched Luz's hand go to the indicator and saw the sign up ahead for the exit road into the dark countryside beyond the highway.

After a while, she recognised the village they passed through. She caught a brief glimpse of light glowing from the windows of the pub, and then they were plunged back into the darkness of winding lanes between tall hedges. Finally, the car slowed and turned in to a gravel drive. Kathy made out the razor-sharp line of a dark wall against the night clouds. They were at Briar Hill, she realised, Luz Diaz's home and Charles Verge's first building.

Luz led the way through the opening in the wall into the glass pavilion, so like the one in Barcelona, and down the spiral staircase into the studio lounge, George Todd following close on Kathy's heels all the while. So far he had said not a word. Luz indicated a seat for Kathy, then threw the short jacket she was wearing over the back of another chair and sat down.

'I'm dying for a drink. Scotch for me please, George. What about you, Kathy?'

'Water, please.' Kathy sat. Beyond their reflections in the glass wall she could make out the shapes of dark tree masses across the fields. They waited while George poured the drinks and then sat down, placing himself, Kathy saw, in the background, between her and the stairs, but also where he could watch her face.

'Kathy …' Luz Diaz leaned forward, cupping her glass in her two hands as if offering something precious to her guest. She fixed Kathy with dark eyes that dilated slightly with concentration, a calculated, rather theatrical effect, Kathy thought. 'What I am going to tell you I will never repeat outside of this room, and will vehemently deny if you repeat it to anyone else. As far as the world is concerned, Charles Verge was murdered on the twelfth of May by his partner Sandy Clarke. As all the world now knows, with the exception of you it seems, he was an innocent victim, an architect of world standing, a tragic loss.'

She sat back, placed her drink on the glass table at her elbow and lit a cigarette. 'Okay. Now the truth. Charles Verge may have been a genius, I wouldn't know, but he was a deeply flawed character. He bullied his colleagues relentlessly, treated his male employees like slaves and female staff with contempt. He was manically jealous of his peers, was obsessed with his public image, and paranoid in his suspicions of disloyalty in those around him. After Gail left him, these tendencies, which she'd more or less reined in, blossomed unchecked. His second wife actually encouraged them, because she thought that, seeing everyone else as potential traitors and enemies, he would rely totally on her.'

Luz took a sip of her drink, drew on her cigarette and studied her listener for a response. Kathy thought the picture made sense, and gave a nod.

'Okay. About two years ago I met up with him — in Barcelona, I think it was, or maybe New York. Anyway, I hadn't seen him for a while and I was struck by how he'd changed for the worse. I guess he was under stress with his work, but he struck me as close to a breakdown. We had a meal together, and the whole time he ranted and raved about how everyone was trying to ruin him. His mother and daughter were driving him mad. Sandy Clarke, who from what I'd heard must have had the patience of a saint, had always just exploited his reputation and was now so jealous of his fame that he was trying to undermine his business, Charles claimed. Worst of all was his wife, Miki, who was hell-bent on destroying his reputation with her hopeless ambition to be recognised as a design star.

'I tried to reassure him, make him see sense, but that just made him angrier, and in the end all I could do was be a good listener, and a good friend when he needed a shoulder to cry on. But I think now, looking back, that it must have been around then that he decided, like Samson, to bring the whole temple crashing down, and destroy them all.

'There was another side to him. Outside his own world he could be an extraordinarily generous person, as both George and I know. I caught up with him again early this year, and he seemed calmer, as if he now was in control of the situation. I, on the other hand, was a mess. I'd recently broken up with a partner who had cheated me badly, taking just about everything I owned. Charles insisted on putting me back on my feet. He offered me this house, the chance to move to England and start again. He made it look as if I'd bought the place, but really it was a gift, an astonishingly generous gift. George has a similar story. Charles befriended him in prison, and set him up when he came out with a home and money. He, too, has been able to start over again, with a new life. So in the end, when Charles needed us, even though we knew that what he'd done was terribly wrong, we had to help him.

'He came here on the Saturday, right after he'd killed Miki. He was very calm. He explained what he'd done and said it had been unavoidable, that Miki had become unreliable and unfaithful, and dangerous to him. He knew exactly what he was going to do, and needed our help. George spent the rest of the day with him, taking his car to the coast, and that night took him over to France in a boat he'd arranged to use. Charles said that he would get Dr Lizancos to change his appearance in Barcelona, then go on from there to South America.

'It was a couple of months before we heard from him again, by phone. He was still in Barcelona, he said, and things had gone terribly wrong. Lizancos had botched the operations on his face, there had been infections and he was ill. The Spanish police were closing in, he couldn't get to South America and Lizancos was panicking. He needed somewhere to hide out, to recuperate. Of course, we agreed. George drove down to Spain and brought him back here. There is a small self-contained flat on the ground floor. He has been there ever since.'

Kathy sat very still, as if expecting Verge's figure to emerge from the shadows.

Luz crushed out her cigarette. 'He was in a terrible state, poor man, when George brought him back. His face was a mess — my God, that Lizancos is a butcher! Charles said he is too old to cut people up, his hands shake. It was a terrible mistake going to him, but he was a very loyal friend of Charles's father and Charles knew he could rely on him to keep silent. And there was something else that upset Charles even more. He said that he had arranged things so that Sandy Clarke should have been suspected of both his and Miki's murders. He had left clues and evidence of financial dealings which incriminated Clarke, the idea being to clear Charles's name and allow him to escape in safety. But somehow the police had been so incompetent that they had apparently overlooked these things. Now everyone believed that Charles was alive, a killer on the run. This preyed on his mind a great deal. As he recovered physically — though disfigured — he became very depressed by the thought that posterity would remember him as a monster.

'Then you came to speak to Charlotte that day, after you had interviewed Sandy Clarke. George saw the files you were carrying, and how upset they made Charlotte, even though afterwards she refused to say what it was about. So he followed you to the supermarket, stole the papers and brought them to Charles, who discovered that Clarke was the father of his expected grandchild. He was very angry. That was when he decided to kill Clarke and make him claim responsibility for Miki's death. He succeeded brilliantly, of course, with George's help, and his reputation was restored just in time for the opening of his last masterpiece.'

'So where is he now?' Kathy asked. Throughout Luz's account George hadn't stirred a muscle, hadn't blinked and hadn't shifted his eyes from Kathy's face.

Luz reached for a magazine on the glass table. 'This is the *Architectural Review* edition featuring Marchdale. It is a wonderful appreciation, the confirmation of Charles's talent. It came out last Wednesday, the day before the opening. That evening he had supper with us. He was very content, and said that everything was now in order. The next day I phoned him from Marchdale to tell him how wonderfully the opening had gone. When I returned I found him downstairs in his room. He had taken an overdose.

'I called George, and together we built a great pyre with timber from the woods. We burned his body and all his possessions, then scattered the ashes.' She turned to the window and gestured. 'He's out there, Kathy, in the air and the water and the soil. You will find no trace of him.'

Kathy said nothing, lowering her eyes, aware of them watching her. Finally George spoke for the first time, softly. 'She doesn't believe you, Luz.'

Kathy looked up, first at him, then at Luz. 'Actually, I do believe most of what you said.'

'Most?'

'The trouble is, Charles has done this so many times before — died and left no body. First in the English Channel, then in some unmarked grave, and now scattered across Buckinghamshire.'

Luz's expression hardened. 'It was necessary that there should be no trace left. You understand that. His reputation must be preserved.'

'Hm.' Kathy didn't attempt to hide her disbelief. She felt grimy and exhausted.

'But there is something,' Luz said. She got to her feet and handed Kathy a small clear plastic pouch. Inside she saw a colour photo of a laughing girl. Turning it over she read the childish printed message, 'To dearest Daddy, luv from Charlotte, XXX'.

'It was in his wallet, and I didn't have the heart to burn it. I suspect it was the most precious thing he had. I dare say it has his fingerprints on it. You can have it.'

'Why?'

'You can use it, perhaps. Tell your bosses that you found it in Lizancos's house, to prove Charles was there and justify your actions. Tell them about what I have said tonight, too, if you like. Maybe they will forgive you.'

'Why would you want to help me? You said you'd deny everything.'

'Of course I will. But I want you and your people to know the truth and then leave us alone. I am betting that your bosses will want to bury it. It is all too late now, and too embarrassing. I have the feeling that, after tomorrow, the police will be thankful to never hear the name Charles Verge again.'

Kathy shrugged. 'Yes. Makes sense.'

'Good.' Luz smiled at her, then turned and nodded to George, whose expression remained as morose as ever.

'I really do feel very tired, Luz,' Kathy said. 'Can you call me a cab?'

'It's not necessary. George will take you home. We owe you that. I'm only sorry that we had to talk so late, but I think you understand now. Good luck tomorrow.'

'Thanks.' Kathy got to her feet and moved towards the stairs, Luz and George ahead of her. As she passed the glass table she stooped briefly, took the cigarette butt from the ashtray and dropped it into her pocket. As she started up the stairs behind them, George turned and took hold of her arm. He then gently slipped his hand into her pocket and produced the stub, holding it up for Luz. The other woman stared down, puzzled.

'What is that?'

'She took your fag-end, Luz. She wants to check your DNA.' He turned to Kathy. 'Right?'

Kathy said nothing, watching the expression go out of Luz's face.

'Oh.' Luz's voice sounded flat. 'That's too bad.' She took a deep breath and began to descend once more. 'We'd better go down to the lower floor. It seems it will be necessary for you to spend the night here, Kathy.'

With George close at her back, Kathy followed the other woman to a hallway near the foot of the staircase. Luz took a key from her pocket and opened a door, reached in to switch on a light, and led them into a small sitting room. There was no picture window outlook down here, but rather a scatter of small windows, like irregular portholes, on the external wall, which was formed of blocks of rough stone. From the outside, Kathy imagined, this storey would look like a rock plinth on which the light glass and steel pavilion above was raised. There was an alcove with an unmade bed, and another with a small kitchen. The furnishings were spartan, as if the room had recently been stripped and scoured.

Luz gestured to a chair. 'Sit down, Kathy. George, I'd like you to wait outside in the hall while I have this conversation with Kathy. Stay close to the door in case I need you, okay?' The Spanish accent had faded.

George nodded and left, closing the door gently behind him.

'That's the only way out, Kathy. George is armed, in case you hadn't noticed. He is very loyal to me, and would kill you without hesitation if he felt it necessary. You understand?'

Kathy nodded and sat. Luz pulled another seat in front of her, so that they were face to face, intimately close within the bare room.

'How long have you known?'

'I saw what kind of operations Dr Lizancos does, Luz.' Kathy felt her throat dry. 'He keeps videos of his finest work. I have actually seen him cutting off your balls.'

'Oh ...' Luz's mouth turned down in a grimace. 'I didn't know that.'

She sat back and lit a cigarette, the flame trembling a little as she held it to the tip. 'You find the idea grotesque, do you? What Lizancos did to me?'

'I think it's rather extreme to change your gender so as to evade the law.'

'Actually, it was more the other way around.'

Kathy frowned. 'You murdered in order to change your sex?'

'Yes, that's what it amounts to.' She leaned closer to Kathy and her voice dropped to an urgent whisper, as if she didn't want George to hear. 'I want you to understand, Kathy. I thought from the very first time I met you, here in this house, that if anyone could understand, it would be you — a young, independent woman, making her own life.'

Kathy felt a shiver of distaste creep up her spine. The other woman was so intense, little flecks of spittle flying from her mouth as she spoke, her perfume too strong at close quarters, that Kathy felt an overpowering desire to back away, but she could only hear the words if she bent her head close.

'You must understand that this is not some kind of desperate last-minute ploy, Kathy. I have felt that I was really a girl from my earliest years. My first memory is of lying in my bedroom with a

292

woman nurse, and feeling certain that I would grow up to be like her. As I grew older and became aware of human sexuality, the idea didn't fade away. It grew stronger, more certain. I didn't want to imitate a woman — I *was* a woman, locked inside the wrong body.

'I told no one, but I read everything I could about my condition. When I read Jan Morris's book *Conundrum* it was an inspiration to me. I remember the year it came out, 1974, the same year I returned to England with my new American wife and began work on this house. Here was a man who had frankly, publicly, discussed his innermost thoughts, his decision to surgically change his body to that of a woman. He had confided in his wife and family, who supported him, and had walked out into the world without shame, a free woman.

'But I didn't have the courage to follow her example. I kept my feelings secret, and the more successful I became, the more I shrank from the idea of going public. I had a young man come to work for me once, a brilliant draughtsman, sensitive designer. He had much the same problem as me, and one day, it being the liberated eighties, he came to work in a frock. The others goggled, then pretended not to notice. They smirked and sniggered behind his back, of course, but he stuck to his guns. He seemed quite self-possessed when he saw the faces of the trade reps and building inspectors and clients turn red when he walked into a room. Then the day came when he had to go out onto a building site. The men had heard about him, and they weren't so polite. That night he hanged himself.'

Kathy's back was stiff from crouching forward to catch Luz's words; she straightened, stretched, and wondered how long this pitiful story was going to last. 'I don't see how this accounts for murdering your wife,' she said.

'It's important you understand the background. I was trapped in a situation I couldn't change, and I hated myself for it. I began to detest Charles Verge. I despised him for his paranoia and egomania. I didn't want to be him. So I invented this other person who I wanted to be: Luz Diaz, the Spanish artist. It turned out to be the most satisfying design project I'd ever done; I created her life story, constructed her career, fabricated catalogues for her brilliant exhibitions long ago. It gave me a secret thrill to mention her to people: "Oh, and I bumped into that Spanish painter the other day in New

York. You know, Luz Diaz, who did that big abstract in our flat. She was very sad, her mother died recently, so we had a drink together at the Hyatt and she cheered up a little." It was a harmless fantasy, I thought, except that it became addictive. More and more I yearned to be Luz. And after my marriage to Gail collapsed I finally rented Luz an apartment in Barcelona and began to act her part, living her life for whole days at a time.

'Then, about two years ago, I met Dr Lizancos at a lunch in Barcelona. He had been a boyhood friend of my father, and one of the other people at the table mentioned to me that he was an expert in reconstructive surgery — cosmetic, but also, more discreetly, transsexual surgery. After the lunch I asked Dr Lizancos if I could have an appointment with him. That was how I began to believe that I might turn Luz Diaz into a reality.

'I was married to Miki by that stage, of course, and the hope that my new wife might cure me of my obsession had not materialised. I decided to go ahead with Dr Lizancos's program of drugs in preparation for future surgery. I envisaged that I would retire from the practice and disappear to Spain, to live Luz Diaz's life, with Miki as my companion. It was a tremendous burden, this secret, especially when the drugs began to take effect. My sex drive diminished, I lost weight, and the whole shape and texture of my body began to alter. Miki began to make comments about how I had changed. Finally I told her everything, about Luz Diaz and Dr Lizancos, about my plans.

'I expected her to be shocked, of course, but I hadn't anticipated the full force of her reaction. She was contemptuous. She thought my lifelong dilemma was utterly absurd; she regarded my fantasy about Luz Diaz as disgusting; she said my plans were impossible, that I could no more become a woman through surgery than she could become a mermaid.

'It took me some time to realise that, not only would Miki never join me in my new life, but that she would do everything she could to ridicule and destroy it. I imagined her regaling our London friends with tales about her ludicrous ex-husband, doing interviews for newspapers and TV shows, writing her memoirs, *My Life with the Freak*, turning me into a national and international joke. And I also saw her destroying my reputation as an architect, taking over the practice, taking credit for my work, and especially for Marchdale.

'When I realised all that, I began to see that another plan would be necessary to achieve my flight from Charles Verge. I made her promise to say nothing until I was ready to make an announcement to my family and closest friends, and meanwhile I began to arrange the destruction not only of Miki, but of the Verge Practice, when I finally departed.'

It occurred to Kathy that he might have changed his sex and his appearance, but the self-absorption, the egomania, were unchanged. 'How did Sandy Clarke deserve to be your victim too?'

Luz waved a dismissive hand. 'Sandy was a mediocre talent who made an extraordinarily good living from riding on my coat-tails for twenty-five years. He was also screwing my wife. It was time for payback. I knew that if Miki died in suspicious circumstances and I disappeared, I would be blamed. I had to provide an alternative explanation both for the murder and for the money funnelled out of the practice to fund my new life. But what the bloody hell were the police playing at? I left the ground thick with clues, and the bumbling plod missed them all. Didn't they find Sandy's glasses in the bedroom, his pen in the bed, for God's sake?'

'Sandy removed those when he discovered the body.'

'Oh.' Luz looked annoyed. 'What about the bed linen? Miki boasted to me that morning when I got back from the States that Sandy had slept in her damn bed. Didn't he leave any traces?'

'She'd already changed and washed the sheets,' Kathy said, but didn't mention the pillowcase that had had such ramifications.

'Well, what about his driving glove? I took that from his car when he picked me up at the airport that morning, and left it in my car at the beach. Didn't you trace that back to him?'

'It had never been worn. It was assumed to be yours.'

'And the missing money? Didn't the accountants pick that up?'

'Only now.'

'Hell.' Luz shook her head. 'I didn't imagine it would be so difficult. I didn't intend for Sandy to die, not until I found out what he did to Charlotte. Perhaps I should have stuck to designing buildings, not murders. But I've always believed that any design problem, no matter how intractable, has a solution, if one only has the imagination and nerve.' She caught Kathy looking at her, the question in her eyes, and am I next? Luz turned away, and in that equivocation Kathy thought she saw the fate in store for her.

'You'd better bed down here, while I work out what to do now,' Luz said. 'There's blankets and linen in the drawers over there.'

'If you threaten the children, Stewart and Miranda, Brock will never rest until he's taken care of you.'

'Of course we shan't touch them. That was a rather clumsy initiative of George's. He was concerned that your boss was going to persist and needed warning off. I promise you, there's nothing to be concerned about in that area.'

Kathy nodded. 'And the same goes for me. I've got an important meeting first thing tomorrow, and if I don't show up all hell will break loose.'

It sounded feeble even as she said it, and she saw that Luz was unimpressed.

'Don't worry, we'll work things out.' She got up to call George in, but Kathy stopped her, wanting to keep her talking.

'I'd like to know what Lizancos did to you, exactly.'

'Everything he could think of. I was the last opportunity for an old man to display his talent, his last masterpiece. He thinks of himself as an artist too, you see, his medium being flesh and bone, and once he'd begun I didn't have much say in the matter.'

Kathy remembered the first time she'd seen Luz in this house, and the rubber gloves. 'Your fingerprints?'

'Yes, he had a go at those too. It was something he'd always wanted to try, he said, to transplant toe pads to fingertips. I'm still having trouble with them. He'd have transplanted my whole hands if I'd let him — they're too large, of course. The most difficult thing has been something he couldn't alter, my voice. I took voice lessons in Barcelona, but I've been terrified that some rhythms of speech, some characteristic sounds, would be there for Charlotte or Madelaine to pick up. But they didn't.' Luz smiled, proud of herself.

'And in the end, did it work? Are you a woman?'

The smile faltered, then was forced back. 'Of course. I told you, I always have been.'

Kathy wasn't convinced. It was a rehearsed answer, she felt, a response to Miki's challenge that what he was attempting to do was impossible.

Luz went to the door and spoke to George, who came in and

checked the windows, taking keys from the security locks. 'Triple glazed, toughened glass,' he told Kathy.

'Sleep well,' Luz said, and she and George left. Kathy heard the lock click, then made a hurried inspection of the room. There seemed no way out. She found cutlery in a kitchen drawer, and although the larger knives had been removed, there was a selection of smaller ones. She chose a couple, wrapped herself in a blanket and put out the light.

30

Kathy stirred with the first glimmer of grey dawn through the little windows. She could hear nothing, no dawn chorus through the heavy glazing, only the soft hum of the refrigerator and ducted airconditioning, and was filled with a sense of dread about the day ahead.

At one point she thought she heard the faint murmur of a vehicle starting up, then nothing but more long silence. Noticing a small intercom grille beside the door, she went over to it and pressed her thumb on the button. After a while the speaker crackled and George's voice said, 'Morning.'

'What's going on, George? It's seven-thirty. I need to go.'

'Patience. There's food in the fridge and cupboards. Make yourself some breakfast.'

'I don't want breakfast, I want ...' But the line had gone dead.

She found some orange juice, and ate a piece of bread and marmalade, discovering that, despite a lingering nausea in the back of her throat, she was hungry.

Eight o'clock came and went, and Kathy experienced an odd sense of detachment, imagining the reactions when she failed to keep her appointment with Commander Sharpe. She tried the intercom again.

'Hello? Luz, George?'

'Patience,' George's voice repeated. 'Watch TV. Read a book.'

She made a cup of coffee, and pictured the scene in Sharpe's office, the angry call to Brock, the consternation in Queen Anne's

Gate. Presumably, Brock had been told about her trouble in Barcelona. What was he thinking now, that she'd done a bunk? The police conference was starting today, she remembered, and she imagined Sharpe and the other top brass in full uniform discussing her case between sessions. The first of the working parties would be presenting their paper that afternoon. Hers was due the next day. She switched on breakfast TV and watched, like a prisoner spying through a keyhole, the normal world outside, remote and unattainable.

Half an hour later she stopped pacing and tried the intercom again. 'George, I want to speak to Luz. Put her on, please.'

'Sorry, she's busy. We're in the middle of delicate negotiations. She says you're to stay calm and not worry. She'll work things out, but it may take some time. And there's no point buzzing me all the time. Save it for an emergency. You've got plenty of grub down there and stacks of channels. Put your feet up, watch a movie.' He clicked off.

What negotiations? Were they bargaining for her life? She paced around the flat again, searching for something, an access cover, a floor duct, anything that might give her an outlet to the world outside. Nothing. The only possibility for breaking out seemed to be to find something to smash through the glass of a window. She felt for the tea-knife in her pocket and stared at the stone wall, wondering how many years it would take her to dig her way out.

By ten Brock was in a cold sweat. He'd had no contact with Kathy since Friday night, sixty hours earlier. She had seemed disappointed that the Verge investigation had been shut down, but not unduly so. Then they had parted and he had thought no more about it until he got the phone message on Sunday afternoon that one of his officers had gone berserk in Barcelona, and would he kindly get his arse back to London. He had had no sleep since. He had gone himself to meet her plane at Heathrow, but a cloudburst had jammed traffic on the M4 and by the time he had arrived the passengers were already dispersing. British Airways confirmed that she had been on the flight, and he had assumed she was making her way back to her flat in Finchley. He drove there, and spent half the night sitting out-side the building, phoning people until his batteries ran down. Her phone wasn't answering, and no one else he could think of — Bren,

Leon, Suzanne, Linda Moffat — had heard from her. At three a.m. he went home, thinking she might be waiting for him there. She wasn't, and he raised the alarm.

When Sharpe phoned at three minutes past nine to find out why the hell DS Kolla hadn't turned up for her appointment, Brock informed him that she was now listed as missing. 'Missing?' Sharpe had growled. 'Missing in the head, or what? Christ, Brock, this was supposed to be your star. What're the rest of your cowboys like?'

When he'd rung off, Brock had sent Bren to Finchley to gain entry to Kathy's flat, to see if there were any clues as to her where-abouts there. Apart from an altercation with a neighbour who thought he was a burglar, Bren had nothing to report. There was no sign that Kathy had returned to the flat, and nothing apart from a scribbled note of plane times to connect to the events of the weekend.

If only she'd got engaged to Leon, Kathy thought, and he'd bought her a very large diamond engagement ring, she might have been able to cut her way through the glass. She lifted the small iron she'd found in a cupboard and extended her arm. In her left hand she was gripping a steel leg that she'd managed to detach from a chair. She swung the iron at the glass. There was a solid bang that jarred her arm and reverberated through the structure of the building; a star formed in the glass. She tried again, and the star spread. With the third blow the glass shattered. But this was only the first of three layers.

She heard feet on the stairs and ran towards the door, dropping the iron and lifting the chair leg to shoulder height. She pressed herself flat against the wall alongside the door and waited. The door burst open and she swung her weapon, but there was no one there.

A voice outside in the hallway said, with a weary sigh, 'What do you think this is, James bleeding Bond? Come on, luv, I've been around too long. Back off.'

Feeling somewhat sheepish, Kathy stepped away from the door and George appeared, a small automatic in his hand, aimed in the general direction of her midriff. 'Ooh ...' he frowned at what she was holding. 'That's an early Eames prototype that is. Worth a bomb. Hope you haven't done any permanent damage. Luz'll kill you.'

'I was thinking that might be the general idea,' Kathy said, her heart thumping from the adrenaline.

He clucked scoldingly. 'I told you to be patient.'

'Where is she, George?'

'Do you want me to cuff you to the bench?'

'No.'

'Well behave then. Watch telly, have some food. You look like you could use it. There's some choice stuff in the fridge. I bought it myself.'

'Why are you getting mixed up in this, George? You're on parole. They'll put you back inside forever. Let me out now and I'll do the best I can for you.'

'Save it.' He stepped back and slammed the door closed behind him.

It was late afternoon before George appeared again. He knocked on the door and pushed it open cautiously. 'Let's go.'

'Where to?' she asked, suddenly reluctant to leave the security of her prison.

'Where do you want to go?'

'Queen Anne's Gate.'

'Okay.' He turned on his heel and she hurried after him. When she reached the top of the spiral staircase she had the impression that the house was deserted. She noticed a large painting had been taken down from the wall of the studio. They continued on up to the entry pavilion, and George held the passenger door of the car open for her. Her backpack was on the seat. She got in and they set off along the misty autumn lanes, passing the village pub, its lights on for the evening trade.

When they reached the M25 Kathy said, 'Come on, George. What's happening?'

'She's gone. You won't be seeing her again, none of us will. She just needed a bit of time to get clear.' He glanced over at Kathy, her expression suspicious in the wash of passing lights.

'What, no amazing corpseless death?'

'No. She always knew it might come to this. After the opening of Marchdale she thought she was in the clear, but she couldn't be sure. There was always the chance of some bloody-minded copper or reporter figuring it out.'

'Thanks.'

'So she had arrangements in place. She's still got her money, of course, and by now she's a long way away and somebody else. There's no chance of catching up with her this time.'

'Are you really letting me go, George?'

'Yeah, really. I advised against it, you might like to know. Loose end, I said, but she didn't see it that way. She wants the cops to know, and not be able to say or do a thing about it. Otherwise, she said, it would be like designing a building and not having anyone know it's yours. She said this was her last big design.'

'What makes you so sure they won't do anything?'

'We'll see, shall we?'

'What about Madelaine and Charlotte? How do they feel about all this?'

'They know nothing. Nobody does, except you and me, and I've got a watertight alibi for the last twenty-four hours.'

Kathy was silent, thinking. They came to the M4, but then, at the next junction, turned off at the signs to Heathrow. 'Hang on,' she said. 'This isn't the way.'

'I'll drop you off at the taxi rank here.' He felt in his pocket and produced some cash that he handed to her. 'Luz told me to look after you. Here you go.' He pulled over to the kerb. 'Goodbye, Kathy. As far as I'm concerned, none of this happened.'

She watched him roar away, then walked over to the taxi queue and caught a cab into town. As it pulled to a halt at Queen Anne's Gate, she looked up at the brightly lit windows and wondered what sort of reception she would get.

The first person she bumped into in the corridor was Bren, who goggled as if seeing someone risen from the dead.

'Kathy! We've been looking everywhere. What happened to you?'

'It's a long story, Bren. Is Brock about?'

'In his office, yeah. You'd better get up there. Are you okay? No damage?'

'I'm fine. Catch up later.'

But Bren came with her up the stairs all the same, as if she might disappear once again.

Dot's desk was empty, and Kathy knocked on Brock's door. There was a muffled 'Come' and she pushed it open. Brock was bending over a pile of papers. He straightened with a cry, and, in a spontaneous gesture that took her by surprise, grabbed her and pulled her to him.

'Kathy! I thought ...' He hugged her for a moment, then stepped back, holding her at arm's length, embarrassed now at this display. 'I really thought ...' Then he seemed to force a frown across his face. 'Dear God, you've had us in a panic. What happened to you?'

Kathy turned to Bren, standing behind her in the doorway. 'I need to talk to Brock alone.'

He nodded and closed the door softly behind him. Kathy and Brock sat down, and she told him her story.

At the end of it he shook his head. 'I don't know where to begin, Kathy. It's like some textbook exercise on how to make every mistake under the sun. They'll be using this at Bramshill for training purposes, and no one'll believe it could actually be true.'

Kathy lowered her head, accepting the inevitable.

'... dashing off without talking to me first. Not saying a word!'

'I thought that would only make things worse, involving you,' she offered, trying to sound contrite.

'No back-up, no explanation. Where did that leave us when things went wrong?'

He went on, twenty-four hours of sleepless anxiety resolving itself into anger and dismay. Kathy said as little as possible, answering the odd point, making necessary explanations about some of the more lurid disasters, the break-ins, the drunk driving.

'And how you could then, knowing what you did, have agreed to get into that car with Diaz and Todd ...'

'I needed evidence,' she said reasonably. 'I knew I was about to be kicked off the force. I needed something concrete.'

He shook his head in despair. 'It's not the first time, Kathy. I sometimes think you have some kind of death wish ...'

But she sensed the anger fade and something else take its place, a sort of astonished admiration, not so much for her as for Charles Verge.

'He really did that? I had no idea. And none of them knew? No one recognised him, his mother, his daughter ...? It's incredible.'

'You do believe it, don't you?'

'Yes ...' He was thinking of Gail Lewis's story of the hermit crab dragging around the wrong shell. Yet she, like everyone else, had misinterpreted the image. 'Yes, I do.'

When the interrogation was over, Brock poured them both a scotch and sat back, thinking.

'Lizancos will have destroyed his tapes and files, we can be sure of that. But Luz Diaz couldn't have lived at Briar Hill for the past few months without leaving DNA traces, no matter how well they've cleaned the place.'

'I thought of that,' Kathy agreed, 'but even if we found Verge's DNA in the house, it wouldn't help, would it? We know he was there before he disappeared.'

'Depends on the traces, and where they are.'

He reached for the phone and called in Bren, instructing him to get a warrant and take a SOCO team out to the Diaz house as quickly as possible. 'It seems she's disappeared. You're looking for her traces and those of third parties. We know George Todd has been there recently, and so has Kathy. We want to know who else has.'

Bren looked curiously at Kathy. 'Are we looking for Diaz, chief?'

'Yes. Put out a full alert.'

'Right. You coming to the house?'

'Maybe later. Kathy and I have another appointment to keep, and some rehearsing to do before we go.'

The façade of the conference venue was lit up with floodlights and carried a large banner bearing the Metropolitan Police logo and the motto *Protect and Respect: Embracing Diversity*. The taxi dropped them among waiting limousines and they made their way up the steps to the entrance. A steward directed them to a side corridor, and they caught glimpses into a main hall filled with suits and uniforms, glasses and canapés in hands. They came to a room marked *Conference Meeting Room Number 2*, knocked and went inside. There was no one there. On the table were sheets of notes abandoned from an earlier meeting. On one Kathy saw the heading *Crime Strategy Working Party*, and realised with a little shock that her own committee must have been here, preparing for its presentation the following day.

The door opened and two men in uniform came in. Kathy felt their unsmiling curiosity as they examined her before they turned to Brock. The first man introduced Brock to the second. Kathy missed the name, but caught the title, Deputy Commissioner, and saw the badge of rank on his shoulders. Then the first man was speaking to her.

'I'm Commander Sharpe, and you must be DS Kolla? Sit down.' He waved to seats at the end of the room. 'You'd better tell us your version of events, Sergeant. Quickly if you please.'

Kathy did her best, but in that setting, faced with the two sombre uniforms, she felt as if she were recounting some kind of lurid fairytale.

'... I was concerned that some sections of the press believed that Charles Verge was still alive,' she said, following a line that Brock had suggested, 'and I thought they might eventually get to hear of Dr Lizancos and his clinic. I thought this was one important line of inquiry that we hadn't been able to complete when the case was closed, and I believed that it might eventually rebound on us. However, I was aware that the Barcelona police, one captain in particular, was shielding Dr Lizancos, and I knew our direct approaches had been fruitless. Given the sensitivity of the matter, I decided to mount an operation on my own initiative, without involving any of my colleagues, as a form of insurance.'

In this fairytale, 'break and enter' became 'covert admission', and the doctor's abandonment of his clinic at Sitges a compelling reason for further 'provident inquiries' at his home in Barcelona. The two senior officers remained stony-faced throughout this, reacting only when she came to the revelation of Charles Verge's transformation into Luz Diaz. This produced a snort from Sharpe, a look of quizzical disbelief from his colleague.

At the end there was a long silence, then Sharpe said, 'I think I can truly say that that is the most outlandish story I have ever heard. Do you believe it, Brock?'

'I'm rather afraid I do, sir,' Brock murmured.

The Deputy Commissioner leaned towards Sharpe and whispered something. Sharpe nodded and said, 'Step outside, will you, Sergeant.'

Kathy got to her feet, feeling angry and helpless, and made for the door. She stood outside in the corridor for twenty minutes, watching the girls pass up and down with trays of glasses. The muffled roar of conversation from the main hall was louder, and she wondered if the members of her committee were in there, Shazia in her Hijab sipping orange juice, Jay with cropped hair knocking back the champagne. Jay — she remembered their broken date for Saturday night, and thought she must contact her, wondering what she could possibly say.

Just then, Commander Sharpe stuck his head out of the door and called her back in.

She took her seat, unable to tell from their expressions what they were thinking.

'As I understand it,' Sharpe began, 'there is absolutely no physical evidence to support anything that you've told us, Sergeant.' He raised an eyebrow, inviting a reply.

'No, but a forensic examination of Ms Diaz's house ...' She stopped, seeing him shake his head.

'DI Gurney has just phoned in. When he arrived at the house he found it ablaze. The fire crews should be there by now, but it seems likely that the building will be completely destroyed ...' He paused while Kathy absorbed this, thinking with a sense of shock how final this was, the destruction of his first house, a sign to her and everyone else that the game was over now.

'... And that being the case, there appears to be no possibility that any kind of corroboration for your story will ever be forthcoming. Am I right?'

'It's possible. But we do know what Verge looks like now.'

Sharpe winced, as if he still found this too much to swallow. 'Correction — we know what Diaz looks like. We only have her word for it that she is, or was, Charles Verge.'

'George Todd knows.'

'Maybe, but will he tell us? Not likely, I think. And so we have decided that it would be damaging and highly irresponsible to make your suspicions known beyond these four walls.'

He saw the protest flare in Kathy's eyes and said coldly, 'Do you want to remain in the service, Sergeant?'

She took a deep breath, feeling the colour burning in her cheeks. 'Yes, sir.'

'I understand that DCI Brock has told you in no uncertain

terms how ill-conceived and dangerous your behaviour has been. By rights you should be the subject of a disciplinary review. However, in light of the somewhat extraordinary circumstances, and the accommodating attitude of the Spanish authorities, we shall say no more. You will tell no one, repeat no one, of the events of the past seventy-two hours, is that clear?'

'Yes, sir.' They just want it all to go away, she thought, just as Luz Diaz had known they would, and for a moment she felt a flicker of sympathy for the stiff men in front of her, imagining them trying to explain to a roomful of incredulous reporters that, yes, Charles Verge was actually alive, but he'd turned into a woman and had disappeared, yet again.

They got to their feet, and as he passed her, the other senior officer, who had so far said nothing to her, murmured, 'Never mind, Sergeant, it was a great story. I look forward to hearing you present your paper to the conference tomorrow.'

Panic seized Kathy. 'Oh no. I won't be doing that.'

'Why ever not?'

'Well, in view of what's happened ...'

'Nothing's happened. Isn't that what we just agreed? Of course you must do it. Robert's out there somewhere. I'll tell him you need to speak to him, shall I?'

31

Of all the humiliations of the past days, this, Kathy thought, would be the worst. She hadn't taken in a single word of the previous speaker's address, and now they were breaking for twenty minutes for tea before it was her turn. She felt a kind of paralysis invade her thoughts as she headed for the toilets.

Robert had had a copy of her speech all ready for her in the pocket of his imposing double-breasted suit. In her absence, the committee had worked long and hard at refining it, he said, and when she read it she could believe that was true. Whatever fresh or original ideas might have been contained were now so buried under convoluted clauses and mind-numbing platitudes that they were well and truly — she felt qualified to use the word — castrated. Jay's radical thoughts, which Kathy had promised herself would get a mention, had been completely erased. Reading it, she wondered who would be the first to fall asleep with boredom during her presentation, the audience or herself. But that was no contest — terror would keep her awake.

As she gripped the tap at the washbasin she remembered some research that she'd read, about people who would rather go into combat than stand up and speak in public. Oh yes, she thought, and yanked the tap so hard that a jet of water shot out of the basin and splashed all over the front of her suit. She was mopping it with wads of paper towel when a uniformed woman came in to tell her it was time to take her place on the podium.

She took her seat, aware that she still hadn't really made up her mind whether to include the additional pencilled notes she'd scribbled on page four, and again at the end.

She was conscious of her name being announced, of applause, and of herself rising to her feet and floating towards the podium. Address a point a few feet above the head of the last person at the back of the hall, Brock had advised, but when she lifted her gaze she was blinded by the spotlights. She began reading from her script, and was suddenly very grateful for Robert's competently constructed sentences and anodyne turns of phrase. Her voice made strong and sure by the amplifiers, she began to feel that she might after all make it to the end before her heart gave out.

Then she came to page four and the margin notes, and felt sufficiently confident to abandon Robert's script. She was aware of her voice changing as she began to ad lib. And she was also aware of a change in the silence of the audience, which had become intense, especially when she repeated some of Jay's slogans, 'male army of occupation', 'militaristic structures and mind-set' and 'degendering the service'. Like a tightrope walker she kept her eyes fixed on Brock's neutral spot between the lights, certain that she would fall if she once looked down into the sea of pale faces.

She reached the safety of page five, and sensed the audience relax again as her voice took on the mechanical rhythm of reading once more. And soon there was only one page left, and she found herself wading through Robert's rather overblown summarising paragraphs, and, below them, her second set of handwritten notes.

'... But although these processes and procedures may offer an important framework to embrace diversity, there is a danger that we end up viewing diversity as no more than a series of stereotypes,' she improvised. 'Every active officer knows that each crime and each criminal is unique, and that stereotypes can be dangerously misleading.' The most fundamental stereotypes of gender, class and race became meaningless, she argued, in the fluid dynamics of the times, in which the criminal personality might flit from type to type, evolving like a virus to confound the overly rigid systems of law enforcement crime strategies.

So there, she thought, and gathered up her papers and sat down. There seemed to be some applause, then someone else was speaking, and Kathy took a deep, deep breath of relief.

Afterwards, Robert came up to her. He was beaming with what looked like amusement.

'Well done, Kathy. That went down well.'

'Did it?'

'Oh yes. And I think you were right to spice it up with a few off-the-cuff thoughts of your own. Senior management likes to sniff a radical thought from time to time. Makes them feel they're in touch.'

'Really?'

'Certainly. The DC thought it was very good. The last bit, against stereotypes, was especially brave.'

'Was it?' Actually, Kathy had felt she'd been stating the obvious.

'Well, I mean, look around you. Every person here represents some stereotype or other. Look at the members of your committee. If there were no stereotypes they'd have no constituencies and they'd all be out of a job!' He chuckled contentedly. 'So it gives them a bit of a buzz to hear somebody saying stereotypes are dangerous. Of course,' he said, bending closer to whisper, 'they haven't had your recent experiences, seeing how easily someone can turn from one stereotype into its opposite.'

Kathy looked at him in surprise. How did Robert know about Verge's transformation? And if he knew, who else did? 'What are you talking about, Robert?'

'Why, you of course! A policeman one minute and a criminal in a Spanish jail the next. Oh, many odd things cross my desk, Kathy; don't worry, I'm the very soul of discretion. But perhaps it should make you think about your own position. Maybe *you're* the one stuck in a stereotype.'

'How do you mean?'

'Oh, Brock's acolyte, working in the shadow of the great detective. One way and another, you've been noticed over the past days, Kathy.'

'Mostly for the wrong reasons.'

'Maybe at first, but it's a fine line between dangerous insubordination and daring initiative, and people have been impressed, believe me. It's time you moved on, into front-line management. You need someone to advise you on your career. Someone like myself.'

He's coming on to me, she thought with a sigh, and was

saved from replying by Jay, who was pushing through the crush towards them.

An old man was holding open the door of the village pub for his moth-eaten black dog as Kathy drove past. It seemed to be a major operation for both of them. She pulled up by the gate of Orchard Cottage, seeing the lights on in the windows. Charlotte seemed surprised but not unhappy to see her. Madelaine Verge, on the other hand, sitting in her chair by the fireside with a magazine on her lap, looked hostile and suspicious.

'We came across something during the course of our inquiries that I wanted to return to you, Charlotte,' Kathy said, handing her the photograph that Luz Diaz had given her.

'Oh, I remember this! Dad kept it in his wallet. Where did you get it?'

'It turned up among some other papers.'

The young woman stared at it sadly for a moment, then placed a hand on her tummy. 'Thanks. I thought you might have come about the terrible fire at Briar Hill. Isn't it awful? Do they know yet what caused it? George says Luz may have left something on the stove, and then with her painting chemicals in the same area, it was bound to go up.'

'I don't know.'

'You do know about Luz leaving, don't you? We're all feeling sad about that, too.'

'Did Luz come to see you before she left?'

'Yes, on Sunday night. We were just about to go to bed, weren't we Gran? She called in to say she'd decided to go back to Spain for a while, but she didn't leave a forwarding address, and until she gets in touch again I don't know how they'll be able to contact her about the house.'

Kathy tried not to stare at Charlotte while she weighed every intonation, every shift of expression. She didn't know, Kathy decided. She had no idea that the painter was her father.

But Madelaine was another matter. When Kathy met her eyes she thought she saw knowledge and anger that shouldn't have been there.

'We don't even know what caused Luz to go so suddenly like that,' Charlotte said.

'I think I do,' her grandmother said, in a voice as tight as the grip of her swollen fingers on the arms of her chair. 'I think she was driven away by the constant harassment of the police, isn't that right, Sergeant?'

Yes, Kathy thought, she knew, had always known.

'Oh, I'm sure that's not fair, Gran. She'll probably be back before long.'

'I don't think so, dear,' the old woman said, keeping her angry eyes on Kathy all the time.

'Well,' Kathy said evenly, 'I hope she does. I for one would really like to meet up with her again, Charlotte. I've become very interested in modern Spanish painting, and I'd love to contact her about it. Will you let me know if you hear from her?'

'Yes, certainly.'

'She's bound to be in touch when the baby arrives, don't you think?' Kathy added, watching the anger darken Madelaine's features. 'I'll expect to hear from one of you then, eh?'

The old dog was tied up outside the pub door when Kathy drove past for the last time. It looked fed up and she wondered how it had disgraced itself. She turned the corner into the lane leading back to the highway, then pulled onto the side as her phone rang.

'Is that you, Kathy? How are you?' She felt suddenly disconsolate to hear the Indian accent.

'I'm fine, Morarji. How are you?'

'Oh, not so bad, not so bad, all things considered. But I'm a little worried about that silly bugger of a son of mine. You haven't been in touch with him lately, I take it?'

'No, why? Don't you know where he is?'

'Oh yes, I know where he is all right. He's right here, and that's the problem. He doesn't go out, you see. He's so down in the dumps. He had a friend — a man, you understand, not a girlfriend — he went around with for a short while, but they don't seem to be friends any more, and now he seems to have no one he can talk to.'

Leon's father was putting on his oh-my-what's-the-world-

312

coming-to amused voice that tended to exaggerate his Hindu accent, but didn't hide his anxiety.

'The silly boy simply hasn't been himself since he and you broke up, Kathy. That's the truth of the matter. He's terribly confused, it seems to me. And I just wondered if there was the *remotest* chance that you might be able to speak to him? As a former friend, you know?'

Kathy could almost hear Morarji squirming with embarrassment, and guessed that Ghita had told her husband to make the call.

'I'm sorry, Morarji. I'm afraid I can't help. I really am sorry. I have to go now.'

The phone rang again almost immediately. It was Brock.

'Kathy? Sorry I didn't get to your speech this afternoon. I've been told it was very well received. Well done. I got caught up in something else, unfortunately. Something rather nasty. And I just wondered how you're placed now?'

'I'm free,' she said, taking a deep breath of the cool evening air.

'Good.' He sounded relieved, as if he'd expected a different answer. 'Incidentally, we checked out the field where Verge kept his glider. The plane's gone.'

'Ah.'

'So I'll see you soon then?'

'I'm on my way.'

Author's note

The book which Brock notices in Sandy Clarke's office in Chapter 4, on the work of Ledoux, and from which the passage on Doctor Tornotary is quoted, is *Claude-Nicolas Ledoux: Architecture and Social Reform at the End of the Ancien Régime*, by Anthony Vidler, The MIT Press, 1990. The essay about architects and the great detective, which Gail Lewis refers to in Chapter 21, is 'Program versus Paradigm: Otherwise Casual Notes on the Pragmatic, the Typical, and the Possible', by Colin Rowe, in his book, *As I Was Saying: Recollections and Miscellaneous Essays: Volume Two*, The MIT Press, 1996.